LETHAL CITY

Detective Cruz stood behind the BMW with his arms folded. Visible over the roofs of a thousand abandoned autos, traffic zipped back and forth on I-45. A worker sat in the driver's seat, started the engine, reached in the glove compartment, and thumbed the trunk release. The lid popped open on well-oiled hinges. Cruz looked away, coughed into his cupped hand and closed his nasal passages against the stench. He took a deep breath and peered inside the trunk.

Something was bundled inside a light blanket that lay against the spare. The blanket was speckled with brownish red stain. There were other items scattered about the trunk, and Cruz bent nearer to examine a severed human hand. There was an elongated object beside the hand. Cruz backed away and gagged. He'd seen enough. Though he averted his gaze from the sight, he was certain that the elongated object was a leg.

ALSO BY JEFFREY AMES

Only one killer has devised the perfect trap for human prey. . . .
Only one person has ever seen him—and survived. . . .

VENOM

"If you liked *Silence of the Lambs* (and who didn't?), you'll want to pick this one up."
　　　　　　　　　　　　—John Lescroart, *New York Times*
　　　　　　　　　　　　bestselling author of *The Oath*

LETHAL CITY

Jeffrey Ames

A SIGNET BOOK

SIGNET
Published by New American Library, a division of
Penguin Putnam Inc., 375 Hudson Street,
New York, New York 10014, U.S.A.
Penguin Books Ltd, 80 Strand,
London WC2R 0RL, England
Penguin Books Australia Ltd, 250 Camberwell Road,
Camberwell, Victoria 3124, Australia
Penguin Books Canada Ltd, 10 Alcorn Avenue,
Toronto, Ontario, Canada M4V 3B2
Penguin Books (N.Z.) Ltd, Cnr Rosedale and Airborne Roads,
Albany, Auckland 1310, New Zealand

Penguin Books Ltd, Registered Offices:
Harmondsworth, Middlesex, England

First published by Signet, an imprint of New American Library,
a division of Penguin Putnam Inc.

First Printing, February 2003
10 9 8 7 6 5 4 3 2 1

Ⓤ REGISTERED TRADEMARK—MARCA REGISTRADA

Printed in the United States of America

PUBLISHER'S NOTE
This is a work of fiction. Names, characters, places, and incidents either are
the product of the author's imagination or are used fictitiously, and any resemblance to actual persons, living or dead, business establishments, events, or
locales is entirely coincidental.

PROLOGUE

The little girl had only a partial understanding of many things. Her mind received and stored information in bushels; the facts were there, but their meaning would only begin to make sense as she grew older. Life to her was a series of lessons.

She understood quite well the meaning of fear. Her mother was very close at the moment, in the front seat behind the steering wheel, and the girl knew that if she made too much noise her mother would cause her pain.

The only lights within the car came from the radio dial and the occasional glow from her mother's cigarette. The little girl hated the smell of burning tobacco—"Smoh . . . bad" was the way her hatred expressed itself—but she liked the disc jockey's voice and loved the music so much she jiggled her foot in rhythm to certain songs. Most of the DJ's banter went over her head—the term "Top Forty" meant nothing to her— but there were certain things the record spinner said to which she related. Number One (she'd been one, but now she was two) on the charts was a song titled "Joy to the World," by Three (on her next birthday she'd be three) Dog (she loved doggies) Night (which was now, when it was dark outside). There was little joy in the two-year-old's life, but she'd heard the song enough times to know that Jeremiah was a bullfrog and was a good friend of hers. Just as she lightly clapped her hands her mother stirred in front, muttered, "Bullshit," and changed the station to a news program. The girl was miffed, but didn't dare protest because her mother would box her ears.

The child didn't like the news—"New . . . bad"—because it was boring. The announcer droned on and on about someone named Nixon who was president and who was the favorite to repeat in the upcoming November elections. None of this information held any meaning for the girl, so she ignored the news as she gazed at the darkened world outside.

She was more than a little afraid and didn't understand why her mother had been parked in one place for so long. If her mother hadn't been ominously near she would have twisted and turned in her seat, but fear held her motionless. In truth they had only been sitting on this lonely stretch of road for a quarter of an hour, but to the little girl it seemed an eternity. She was cross, tired, and ready for bed. The place where they'd parked was on swampy riverbottom land in South Dallas County, with lights twinkling over Loop 12 in the distance. She whimpered softly as she looked upon a damp creekbed and, farther on, scrubby bushes and trees in a line that faded in the darkness into nothingness. The backseat window was rolled down an inch and a warm breeze blew on her cheeks. All around the girl's face and arms, mosquitoes buzzed and bit.

There was a sudden flash of light in the creekbed a quarter mile to the west, followed by a muffled explosion that rumbled through the night. The girl's eyes widened *and her body stiffened. Her mother slid across the front seat with a whisper of gabardine over velour, rolled down the window and poked her head outside. The child felt her mother's excitement and the feeling was contagious; the two-year-old wiggled in the seat and strained for a better look. Her mother took a final drag from her cigarette and flicked the butt off into the weeds.*

The child's interest picked up even more as she squinted down the length of the creekbed. She could barely make out the outline of a second auto, up to its rims in silt. There was movement as well, a shape-changing shadow moving from one side of the faraway car to the other. One clanking noise and then another reached the girl's ears, and the stench of burning gasoline caused her to frown. Her mother's breathing was rapid and loud. A spark flashed in the distance like a firefly, and then there was . . .

The girl forgot all about her mother for an instant and instinctively clapped her hands. It was . . . it was . . .

Fire. Pretty, pretty fire, crackling low in the creekbed, flames dancing and licking around the faraway auto, enveloping first its trunk, then the roof and hood. There was a second explosion, this one louder than the first, as a ball of flames engulfed the car and blackened the underbrush. Pretty, pretty fire. The child giggled and stretched out her chubby arms as if to hug the flame to her breast.

There was more movement; the shadow appeared again and all at once became a man, his shape outlined in the inferno's background as he charged through the creekbed toward the little girl and her mother. The child's mother yanked on the handle, opened the front passenger door, and slid back toward the steering wheel. The man was upon them, his legs pumping, his feet churning sand and tiny rocks. The child grinned in recognition. Uncle Eddie had come to play with her! The girl murmured, "Unc . . . Ed-dee," as the man climbed in beside her mother and slammed the door.

Her mother said breathlessly, "Is he gone? Is the bastard really gone?"

And Uncle Eddie answered, "Dead, baby. Fuckin' dead."

The child whispered, "Fuh . . . dead," and held out her arms in Uncle Eddie's direction.

But Uncle Eddie ignored the girl just as he always did. The child's mother buried her face in the hollow of Uncle Eddie's shoulder. There were rustlings, the pop of snaps being opened, the rasp of zippers. Uncle Eddie moaned, "Oh baby. Jesus, baby! Jesus fucking Christ! I . . ."

And the girl, her eyes wide, mimicked, "Jee . . ."

The child's mother rose to straddle Uncle Eddie, her eyes in slits, her lips parted wantonly. There was a wet sliding noise as her mother hissed urgently, "Yes, baby . . . yes . . . yes . . ."

The woman hunkered down until all the girl could see were her mother's face and the back of Uncle Eddie's head, his bald spot shining. The man and woman bucked violently together, rocking the car, and the sight was frightening to the child. Her mother bared her teeth. The girl stared wide-eyed.

Her breath coming in gasps, the mother grinned at her daughter over the seatback. "Mommy's fucking, you little cunt," the woman said thickly. "Want to watch Mommy fuck, you dumb little bitch?" Then her body trembled and she screamed in the girl's face, "Oh God, Eddie, you're . . . oh God, God, God . . ."

An odor that the baby associated with the fish that the cook deboned in the kitchen filled the car. She hated the smell and wrinkled her nose. "Mommy . . . fuh," she said and then couldn't watch any longer.

She turned her face to the window. Far in the distance, the flames leaped higher as the abandoned auto burned.

"Fire," the baby said clearly. "Pretty, pretty fire."

1

On a frigid night in the middle of December, Dallas Patrolmen Roscoe Wheat and William Hines stopped for a light at the intersection of Illinois Avenue and Westmoreland Boulevard, one of the meanest corners in the city. Wheat was driving. The black-and-white cruiser's motor rumbled as the officers waited for the light to change. The shift had been slow and the pair were bored enough to argue over politics. Patrolman Wheat, a married man with a daughter in high school, thought that a confessed womanizer such as Bill Clinton should never have been elected and, hell with 'im, hoped that Paula Jones ended up owning the guy. Patrolman Hines, three times divorced over his own screwing around, opined that a man's personal affairs were his own business. Patrolman Wheat interrupted his partner's discourse by tapping Hines on the arm and pointing out the window. Patrolman Hines stopped talking and turned around.

The shiny midnight blue BMW idling alongside the cruiser seemed out of place among the shabby apartment houses, seedy beer joints, pawnshops, and check-cashing emporiums, and the men in the Beemer's front seat didn't go with the car any more than the car went with the neighborhood. The driver was white, his filthy blond hair strung below his shoulders, his spindly tattooed wrist draped over the steering wheel. Middle of the winter, and the guy was wearing a grimy white T-shirt. The passenger was a black man wearing a stocking cap, and he seemed intent on something in his lap. Neither man made eye contact with the policemen.

The light turned green and the BMW proceeded slowly east on Illinois. Too slowly. Patrolman Wheat hung back, moved over a lane, and got in behind the Beemer. Brake lights flashed as the other driver slowed, then held his speed at a steady fifteen miles per.

Patrolman Hines called for a make on the expensive car's license tag. He learned that the BMW's legal owner was a Ms. Morgan Annette Masters, who lived in Plano, way the hell north up Highway 75. Obviously, neither occupant of the vehicle was Ms. Masters. Wheat flashed his roof lights and gave a single blast from his siren. The BMW pulled to the curb.

Wheat opened his door partway, clicked on the cruiser's bullhorn, and ordered both of the BMW's occupants to step out and stand away from the car. The suspects complied. The white guy moved toward the middle of the street with his hands spread, and the black man stood on the curb with his back to the policemen, as if both suspects had been in this situation before and knew the drill. Wheat, a redhead with a mole on his chin, approached the driver. Hines, a skinny drink of water with a knock-kneed manner of walking, went up to the black guy. Both policemen's breath fogged in the night air. Wheat noted that the man in the T-shirt didn't seem to be shivering despite the twenty-degree chill.

Wheat said warily, "Evening. See your license?"

The suspect's nose dripped. He pointed toward the BMW. "Front seat in there." His voice cracked, his speech rapid and slightly slurred. " 'S trouble, Officer?"

"Just the license, please." Wheat glanced toward his partner. Hines had ordered the black man to place both hands on the roof of the car.

"Got a pipe on 'im," Hines called out.

Wheat nodded, unsnapping his Sam Browne holster. The blond suspect leaned inside the car, fumbled on the driver's seat, and turned around holding a wallet. Wheat said, "Take out the license and hand it over."

After the suspect complied, Wheat examined the laminated form with the aid of his Maglite. The driver's license belonged to Rudolph Burns, who had an address in Mesquite. The photo showed a blond man with a thin face who might or might not have been this particular suspect. Wheat's forehead tightened. "You Rudolph Burns?"

The suspect grinned. "That's me. What? Was I speeding or something?"

Wheat dropped his hand to his side. "What's your address, Rudolph?"

The suspect's chin tilted. "Well, now, I done moved. What's the license say?"

"Moved. How many times you moved, Rudolph?"

"Hell, man, four or five. Me and my old lady got difficulties."

"Mmm-hmm. Think hard. When you got this license, where were you living?"

The suspect scratched his head. "I don't remember. Could have been—"

"Is that your car?" Wheat pointed at the BMW.

"Belongs to a friend of mine."

Hines interrupted, calling out from the curb, "Nothing here I can see." His flashlight's beam swept around inside the car.

Wheat frowned. The crack pipe had been on the black man's person, and Wheat wasn't sure if drug paraphernalia possession gave him probable cause to toss the BMW. He turned back to the T-shirt–wearing blond. "What's your friend's name that owns this car?"

The suspect didn't answer and now hung his head as his body trembled. Wheat noted that, in addition to the runny nose, the suspect's nostrils were inflamed.

"Hey," Hines yelled. "They popped the ignition. Hubcap puller on the front floorboard."

Wheat drew his service revolver.

The blond raised both hands in defensive posture. "Now look."

Wheat pointed to the BMW's fender. "Okay, over there. Bend over the car and spread 'em."

"You're making a mistake, man. We ain't done nothing." The blond sniffled as he assumed the position across the fender.

Wheat kept his pistol trained on the suspect, at the same time approaching the driver's-side window and looking inside. Hines' flashlight shined on a hole in the steering column where the ignition lock should have been. The patrolmen now had their probable cause.

Wheat plucked handcuffs from his belt, walked up, and pulled one of the blond's wrists around behind. "Your friend that owns this car," Wheat said. "Until he shows up, you guys are going to have to sit with us a while. Just a precaution, okay?"

*   *   *

As Patrolman Hines held the suspects in the back of the cruiser and called for a wrecker, Patrolman Wheat searched the BMW. Under the front seat he found a Ziploc bag containing a hard chalky substance that Wheat believed to be crack cocaine. It bugged him that there wasn't more dope; a single rock didn't contain enough toot to amount to a felony. One rock of crack, one stolen vehicle. So what? The instant Wheat had cuffed the blond suspect, the creep had yelled for his attorney. Lawyered up, the pair would plead the whole thing down to a couple of weeks in lockup. Wheat twisted around and shined his flashlight onto the backseat. The beam reflected off plush new leather. *Smells nice in here,* Wheat thought, *a sixty-fucking-thousand-dollar auto if it's a nickel.*

He thumbed the latch and the compartment between the bucket seats opened easily. Wheat removed one of his gloves and withdrew a stack of papers, which he held in his lap as he looked the documents over one by one.

The license receipt showed that the car still belonged to Morgan Masters of Plano, with the same address Hines had obtained over the radio. The receipt identified the BMW as last year's model. Nestled in the console was a cell phone, and Wheat made a mental note that detectives should check with the phone company to see how many calls the suspects had made as they tooled around in this hot car.

Wheat laid the owner's manual and warranty aside and concentrated on the bulky pouch envelope, which was the only item remaining from the stack of papers. The envelope, which had a reusable sticky flap, was the same kind of container in which photos generally came over the supermarket counter. This particular envelope was blank, with no identifying logos. Wheat opened the flap. Inside was a pile of glossies, which

Wheat removed. He shined his flashlight on the top picture. He blinked in surprise.

The photo showed the interior of a male strip club, with tables full of women applauding and raising hell as a guy performed onstage in a G-string that looked as if a wad of Kleenex might've been stuffed inside the crotch. The G-string was bright red stretch material. A Lone Ranger mask covered the man's eyes and nose. He was posed with his pecs and arms flexed, and the women in the audience seemed on the verge of orgasm. The picture was dark, not of good quality, and Wheat suspected that the camera had been a cheap flash disposable that someone had smuggled in. Strip clubs were touchy about pictures being taken, lawsuits being what they were these days. Wheat shifted the photo to the bottom of the stack and looked at the next in line.

This was the same man—the stripper, mask and all—on his knees with a pair of tensed female thighs hooked over his shoulders. Just as in the first picture, the background wasn't clear, but this photo was shot in a private room. Visible behind the stripper was the foot of a bed. From the angle of the photo, it was obvious that the lady with the legs had held the camera. The guy's tongue was extended toward her genitals. Wheat went on to the next picture.

Here the Lone Ranger sucked a female breast, this time with the woman holding the camera above her head, her extended upper arms visible in the picture. Female legs were visible in this pose as well, and Wheat confirmed that they were the same legs as in the first shot by the butterfly tattooed on the woman's left inner thigh. Patrolman Wheat expelled breath as he reached for the trunk release button. Before he pushed the button, red lights flashed behind him as a backup police cruiser pulled to the curb.

Wheat climbed out of the BMW as the city wrecker parked behind the backup cruiser, two cop cars and a tow truck now lined up behind the Beemer on Illinois Avenue. A small crowd had gathered on the curb, black faces for the most part, their expressions unfriendly. Wheat approached the wrecker as a man in coveralls climbed down, hauling chains and hooks.

Wheat extended the envelope of photos toward the wrecker driver. "Have a look, huh?" Wheat said. "Jesus, you won't believe what I found in there."

The backup cruiser hauled the suspects, still yelling for their lawyers, to the Oak Cliff precinct while the wrecker towed the BMW over the Trinity River to the auto pound. The pound's entrance was on a side street beneath I-45. After backing the Beemer into a slot between a sixties-model pickup and a Dodge Caravan, the driver carried the BMW's registration papers inside to the office. Mission accomplished, he then went off to warm his insides with coffee until the next call came in.

The office dispatcher rummaged through the papers, found a telephone number, and called the BMW's owner up in Plano. A recorded female voice told him that he'd reached the Masters residence and that he should leave a message after the tone. The dispatcher complied, informing the machine that the BMW was at the auto pound. Then he hung up and wrote a report on the Beemer. It was a busy night, and he still had a lot to do.

Thirty-six hours later the carjackers were still in jail, and the BMW continued to occupy space in the auto pound. The two scuzzes had refused to give their names at the Lew Sterrett Justice Center booking desk, and other than one phony driver's license and a couple of hot credit cards they had no ID, but were identified through fingerprints taken during in-processing. The display on the National Crime Information Center computer screen read: EDDIE RALPH MACON, W/M, DOB 4/7/74, and DARNELL JEROME MAKE-PIECE, B/M, DOB 8/6/69. Macon had recently served twenty-two months in the Texas Department of Justice system for strongarm robbery, and he was a fugitive from a Harris County warrant issued when he'd failed to report to his parole officer. Makepiece was doing ten years' probation for sale of a controlled substance—to wit, cocaine—and was currently on the street as a result of his cooperation with the Dallas County DA in busting his partner in the drug operation. One badass and one snitch—nice to know in case the police needed for one suspect to roll on the other. Despite the fact that the BMW's owner hadn't turned up to sign a complaint, the circumstances of the arrest had allowed the cops to charge the pair with auto theft. Harris and Dallas County authorities had placed warrant holds on both men, so in the near future Eddie Ralph Macon and Darnell Jerome Makepiece weren't going anywhere.

A Crimes Against Property detective named Harold Cruz caught the assignment on the car-theft beef. Cruz' caseload was lighter than usual, so he had more time to screw around with a pissant hot auto case than he normally would have. He placed numerous calls to Ms. Morgan Masters up in Plano, and when she hadn't responded by the second afternoon, he decided that a personal visit was in order. Plano was outside the Dallas cops' jurisdictional limit, so Cruz asked Main Headquarters to send someone, he didn't care whom, to Ms. Masters' Stonebridge Ranch home to look around.

*   *   *

Plano was no burg. It was a city-within-a-metropolis with a quarter million residents, a third of whom lived in upscale golf course communities. Geographically it was part of Collin County, though Plano bore no more resemblance to the sleepy rural towns of McKinney and Allen than to the Oak Cliff neighborhood where the police had spotted the BMW. The Plano upper crust carried mucho political stroke, so in dealing with the residents, law enforcement walked on eggs.

All of which explained the Dallas cops' reluctance to follow standard procedure and send a couple of uniformed officers out to Morgan Masters' place in a squad car, after first clearing the jurisdictional invasion with the Plano Department. Unis showing up at one's door tended to set tongues a-wagging, a no-no up in Plano. So the dispatcher checked the duty rosters to find a plainclothes who wasn't currently occupied. Eventually she settled on the newest assignee to the Metro Squad, which was an elite group of detectives with investigative authority throughout the Dallas–Ft. Worth Metroplex. The assignee was a thirty-eight-year-old detective sergeant named Ham Benno, a slender man who jogged, lifted weights, and kept to himself in his private life and who was so new to the department that no one had yet partnered up with him. A cushy Metro Squad assignment for a new hire was practically unheard of, and rumor had it that Benno was connected at City Hall. Benno felt his co-workers' resentment every time he entered the squad room. A trip to Plano would be a relief for him, if only for a little while.

Benno checked his assigned Mercury sedan out of the motor pool, where he'd left the car for an oil change, and drove up Central Expressway with snowflakes whipping against the windshield. The temperature was a couple of degrees above freezing and the snow wasn't expected to stick, though there was precautionary sand on the bridges and a few slick patches on the freeway shoulder. He arrived in Plano around two in the afternoon and had to stop for a Christmas parade on Stonebridge Parkway. Benno watched without much interest as the Nativity scene passed by. Religious holidays held little meaning for him; he was a backsliding Jew who hadn't visited the synagogue since his eighteenth birthday and who hadn't recited the *kiddush* or partaken of the honeyed apple of Rosh Hashanah in all that time.

Morgan Masters' home was in a new built-to-look-old subdivision. Benno wasn't crazy about the neighborhood; he thought the houses overbuilt and suspected they were grossly overpriced. There didn't seem to be any architectural pattern to the area; mammoth Tudors with arches and spires sat alongside Spanish-styled homes with red-tiled roofs, all built to within yards of the street so that lawns were tiny if they existed at all. As he drove along curved avenues, Benno had glimpses of country club fairways. At one intersection he had a straight-on view of a magnificent Colonial-style clubhouse.

The Masters place backed up to what Benno imagined was one bitch of a par-three that had to be a two-hundred-yard carry over water. The elevated tee was visible through an opening between the Masters home and the house next door. He sat in the driveway for a moment, peering through falling snowflakes, picturing himself up on the tee selecting a club. Winter golf was the main thing that Benno missed about California. While in LA he'd played Griffith Park or Rancho just about every day off, and once he had even toured Lakeside CC as a pro-am guest. He cut the engine and approached the Masters house, his breath fogging in the cold.

The front yard was bigger than those on the rest of the block, and before the house stood a circular exposed aggregate drive and fountain. Two-story Roman pillars fronted a modest-sized porch, and the massive oak door was centered beneath a floor-to-roof leaded-glass picture window. A blue four-door Mercedes sat in the drive behind a dented Ford Escort. The Ford seemed out of place, and Benno decided that the heap belonged either to a maid or to a teenager. He peered in at the entry hall. At the foot of a wide stone staircase was a six-foot-tall grandfather clock with its pendulum rocking back and forth, ticking and tocking. The floor was marble tile, with a gaudy Oriental rug laid out in front of the doorway. Benno pressed the doorbell and listened to the chimes ring. It was cold as a bitch outside; he blew on his fingers and thrust his hands into his overcoat pockets.

Two minutes crawled by. Benno rang the bell a second time and jumped up and down to shock some feeling into his feet. Still there was no movement inside the house. He went out and felt the Mercedes' hood, then the Escort's. Both engines were cold.

Benno's only instructions were to inform the lady that police had recovered her missing BMW and that the car was in the auto pound. He debated over leaving a note wedged into the front doorframe. Then he shrugged his shoulders and walked around to the side of the house and approached an eight-foot-high stockade fence with rounded pickets.

Close to the fence and snugged up to the house, set in ornate brick, was the electricity meter. Benno stepped up and down on the bricks to be certain they'd support his weight. Then he climbed up on the meter and peered over into the yard. Loud barking ensued. A chocolate Labrador retriever ran into view.

The dog charged the fence and reared up on its hind legs. Though its barking continued, the Lab's manner didn't seem threatening. Benno cautiously held his hand a couple of inches from the trembling snout. The Lab whimpered, wagged its tail, and licked his fingers.

Benno put one foot on top and hoisted himself over, thudding to the ground, righting himself on winter-dead Tiff, reaching out to pet the dog. The Lab tried to lick Benno's face. He pushed the animal down and went along the side of the house with the Lab at his heels.

In seconds Benno stood beside a teardrop-shaped swimming pool, complete with treated cement banks and a low diving board. The deck furniture was expensive redwood. A small outbuilding, probably a dressing room, stood behind the diving board. Steam rose from chlorinated water. Benno brushed melted snow from his face. The bushes around the perimeter of the yard whitened as snowflakes clung to the branches.

He trudged toward the house on a stone pathway. The Lab trotted ahead, whining over empty food and water dishes. Benno opened a plastic container and found a bag of dog food with a scoop inside. He filled the dog's bowl, then located a faucet and filled the water dish. The dog lapped thirstily. Benno stepped up on a tiled back porch and peered through a glassed-in door into a kitchen.

The kitchen was half again the size of Benno's apartment, with an island stove and rows of overhead cabinets. Big pots, pans, and skillets hung from a rack above the sink along with a row of meat forks and butcher knives. The room was spotless except for a pile of towels on the counter. Benno lifted a hand to shield against the glare from the window glass. The towels were wadded together and darkly stained. There was a wall-mounted cordless phone connected to an answering machine, the red message light blinking.

He rapped on the window and waited. He thought about breaking the glass, reaching through the opening and releasing the deadbolt, but there was a security panel just inside the door. If he triggered the alarm, there'd be hell to pay. He backed away and retraced his steps, leaving the dog munching away in the yard. Benno then climbed the fence and went back around to the front. He scribbled a note on his business card and poked the card into the front door crack.

Two minutes later Benno stood on the porch next door and rang the bell. This home was a rambling one-story with a bay window and a huge mahogany door with a brass knocker. A peephole opened and closed. The door opened the length of a chain and a Hispanic maid peered out. She was a youngish woman with a pretty round face; she wore a gray uniform with a white starched collar.

Benno opened his wallet and flashed his shield. "Dallas Metro detective, ma'am. I've been trying to reach the people next door."

The woman raised a curious eyebrow. "Tha's over to Miss Masters'?"

"Right. Does she own a midnight blue BMW?"

She nodded. "Spor'scar. Why you ask?"

"Police business. You wouldn't know if anyone was home over there, would you?"

"Got no clue, mister. Miss Masters, she comes and goes. All hours."

"She's not married?"

The maid rolled her eyes. "She's had men livin'

over there. But I don't think she's together with anybody now—you know what I mean?"

Benno rubbed his numb hands together. "Have you
seen her?"

"Not this week."

"Are you sure she hasn't moved?"

"No, she's still there." The maid gave a chatty blink.
"I'll tell you something, Mr. Detective: Miss Masters,
sometimes she's home, sometimes she ain't. The way
she runs around, I'm not sure that lady even knows
where she lives."

Benno drove back downtown and entered the precinct's new office building through the rear. He went
upstairs to the Metro Squad room, sat alone at his
desk, and wrote up a report, then called Crimes
Against Property Detective Harold Cruz. He got Cruz'
voice mail and left a message. Benno couldn't complete his report without Cruz' case number, so he
tossed the form into his in-basket. He massaged his
temples and rubbed his eyes. He couldn't shake the
feeling that, when he'd visited Masters house, someone had been home but hadn't come to the door.

Detective Cruz wasn't at his desk when Benno
called, and he didn't respond to his voice mail for
several hours, because he'd gotten a call from the auto
pound. As the unseasonably cold weather had continued, the auto pound workers grew tired of freezing to
death, and just that morning, they'd finally gotten the
okay from the administrators downtown to fire up the
heaters around the lot. One of the heaters was located
seven feet from the BMW's rear bumper, and as the
hot flame licked the air, the area around the sportscar
had begun to smell. According to the auto pound dispatcher, the odor was incredibly foul.

At the precise instant when Benno was leaving his voice mail message, Detective Cruz stood in the auto pound yard behind the BMW with his arms folded. Visible over the roofs of a thousand abandoned autos, traffic zipped back and forth on I-45. A worker sat in the driver's seat, started the engine, reached in the glove compartment, and thumbed the trunk release. The lid popped open on well-oiled hinges. Cruz looked away, coughed into his cupped hand, and closed his nasal passages against the stench. He took a deep breath and peered inside the trunk.

Something was bundled inside a light blanket that lay against the spare. The blanket was speckled with brownish red stain. There were other items scattered about the trunk, and Cruz bent nearer to examine a severed human hand. There was an elongated object beside the hand. Cruz backed away and gagged. He'd seen enough. Though he averted his gaze from the sight, he was certain that the elongated object was a leg.

2

Benno didn't think that Darnell Jerome Makepiece liked having his dinner interrupted. Finally Makepiece said as much. "Fried steak an' Tater Tots is the only thing worth a shit they give us. Time I get back, some dude's gonna eat alla mine."

Detective Harold Cruz was acting as spokesman during the interview, and Benno was just as glad. A detective from Metro was an outsider here: The stolen BMW was a local matter at this point, and working-stiff cops hated for some elite unit to stick its nose in. True in LA, true in Dallas, and true in every major department in the country.

Cruz said to the prisoner, "We'll have them save you a plate. The thing I don't understand, Darnell, a guy like you selling a few papers of toot, you oughtta be able to do probation standing on your head. So why you want to hang out with a badass? You trying to graduate or something?"

Makepiece's handcuffs clanked as he tugged his ear. "Naw, man, I quit in eleventh grade."

"I'm not talking about graduation from any fucking

public high school. I am talking about you climbing to new heights of crime. Do you know who I am?"

"Some other cop dude. Alla same." Makepiece had a purple birthmark on his cheek. Otherwise his skin was without blemish, the color of bittersweet chocolate, glistening in the light from the ceiling lamps.

Makepiece and Cruz were on opposite sides of a table in the interview room, where a uniformed cop had delivered the prisoner just moments ago. Cruz was in his thirties. His head was shaved. He had tight, smooth facial skin and an olive complexion, and he wore a white shirt with the collar undone and his tie yanked down. Benno lounged off to the side in an observing posture. Directly across from him was a detective he didn't know and wondered about, a young, lithe black woman with short straightened hair. Wearing a gray business dress, whose skirt stopped modestly at her knees, she regarded the prisoner with an earnest deadpan look.

Cruz shook his head. "Well, yeah, Darnell, if you're only talking about me, I might be just some other cop. I'm just plain old Detective Cruz. Robbery, burglary, auto theft—you know, things like that. But these people are Detectives Ham Benno and Tina Drummond. They're from Metro. They investigate the same things I do, plus murders. They might be a bigger problem for you."

Benno's chin lifted. When Cruz had called him to relate the discovery at the auto pound, Benno had come to the jail alone to find Tina Drummond waiting. Cruz hadn't introduced her, and now Benno knew why. Cruz had assumed that two detectives from the Metro Squad would already be acquainted. As he looked at Detective Drummond she smirked at him. Benno shrugged.

Makepiece looked from Benno to Drummond and

back again. "I ain't done no murder. I ain't done nothing. I barely know the dude I was with."

Cruz tilted back in his chair. "You mean Eddie Ralph Macon? Your partner?"

"That his name?"

"That's the name we came up with. Why? You got some street monicker for the guy?"

Makepiece showed Drummond a conspiratorial look. "Sister, you gonna let this dude go on hasslin' me?"

Drummond looked at her knees, then raised her gaze. She spoke in a calm, unaccented alto. "We'll have something straight here, sir. I am not your sister. Nor am I your homegirl, and I am sure as hell not your girlfriend. I am here investigating a possible homicide, and you are the very suspect we are investigating. You may call me Detective Drummond and I'll refer to you as Mr. Makepiece. Mutual respect, okay?"

Makepiece screwed his features into a leer. "Ain't no call to go dissin' me."

Tina Drummond had a full mouth above a square chin, and she wore pinkish lipstick. "I'll show you dissing if you want, Mr. Makepiece. But this room isn't divided along racial lines. We're the cops. You're the bad guy. Three against one."

Makepiece watched the ceiling. "I told you, I barely know that other dude. I never saw him before that night the *po*-leece stopped us."

"Never saw him. Right." Cruz moved in closer to the table. "The two of you met and said howdy, then decided to steal that BMW."

"I don't know nothin' about that car. Dude was just lookin' to score some toot."

"Which you were holding in your lap when the officers stopped you," Cruz said. "At least you were holding the pipe. The crack was in a Baggie. I gotta ask you, Darnell. A guy that's been around as much as you, you think these Metro detectives are here over a Baggie with one lousy rock in it?"

"Maybe Ralphie done some bigger shit. I don't know nothin' about what he done."

"Ralphie? *Ralphie?* Are you talking about the guy you just met that night?" Cruz glanced at the prisoner's rap sheet. "They call you Skitter?"

"My crew might." Makepiece eyed the computer printout as if he was trying to read upside down.

"Just your crew? What's Eddie Ralph Macon call you?"

"He don't call me nothin'. Mostly he just say, 'Get that pipe smokin'.' " Makepiece waited for a laugh from his audience, got none, then resumed his study of the ceiling.

Tina Drummond spoke up. "That's an awfully nice car you two strangers used to get acquainted in, Mr. Makepiece. Got a lot under the hood."

Benno watched her. He liked the way she was getting into the main topic. She had steady brown eyes under brushed lashes.

Drummond kept her voice calm. "Got a lot in the trunk, too."

Makepiece never batted an eye. He fished for a toothpick, which he poked into his mouth.

Cruz continued the one-two punch. "Come on, Skitter. Who do you think you're fucking with? You two boost this nice auto, the first thing you're gonna do is pop the trunk to see what's in there you can fence."

"Shee-it. I done told you that was Ralphie's ride. Dude was drivin' it when he picked me up."

Benno kept silent. This was Cruz' show, with Drummond as backup. But the scuzz had just trapped himself, and his sudden downcast look said that he knew it. Had Benno been conducting the interview back in LA, Darnell Jerome Makepiece would be about three questions from toast.

Drummond took over, never raising her voice. "You never saw him before, yet you call him Ralphie. He picked you up while you were just walking down the street minding your business. Are you a boy toy, Mr. Makepiece? I'm really going to start dissing you if I think you drop your pants and bend over for money."

Makepiece started to lose it. "I never done nothin' like that. Don't hassle with no sissies."

"Well, it's got to be one or the other. Either he picked you up or you were with him when he got in the car. So either you're a whore or you're a car thief. Which is it?"

"Ain't no ho." Makepiece pounded the table.

"Okay, we've established that you're a car thief."

Makepiece looked down at the table. "We boosted the ride over by Cedar Crest Golf Course."

Cruz leaned back, intertwining his fingers behind his head. "That's no Oak Cliff auto, Darnell. That's an uptown ride."

"It was sittin' in a vacant lot, man. Just sittin' there."

Drummond thumbed through the photos that the officers had found inside the BMW. "The car was abandoned?"

"Ralphie boosted it. I met him 'cause he needed a score. It's what I do, lady. It's all I do. Don't do no stealing."

"Mmm-hmm. What about the lady that owns the car? I suppose you never saw her, either."

"Never saw nobody. I don't mess with no face-to-face robberies."

"I thought you didn't mess with robberies at all, Mr. Makepiece. Of any kind."

"Well, I don't. But if I did, it wouldn't be with the person standing there."

"Not because you're afraid to face them, right? You just don't like having witnesses to these thefts you never participate in."

"I don't know nothin' about all that." Makepiece stared at the far corner of the room.

Cruz knocked once on the table. "Sure you don't, Darnell. Just like you've never been a snitch."

Makepiece folded his hands and didn't answer.

"I think you know what's coming now," Cruz said. "So before you get behind this—you've been yelling for your lawyer for three days now. Yet no lawyer has appeared. Where is this person?"

Makepiece bit down on the toothpick. "Don't 'zactly have no permanent lawyer."

"As in, you can't afford one, Darnell. So we're offering. One will be appointed. Once a lawyer is appointed, he'll tell you not to talk to us. You know that and I know that. You and Eddie Ralph Macon are going down hard. What you say in the next thirty seconds is going to decide which one goes down the hardest."

Makepiece's tone went up a panicked octave. "Man, I never seen no woman. Don't know nothin' about no woman."

"Are you waiving your right to counsel?" Cruz shoved a form and a ballpoint over in front of the prisoner. "Sign on the line if you are. Otherwise we've got nothing to talk about."

Makepiece snatched up the pen and scribbled, without bothering to read the form. *He's signed a lot of those,* Benno thought. *The fuck has the drill memorized.*

Cruz took the form and showed it to Drummond, the other two cops leaving Benno out of the loop. Drummond brushed hair back off her forehead. "We're interested in what was in the trunk, Mr. Makepiece."

"I never saw no woman. It was all Ralphie that done that."

Drummond and Cruz exchanged a look. Drummond said, "If you never saw anything, how would you know who did what to who?"

"Ralphie told me. That's a statement against penal interest."

Cruz laughed out loud. "You a lawyer, Darnell? Or you just been down this road a lotta times? Be straight here. Eddie Ralph Macon killed the lady and put her in the trunk. Is that what you're telling us?"

"Ain't sure if he stabbed her or shot her or what. He just told me he done it."

Cruz seemed amused. He reached over and rapped on the door. The uniformed cop who'd delivered Makepiece to the interview came in and stood by.

Cruz sat forward and watched the prisoner. "We'll be in touch, Darnell."

When the uni boosted the prisoner up, Makepiece's look was suddenly wild. "Ralphie's one bad dude, man. I know other shit he done."

"Well, if you think of any more, let us know." Cruz turned to the uni. "We're through with this guy."

"Ralphie done killed a lotta dudes," Makepiece said.

"Sleep tight, Darnell." Cruz held the door while the uniformed cop escorted the prisoner out. After Makepiece left wearing a confused expression, Cruz shut the door and said to Drummond, "That tells us they never looked in the trunk at all."

Drummond nodded. "Puts us back to square one. Makes a revisit to Plano mandatory."

"Right."

Benno scratched his head in confusion. "The guy was about to give it all up. So how come you ended the interview?"

Cruz shrugged with his hands. "I had a long talk with Detective Drummond before you got here. Sorry we didn't have time to fill you in. Sure, Darnell would say black was white—anything to help himself and screw his partner. But Darnell don't know shit from Shinola about this case. The body parts in the trunk belong to a guy."

3

Benno and Drummond talked some on the twilight
ride up to Plano. Benno felt a little silly having to get
acquainted with a detective in his own unit. He knew
the shift lieutenant, DiAngelo, a surly guy who stayed
to himself inside his office and who made no bones
about not liking new hires shoved down his throat.
An Asian-American cop occupied the desk beside
Benno's, but Benno had never spoken to him other
than to say hello on his first day there. The guy was
in his mid-twenties, a youngster with slicked-back hair
who spent most of his down time telling the other
detectives that his mostly Asian neighborhood needed
one of their own on the City Council—as if all these
Anglo, black, and Hispanic policemen gave a shit. Dallas, Texas, was one of the racist capitals of the world
and Benno was the only Jew in Metro, but he knew
that ethnicity had nothing to do with the deep freeze
he was getting from his coworkers. Cops as a rule
treated each other as equals on the job and reserved
their slurs for private moments when they were with
their wives, girlfriends, or drinking buddies. Tina

Drummond was the only woman Benno had seen in the unit, though there could have been others on the late shifts; Benno hadn't been on board long enough to work nights and wasn't looking forward to it when he had to.

Drummond said, "If you talked more, you'd get along better." She was in the Mercury's passenger seat, Benno driving because he already knew the way to the Masters house. Tina Drummond shifted her long legs, her knees on a level with her waist, her shins practically touching the dashboard.

Benno didn't answer. He hoped his silence made him seem deep and mysterious, though the truth was that he didn't know what the fuck to say to this woman.

"Unless it is that you just don't want to talk," Drummond said. "It'll be a bitch for me to work with Silent Sam."

Benno did like to talk, and he considered himself a personable guy. He was also a first-rate detective, which was the main reason that Deputy Chief Jeff Rubin had given him a chance in the first place. A secondary reason had to do with Rubin's relationship to Benno's father, though Rubin had been tactful not to remind Ham that Japeth Benno was his cousin during the interview. Rubin had cautioned Ham, "Your past will come out. There is too much chitchat between departments for it not to, but you shouldn't be the one to tell. First you gain respect. Then Dallas will be more likely to take what happened in California in stride."

None of which responded to Tina Drummond's worries. Benno rubbed the side of his face. "I apologize. I got wrapped up in thinking about the case."

"According to you, you went up to Plano and found no one at home. You talked to a neighbor's maid, who told you she didn't know Miss Masters' whereabouts. So what's to be wrapped up in?"

"My concern for the woman."

"You don't know that anything's happened to her."

"I heard enough, and we should be worried. We've already got one stiff. So how do we know Miss Masters isn't dead just like the guy? For all we know, Makepiece was just confused about which one they stuffed in the trunk."

Drummond shifted her position so that her back was to the door. "That's a possibility, but this one case in itself isn't what we're discussing. Right now my concern is about the guy who I may be depending on to watch my ass. I may be permanently partnered with you."

Benno looked at her. The Merc drifted to the right. Benno did an eyes-front and steered back into the proper lane.

"I said, 'May be,' " Drummond said. "It's not up to me in the long run, but I have input. Lieutenant DiAngelo sent me over to get acquainted with you. So far all I've gotten is you staring morosely out the window and telling me you're concerned for some woman you've never met. Let's cut the bullshit, okay?"

"You don't have a regular partner?"

"I've had several."

"You must be particular."

Drummond chuckled. "*They* are. I am drowning in a sea of testosterone. All these guys, only one chick, especially a black chick . . ."

"You could be overreacting."

"If it only happened once, maybe. But after four guys giving all these lame excuses for wanting a change? Face it. You and I together would be a pairing of misfits."

Benno tried not to resent the remark, but did. "I'm a damned good detective, in case you—"

"Sure you are. Getting a new-hire assignment to the Metro Squad, it goes without saying that you are. Being good has nothing to do with it." Drummond was half facing him with her arm draped over the seat. "But how good are you, Benno?"

He released the wheel and shrugged with his hands.

"Ever draw your weapon on duty?" Drummond asked.

Benno regripped the wheel. "Yes, I have."

"Fire it?"

"A couple of times."

"Hit anyone?"

"I shot two guys, okay? One I killed, the other I didn't. I don't think that makes me any better or worse as a cop. A lot of assholes in the penitentiary have killed people. There's a helluva lot more to being a cop than shooting someone."

She studied him thoughtfully, adjusted her position once more, and showed him her profile in the shadows cast by the freeway sodium lights. "Yeah, there's more. Time's gonna tell about you. I don't know how much time, but believe me it will."

The neighborhood seemed different at night. The mansions were dark hulks against the horizon; the Mercury's headlights illuminated shadowy images of trees. Benno parked at the curb in front of the Masters home, imagining the golf course beyond, fairways and greens fading in the distance into vegetal gloom. The Mercedes and the Escort were in the identical spots where they'd been that afternoon. Drummond collected her handbag from the floorboard.

"There's a Labrador retriever in back," Benno remarked.

Drummond opened the door and swung her legs
out. "I hope we can go in through the front, then.
Dogs scare the shit out of me."

Benno watched her stand. "You don't seem the type
to be afraid of animals."

"The two-legged kind, never. But a big mongrel cur
on the block bit me when I was little. Ah hell, though,
with you to protect me . . . ? Come on." She slammed
the door.

Benno hesitated, watching Drummond's slim back
and straight shoulders as she moved into the yard.
He'd accepted the other cops' distrust and even halfway understood it, but Drummond's posture was
somehow different. He'd have to work on his ap-
proach with her.

His confidence would grow with time. Once he got
his feet under him, it would be like the old days before
the blowup in California. Given time, he could be as
good in Dallas as he'd once been in LA. He drew his
overcoat tight around him and stepped out in the cold.

They didn't see a light on inside the house. Benno
rang the doorbell three times, but no one answered it.
At the first sound of chimes, the Lab began to bark,
raising a ruckus beyond the fence, and other dogs
throughout the neighborhood soon joined in a chorus
of yelps and growls.

"I guess we could go on in and later argue that we
feared imminent danger," Benno said. "A dead guy
hacked to pieces, the lady unaccounted for . . ."

Drummond was a step ahead of him. She hauled a
hammer out of her purse and shattered the leaded-
glass window. Shards tinkled onto the porch. Benno
asked why Drummond was carrying a hammer. She
just wrinkled her nose at him as she reached inside

and opened the door. Benno pointed his flashlight inside. The beam reflected off polished marble tile. He followed Drummond across the threshold, past the antique grandfather clock, and made it halfway to the staircase when a siren blared.

In the confined space the noise was deafening. Benno dropped his flashlight and stumbled in pursuit as it clattered across the tile. Drummond punched the police code into the security panel. The siren ceased its wailing at once. Benno caught up with the flashlight while Drummond called the Plano cops on her cell. She gave her badge number to the dispatcher, who recalled the 911 car that was already on its way. Benno led the way to the back, his hands shaking.

They passed through a richly furnished den, complete with leather-upholstered sofa and chairs, a monstrous saltwater aquarium, a sixty-inch rear projection TV, and a white bearskin rug. "Will you look at this shit?" Drummond muttered.

They made it into the kitchen. Drummond surveyed the room with hands on hips. "You mentioned a pile of rags or something?"

Benno swept the counter with the flashlight, shined the beam on clean white Formica. No stained and wadded cloth. Had he been imagining things earlier? The portable wall phone he'd seen from the porch hung on his left. The red light on the answering machine continued to blink. If he hadn't imagined the phone, he hadn't imagined the darkly stained mound of rags. He jumped and very nearly dropped the flashlight again as something cold and wet touched his hand at waist level, accompanied by the sound of rapid panting.

Christ, the dog was in the house. The Lab nuzzled his palm and licked his fingers. Benno scratched the

animal behind the ears. Its tail thumped back and
forth. Drummond murmured, "Nice doggy." There
was fear in her tone.

Benno grabbed the Lab's collar and led the animal
to the back sliding glass door. The door stood open
and an icy draft blew on his face. He put the dog out
and, using his handkerchief, slid the door into the
closed position. "That was locked this afternoon," he
said. "If someone left it open, why didn't it trigger
the alarm?"

Drummond came up beside him and pointed at the
security panel. The light above the numbered buttons
was green. "Zoned security. It's separate, so you can
leave the alarm on in front while you're messing
around in the backyard."

"Meaning someone's been in or out since this afternoon, which explains why that pile of rags has
disappeared."

Drummond bent near the counter and sniffed.
"Smells like Jet Bon-Ami." She looked down the
room lengthwise, said, "Wonder who's called," then
reached over and depressed a button on the answering machine.

A mechanical female voice said, *"Five messages."*
Then there was a series of clicks and whirs. Benno
took out a pad and pen and pointed at the flashlight.
Drummond trained the beam on the writing pad.

They listened to the call from the dispatcher telling
Ms. Masters that her Beemer was in the auto pound,
followed by three messages from Crimes Against
Property detective Cruz. After every message, the mechanical voice cut in with the day and time. Benno
yawned and scratched his nose.

Now there was a beep, followed by a soft educated
female voice saying, *"Morgan, it's Jessica. I've been
out of town and just got your message. Come on, pick*

up, will you?" After a short pause, the voice continued with increasing urgency: *"Please, Morgan. Don't do anything stupid."* Then, after a second, longer pause, the voice said, *"I'm here for you, babe. I'm carrying my cell, so call me as soon as you can. You can get through this, Morgan. Call me, okay?"* The computerized voice droned, *"Tuesday, five twenty p.m. No more messages,"* and then the machine clicked to a standstill.

Drummond knocked in disgust on the counter. "That call was from this afternoon. Shit, she didn't leave a number."

Benno pointed at the wall phone. "Don't those things have caller ID?" He picked the portable out of its cradle, found the inch-square computer screen above the dial pad, and pressed the SCROLL DOWN pointer. He skipped over the auto pound number and Cruz' office line—which appeared three consecutive times—and then squinted at the liquid crystal display reading, "BALDWIN, JESSICA," followed by a number in the 214 area code. He jotted the name and number down, then put his pad and pen away.

"Bitchin' detective work, Benno," Drummond said. She drew her weapon, banged home the clip with the heel of her hand, and moved the slide back and forth with a sharp *click-click.* "What do you say, partner?" she said. "Someone came through that door and could still be in the house. I think we oughtta have a look upstairs."

Benno felt like a thousand kinds of asshole as he allowed a woman to lead the way in a tense situation. He followed Tina Drummond upstairs with his own .38 Special held ready. He pointed the flashlight's beam on ahead of her. He told himself that Drummond would resent it if he took charge of the situation. He'd worked with female officers in LA, but Benno had always been the one to call the shots. In his work, his three-year marriage, in all kinds of relationships with women, Benno had always led the way.

There'd been one dominant woman in his life, his grandmother, but he'd been a little boy back then and easily led. He now pictured the old woman, stern hooked nose and hair gone completely gray by the time she was fifty, and also pictured himself standing humbly beside her on the Sabbath as the rabbi removed the Torah from the synagogue's ark. She'd been Benno's only symbol of authority and his last voluntary contact with religion; in his own mind Benno marked his grandmother's passing as the time when he'd become a man. At fourteen he'd stood between his parents and looked down at his grandmother in her casket, his father's yarmulke level with his tall son's shoulders. He recalled the funeral as if it had been yesterday, remembered well that his eyes had been dry and that he'd read over and over the little blue numbers tattooed on his grandmother's arm. Odd that he'd never really looked at the figures before that day, but now, at thirty-eight years of age, he still could recite them from memory.

The second level was built around a corridor that encircled the stairwell. Benno and Drummond acted on instinct; they both knew the drill even though they'd never worked together. They alternately covered each other's back as they moved cautiously through two bedrooms with a connecting bath. The furniture was strictly fat-cat material: queen-sized beds with quilted comforters, pewter flowerpots, and ornate phones on mahogany nightstands. They looked under beds and inside closets, but found no one. The detectives went down the corridor and through another door.

They were now in the master bedroom, half again larger than the sleeping quarters they'd just passed through. Benno glanced quickly at a king-sized bed with the ruffled spread thrown aside and the covers kicked around, then he swept the flashlight over a recessed French door leading to a balcony. He went into the master bath and turned the beam on two separate shower stalls and a sunken tub with gilt fixtures. The fixtures were in the shape of a goose and two goslings. From out in the bedroom Drummond called, "Something here."

Benno looked out. Drummond stood by the bed, bent from the waist, peering down. Benno went up beside her. The pillowcase and sheets were covered in blood. The blood had dried in spots; in other places it shimmered in bright red pools.

"Like a butcher shop," Drummond said.

Benno shined the flashlight on the floor. "No spatter trail. I guess we've got to assume a connection between this and the body parts in the BMW. If anyone carried a body out of here, it was wrapped in something."

Drummond pinched her chin in thought. "The stiff's torso was in a blanket."

"A porous blanket. Which would leak. We should be looking for something waterproof. Plastic sheets, maybe something in the garage."

"Assuming this mess oozed out of the guy found in the car and not Morgan Masters."

Benno nodded agreement.

Drummond put her thumb over Benno's and turned off the flashlight. "Regardless of who did the bleeding here, it's apparent that nobody's home. Save your batteries. I'm turning on the lights."

As she moved away in the darkness, a headlight beam suddenly stabbed in through the window and moved across the ceiling.

"Hold it," Benno said sharply. He turned his flashlight back on and swept the beam across the room. Drummond froze with a pencil touching the light switch. The detectives walked quietly over and peered down out the window.

The moon had broken through the clouds. In the ghostly yellow light, a taxi pulled into the driveway and stopped behind the Escort. A man and a woman got out. The woman wore an ankle-length coat while the man was dressed in jeans and a jacket with a fur collar. The cabbie opened the trunk and stacked luggage on the porch. The man loaded a suitcase into the Ford Escort while the woman paid the fare. The taxi backed into the street as the couple approached the house and disappeared underneath the porch overhang.

Benno and Drummond crept out of the bedroom and waited at the top of the stairs while the front door opened. Lights came on in the entry hall. The two cops hid in the shadows.

From downstairs came the shuffle of feet and then the rustle of clothing. The woman said in a husky voice, "Hurry. Hurry . . . God."

"Jesus," the man groaned, followed by the sound of a zipper sliding down.

Benno bit his lip. Here he was working with a woman he didn't know well enough to tell an off-color joke, and now this couple downstairs was ready to get it on, right here. Benno looked at Drummond. She grinned from ear to ear.

Now the man downstairs grunted, "Oh, baby, I . . ."

Drummond whispered, "I almost hate to break this

up." She came out in the open and started downstairs. Benno followed, hanging back a respectful distance.

Drummond reached the bottom, turned left, and went out of sight. "Miss Masters?" she said.

There was more urgent rustling. The woman replied, "Yes?" Her tone was oddly calm. "I'm Morgan Masters. And who the hell are you?"

Benno came around the corner. Drummond's back was to him, and beyond her, the woman was on her knees, with her coat crumpled on the floor and her blouse open to the waist. She had creamy breasts inside a lacy black bra. She was young and pretty with a firm body. She looked curious, but wasn't afraid. The man was hastily zipping his fly. On the floor beside him sat a portable video camera. He turned around and faced the detectives. He had rugged good looks and hadn't shaved. Underneath his jacket he wore a tank top, showing off his well-muscled physique.

"And this is . . . ?" Drummond said, pointing at the man.

The guy looked as if he'd like to make a run for it. "Uh, Gerald."

Benno stepped up beside his partner. "Can you tell us where you've been for the past few days, ma'am?"

Morgan Masters seemed only vaguely aware of Benno looking at her breasts. He tried to concentrate on her face. Morgan buttoned her blouse as if she was in no hurry to do so. "Out of town. Look, if you're here to rob me . . ."

Drummond showed her badge. "Metro detectives. And trust us, it's important that we know where you've been."

Morgan glanced at Gerald, who stood there scowling. She said, "Where I've been is none of your business."

"Oh, yes, it is," Drummond said. "I have to tell you this is serious, and as of now, everything about you is our business."

"You think so, huh?" Morgan thought it over. "Fuck you. I'm calling my lawyer."

"Your choice," Drummond said. "But if we're getting lawyers involved, then let us call ours."

"Yeah, okay. As soon as I talk to mine." Morgan picked up the phone and punched in a number she had memorized.

Some victim, Benno thought.

4

The riding DA was Randy Dunst, a young guy with greasy black hair, dandruff, and a habit of snuffling. He paced back and forth in Morgan Masters' den. "This is Collin County. Jesus Christ, I'm not even supposed to be up here. I could get in a world of shit."

Drummond sat calmly in a recliner with her feet up. "Great, Randy. We've got a couple of suspects in there. They're the ones who are supposed to be in a world of shit, and now we're finding out it's really us that's in trouble." She thumbed toward the kitchen, where Morgan Masters and her friend sat across from Morgan's attorney. Her lawyer was named Harold Stein, and he seemed pretty sure of himself. "Hey, Benno," Drummond said. "Maybe we should join the other team."

Dunst continued to pace. "I can't believe this. Two policemen without a warrant—and *way* outside their jurisdiction—go breaking into a house where no one's home. You've got blood out the ass upstairs, but we probably won't be able to use it."

Benno was getting fed up with this guy. He sat on

the sofa and crossed his legs. "Use it where? Look, Counselor, we had a woman's car in the possession of two real badasses, and it turns out there's a body in the trunk sliced up to hell and gone. We still don't know whose body, but excuse us for suspecting that maybe there'd been some foul play in this case. Also excuse us for not detouring by the law library before we checked to see if she was still alive. If we'd known what was coming we would have acted differently."

"We haven't even identified the stiff?" Dunst asked.

"There are times when you've got to assume," Benno said. "We have the corpse's fingerprints. If Miss Masters would cooperate to the extent of telling us who might've had access to her BMW, we might have a shot at dental records. The point is, we had one body on our hands and no one could locate Miss Masters. I think we had fear of endangerment as just cause." Drummond gave Benno a sudden look of respect.

Dunst peered into the breakfast room as if trying to eavesdrop; then he turned to Benno. "That'd be great," Dunst said, "if you'd found her dead in here. But she's now a suspect. Different ball game."

Drummond broke in. "We didn't know she was a suspect. And what makes her one?"

"Come on, Detective. There's a body in the trunk of her car and she's running around with this guy."

Drummond straightened the recliner and put her feet on the floor. "Sounds like Nail'emville to me. Gives us even more probable cause."

"In some instances. But not with people who have this kind of stroke."

"What kind of stroke?" Benno asked.

Dunst looked as if Benno had just dropped in from Mars. "Jesus Christ, you don't know?"

Benno rubbed his temples. "I'm just in from out of town."

"Well, I'm from *in* town," Drummond said. "And I never heard of any Morgan Masters, either."

Dunst placed hands on hips in a slightly girlish pose. "Don't think Morgan, people. Does LaVon Masters ring a bell?"

Benno rubbed his forehead. He'd never fucking *heard* of LaVon Masters. Jesus, until a month ago he'd never set foot in Texas. He supposed that LaVon Masters was some local big deal. He thought it was peculiar that Randy Dunst could have the social register memorized, yet still could not do diddly about law enforcement's position in this case.

Drummond licked her lips. "LaVon Masters, the art lady?"

Dunst seemed more in his element now that he didn't have to give his legal opinion. "Right. As in paintings donated to the Dallas Museum. As in a wing in the concert hall."

Benno had a sudden nervous twitch in his eye. Big-name people meant big-time publicity. The last thing Deputy Chief Rubin had told him was to avoid the media like a plague, at least until he got his sea legs. He didn't know whether to back off right now or to wait for the shift lieutenant to replace him on the case. He kept quiet.

Drummond stood up. "Hey, Stonebridge Ranch is nice, but Highland Park it isn't. People like LaVon Masters—"

"Live on Beverly Drive," Dunst finished for her. "Or down by Preston Trails. LaVon Masters does a little of both. Winters she stays next door to Dallas Country Club. Summers she's on Vancouver Island up in Canada. This little dump is just the place where her daughter lives." He thumbed toward the breakfast room. "How do you think the young lady in there affords Harold Stein as a lawyer? You think this guy makes house calls on a regular basis?"

"Oh hell, Randy," Drummond said. "Lawyers are lawyers."

Dunst smirked in irritation. "No, Detective, lawyers *aren't* lawyers. Put it this way. If the CEO from Texas Instruments calls, Stein sends one of his associates. For LaVon Masters he comes in person." He started his pacing again. "Christ, Christ, Christ! Now we've got to go in there and explain to this guy why we're busting into his client's home without a warrant. We'll be lucky if heads don't roll."

Benno couldn't take any more. "Bullshit. We're in bounds. You're overreacting."

Dunst actually shivered. "You think so? One call from this woman's mother, we're all toast."

"Look," Drummond said. "Miss Masters knew that no one was in this house, at least nobody alive. Whether she knew anybody was dead is a different question, but she didn't expect a soul to be in the house."

"Oh?" Dunst looked at Drummond as if she'd just misbehaved. "Are our detectives into mind reading now?"

"Not exactly, but it's more than my woman's intuition. If she expected to run into someone, why would she be blowing a guy in the entry hall?"

Dunst's jaw dropped. "Doing what?"

Drummond grinned seductively. "Come on, Randy, you know what a blow job is, don't you? Don't expect me to demonstrate here."

Dunst looked hopeful for an instant, then frowned. "I wouldn't be putting that in any report. These people might be suing the shit out of us as it is. Come on, let's talk to them. Maybe I can get on their good side." He stepped toward the breakfast room, stopped, and muttered, "A blow job?" Then he led the detectives out of the den with Drummond laughing out loud.

Dunst entered the kitchen, paused, and cleared his throat. "A word, Mr. Stein? I'm Randy Dunst, with the Dallas DA's office. Maybe we can resolve this with a minimum of trouble."

Stein, a man in his fifties with iron-gray hair, seemed a whole lot more at ease than Randy Dunst. He was seated at the breakfast table between Morgan Masters and her boyfriend. He stood and placed a restraining hand on Morgan's shoulder. "Oh, we're going to resolve it, Mr. Dunst. How much trouble we're going to have is up to you."

As Dunst bowed and scraped before Harold Stein, Benno studied Morgan Masters. Now here was a head scratcher. According to her driver's license—which Detective Cruz had run up on the computer screen earlier—Morgan was twenty-nine. She looked several years younger than that, even college age, her frosted hair just-so, dressed in five hundred bucks' worth of navy slacks, white velour blouse, and khaki London Fog. What he'd seen of her body—which was quite a bit, at least from the waist up—was stunning, but this was no dim-witted Barbie doll. She had intelligent, deep-set eyes and radiated cool sophistication along with a rich woman's confidence. So where in hell had she come up with the boyfriend?

The guy might've been a step up the food chain from Darnell Jerome Makepiece, but no more than a step. Morgan's stud, a bodybuilder with the personality to go with it, had dull, stupid eyes with a sort of where's-the-nearest-mirror look about him. While the detectives had waited for the lawyers to arrive, Benno had asked for the guy's full name. Gerald Trafficante. Strong of back, weak of mind.

Christ on a crutch, Benno thought. *This is the guy who Morgan Masters, daughter of privilege, has been fucking?* The idea made less sense the more Benno thought about it. Some senator or congressman maybe, but *this guy*?

Riding DA Dunst was saying, "Come on, Mr. Stein. These detectives were just doing their jobs. Under the circumstances, who could blame them?"

"Under what circumstances?" Stein had clipped gray eyebrows. He wasn't over five five, and half a head shorter than Dunst, but Benno had the impression that Stein was the one looking down on the other man.

"The blood," Dunst fumbled. "The mess upstairs."

"Which they found after they'd already broken in."

"They feared for your client's safety. They had a burden to look around."

"Oh, you haven't seen burden yet."

"Maybe I'm not understanding, Mr. Stein. Doesn't your client want this all cleared up?"

"Of course she does. She just doesn't want to come home and find this pair lurking around without a warrant." Stein appeared deep in thought. "All right, Mr. Dunst, we'll give you this much: Miss Masters has been out of the city. Apparently while she was gone, someone made off with her auto. She doesn't know who. She knows nothing about any crime committed here in her absence. End of story. Now let's discuss why your officers have created this embarrassing situation for her."

Dunst continued to grovel. "I can understand that she might be upset."

"Apparently your officers couldn't." Stein looked down his nose at Drummond and then at Benno.

Benno had had it up to here. He stood up. "You're sure right about that, Mr. Stein. We're not understanding any of this. The main thing that escapes us is why, after we busted our asses trying to make sure this lady wasn't shredded up the same way as the guy in the trunk of her car, she's now shitting on us with your assistance."

Dunst gaped at Benno. Stein frowned. Morgan Masters' lips curved in an inquisitive half smile. Trafficante continued to stare off into space. He flexed his arm and looked down at his biceps.

Benno pictured Deputy Chief Rubin firing his ass, cousin or no. But Benno stood his ground. "I'm having the crime scene unit come out here. Now." He dug out his cell phone.

Dunst's nostrils flared. "Are you out of your mind, Detective?" He looked to Stein as if for approval.

"I might be," Benno said. He turned to Stein. "The lab techs will be here shortly. If you can get some kind of restraining order to keep them out, more power to you." He made the call and, with Stein gaping in disbelief, gave the dispatcher Morgan Masters' address.

Stein wagged a finger in Dunst's face. "I'm holding you responsible for this."

Dunst's breathing quickened, and for just an instant, Benno wondered if the riding DA might pass out cold.

Benno stepped in between the two lawyers and faced Stein. "I've got no idea who's done what here, Mr. Stein. And I admit I've never come across a crime scene quite like this, where there's no victim on the premises and the person we thought might be a victim gets up in our faces and tells us to fuck off. But I'm betting if this was some creep's house over in Oak

Cliff, we wouldn't be having all this chitchat." He shifted his attention to Dunst. "And I do know who's in charge of the scene, and for now, that's me and Ms. Drummond over there. And we're going to gather evidence. I guess it'll be up to Mr. Stein to make us eat the evidence if it comes down to that. And while we're waiting for the crime scene unit, Detective Drummond and I will be asking a few questions."

Stein stepped over beside Morgan Masters. "You won't be asking them of my client."

"Wouldn't dream of it, Counselor." Benno eyed Trafficante, the bodybuilding freak. "We intend to question this guy."

Trafficante looked slowly up from inspection of his biceps. He said to Stein, "I gotta talk to them?"

Stein opened, then closed his mouth.

"Right, Counselor," Benno said. "Mr. Trafficante doesn't happen to be your client, does he? Come on, Mr. Trafficante, join me and Detective Drummond out in the other room. I expect you've heard some of our questions before."

Trafficante's lip curled. "And what if I just sit right here?"

"Then we'll haul your ass downtown. Everything they say about us is right on, Mr. Trafficante. People without their lawyer present get taken advantage of."

Now that Benno was over the line, he decided that no matter what he'd keep on keepin' on. He led the way into the den walking fast, coattails flying. Tina Drummond followed more subdued than before; she sat on the sofa while Benno directed the weightlifter to a chair. Drummond dug in her purse for the photos from the BMW's glovebox, the ones taken inside the strip club, and compared the masked man in the pic-

tures with the hulk seated across from her. She gave
Benno the thumbs-up; this indeed was the guy. Benno
had a surge of satisfaction. He bent over the couch,
leaning on his hands. Visible through the doorway,
ADA Dunst had a hangdog look as Stein read him
the riot act.

Benno faced Trafficante. "You want your own
lawyer?"

Trafficante put both hands around his thigh and
squeezed, obviously happy with his own physical de-
velopment. "I might. Depends."

"On what?"

"On what the beef's about. I ain't done nothing to
get busted for."

"Then you shouldn't need a lawyer. Look at me,
Gerald."

Trafficante's upper lip twitched.

Benno said, "We got to run a sheet on you, or you
want to save us the trouble?"

Trafficante gave a so-what shrug. "So I done time
once. Everything else on me is minor shit."

Drummond hauled out a notepad and butted in.
"Dope? Armed robbery, what?"

Trafficante glared at Drummond, then at Benno.
"I'm going to answer anything more, I'm talking to
you. Guy to guy."

Benno mentally held his breath. In his brief talk
with Tina Drummond he'd noticed two chips on her
shoulder: the racial chip and the female chip. He suspected that the female chip was the biggest. All Benno
needed was for his partner to get into a battle of the
sexes with the interviewee.

He needn't have worried. Tina Drummond shifted
her position on the couch and smiled sweetly at the
guy. "Imagine I'm your secretary, Mr. Trafficante, and

that I'm taking dictation. Now were your legal problems based on drugs or some other misunderstanding with the police?"

Benno felt relief. Drummond's professional chip outweighed the other chips, and then some.

Even Trafficante had to grin. "Yeah, okay. Porn distribution."

Drummond arched an eyebrow. "Oh? Starring yourself?"

"I done a couple of 'em. Why, you in the market?"

"Why should I buy your naked pictures, Mr. Trafficante, when I can already see your ass showing in this interview?"

Trafficante scowled. "Hey, I was hard up."

"Well, now that you've seen the error of your ways, done your time and all," Drummond said, "what is your current occupation?"

"Dancer."

"Wow, I'm impressed. *Cats*? *Miss Saigon*?"

Trafficante's eyebrows moved closer together. "Huh?"

"Broadway shows, sir. Surely you've heard of them."

"Oh yeah. Naw, not yet. Just a few gigs around."

"In ladies' clubs?"

"A couple."

"Everyone has to start somewhere," Drummond said, then looked around as Benno touched her shoulder.

Benno sat beside his partner. He rested his forearms on his thighs, leaned forward, and looked at Trafficante eye to eye. "That your car out there, Gerald? The Escort."

Trafficante looked embarrassed. "For now. Just till I get a better ride."

"I know the feeling," Benno said. "We noticed you

and Miss Masters had luggage you left outside. Been on a trip?"

Trafficante seemed confused. "You talking about Morgan?"

"You don't know her last name?"

Trafficante relaxed and draped one arm over the back of the chair. "She took me over to Bossier City to party. Do the casinos. Women take me lots of places."

Drummond sighed. "I'll just bet they do, big boy. What's your standard fee?"

When Trafficante scowled at her, Benno cut back in. "You meet Morgan in one of the clubs where you, uh, dance?"

"Yeah. A friend innerduced us."

Benno gave Drummond a sideways glance. She nodded and held up the photo taken inside the strip club of the guy dancing in a G-string while women whistled and clapped like mad. "This you, Mr. Trafficante?"

Trafficante squinted at the photo, then looked down and rubbed his triceps. "I don't know as I should say."

Benno tilted his chin. "And you were doing so well, Gerald. So you'll know, and so you'll understand why you *should* say, this is a murder investigation. Never mind whose murder. It's enough to say the lady is a suspect and that we also suspect that someone helped her. You'll excuse us if we're considering that the someone could be you. Not that your circumstances are suspicious or anything."

"*Murder*? I ain't never murdered no one in my life."

Drummond held the picture out. "So now that we've established that you draw the line somewhere, Gerald, have another look. Could this possibly be you in this picture?"

Trafficante nervously scratched his nose. "Okay. Could be. On the job they call me Zorro."

"How blinking original," Drummond said. "And you strip where, Mr. Zorro?"

"Come on, now. Dance."

"Have it your way," Drummond said. "I don't care if you do *Swan Lake*. I want to know where you work."

"Place called Muscle's, out in Grand Prairie."

"Ah, the burbs. And Morgan is your number-one fan, yet you don't know her last name?"

"We don't tell each other that kind of shit," Trafficante said. When Drummond looked at him, Trafficante spread his hands. "She don't know my real name, either—just that I'm Zorro. It's better we don't communicate in that regard, if you know what I'm saying."

"Ah, that I do," Drummond said. "Keeps the relationship on a professional level."

"Yeah, right. Look, Morgan comes by the other night, okay? Said she wanted me to go to Bossier City with her for a few days. I had some days off and I needed the money. Morgan give me this address, so the next morning I drove up here to Plano and found it. We took a cab to the airport four nights ago and just got back."

Drummond exchanged a look with Benno. She said, "Gee, a lovely couple like you two and you don't even know each other's full names."

"Morgan don't give a shit," Trafficante said. "She just wants somebody humping her. Don't matter who."

"I suppose that works for me." Drummond wrote something down.

Benno leaned back and rested his ankle on his knee. "Let's talk about Morgan for a minute, Gerald. We understand you get offers, and we're cool with that.

But isn't Morgan a little different than your usual trick?"

"You got that right. Usually it's some old cunt. But you'd be surprised who's paying for it, Ace. Look at Hugh Grant."

"Yeah, but Hugh's into women," Benno said. "And let's assume there aren't a raftful of starlets looking for a stud like you. On the average, wouldn't you think someone like Morgan in there could get whoever she wants whenever she wants them?"

Trafficante glanced toward the breakfast room. He lowered his voice. "Just looking at her, yeah. But she can't get just anybody into her scene. This is one crazy bitch—you understand what I'm talking about?"

Benno put both feet on the floor. "No, I don't. Fill me in."

"She's into photography, man. Wants a picture of every-fucking-thing."

Drummond picked up a picture of the masked man giving oral sex to the woman. "Like these?"

"Those are nothing. We'd be, like, laying there ready to get it on, and she'd jump up and check the video camera. She'd be panting for it one minute, but if the camera went off it was like she was turned off, too."

"You mean, she was faking it with the passion?" Drummond asked.

"No way. I've been around plenty and I can spot a fake. That bitch is hot. It's just that it ain't a man that gets her that way. It's that fucking camera."

Drummond gave a sympathetic pout. "Poor baby. Must be tough learning it isn't you."

"I don't give a shit one way or the other," Trafficante said. "Just pay me, you know? I'll whip your ass, whatever you want. But this woman's whole scene is weird. Even when we weren't doing it, she kept ordering me around. At dinner she made me sit at a separate table, shit like that. Like I was her servant."

"Well, weren't you?" Drummond asked. "If you assume the role, you have to play it to the hilt."

"Hey, I know my place. A lot of these rich women want to hide you in the closet till they're ready to moan all over you, then clean up and leave looking like they've been shopping or some shit. But this bitch is different. Like, you know when you came downstairs when she was blowing me?"

"I'll never forget it, Gerald," Drummond said, "not if I live to be a thousand."

"Okay, right there. She had me holding this camera to get her taking it in the mouth. I mean, it's her gig, right? And she was hot—goddamn, was she ever. But the second you walked in and I shut off the camera, it was all over. In one second she was cool as cool. Weirdest thing I ever saw."

Benno chewed a thumbnail. "And outside of your, uh, relationship, you two aren't really that close?"

"I told you already. First she shows up at Muscle's. I done a couple of private parties with her—meaning I fucked her six ways from Sunday. Then she took me to Louisiana. I've been with that bitch maybe five days in my life, total. I fucked her and let her blow me. Otherwise I don't even know the woman."

Benno made a mental note to verify the trip, the plane departure, and hotel stay. The BMW had stayed in the pound for a day and a half before Detective Cruz had had the trunk opened. If Trafficante was telling the truth, he was clear as far as any murder was concerned. Benno flipped through his notes until he found the phone number he'd copied down from the caller ID back in the kitchen. "You ever hear her mention anyone named Jessica Baldwin?"

"That's some woman she met at the club where I dance. Morgan called her a couple of times from the hotel."

"But you don't know this woman?"

"Might have seen her around the club, but I ain't sure. Morgan thinks she's some kind of guru and she spills her guts to this woman over the phone. Personally I think it's all a lotta bullshit. I got these women's guru, right down between my legs."

"Or between the cheeks of your ass," Drummond said. "Where are these videotapes of you and Morgan?"

Trafficante jerked a thumb toward the front of the house. "With the luggage."

Drummond and Benno exchanged a look. As long as the tapes were outside the house, they could take them without a warrant, assuming Trafficante turned them over.

Drummond leaned up in bargaining posture. "Say we let you walk. You turn over the tapes?"

Trafficante grinned. "You let me walk, I might even go down on you, lady."

"Now that would be sure to get you locked up," Drummond said. "I'd probably never let you out of my sight again."

Benno handed the bodybuilder one of his business cards and a pencil. "Write down your address and phone number, Gerald. If your story's true, then you got nothing to worry about. And two things. Once you leave here, you're ours. You're not to communicate with Morgan Masters again without my okay. Also, if I find out any of your story's bullshit, I'll bust your ass double."

Trafficante bent to write. "It's true. I ain't lying. In all my fucking life, this is the weirdest bitch I've ever seen."

5

There was a side exit leading from the den. Benno let
Drummond and Trafficante out so that she could get
the videotapes and he could sneak away in his Escort.
Benno watched them walk into the cold, Drummond's
hips gently undulating and Trafficante in a tough-guy
slouch. Then he shut the door and returned to the
breakfast room. He stepped across the threshold and
froze in his tracks.

Quite a crowd had gathered. The crime scene unit
was at work, opening cabinets, squinting at the floor.
Two techs were visible in the entry hall, already climbing the steps on their way up to the master bedroom.
Harold Stein glared from his seat at the breakfast
table. Randy Dunst helplessly massaged his forehead.
Morgan Masters sat beside her lawyer. She met
Benno's gaze, then looked away. Benno crossed the
kitchen and approached one of the techs, a dishwater
blonde standing on tiptoes, peering on top of the refrigerator. He tapped her on the shoulder. She sank
down on her heels and turned to him.

"Detective Benno," Benno said. "Metro Squad. Who's in charge of you guys?"

A hoarse male voice said from the doorway, "I am."

Benno turned. A sturdily built bald man stood there wearing a lab coat. He had a pair of glasses dangling by an earpiece from the breast pocket. The guy held out his hand. "Sergeant Katz."

Benno gripped the hand. "Ham Benno. The riding DA let you in?"

Katz looked about to laugh. "Didn't act like he wanted to."

"Yeah, well"—Benno walked closer and lowered his voice—"we got an odd situation here."

"We just collect and bag it, Detective." Katz pointed in the general direction of the front porch. "Any explaining you have to do, you should be talking to them."

"To who?"

"More brass than I've seen since last Memorial Day. To tell the truth, I don't think that ADA would have let us on the premises without the okay from one of those captains out there. Plus John Hoermann, in person."

Benno scratched his head. "John Herman?"

Katz gave a crooked grin. "You got the pronunciation. He spells it like the Germans—H-O-E-R-M-A-N-N."

"Look, I'm a two-week veteran of the department. Who's John Hoermann?"

"Chief prosecutor. You might as well say he's the DA, since the DA spends all his time politicking."

"What's a guy like that doing way up here in Plano?"

Katz spread his hands, palms up. "The same thing all those TV and newspaper people are doing up here.

Somebody leaked something. You got switchboard operators, dispatchers, everybody with their hands out to the newspapers. A case this big, plus with what happened before—who knows? Like I said, we just collect it and bag it. You called for us—we're at your service."

He started to walk away, but Benno stopped him. "What's so big about this case?"

Katz wiped his forehead with his coat sleeve.

"What's big about it?" Benno asked again.

Katz looked tired. "It's been a long time, but looking at you I'd say you were over thirty. Anybody around here your age who doesn't remember the Masters killing must be from Mars."

"Not quite Mars," Benno said. "Just California."

"Same difference." Katz hauled an empty evidence bag out of his pocket. "I don't envy you, Detective. This is gonna be big. At times like this, I'm glad I do what I do and keep out of the way." He went out into the entry hall and climbed the stairs toward the master bedroom.

Benno went to the front door and looked out through the glass. Jesus, it was like a convention out there. On the porch stood two full captains, one from DPD and the other from the Plano force, with gold trim on their cap bills. In between the captains was a tall skinny man wearing an overcoat and muffler. Visible beyond the trio were three or four guys toting minicams and two on-the-spot reporters—a coiffed blonde in a red jacket and a beautiful black woman—both of whom Benno recognized from the ten o'clock news. Their breath fogged. Two mobile TV trucks sat in the drive, flanked by three print reporters with notebooks and a still photographer. A flash ignited as the photographer took pictures of the captains and the man with the overcoat.

Benno hung back until he saw Tina Drummond emerge from the darkness, casually holding two rectangular boxes. The Ford Escort's lights came on and Trafficante drove away, easing carefully around the news trucks. One of the TV reporters said something to Drummond. Drummond ignored the reporter and approached the police captains.

Benno walked out onto the porch, inhaling icy air. He walked up just as Drummond introduced herself to the captains. The guy in the overcoat asked Drummond, "Who's the lead detective here?"

Benno and Drummond shrugged at each other. Benno said, "We haven't discussed that. We came here originally to report we'd located a missing auto."

"And found a helluva lot more than you'd bargained for," the tall man said. He extended a hand to Benno. "You'll do. Hi. John Hoermann."

Chief Prosecutor John Hoermann was no Randy Dunst. Hoermann was every bit as sure of himself as Morgan's lawyer. He looked around sixty, judging from the wrinkles in his face, but he carried himself like a man thirty years younger. He had a sharp nose and intelligent eyes, and he stood a good three inches over Benno's six one. "We can have jurisdictional problems here," he said in an educated Texas drawl.

"Sure," Benno said. "Different police departments."

"That isn't what I'm talking about. You detectives were in your rights coming up here investigating a stolen auto found in Dallas. But we're in an entirely different county, meaning a different DA might have jurisdiction over any murder. I want to be certain I'm not stepping on toes before I go giving interviews to the media. So let me be sure I've got it straight. The body was found in the Dallas city limits, wasn't it?"

Benno adjusted his collar. He looked to Drummond. No help there. Benno said, "To be precise, Mr. Hoermann, the body was in the trunk of a BMW in the Dallas auto pound. Patrolmen stopped two suspects driving Miss Masters' vehicle in Oak Cliff, but it was a couple of days before anyone looked in the trunk and found the body."

"But within our jurisdiction, right?" Hoermann glanced at the two uniformed captains, who stood by mute, hands in pockets.

"As far as it goes," Benno said. "I should tell you there's also evidence that the crime itself occurred here in Plano. I don't think we've got an ID on the vic, but—"

"Enough for now," Hoermann said. "We can fill in details later. The penal laws allow a murder to be prosecuted in the jurisdiction where the body turns up. That's all I need." He stepped over to the edge of the porch, faced the media people and raised his voice. "Sorry to keep you waiting." The two captains went up to stand on either side of the prosecutor.

The reporters approached, mikes and notepads ready, minicams rolling.

Hoermann flashed a politician's smile. "First and foremost, know the investigation is in its preliminary stages, so please keep your questions general."

All hands went up except for those of the cameramen, who continued to grind away. Hoermann pointed to a heavyset young woman with scarlet lipstick. "Mr. Hoermann, is there any connection between this investigation and the death of Harry Masters?" she asked.

Hoermann waved her off. "Now there you go, dredging up ancient history. I can't comment on that." He pointed toward another upraised hand.

Benno watched three reporters scribble notes. Who was Harry Masters? Must be related to Morgan. And LaVon, Morgan Masters' mother, aka the art lady. Benno wished he knew what the fuck was going on.

The blonde on-the-spot television lady lowered her hand and pointed her microphone. "Mr. Hoermann, is Morgan Masters a suspect here?"

"We can't name anyone as a suspect," Hoermann said. "Let's stick to what is known, shall we?"

"And what is that?"

"That a man is dead. That his body turned up in the trunk of an auto registered to Morgan Masters. And don't bother to ask—the victim hasn't been identified."

A short wiry man waved his notebook. "Okay, sir. Isn't Morgan Masters LaVon Masters' daughter?"

"I can't argue with that," Hoermann said.

"Well, then, you've said the body was in her car. Have you ruled Morgan Masters out as a suspect?"

"No comment," Hoermann said. "And that's all I can give you for now." He reached behind him and hauled Benno up front. "This man is Detective Benno from Metro. He's heading up the investigation, and as it progresses, he'll keep you as up-to-date as possible. Without compromising what the police are doing, of course."

Benno felt like a jackass, standing there with the chief prosecutor and two captains. He'd only wanted to tell the lady they'd found her car, for Christ's sake.

One reporter yelled, "Benno? How do you spell that?"

Benno was speechless. Deputy Chief Rubin was going to have a—

"B-E-N-N-O," a voice called out. The speaker was the wiry reporter who'd asked the previous question, and looking closer, Benno sort of recognized the guy.

The newsman was slightly bucktoothed. He spelled Benno's name a second time, then grinned. "Ham Benno, isn't it? Nice to see you again, Detective."

Benno tried to smile. "How you doing?"

"I'm all right. I can see you don't remember me." The reporter took a step forward. "Bill Nordstrom, with the *News*. For a while I was with the *LA Times*."

Benno's heart sank into his midsection. "Good to see you," he said weakly.

Nordstrom chewed his lip. "Not half as good as it is to see you, Detective Benno. You can't imagine how dull things have been without you around."

6

The media packed it in and left, as did Hoermann and the police captains. The reporters had a story, Hoermann and the captains had the maximum in public exposure, and the silent understanding between press and politician lived on.

Benno went in and hung out with Drummond while the crime scene unit finished up. The day shift had ended several hours ago, and both detectives were now on overtime. A heads-up Main HQ personnel clerk buzzed Drummond to say that relief was on its way. Benno barely noticed. Ever since Nordstrom the reporter had recognized him, butterfly wings had battered his insides like propeller blades.

He went through the motions, following Drummond from room to room while the techs soaked up blood swatches, vacuumed carpets, and dusted for prints in the bath- and bedrooms. In the utility room they found towels and rags freshly washed and dried, items that Drummond told the techs to take to the lab for testing. At the same time she sent two unis out back to scour the perimeter, telling them to be careful not to leave prints on the sliding glass door. She also said to watch out for the big dog. Benno winked at the guys and shook his head; the dog was a pussycat in disguise. In the kitchen they found a wooden knife display with two of the larger knives missing, and they made sure the techs dusted the display for prints. Harold Stein did his best to be everywhere at once, staying on the crime scene unit's heels while Randy Dunst brought up the rear like a basset hound. Twice Benno had to step out of the lawyers' way.

Finally Benno went downstairs alone and stood looking out the window with his hands in his pockets. It was still snowing; the flakes, now bigger and fluffier, were beginning to stick. Christmas lights blazed up and down the block, but there were no decorations inside Morgan Masters' house. The heat was turned up. Benno looked around for a place to discard his overcoat. Someone tapped him on the shoulder. He turned around.

Morgan Masters had changed into a clinging silk blouse and velour slacks. Benno peered beyond her, searching for her lawyer. Stein was in the breakfast room, talking down to Randy Dunst.

"Hey, can we talk?" Morgan said softly.

Benno pictured her as she'd look on videotape with Trafficante the bodybuilder. Didn't make sense, a woman like this one. "We shouldn't speak, miss. You have an attorney."

She watched him calmly. She had seen-it-all blue eyes. Through all the rich-girl veneer, the lady was tough as hell. "I don't care," she said. "I want to tell you something in person."

"This is for your own good. I'd suggest that, if you have anything to say to us, you come to headquarters with your lawyer. We can have a steno there."

"I don't care about all that legal bullshit, either. I care about what's happened."

She switched to a melted look, anxious and vulnerable. Benno reminded himself that this was the woman who'd been blowing a guy in her entry hall the first time he'd laid eyes on her. A scuzzy, nasty guy. Benno said, "Sorry. Not without your lawyer." He thought about calling out to Stein. Or Dunst.

She stepped in closer. "I don't want my lawyer. I want you to know, personally, that I don't know a thing about what's happened around here. Hey, Detective, I wasn't really looking to get walked in on. If you'd said up front about all that blood upstairs . . ." She started to touch his arm, then dropped her hand.

Benno was conscious of her scent and could feel her body heat. *Christ.* He backed away. "I've listened to you more than I should have, Miss Masters. Now please walk away from me. Otherwise I'm going in there and bringing your lawyer in on this. You can ask his advice, and if he tells you to repeat what you've just told me, I'll listen a second time. Only then my partner Detective Drummond will listen in."

Something flashed in her eyes. She looked down, then slowly back up. "Are you sure?"

Benno swallowed hard. "Sure about what?"

She took a deliberate step closer. "That you want me to walk away. Not many guys ask me to walk away. Don't you want to touch me?"

Benno stood frozen. Beads of sweat popped out on his forehead.

"This is what I'm talking about, Randy. This sort of thing," Harold Stein said loudly from the doorway.

Benno looked past Morgan. Stein was pointing at him. Dunst was there as well, looking terrified. Morgan continued to smile, a dangerous come-on grin.

Benno stumbled backward, then righted himself. "Look, she came up to me."

Stein came over, grabbed Morgan's arm, and pulled her back. "Maybe you didn't understand me earlier, Detective. You're not to talk to Miss Masters out of my presence. If that isn't clear, I can make it clear."

"She came up to me," Benno said again.

Stein didn't answer. He took Morgan with him and swept past Dunst, heading for the kitchen. "You'll hear more about this, Randy," Stein said. Morgan peered at Benno over her shoulder. As Stein pulled her through the door, she coyly waved.

Dunst watched openmouthed until Stein and his client had left; then he turned and faced Benno. "Jesus Christ, Benno, what the hell are you pulling here?"

Benno started to speak. He closed his mouth. He took a deep breath, trying to control himself. "Aw, fuck you, Randy," he finally said. "I already told you the woman came up to me."

The unis came in from the back, and one carried a heavy-bladed ax with a cloth wrapped around its wooden handle. The handle was worm-eaten with most of the paint flaked away. The blade was rusty and covered with what looked like dried blood. The uniformed guy exhibited the ax to Drummond and Benno. "Found this next to the fence," he said.

Drummond waved one of the techs over. "Bag it and tag it," she said. "Special care with that item, okay? And send some people with these officers out to the back fence where they found the hatchet. Someone exited through the back door and might've gone over the fence out there."

The tech nodded and carried the ax toward the exit. Drummond shuddered as she turned to Benno. "Bastard could do some damage, huh?" she said.

Two Metro plainclothes eventually showed up to spell Benno and Drummond—a white guy named O'Doul and a black guy named Whitley, night shift men whose look said they'd heard of Benno and didn't trust him. A new-hire assignment to Metro was a big deal, sure to cause a lot of speculation. Benno knew cops and understood that the stories would range from his being Deputy Chief Rubin's illegitimate son to his being a snitch for IAD. He shook hands all around and stood by while Drummond filled in the newcomers. There wouldn't be much for O'Doul and Whitley to do; the crime scene unit was about finished and Harold Stein was about to take his client to a hotel to spend the night. Dunst helped Morgan pack, likely the first time in history that the riding DA had acted as the suspect's lackey. Benno followed them out to the curb and stood by while Dunst loaded a suitcase into the trunk of Stein's Mercedes.

Benno called Dunst aside. "Does the DA's office have any investigators to spare?"

Dunst glanced toward Stein, who was around on the other side escorting Morgan into the backseat like a footman. Dunst whispered to Benno, "Maybe. Why?"

"That woman's a suspect, Randy. You need twenty-four/seven on her, beginning now."

"He's taking her to the Doubletree Inn. Jesus, you don't think Harold Stein would chance—"

"I got no idea what he'd chance," Benno said. "I'm more worried about what *she'd* chance. Listen, would you rather I talk to Hoermann?"

Dunst looked as if he'd just swallowed a grapefruit. "John Hoermann?"

Benno slowly shook his head. Jesus, what was wrong with this asshole? "Yeah, John Hoermann. I'm going to say this once, Randy. You just let a major suspect waltz away from a crime scene because you're scared shitless of her lawyer. So I'm wondering if you're more scared of Hoermann than you are of Harold Stein."

"Jesus Christ. *Hoermann?*"

"Hoermann. Last chance, Randy. Do you make the call, or do I?"

Dunst expelled a long sigh. He dug for his cell phone. "Good idea, Detective. I'll get a couple of people over to the hotel to keep an eye on her."

"Glad you thought of that," Benno said.

Drummond and Benno left. On the ride downtown Drummond asked him, "Well?"

Benno had both hands on the wheel. "Could still be the scuzz, but I doubt it. The guy Makepiece would have rolled on his partner in a second if he'd known what was going on."

Drummond adjusted herself so that she was sitting on her ankles. She laid her arm across the seatback and rested her chin on her biceps. "I wasn't talking about the case. I was talking about us."

"As partners?"

"Sure as hell not as husband and wife. I grew up in San Antonio, Benno. I have two years at St. Mary's U. Now you know my background."

"Yeah, sure," Benno said. "Know you like my sister."

She moved quickly on. "I was also married. No kids. Got divorced after I was on the job. Standard police life story. I'm open about everything except my age."

"You're under thirty," he said. "Closer to twenty-five."

"Which you determined how?"

"You look young, except for your eyes."

She grinned, straight white teeth flashing. "Because

of the seamy side of life I've seen? Come on, that's corny."

"I was about to say, that your eyes give you a look of intelligence beyond your tender years."

"My years haven't been that tender, Benno. And my guess is yours haven't either."

"I'm thirty-eight."

"The bullshit going around is that you just blew in from the West Coast. That you're related to someone at City Hall who gave you a leg up on starting out as a Metro detective. How accurate is that?"

Benno took the ramp from southbound Central onto Woodall Rogers Freeway as he considered his answer. Finally he said, "Pretty close."

"And you're related to who?"

"Jeff Rubin. He's originally from California and he's my father's first cousin."

"A deputy chief, yet. So Ham is short for what? Hamilton or . . . ?"

"It's just Ham. My father is Japeth. I've got a cousin Shem someplace. Biblical names."

"Sure, Noah's sons," Drummond said. "I took religions of the world in my sophomore year, before I dropped out. You do know it was Ham who caught his father in bed with his two sisters, don't you?"

"Of course. I grew up with the Torah under my pillow."

"The story goes that Noah cursed Ham for breaking in when he shouldn't have. A lot of scholars believe he turned Ham black. It'd be sort of ironic if you and I partnered up. The Jew and the African against the world. Might put you in some neighborhoods where you're not accustomed to going."

"Wouldn't be the first time," Benno said. "I had an uncle that ran a wholesale kosher foods distributorship in East LA. After school I used to drive his delivery truck all over, good neighborhoods and bad. Grocery stores and what delis there were. I used to hide my yarmulke under the seat when I'd drive through Watts. The black guys didn't cotton to little Jewish boys."

"Orthodox?"

Benno rubbed the top of his head. "Worse. Hassidic. We wore the whole black outfit. I'm not a practicing Jew any longer. When I was first out on my own I used to drive around on Saturdays because for the first time in my life, I could. When I was a kid, walking everywhere on weekends used to embarrass the hell out of me."

Drummond's voice lowered an octave, her tone more questioning. "So what are you doing in Texas?"

Benno expelled a long low sigh. "It's a pretty long story, beginning with something that happened on the job in LA. Hey, I'm not being evasive, but I'd as soon not talk about it."

"Sooner or later you'll want to. Everybody wants to talk to somebody. If you need a shoulder . . . Hey, I can be like the guy that says, 'Forget it, Jake. It's Chinatown.' How would that be?"

"Huh?"

"It was a movie I must have watched a hundred times as a teenager. Jack Nicholson's partner, right after Faye Dunaway gets killed, he says—"

"I know *Chinatown*," Benno said. "It's not exactly like that, Tina. But then in another way, maybe it is. I don't want to talk about my own private Chinatown, okay?" He looked over to find Drummond convulsed in silent laughter, her shoulders heaving. "What's so funny?"

She chuckled out loud as she straightened her posture. "I was just thinking how much cooler it sounds when you're talking about places in California. Here in Dallas it'd be 'Forget it, Jake. It's Oak Cliff.' Or Forney, Mesquite—someplace like that. No wonder nobody sets any movies around here. Takes a lot of the romance out of it, huh?" She turned serious. "If you don't want to talk about it, don't. But maybe you should think about it. If we're going to work on this case together, maybe there are things I should know that other people don't."

Benno took the ramp leading down onto north-bound Akard Street, the converted warehouses that formed the West End District now visible on his left. "You should know that the odds of us continuing together on this case are pretty slim."

Drummond folded her arms and looked down. "Because you prefer a guy?"

"At the risk of turning you against me," Benno said, "I've got to tell you that you need to get rid of the chip on your shoulder. Who you are's got nothing to do with it. It's who I am. A reporter back there recognized me. There will likely be some things in the paper that'll remove me from the case."

"What things in the paper? All about your Chinatown?"

"Something like that," Benno said.

She studied him. "I suppose that's your business, at least for now. But unless that happens, let's assume that this mess is about to become our number-one priority, with you as lead investigator."

"Yeah, I appreciate the hell out of Hoermann for designating me," Benno said. "Remind me to do him a favor sometime."

Drummond laughed. "I never want to be lead. This way you're responsible for my fuckups." Her gaze drifted to the right, toward One Main Place as they continued south on Akard Street. "I don't fool around on the job, Benno," she said.

He looked at her. The Mercury drifted to the left. He jerked the wheel to steer into the proper lane.

"Don't misinterpret what I'm saying," Drummond said. "I don't sense any feelers coming from you or anything. But it's messed up more than one partnership for me. Knowing things up front, I think that's the best way to go. Don't you?"

Benno let Drummond off on Akard beneath I-30 and watched her take the walkway between City Hall and the Municipal Building, losing her in shadow for an instant before she reappeared in the floodlight beams. She hustled around the corner of City Hall and was out of sight. Benno then put the Merc in gear and headed for home.

He rented an apartment at the rear of a fireman's widow's home on Monticello Street off Lower Greenville Avenue. He went in through his private entry, hung his overcoat on a hall tree, turned up the heat, stripped down to his boxers and sat around in his underwear. He left the television off; he never turned on the set except to watch the news. His chest was hairless, his stomach flat from situps thrice-weekly after his runs. He had a narrow face, a large hooked nose, and short brown hair combed back on the sides. His neck was firm, molding tight around his Adam's apple.

A half hour later Benno boiled water in a kettle, dropped a teabag into a cup, and poured the water over the tea. As the brew steeped he filled a glass with ice and, when the tea was strong enough for him, he poured it over the ice and added sugar. He'd learned to drink iced tea while living in California, shortly after quitting the booze. He'd tried eliminating sweetener several times, but never acquired the taste.

He went into his bedroom, opened a trunk he had stashed in the corner, took out his yarmulke and prayer shawl and laid them on the bed. He hadn't touched the religious garments in years, but now sat staring at them, side by side on the mattress, for an hour or more while drinking his tea. He picked up the phone, dialed the area code and four digits of his father's number, but then replaced the receiver in its cradle. His vision blurring slightly, Benno carefully folded the yarmulke and prayer shawl, replaced the items in the trunk, and went to bed. He tossed and turned through the night, kicking the covers into pretzels of cloth.

Ham Benno was thirteen when he decided that he didn't want to live his life as a Hassidic Jew. When he recalled his Bar Mitzvah he had three distinct images; the first was of a pleasantly rounded fourteen-year-old girl named Sarah Angrist who, accidentally on purpose, sat beside him for a time pressing her thigh against his and giving him a hard-on. All these bearded men in black dress and yarmulkes sitting around, and Benno with a boner up to here.

His second distinct impression coming from his Bar Mitzvah had to do with his grandmother, Ruth, who a year short of her death was bedridden with the cancer that would eventually kill her. One by one the adults went into the back bedroom to pay Ruth homage, and each came out sadly shaking his head. There was a lot of conversation through the afternoon about Ruth Benno and how she was the final living family member who'd survived the Holocaust. The consensus was that Ruth's passing would mark the end of an era, and Benno recalled that everyone seemed saddened by Ruth's condition except for Benno's mother, Sally. Oh, Sally would never come out and say she looked forward to the old lady's death, but her eldest son could sense his mother's attitude. Ruth had lived with the Bennos ever since her release from the concentration camp, and as the only other female in the family, Sally had become sort of the older woman's servant— fixing the various kosher broths that Ruth loved, cleaning her room, sitting mute as Ruth educated the children on the Torah and Talmud. Ham Benno knew, deep inside, that only with his grandmother's passing could his mother assume first place in the family chain of command.

Benno's Bar Mitzvah was also one of the few times he'd been around his cousin Jeff Rubin, who came to the celebration wearing his LAPD uniform. Later Rubin would move up in the ranks and eventually get a big transfer to the Dallas force that would put his name in the paper. But on Benno's thirteenth birthday Rubin was still an LA patrolman. Jeff Rubin had a wife and a couple of kids of his own, and he almost never stepped over the Benno threshold; the two families never socialized, mainly because Japeth Benno resented that his nearest cousin, Jeff, had become a Reform Jew. Ham didn't yet know the differences between the various religious groupings of American Judaism, mainly because Japeth Benno had taught his offspring that the Hassidic way was the only way, but he did understand that Reform Jews didn't wear the skullcap, even during worship, that men and women sat together at the synagogue, and that Reform Jews didn't wear any sort of traditional garb. Benno hated the Hassidic getup; passersby on the street gaping as if seeing a freak show embarrassed the hell out of him. As such, as an early adolescent, Ham Benno secretly thought that being a Reform Jew must be pretty cool.

Jeff Rubin stayed pretty much to himself at the party. He spent most of the evening talking to Ed Schwartz, a slope-shouldered bald guy whom Benno's father had described as an infidel. Schwartz wasn't a relative. He was making his living downtown as a bail bondsman and never went to temple, Reform or otherwise. Originally he wasn't on the guest list at all, and he only got invited because his sister was married to Ruth Benno's brother. Thirteen-year-old Ham Benno stayed as close to the two outcasts as he could without his father noticing and eavesdropped on their conversation whenever he could. The gold buttons on his cousin's uniform impressed him. By the time his Bar Mitzvah was over, Benno'd decided that, if being a Reform Jew and a cop would set him apart from the rest of the family, he'd be both.

7

Harold Stein drove grimly up to the North Dallas Tollway booth, applied the brakes, and poked a ten-dollar bill through the window at the attendant. He bristled impatiently while the attendant made change; then he rose up to shove the change in his pocket as he accelerated into the toll road's southbound lanes. He turned his ear to the backseat as Morgan Masters said, "Shit, Steinsy. What a fuckin' zoo."

Stein's grip on the wheel tightened into a stranglehold. Thirty-five years in practice, the last twenty as senior partner in Stein and Bromberg, LLP, seventy lawyers on the payroll, judges looking for campaign donations groveling at his feet like beggars, public-employee assholes like Randy Dunst cringing in intimidation—and yet this simple-minded cunt continued to call him Steinsy. *Steinsy?* Christ, no one else would have the nerve. Stein forced his hands to relax. Practicing law had taught him one important lesson: At three hundred and ninety dollars an hour, Harold Stein could take a lot of shit. And cackle in glee whenever the bill went out in the mail. He returned his gaze to the road ahead and didn't say anything.

Morgan leaned forward until her chin rested on the seatback. "We're gonna sue their ass, Steinsy. Collect a fuckin' fortune." She made a snuffling noise.

Stein glanced in the rearview. Morgan had one finger over her nostril, snorting cocaine. He didn't know how much powder she'd stuffed up her nose back there, but she was already high, slurring her words. The twit was a bomb waiting to explode. She'd just left a murder scene where she was the number-one suspect, and on her way out, she had carried a vial of coke past half of the fucking police department. Could Stein look the other way while his client did dope in the backseat of his car? At three hundred and ninety dollars an hour, you bet he could.

"Sue their fuckin' asses," Morgan said.

Stein put on his best grandfatherly tone. "You might want to think twice about that."

"They have, like, violated my constitutional fuckin' rights. I heard you say so."

"You heard me say that to the prosecutor, Morgan. To tell the truth, I'm not sure the police are out of bounds here. I'd have to research the matter."

Morgan leaned back against the cushions. "They can't just bust in people's houses. I know that much about the law."

"They can under certain exigent circumstances. The bloody mess in your bedroom may constitute one."

"I don't know shit about that."

"I'm hoping you don't."

"And what the hell does that mean, Steinsy?"

"Call it past experience. Never mind. We need to account for your whereabouts for the past few days."

Morgan sounded suddenly sleepy. "I've been outta town. Zorro will tell them."

"I, uh, don't think that individual will make the most believable witness. You need motel receipts, credit card vouchers."

"I paid cash. Money talks and bullshit walks in Louisiana." Visible in the rearview mirror, Morgan tossed a bundle of money up in the air. A few bills drifted over the seat and landed on the floorboard.

"Christ, Morgan, that's even more suspicious. Nobody pays cash these days."

She sounded suddenly fearful. "I'm not going to jail, am I, Steinsy?"

Stein didn't want to answer that one. Over the past few years Morgan Masters' tits-and-ass behavior had earned Harold Stein several hundred thousand dollars in legal fees, all forked over from her mother. With Morgan in jail that river of income would dry up. Should she go to jail? Probably, for something. But *would* she? As long as the checks didn't bounce, he'd do everything he could to keep her breathing free air. He said, "You need to make a list of who has access to your house. Someone made that awful mess in there."

"I sure didn't. What do you think about that cop?"

"What cop?"

"That detective. He's cute."

"Morgan. You have to stay away from any police, at least until we can straighten this out. Who's got a key to your place?"

She pouted in thought. She began to giggle. "Do you have a phone book?"

"Christ."

"I can't help it if I'm popular."

Popular? Spread your legs wide enough, Stein thought, *and the whole world rushes in under your skirt.* He said, "Maybe you should have your locks changed. I'll need a list of some kind. All the names you can think of."

"I don't know all of their names, Steinsy. Take Zorro."

"You take Zorro. You shouldn't be counting on him too much."

She began to cry. "I can't fuckin' go to jail."

"It's a long way from that," Stein said. "They'll need a whole lot more evidence than I've seen so far. They'd have to place you at the scene in the right time frame, for starters."

"Well, I wasn't fuckin' there." Morgan scooted forward and peered out the window. "Where are we fuckin' goin'?"

"We're fuckin'—" Stein cut himself off and cleared his throat. "You'll be staying at the Doubletree Inn until the police release your house as a crime scene and you can go back home. Three or four days."

"Hotels bore the shit out of me. Take me back so I can get my fuckin' car."

Stein slammed his palm against the steering wheel. "No car! No leaving the hotel! You are to stay there until I get back to you. Order anything you want from room service. Watch television, but do not leave."

"You givin' me fuckin' orders?"

"What does it take to get through to you that you're a murder suspect? I don't control you, Morgan, but I can get your mother involved."

"LaVon? Now that *really* scares the shit out of me."

Stein threw up his hands. "Be scared. Don't be scared. But stay in the hotel. If you get really bored, Morgan, perform oral sex on the bellman."

"Now that's an idea," Morgan said.

The Doubletree Inn loomed on the right, a thirty-story parabola with twinkling lights from top to bottom against a sky blackened by sooty smog. Stein moved over into the exit lane. "You get whatever ideas you want to, Morgan. But if I have to hire someone to guard the door, I'll do it. Do not leave the hotel. Absolutely, positively. Do not even stick your nose outside."

Stein used his Amex to check Morgan in, then shook off the bellman and toted her luggage to the elevator with her marching grumpily along beside him. She listed some names as they walked. On the ride up, two fortyish women looked down their noses at Morgan, then favored Stein with glares that could melt cobalt. Stein ignored the women.

Once he'd found Morgan's room he slid the card through the slot, waited for the tumblers to click, then ushered her into a suite with two king-sized beds. He placed her luggage on the rack, laid her card key on the dresser, cautioned her not to leave once again, said good night, and marched toward the door. She flounced onto the bed, said, "Fuckin' Nazi," and clicked on the television.

Stein rode down on the elevator and exited through the lobby, shooting furtive glances around to make sure no one recognized him—some of his corporate clients held meetings in this hotel. He'd left his Mercedes parked under the canopy just outside the main entry. As he slid behind the wheel, two men in rumpled suits got out of a pedestrian-looking four-door— a Ford or a Mercury, Stein didn't know one cheap make from another—and hustled into the lobby. *They're cops,* Stein thought, *or DA's investigators, out to keep an eye on my client.* So if Morgan should wander outside the hotel, the two plainclothes might even arrest her ass. Great, Stein thought as he drove away, it would serve her right if they did.

* * *

Morgan Masters hated Harold Stein. She also hated her mother, the bitch LaVon, and she now despised the entire fucking police department. The thought that she'd let the guy—what was his name? Zorro? Yeah, whatever. The thought that she'd let Zorro touch her made her want to vomit. She could practically smell the bastard and feel his disgusting erect penis slide into her mouth. Oh fuck, she'd degraded herself once more. She'd vowed over and over, never again, but couldn't seem to stop. Male whores turned her stomach, but right now Morgan Masters turned her own stomach even more. What was wrong with her? She had to be as crazy as hell.

She changed channels on the television, pressing on the remote so hard that she chipped a nail. She had no idea what program she was watching and didn't even care. She hated television as well, and her vision was too blurred by tears for her to make out what was on the screen even if she'd wanted to. Once the coke wore off she might do another line, but only so she'd remain in a hazy state. She wasn't hooked on drugs, and the only time she ever touched cocaine was after one of her crazy spells. The dope made her high and made the pain easier to bear. She hated liquor as it often made her violently ill, but sometimes after one of her crazy spells she'd get drunk in addition to doing drugs. She wanted to talk to Jessica, but was too ashamed to face her. Of all the people in the world, only Jessica understood.

Morgan knew she wasn't really a bad person, but sometimes she just couldn't help herself. Sometimes she could black out the awful memory, but when she slept it would all come back in a nightmare. Her problems with sex went back as far as she could recall. Her earliest memories began around the age of seven, and everything before that was a total blank, but she thought she'd probably had the sexual problems since the day she was born. In her entire life she'd never had any normal relationships with men. She knew she looked good, and normal men from normal backgrounds often came around, but Morgan would never have anything to do with those guys. She'd go through weeks and weeks of total celibacy, but then she'd go off the deep end once more and head for the male strip clubs. More than once she'd thought about suicide, and once she had even gone so far as to take a bottle of sleeping pills. On that occasion she'd lost her nerve, called 911, and ended up in a hospital emergency room having her stomach pumped. After that she'd spent two months in a psychiatric hospital, but when she was back on her own she'd returned to her old destructive behavior.

Jessica was definitely helping, but now Morgan had let Jessica down. Facing Jessica was Morgan's greatest fear.

She'd told Detective Ham Benno the truth: She didn't know a thing about what had happened in her house while she was away, but she did have memory problems over the past few days. She recalled snatches of the trip with Zorro—the plane ride, the casino gambling, the wild journey home—though she'd managed to blank out most of the sex with the sleazy fuck. But somewhere in her subconscious were vague memories of Zorro on top of her, snorting and bucking in lust, his stench so strong in her nostrils it made her gag. *Oh Jesus* . . .

She lurched up from the bed and hurled the television remote across the room. The remote hit the wall and shattered, plastic and tiny batteries scattering over the carpet. Morgan yanked the minibar open and pulled out a bottle of Scotch. She poured the Scotch into a glass, no water, no ice, and curled up in a chair with her drink in both hands. She had a long swallow, shuddered, and began to sob. Tears rolled down her cheeks. She chugged the rest of the liquor, smashed the glass against the wall, sank back on the bed, and hugged herself. She was shivering. Her lips quivered and her legs twitched as if in convulsion. She felt as if she were freezing to death.

Harold Stein had a stop to make before he went home. From the Doubletree Inn he took Preston Road south all the way to Beverly Drive and turned left at the southern boundary of Dallas Country Club. The traffic ahead was bumper to bumper, as pickups and SUVs cruised Beverly Drive so that drivers and passengers could ogle the millionaires' Christmas lights. The mansions on both sides of the street were lit up with shimmering points of fire. Here and there, on lawns the size of polo fields, stood life-sized Nativity scenes, mechanical waving Santas, and reindeer made of burnished bronze. Traffic crawled along at ten miles per as moms, dads, and tots alike gaped at the lights and *oh*'ed and *ah*'ed. Stein resisted the urge to ride the horn in order to get the dim-wits moving.

Three blocks beyond the country club he cut down a side street, made another left, and pulled into a circular exposed aggregate driveway. Between the drive and the street stood a fountain with granite cherubs around the perimeter, spewing water from monstrous seashells held in chubby stone hands. The house was a redbrick three-story Colonial with a white-pillared porch, and an eight-foot-high hand-carved front door with a brass knocker. At this home there were no Christmas decorations.

Stein went up on the porch and rang the bell. Chimes played the opening five bars to "New York,

New York," little-town blues melting away and all that crap. Stein didn't much like the song. He didn't like music in general, and he thought that New York City was an overrated piece-of-shit town. He hunched his shoulders and shivered in the cold.

In minutes a peephole opened and closed, chains rattled and deadbolts slid, and then a uniformed Hispanic maid opened the door and let Stein inside. She was rail-thin and kept her chin tilted down. He followed her starchy walk to the back of the house, past Egyptian pewter urns and paintings by Dali and Dimitri Vail. In every room and corridor, at least one mirror hung. The maid led Stein to double French doors and left him. He knocked softly and went on in.

LaVon Masters sat at a rolltop desk, writing a check. Though Stein knew her to be fifty-eight years old—she'd threatened him with mayhem enough times over the years if he told anyone her age—she was still a stunning woman. Her face was an older version of Morgan's, her eyes the same piercing blue. Her cheeks were free of wrinkles, the collagen injections undetectable; her chin and neck were firm, and her breasts and legs were good under clinging pale blue silk lounging pajamas. Her breasts were implants, of course—Stein had arranged the reconstruction along with a tummy tuck and had bought the surgeon's silence with a tip of a few thousand bucks or so. Her toned legs were the result of daily trainer-assisted workouts. Her hair was honey blond all the way to the roots, as weekly appointments at Neiman's kept the strands evenly colored. LaVon turned heads on the street and, as long as the cosmetic surgeons and beauty consultants held out, likely would for a number of years. Stein sat in a cushioned velvet chair on her left. LaVon never looked up. "I've been sittin' here plannin' my garden next spring."

Stein wasn't sure what to say. LaVon Masters' sudden interest in gardening was a well-known joke around the wealthy community—behind her back, of course, but a joke nonetheless. The previous fall she'd spent a small fortune constructing a greenhouse connected to the back of her mansion and had bought every kind of exotic flower and vine that the plant hustlers had to sell. Stein knew nothing about botany himself, but his wife had told him that LaVon's choices were inane—something about growing caladiums in the same bed with a supertough Argentinean vine that would choke the caladiums all to hell and trying to plant impatiens in shade. Just last week, Stein knew, LaVon had paid thirty thousand dollars for a single plant, which now resided in her greenhouse; the overpriced bush sprouted flowers so vile-smelling that it was difficult to stay within a hundred feet of the damned things. Two days earlier LaVon had dragged Stein into the greenhouse for a personal whiff, and he'd yet to get the odor completely out of his system. As far as Stein was concerned, LaVon, after all these years, was still the original Beverly Hillbilly when it came to taste. But she could afford whatever she wanted to buy, and if she wanted to think her fucking garden was going to be a showpiece, Harold Stein wasn't about to disagree.

He opted to say, "I hope the project's going well for you."

"Comin' along," she said. "You got anything good to report?"

Stein unbuttoned his coat and crossed his legs. "Won't know for a while. The police have a problem with opportunity. We can place your daughter out of town at the time of death. It's our story and we're sticking to it."

LaVon signed her name with a flourish, tore off the

check, and reached for an envelope. "Where is the little cunt?"

"I've parked her in the Doubletree. When I left, a couple of plainclothes cops were heading into the lobby. She won't be going anywhere. She wanted her car—can you believe it?"

"I thought her car was in the auto pound," LaVon said.

"The BMW. She's still got the Mercedes at her house."

LaVon dropped the check into the envelope, sealed the flap, and handed the envelope to Stein. "I don't want her runnin' around town, Harold."

Stein put the check in his inside breast pocket. "Trust me. She won't be."

"I got enough problems without her struttin' her ass through them strip clubs."

"She took one of those guys on the trip with her. A pretty schlocky character."

"Ain't they all? What's gonna happen now?"

"We wait for the other shoe to drop. You can expect the police to call in the next few days. They'll be interviewing everybody and anybody connected to Morgan—that you can count on."

"Oh shit. I gotta talk to those assholes?"

"I'd advise you to," Stein said. "They'll hound you till you do. You don't know a thing, LaVon. You haven't seen Morgan lately and haven't a clue where she's been or what she's done."

"I'm that smart, Harold, thank you very much. Fuckin' cops make me nervous."

"They make everyone nervous. Invite them in. Talk to them in the sitting room, and don't use words like fuck and shit. Put on your regal front, LaVon. You're good at it. Pretend they're representatives from the concert hall. If you're convincing enough, they'll leave you alone after one session. They sure as hell don't consider you a suspect. They'll be grilling you about Morgan. She's all they're interested in."

LaVon pushed back from the desk. "Don't be fillin' me fulla shit, Harold. They ain't forgotten the past."

"It's been over twenty-five years. Every cop that was on the force then is either dead or retired." Stein rubbed his eyes. "Thanks for the check. I've had a long day."

"You know the way out," LaVon said, and as Stein rose and walked toward the exit, she said, "Hey, Harold."

Stein turned back to her with eyebrows raised.

LaVon sat intensely forward. "Do you think she knows?"

"Morgan?" Stein rebuttoned his coat.

"Hell yes, Morgan. Does the little cunt know?"

"I don't think there's much of a chance of that. If she does, she didn't let on to me."

A line of tension appeared on LaVon's forehead. "Much of a chance? *Much of a fuckin' chance?* I don't want any chance at all, you bastard."

Stein expelled a long slow sigh. He put on his best mentor's posture and held out his hands, palms toward her. "You've got to learn to relax," Stein said. "I told you. She doesn't know. Trust me. I'm your lawyer. As of this moment, she doesn't know a thing."

After Stein had left, LaVon capped her pen, put it away, and closed the rolltop desk. She turned off the lights, left the study, and locked the French doors with a key that she kept on a chain around her neck. She went through a floor-to-roof atrium with a glass ceiling and mounted a floating staircase. On the bottom step she paused to yell out, "I'm goin' to bed, Carlotta. Don't fuck with me the rest of the night, y'all hear?"

Two corridors away, the maid closed the door to her
own small room.

LaVon climbed the steps, silk fluttering and folding
around her legs, and paused halfway up to examine
herself in the banister-mounted mirror on her right.
She touched her hair, then continued on. At the
second-story level was another mirror, this one on her
left. She touched her hair on the other side of her
head.

LaVon Masters liked what she saw. When she
reached the point that her reflection no longer pleased
her, she'd have the mirrors removed.

There was a suspended walkway leading to the
second-floor corridor. She took the walkway and entered her bedroom. The bedroom contained a sitting
area with leather furniture and a marble vanity with
a big round mirror. There was a bay window overlook-
ing a rose garden. On the vanity sat spray bottles of
perfume and seven different brands of skin cream.
There was a king-sized four-poster bed with a canopy
and curtains. She switched off the overhead lights and
turned on the muted fluorescents at the head of the
bed. She parted the curtains, sat on the mattress, and
took off her shoes.

Gerald Trafficante aka Zorro was propped up
against the headboard, wearing light green Jockey
shorts that molded his privates. His muscular legs were
crossed at the ankles. He was reading a weightlifting
magazine, which he now tossed away.

LaVon arched an eyebrow as she looked at him
over her shoulder. "Where'd you park?" she said.

"Out back in the servant's driveway, by the Mexican
bitch's car. Same place as always. Why? You afraid
somebody's gonna see me?"

"You never know. Somebody just dropped by."
LaVon stood and stripped off her pajama bottoms.

She was naked underneath. Her pubic hair was trimmed into a sharply defined V. "You gotta leave before daylight. How was the trip?"

"It was a trip."

"You know what I mean. How was she?"

Zorro propped his elbow on a pillow and rested his chin on his lightly clenched fist. "Okay. Pussy's pussy. The cops were already there when we got back. I give 'em some video tapes."

LaVon removed her top and tossed it away. "Can you see her face in them?"

"I ain't looked. But, yeah, I think so."

LaVon stretched out on the bed and pointed her toes. "Is that what you say about me?"

"What's that?"

"That pussy's pussy?"

Zorro reached over and slapped her ass. "Naw. I tell 'em your pussy *ain't* pussy. That what you want to hear?"

"What I want to hear is that I'm better in bed than she is."

"Yeah, whatever," Zorro said.

LaVon rolled onto her side, facing him, and hooked one leg over his. "Turn off the lights, you fuck," she said.

Outside it had begun to snow, big fluffy flakes that drifted in the gentle wind and whitened Santa caps and Nativity scenes throughout the neighborhood. Trucks and SUVs left Beverly Drive and its Christmas lights and headed for home before the roads got slick.

The three-story house with the circular drive and fountain was now dark in front, except for a single security light that cast its beam on the pillars and porch. Out back, snowflakes settled onto the green-house roof and on dead rose petals and thorny branches in the outdoor garden. There was an eight-foot-high stockade fence with an electronic gate and a security panel. Beyond the gate was a narrow driveway leading in from the alley. A rusty twelve-year-old Chevy Celebrity sat nose-on to the gate, and behind the Chevy was a dented Ford Escort—Zorro's car.

A shadowy figure moved alongside the Escort. A flashlight came on, illuminating the seat and steering wheel. Then the beam crept its way down the side of the car and shined on the rear bumper. The flashlight went off. Gloved hands affixed two strips of tape to the bumper, forming a cross. The flashlight clicked back on. The tape reflected bright chartreuse in the beam. The light went off a final time; then footsteps crunched away through the thickening snow.

Trafficante got ready to leave LaVon Masters' place at four in the morning. LaVon slept on her stomach with her ass sticking up and her head turned to one side on the pillow. Her ass was fairly tight but it showed saggy lines and a couple of tiny surgical scars. Her face, relaxed in sleep, looked puffy and droopy. This broad was fucking *old*.

Trafficante dressed in a hurry and found the three hundred-dollar bills she'd left him on her bedside table. As if when she didn't hand him the money in person he was really humping her for love. Her game, her rules. Trafficante didn't really give a shit as long as he got paid. He wondered who was crazier: the old cunt or the young one. He thought it was probably a toss-up. While he'd been over in Louisiana there'd been a murder in the young one's house, and now the police were on his ass. As for the young one, he wouldn't touch her again with a ten-foot pole, not for any amount. Absolutely, positively, no fucking way. The videotapes he'd given the female cop could mean trouble in the future; Trafficante'd been around the justice system enough so that he understood he might even have to testify. If it came down to that, he'd simply leave town and find another gig in some distant part of the country. Trafficante didn't testify. *Snitching,* yeah, but *testifying* created too much exposure. Trafficante didn't want his name in the paper, no fucking way.

He left the bedroom and went down the steps two at a time, pausing twice on the way to examine himself in the mirrors. Buff. Stud. The kind of body that had women creaming all over themselves.

On his way out he wondered briefly how LaVon had gotten this fucking rich. High-dollar paintings hung all over the walls, and there was crystal on display that went for a couple of hundred bucks, retail, for a single goblet. He thought about stealing some of the stuff, but quickly changed his mind. Crazy old woman likely kept some kind of inventory.

He passed the study and went down a thirty-foot-long hallway toward the back of the mansion. More oil paintings were on display on both sides of the corridor. The woman was a fucking money machine.

He pushed out through double swinging doors and exited through the greenhouse. Rows of heaters kept the temperature in the greenhouse at eighty degrees, and the humidifiers made little hissing noises. Overhead fluorescents cast a ghostly light. Trafficante shuffled along in a tough-guy slouch, sneering as he passed caladiums on his left and rows of boxes where impatiens grew. The woman had gardeners, maids, all kinds of servants running around to take care of this house and grounds—just so she could keep on making her game as some big society whore. But deep inside, Trafficante knew, she was just another horny old cunt begging for services such as only guys like him could provide. Just thinking about it gave him a laugh. About three-quarters of the way down the greenhouse aisle to the exit, he paused and scratched his head.

Growing out of a floor-level box filled with potting soil was a green bushy stalk six or seven feet tall. Big purple flowers sprouted from the plant. The flowers were shaped like roses, only bigger than any rose Trafficante had ever seen. The petals were light purple around the edges and deepened in color nearer the stalk.

If LaVon had been telling the truth the other night, here was something a man might steal and get away with it. The last time he'd sneaked in here in the middle of the night, LaVon had been waiting inside the greenhouse looking at this plant, an expression nearing lust on her face. As if she was *horny* for this fucking bush or something. She'd told him all about it as they'd gone upstairs. She'd ordered the bush from some rare plant grower in Massachussetts, had paid thirty grand for the fucking thing, and next spring planned to have these bushes growing all over her yard.

Jesus Christ. Thirty fucking grand.

Trafficante had never seen thirty thousand dollars all at one time in his whole worthless life. He knew nothing about plants, but he did know something about thirty grand. It was enough money for him to live a while without servicing stupid cunts like LaVon Masters and her crazy fucking daughter.

And Gerald Trafficante knew something else.

He was marginally acquainted with a guy who lived in Fort Worth. If something had any value whatsoever, this guy knew where to unload the fucking thing. Eddie Von was the man's name, and Eddie was no normal fence. Eddie moved shit that no one else would touch. Eddie had style. Eddie also had a house with a swimming pool, and he played golf at Colonial Country Club. Hell, Trafficante knew someone who'd fenced some stolen *lightbulbs* through the guy. Bunch of expensive plants, no sweat.

Trafficante considered himself smarter than most. Fuck, he'd almost graduated from high school, hadn't he? He pulled out a Swiss army knife, opened a blade, and sawed two of the flowers off of the stalk. He wrinkled his nose. The flowers stunk—Jesus, did they ever. He thought LaVon had probably been lying about the plant's value, bragging about all this money she'd spent. But so fucking what? *Nothing ventured, nothing gained,* Trafficante thought. He'd show the flowers to Eddie Von, and if Eddie showed any interest, Trafficante knew where to get more. A whole lot more.

He bounced the big purple flowers up and down in his hand as he exited the greenhouse and stepped out into the cold. He hunched his shoulders against the frigid breeze and cursed every snowflake that floated past in front of his face. Texas weather sucked bigtime, freezing in winter, the summer sun roasting your ass. Trafficante slouched on through LaVon Masters' backyard, wondering where he could go if he could get his mittens on thirty fucking grand. Florida, maybe, or even some island in the south fucking seas.

He dropped the flowers on the seat beside him and shivered as he tried to start his Escort. The engine took several tries before it finally cranked, and then it died as soon as he dropped the lever in gear. The snow was piling up now, drifts beginning to form in spots. He cranked the engine once again, turned on the heater, and waited for the air to warm inside the car. At the first hint of warmth he dropped the lever in gear again, and this time the motor kept on running. On the way down the alley to the street the tires spun in slush, and the Escort's rear end fishtailed.

Trafficante was beginning to feel sorry for himself. No way should a buff stud like him have to drive through this rich man's neighborhood in this fucking heap of an Escort. He added a car to the list of things he'd buy with the thirty grand.

As he drove alongside the creek at a snail's pace, he passed a row of cars on his right. As the Escort crept past, the lights of one of the parked autos came on. The headlights reflected from a bright chartreuse cross on the Escort's bumper. The parked car pulled out slowly and drove the slippery street at a speed equal to the Escort's. Gerald Trafficante, aka Zorro, was so intent on choosing his future boss set of wheels he never noticed that he'd picked up a tail.

8

In the dream, it was always the SWAT youngster's eyes. Gray and crystal clear, shifting from side to side under the blocked-off hat. Excited. Eager. Ready for anything. But at the same time, tense. Frightened . . .

And seconds later, dead. Staring up at nothing in the echo of gunfire. And another noise . . .

The footsteps thudding over hardwood, coming fast.

A single emotion rose in Benno's subconscious as he looked down on the dead young man, the vacant staring eyes. The emotion wasn't anger. Nor sorrow, nor anticipation.

Only fear.

Benno worked out in gray half-light at seven in the morning, pushing himself, kicking out the last hundred yards before he reached the twenty-four-hour deli across from the Granada Theater on Greenville Avenue. The temperature was twenty-two degrees and a good six inches of snow lay on the ground, yet sweat covered his body and steam rose from his warmup suit. His chest rose and fell in labored breaths. He

bought an onion bagel in the deli, picked up a copy
of the *Morning News,* and cooled down as he walked
home through a neighborhood of eighty-year-old re-
furbished houses with snowcapped roofs, moving his
arms around, loosening his shoulders. Once in his
apartment he flipped on his coffeemaker and did two
hundred sit-ups while listening to the hot liquid hiss
and drip. He poured a cup, added sugar, and flopped
down at his breakfast table to scan the paper. He bit
into the bagel and chewed as he read.

It was even worse than he'd expected. MURDER POS-
SIBLY LINKED TO HARRY MASTERS KILLING was
stretched across the metro page in huge type, and his
own picture appeared beneath the headline, Chief
Prosecutor John Hoermann pushing him into the lime-
light. Benno frantically searched the opening para-
graphs of the story, hoping against hope that they'd
omitted his name. Nope, there he was, the spelling
perfect: Detective Ham Benno, lead investigator. He
pictured Deputy Chief Jeff Rubin at home, reading
his own copy of the paper, spilling his morning coffee
all over the floor and dying of apoplexy.

The story itself was sketchy at best, but it still managed to hint at plenty. Police would neither confirm
nor deny that LaVon Masters was a suspect, ditto her
daughter, Morgan, but Detective Benno would have
more for the public as the investigation progressed.
Benno checked the byline over the article; he didn't
recognize the reporter's name, but it wasn't Bill Nordstrom's story. That would come later, likely in the next
day or so, a followup article wherein Nordstrom would
report Benno's history in LA. That was when the shit
would hit the fan.

The third paragraph was plain-vanilla bullshit, a
rundown on the current situation—or at least the parts

that law enforcement had let leak, such as the unidentified corpse found in the BMW's trunk as it sat in the auto pound. There was nothing about the body's dismembered condition, of course, as that was a detail only the killer could know. The reporter let it drop that the car was registered to Morgan Masters and left the rest to public speculation. The article continued further on in the paper. Benno flipped through the pages, found the jump page and continued to read.

The wrap-up was longer than the front-page portion, a rehash of Harry Masters' murder twenty-seven years ago. Harry had been an LA transplant, building his Hollywood connections into a near monopoly on movie distribution throughout Texas in the days before multitheater complexes and studio-controlled distribution deals. In addition to All-Star Distributing, Harry had owned a chain of theaters with five locations in Dallas, three in Fort Worth, and three each in San Antonio and Houston. The Masters movie houses had been the scene of numerous premieres in the fifties and sixties, and the stars had turned out in force to hawk the productions. Harry himself had hung out with Sinatra and the Rat Pack, gone big-game hunting with McQueen, hosted fund-raisers alongside Bogart and Edward G. Robinson. In 1968 he'd married one of his popcorn vendors, LaVon Greene, a little girl from Little Rock, and transformed her into royalty. Benno scanned a layout of photos beneath the story: Harry and LaVon in Times Square, Harry and LaVon posing with a strung-up marlin on Harry's yacht, Harry and LaVon in their Circle Suite at a Cowboys game. Their daughter's birth had spawned more headlines. Benno squinted at the image of LaVon, picturing in his mind's eye Morgan Masters as she'd approached him last night in her living room.

The ancient photos were fuzzy and not of good quality, but the family resemblance between mother and daughter was striking.

On the eighth of July in '72. Harry Masters had left his Highland Park mansion around nine p.m. and had gone off to make the rounds of his movie houses. There was nothing unusual about this procedure; according to the *News,* Harry appeared at each of his locations once a week—even taking turnaround Southwest Airlines flights to Houston and San Antonio, often late at night, picking up the box office receipts and making the bank deposit the following day. Here Benno read between the lines; since the theater managers never knew on which night Harry was coming to call, the odds of hands being in the cookie jar lessened considerably.

On this particular evening Harry Masters arrived at the Grand between nine thirty and ten. After he secured the money from the box office till he had a brief conversation with the manager, a Mr. Otis Rigg. According to the manager, the topic of conversation had to do with converting the theater ownership into the name of a trust; under the terms of his employment Otis Rigg had received profit sharing in the form of stock, which Harry wanted to buy. The manager had quoted his price and the two parted on good terms, and then Harry exited into the neon brilliance of Elm Street. He never made it to his other movie houses that night, and he was never again seen alive. Two thirteen-year-olds were fishing under a bridge on South Loop 12 a couple of days later when they noticed a charred abandoned auto in a field. It was the hood ornament that attracted the kids; the car was a late-model Lincoln. Human remains were inside, burned beyond recognition. Police had identified Harry through dental records.

The story had a chopped-off ending—writer versus editor, Benno knew, the writer with eloquence as his goal, while the editor's eye was firmly on the story's length in column inches—and Benno wished there was more detail. He formed questions in his mind even as he read. LaVon Masters had eventually become a suspect (*Why?* Benno thought) and the Dallas County DA had indicted her a year after the murder. (Benno wondered why the charges had been delayed, and what evidence had finally led the DA to move on the case.) There had been humongous publicity surrounding LaVon's arrest and trial, and in the end the judge—whose name was Arthur Bigelow, according to the article—had saved the lady by taking the verdict out of the jury's hands. After both sides had rested, the judge had ruled that the prosecution hadn't proved its case. Exit LaVon Masters from the justice system, never to be charged again by virtue of double jeopardy, to the eventual benefit of the Myerson Concert Hall, the Dallas Art Museum, and numerous charities around the metroplex. Benno's experience with the LAPD spanned fourteen years, over half of that time in the Robbery/Homicide Division, and he'd testified in more than fifty trials. It was SOP for the defense to make an instructed-verdict motion at the close of testimony, but Benno had never seen a court grant such relief. The judge's decision in the Masters case—particularly considering the publicity surrounding the trial—was curious as hell.

Benno got out a pad and pen and closely read the article a second time, making notes as he went along. He performed this function by reflex, the detective in him taking over, committing every detail to writing. Even as he worked, however, he had an empty feeling in his belly. He thought that last night's exposure would be more than Deputy Chief Rubin could stomach, and that he, Ham Benno, would be removed from the case.

Ham Benno arrived on the job at ten minutes before ten. He wore a pressed blue suit, white shirt, and crisp red tie. He shrugged out of his overcoat and folded the garment over his arm as he came in through the street-level entrance and proceeded to the elevator. Every day on the job thus far he'd showed up exactly ten minutes early for his shift. In this manner he avoided the early arrivals hanging out in the coffee shop, shooting the shit until they reported for work, yet he was always on time so as to not piss off the graveyard shift people who were anxious to go home.

He walked into the Metro Squad room and paused at the rail, his eyelids raised in curiosity. The Chinese-American detective had moved. He was methodically stowing his gear into desk drawers closer to the front of the office and also bending an ear to the night shift guy who was filling him in on the graveyard details. As Benno watched, the Asian placed his nameplate on the desk top. Benno read the name: SONG. Odd that, in the two weeks prior to today, Benno had never known what to call the guy. Song glanced up, then looked quickly away. Benno went through the gate and to the back of the squad room.

His office was a cubicle enclosed by partitions with plastic inserts. Song's former desk butted up to Benno's; it now was vacant. Benno hung his overcoat and jacket on hangers, his blue nylon holster nestled under his armpit, and sat down. There was a stack of call slips on his desk with a handwritten note on top. The note read, in curt cursive:

Don't return any of these. See me.

The signature was "DiA" followed by a slash. Di-Angelo was the shift lieutenant. Benno peered out of the cubicle. DiAngelo's door was closed. Benno thumbed through the call slips.

There were ten calls, all from newspaper and television people. Benno laid the media callbacks aside. There was a scraping noise just outside the cubicle. Benno looked up as Tina Drummond came in.

Wearing slacks and a sweater, she was laden down like a pack animal, a foot-high stack of files balanced on one arm, her nameplate in the crook of the other arm, a cup of coffee in her hand. She breathed in through her nose and said, "Look, could you . . . ?"

Benno jumped up, took the stack of files, and flopped them down on the vacant desk.

Drummond set her nameplate beside the files, sat in the chair, and tilted back. She sipped her coffee. "Not my idea, in case you're wondering."

Benno parked his rump on the edge of the desk. "Actually I wasn't. We're officially partnered now?"

"As much as anything's official around this dump. All I can say is, I came in. DiAngelo had left marching orders on my desk, so here I am." Drummond's gaze drifted to the call slips. "Whatcha got?"

"Ten calls from reporters," Benno said.

Drummond grinned. "Ain't it neat being the lead detective?" She tilted forward in her chair. Her gaze shifted past Benno toward the cubicle entrance. "Yes, sir?" she said.

Benno swiveled his head and saw Lieutenant Di-Angelo leaning against the partition. He had a full head of dark wavy hair and a gut that pooched out over his belt. Forty years old, he had a prominent jaw and a double chin. His brow knitted in a scowl. "You two."

"Hi, Loo," Drummond said brightly.

"You . . . two," DiAngelo repeated, this time drawing it out. He crooked a finger. "Both of you."

Benno pointed at the call slips. "Look, about that stuff in the paper, and about those call messages, I didn't—"

"Fuck the call messages," DiAngelo said. "And fuck the newspapers. You two are wanted in the chief's conference room. Get moving." He stepped toward the squad room exit. "And so you'll know, this ain't my ass. Your ass, maybe. Not mine."

There was a saying around Main Police Headquarters that the higher one rose in the building, the more brass one was likely to encounter, thus prompting the rank-and-file detectives to stick to the lower floors. Benno and Drummond rode all the way to the top in the elevator. When the doors opened, Drummond exited first and led the way down a carpeted corridor with Benno a step behind.

Benno thought about DiAngelo's parting shot. He hadn't grown to like DiAngelo much during his short time in Metro, and at the moment, he hated the guy. The last time he'd felt like this was seven years ago in LA, just before he'd gone before the disciplinary board. Back then he hadn't been in suspense; he'd already known he was getting the ax, and the only question was how much of his pension he was going to keep. That deal was different. In fact, comparing then and now, Benno thought that he was an entirely different guy with entirely different goals. So okay, in LA he'd been a royal fuckup, but here he'd only been following orders when he'd driven up to Plano in the first place. Getting the shaft when he was innocent would be even harder to take than when he'd had it coming.

Midway down the hall, among strong oak doors with gilt lettering, was a conference room with a window looking in. Benno and Drummond peered inside. There was an oval conference table in there, with ten cushioned armchairs. There was also a rolling server bearing coffee, water, and a stack of Styrofoam cups. Photos of the mayor and the police chief were on the wall, along with the city crest. Five of the seats had people sitting in them.

Benno winced as he recognized Deputy Chief Jeff Rubin. Apparently Rubin hadn't died from apoplexy while reading the morning paper, though the expression above his uniform collar was appropriately grim. To Rubin's right sat the two captains who'd appeared last night at the crime scene, along with Chief Prosecutor John Hoermann. Hoermann's look was somber. Next to him, looking confused, was riding DA Randy Dunst. Drummond murmured, "Well, here goes." Then she knocked on the door and the two detectives went inside.

Benno and Drummond faced the table from just inside the entry. The two police captains showed stoic looks. One was a slim white-haired man and the other was Hispanic, with dark eyes and black hair combed in a widow's peak. Deputy Chief Jeff Rubin flicked a glance in Benno's direction, then studied the polished mahogany surface before him. Chief ADA John Hoermann sat up straight. Dunst looked frightened. For ten full seconds, no one uttered a word.

"This is an embarrassment," Hoermann said finally and the captains nodded agreement. "It's going to require a lot of damage repair."

Benno swallowed back a lump the size of a grapefruit in his throat. He pulled out a chair and sat down across from the brass. Drummond did the same.

Hoermann folded his hands. "I think we should first agree on where the breakdown in communications came about. You detectives will need to explain how all those details wound up in the morning paper."

Benno chewed his inner cheek. How the hell was he supposed to answer that one? He'd walked out on the porch, listened to Hoermann tell the press that he, Benno, was the lead detective on the case, and then Hoermann had shoved him to the front with no fucking warning at all.

Tina Drummond said, "Begging your pardon. But I don't think that's anything for us to explain."

Hoermann's look said that this wasn't the answer he'd been looking for. One of the captains eyed Drummond with growing interest. The other captain flashed an inquisitive look at Jeff Rubin. The deputy chief continued to watch the table.

Drummond continued. "The first public announcement came from your lips, Mr. Hoermann. If you'll recall, neither Detective Benno nor I had spoken to you beforehand."

Hoermann looked trapped for an instant; then he firmed his mouth. "I'll have one thing clear in this. I don't jump into anything. I had information that those reporters already knew most of the story. Otherwise I wouldn't have uttered a word to them."

Drummond smiled. "I'm sure you had information from somewhere, sir. I just want to qualify that the information didn't come from us. We'd only begun the investigation when you arrived on the scene."

Now the captains appeared confused. The Hispanic said, "If these detectives didn't tell you, John . . ."

"The hell should I know?" Hoermann was shouldering none of the blame, no way. "Look, the call comes in to my home. The police dispatcher told me that the media was already at the scene. If someone hadn't tipped them off as to the parties involved, what were all those reporters doing out there?"

The captain pointed a finger. "That's a little bit different than what you just told the mayor's office in that conference call. Now the mayor's going to give misinformation to LaVon Masters' lawyer and wind up with egg all over his face. What you said not five minutes ago, John, was that you'd see that these detectives got their act together. Now you're saying it isn't even their fault."

"Now look." Hoermann was defensive, his eyes narrowed. "I'm saying no such thing. I'm saying I got the word from the dispatcher. Ultimately her information had to come from the people investigating."

"Oh bullshit," the captain said. "Rumors fly around a police station just like anyplace else."

Benno also wondered where the word had come from and thought it probably came from Cruz, the Crimes Against Property cop who'd conducted the jailhouse interview with Darnell Jerome Makepiece. Benno felt he should interject, but didn't know what he could say without pointing the finger in another officer's direction. So he kept his mouth shut.

"That's not the situation in my shop," Hoermann said. "We don't spout off until we have our ducks in a row. If the mayor's going to chew someone's ass, it's not going to be mine."

"Yeah, right," the captain said. "If you—"

"If *you*," Deputy Chief Rubin suddenly spoke up, placing a hand on the captain's arm, "and you"—looking now directly at Hoermann—"will cut out the sniping, you'll realize that what who told who doesn't matter. All of you are missing the point."

Benno felt more relaxed now that his cousin was taking over. Jeff Rubin had a square jaw under a hooked nose; he was a no-nonsense guy whom everyone respected. Hoermann and the two captains sat at attention. Tina Drummond crossed her legs under the table.

"Who is it you're kowtowing to?" Rubin said.

"There are retired cops all over town that remember when LaVon Masters wasn't an icon. They remember when LaVon Masters was a murdering bitch that made asses out of the entire department. So why are we bowing and scraping to this woman?"

Hoermann raised a hand, palm out. "Now hold on, Jeff. I didn't see anyone assuming an inferior posture here. I thought we put up a unified front."

"Balls." Rubin never raised his voice. "The only thing unified was all three of you needing kneepads, trying to explain to the mayor why all that shit about LaVon Masters got in the *News*. And all three of you agreeing that the foul-up had to be the fault of these two detectives here, who it now turns out are blameless parties. This is a murder investigation. It isn't a solicitation for donations to the mayor's or the DA's reelection campaigns. The only purpose for Harold Stein's call to the mayor was to put the whole county on the defensive, which he accomplished. So anyone see anything odd about the questions the mayor's people are asking?"

The captains and Hoermann seemed confused. Benno watched his cousin with respect.

Rubin said, "We're all supposed to be trained observers. What did we observe? What's missing here? We got Harold Stein, who last night was the suspect's lawyer, now calling the mayor in his capacity as the suspect's *mother's* lawyer. So how come he's not calling on behalf of the suspect, Morgan Masters? You don't find that odd? The purpose of that call was to blow smoke up our asses, gentlemen. And in the case of you three so-called higher-ups, the scam has worked like a charm."

The white-haired captain spoke up. "We're looking out for the interests of the department, Chief."

"What you are looking to do is cover your ass,"

Rubin said. "Tell me, class, what question did Stein forget to ask when he called the mayor?" He looked around at the room in general.

Benno was stumped. Drummond said, "We didn't hear the conversation, Chief. Detective Benno and I."

"Right, you didn't," Rubin said. "In retrospect, the investigating detectives were left out of the loop, which shouldn't have happened. Harold Stein read the mayor the riot act, but never showed the slightest interest in who the dead guy happens to be. Shouldn't Stein be interested in that? I damned sure would be if I was him. We got a bloody mess upstairs in that house, yet nobody seems to wonder whose blood it is?

"Right," Rubin said. "You're chasing your tails here worrying about what LaVon Masters might do to you, when what you should be doing is finding out about the dead guy." He popped a folder open and rummaged through the papers inside, finally pulling one sheet out and waving it around. "Jesus Christ, doesn't anybody read any autopsy reports? Your cut-up stiff had a prostate the size of a grapefruit and emphysema, not to mention an artificial knee. The medical examiner places the deceased's age somewhere between sixty-five and seventy-five. So who wants to kill an old fucker like that? Did anybody bother to print the corpse?"

Hoermann and the captains looked nervously at each other. Hoermann said, "I'm assuming it was done."

"You assume. Anybody look for a murder weapon?"

"The bloody ax in the yard . . ." Hoermann trailed off.

"Which was conveniently left in open sight," Rubin said, "and also forms a matched set with the two smaller hatchets hanging in the garage. So far so good. According to this report, the guy got dismembered post-mortem with a heavy instrument, probably an ax. But what about the four stab wounds in the victim's torso and the two knives missing from the kitchen? Anybody look for the second weapon used on this guy?"

Hoermann hitched uncomfortably around in his chair. "We assume the crime scene unit . . ."

"Yeah, right," Rubin said. "Well, I'm through assuming. I'm going to make sure we run the proper make on the dead guy. The bullshit is over, gentlemen. We are going to get our asses in gear taking care of this case. I'm instructing these detectives to do just that, and I don't give a shit who they have to question or whose nose gets bent out of shape. Over twenty-five years ago LaVon Masters got away with killing her husband. Like Don Rickles said about Doris Day, this department knew LaVon before she was a virgin. Trust me, folks. As long as I got a heartbeat, she ain't gonna hose this community a second time."

Rubin laid down the law. He told Benno and Drummond to give him a daily written report on the case. Then John Hoermann got miffed over being left out, so Rubin told the detectives to send a copy of the report over to the DA's office, at the same time managing to sound as if he was doing Hoermann a favor. Hoermann told Benno and Drummond to coordinate everything with Randy Dunst. Drummond whispered to Benno, "Great. All we fuckin' need."

The meeting adjourned. Hoermann stalked out with a sour look, followed by the captains. Dunst brought up the rear. Drummond and Benno started to leave as well. Rubin said, "Detective Benno?"

Benno turned. Drummond halted partway out the door and turned as well.

"You and I need to talk," Rubin said.

Benno was torn. He didn't want Drummond to think anyone was taking her out of the loop.

Rubin already had the picture. He smiled at Tina Drummond. "This has got nothing to do with you, Ms. Drummond. Or this murder case. Family business."

Drummond eyed Benno. She shrugged, then went out and shut the door. Benno wished like hell he could have gone with her. He went back to the table and sat down.

Rubin leaned back and propped his shin against the edge of the table. "I read the paper. Seems you've already stepped in a little shit here. I thought we had an agreement." He set his gaze and waited for Benno to say something.

Benno unbuttoned his coat and yanked down on his tie. "You going to give me a chance to explain?"

Rubin spread his hands. He didn't answer.

"The way it started out," Benno said, "I went up to Plano to tell the Masters woman her stolen BMW was in the auto pound. That's all I was going to do. I didn't find anybody at home, so I came back and wrote a report. In the meantime, the cop chasing the stolen car report found the body in the trunk. One thing led to another."

"And put your name on page one," Rubin said. "The *Dallas Morning News* has got nationwide circulation. Police departments everywhere read all this shit, got people on the payroll looking at it every day. How long you think it'll be before we get a call from Los Angeles?"

Benno pictured Nordstrom, the reporter who used to be in LA. He hesitated about bringing the guy up, then decided that Rubin would find out anyway. Benno said, "Even if you don't, there's already a guy reporting on the case that knows who I am."

"Jesus fucking—"

"Also something I couldn't do anything about," Benno said. "Look, I'm minding my own business. Hoermann announces to all those reporters that I'm the lead detective on the case. Then he shoves me out in front of them. One of the reporters collars me. I sort of remember the guy from Los Angeles. He'll write me up in the paper sooner or later."

"Bill Nordstrom—is that the guy?" When Benno nodded, Rubin looked at the ceiling. "Ah shit. I knew Nordstrom. Used to work for the LA paper. All those newspaper guys owe us. Maybe I can cut him off."

"You already stuck your neck out too much for me," Benno said.

Rubin waved a hand dismissively. "My neck isn't out. I got a helluva pension here. The department as a whole thinks *its* neck is out, but I don't happen to believe that kissing LaVon Masters' ass is going to accomplish anything in this case. Your neck is out more than anybody's. So okay, I got you hired, sort of indirectly. But now that you're on board, there's about three guys down the line who can fire your ass. If one of them does, I can't step in."

"It's out of your control," Benno said. "Maybe that's best."

"If I thought it was best you got fired, I never would have got you hired. Let me talk to a few people."

"I put you out too much already, Jeff."

Rubin pointed a finger. "That's not my name when we're on the job. Chief Rubin to you, okay? And I'm not being charitable here. I want you on this case."

Benno didn't try to hide his surprise. "Even with the publicity?"

"I'm weighing options. Your name in the newspaper—that's bad. Having a detective on the case that LaVon Masters isn't going to scare the shit out of—that's good. From what her record tells me, that's also

Detective Tina Drummond. Even the chief of police shits his pants just thinking about that woman, but not you two. You talked to your father?"

Benno lowered his gaze. "No."

"Since he's calling me, I could've figured that out. Japeth Benno hasn't left me a message in twenty years. Since your grandmother's funeral I've seen him maybe five times, all by accident, yet here he's leaving me messages. So I thought you should know. Likely Japeth's heard you moved here and got a job. Since he knows I'm in Dallas, too, that's why he's calling me."

"Even if he knows it," Benno said, "I'm surprised he'd try to find me."

"I suspect he'd like some contact with his grandchild," Rubin said.

"I've barely got any contact with my kid myself, though it's getting better since I'm sort of back on my feet. I haven't missed a payment in two or three years, and Jan says Jacob can visit me after Christmas. My old man stepping into the picture might change all that."

"Your wife's celebrating Christmas? She's not a Jew, then."

"Ex-wife. She's a California girl who goes to the Methodist sometimes, Christmas and Easter mainly. She knows about my growing up. She'd be terrified my old man would try and make a Hassid out of the kid."

Rubin rested his cheek on his lightly clenched fist. "Maybe he wouldn't. If you laid some ground rules . . ."

"Come on. You and my father haven't been tight for—what? Thirty years? So how come now you're campaigning?"

"We get older. We want to make amends. Japeth is strong on *tzedakah,* the good deeds. He and I are a lot alike in that regard."

"My old man's idea of a good deed," Benno said, "is different than someone else's. His idea of a good deed is leading an infidel to the tabernacle."

"Evangelism isn't part of the Jewish faith. You haven't been strayed so long you've forgotten that."

"I'm not saying he'd go down the street buttonholing people. But in my case he'd never let me rest until I was dressed in black. Look at you. He practically X'd you out of the family just because you're Reform. I can't take the chance of putting him together with my kid. It might end my own contact. Wipe out the strides I've made."

Rubin seemed resigned for a moment, but then he said, "You'll be sorry someday if you don't patch things up. I won't tell you how to go about it—that's up to you." His look saddened. "Hanukkah could be a good time for it."

Benno looked at the wall calendar. "That time already? I don't even keep up with the dates any longer."

"It comes around faster the older you get," Rubin said. "Seems like just the other day you were a kid, spinning the dreidel."

"And landing on *nun*," Benno said. "Or sometimes matching the pot. I was never very lucky." He expelled a sigh. "Someday there might be a chance to get together with my pop. Now isn't the time."

"If enough time passes," Rubin said, "then it might be too late."

"I respect what you're saying. You're responsible for two jobs I got: one in LA when I first became a cop and now this one, giving me another chance. Almost anything you asked me to do, I'd do my damnedest. But any reunion with my father would be on his terms, including me returning to the synagogue. I can't do that."

"If that's the situation, that's the situation," Rubin said. "I'll stick my nose in no more. I've delivered the message that Japeth's calling me. It's all I can do."

"Thanks for filling me in." Benno looked toward the exit. "We finished here?"

"Yeah, for now. Beginning this moment, though, you watch your ass. Anybody tries to tell you to compromise your investigation into this murder, you send 'em to me. And some of these political assholes will try—that you can count on. They'll all be bowing and scraping to LaVon Masters. Don't take my word for it. Talk to some old cops that live around here. A colder bitch than LaVon Masters ain't never lived in this world."

Benno hustled out of the conference room and almost ran headlong into Tina Drummond. She'd just raised a hand to knock and carried a stack of papers fresh from her computer printer. She stepped back, looked up at Benno, and said, "The *Dallas Morning News* archives show four hundred twenty-seven hits on Masters, LaVon. I'm eliminating everything after 1980. This should give us most of the details on the Harry Masters killing—at least what's public knowledge."

Benno left the door partway open, conscious of Jeff Rubin still seated at the table behind him. "Great," Benno said. "Shouldn't identifying the current body be our priority, though?"

Drummond pulled a couple of sheets from the stack and waved them. "Already done. I stopped off at the lab and picked up the NCIC fingerprint report. Our dead man is a Mr. Edward Payne. Seventy-seven newspaper hits on this guy, not to mention a rap sheet going back a half century or so. Would you like a thumbnail summary?"

Rubin called out from within the conference room, "I think we all would, Detective Drummond."

Benno and Drummond went in and sat down across from Rubin. Drummond spread the report out on the table. "Edward Henry Payne aka Uncle Eddie Payne. From 1948 until the late seventies he was a suspect in seventeen different homicides. All charges dismissed. You've got to read between the lines, but the inference is that witnesses were somewhat reluctant to testify against the guy. There was one murder-for-hire case where they had both him and a Highland Park woman in custody over killing her husband. She made a deal to roll over for the prosecution. While she was in jail she had a sudden heart attack."

Rubin threw up his hands. "Christ. How does an old-time asshole like that fit in the picture?"

"Today's picture?" Drummond said. "Or this murder back in the seventies?"

"Both," Rubin said. "Bet me he was somehow connected to LaVon Masters around the time of her husband's killing."

"There are no newspaper hits on him since 'seventy-nine. Wonder where he's been since then."

Rubin studied his knuckles. "An old-time hardass like that should be dead."

Drummond waved her folder. "This is an autopsy report, sir. He *is* dead."

"No, I mean years ago. There're no more guys like that left anymore. Ah, the old days. So this is our dead guy?"

"Apparently so," Drummond said.

Rubin's forehead tightened. "What was Uncle Eddie Payne's birth date?"

Drummond checked the record. "In 1922."

"Gives him what, twenty-some years on LaVon? At the time of Harry Masters' killing, Uncle Eddie woulda been late forties, early fifties." Rubin seemed deep in thought. He pointed a finger. "Who's seen that information, Detective Drummond?"

Drummond shuffled the papers around in her lap, straightened the pile. "As far as I know, just the medical examiners and me."

"I'll be on the phone to the medical examiner to make sure that's as far as it goes for now. Hoermann's office is out. I don't want Uncle Eddie Payne's name in the newspapers. For public consumption, the dead man's identity remains a mystery, and I don't want Hoermann spilling the beans until I can roust a few guys. I'm betting Uncle Eddie Payne and LaVon Masters are connected somehow. It'll take some digging in the dead case archives."

Benno opened, then closed his mouth. He wondered if Rubin's obsession with the Harry Masters case might be sending the deputy chief off the deep end. Finally Benno said, "The cases aren't necessarily connected."

"They are connected," Rubin said. "For now, you two report directly to me. This will put Lieutenant DiAngelo's underwear in a knot, but I'll handle that. I'll talk to the guy. While I'm doing some stuff on the q.t., you go on with your rat killing. You got this male stripper as a witness?"

"Gerald Trafficante alias Zorro," Benno said.

"Okay, Detective Benno, your assignment is to check out the stripper's story from A to Z. Start with his employer. Detective Drummond, while your partner is doing that, I want you on the county property records. I want a list of every tangible asset listed belonging to LaVon Masters."

When Drummond lowered her gaze, Rubin grinned. "Before you start sending for the butterfly nets, listen to something. Women like LaVon Masters are all about money. Harry Masters is dead because his wife wanted his money. If somebody else is now dead, it's about LaVon Masters *keeping* that money. I'm not saying the daughter's not involved, and at this point assume that she is. But LaVon's behind it. Mark that down, and if I'm wrong, you can call the funny farm to pick me up."

"What about interviewing the daughter?" Benno asked.

"Eventually, yeah, but you don't touch that with a fifty-foot pole for now," Rubin said. "Talking directly to her will do nothing but get Harold Stein riled up again, and we'll have all kinds of political assholes sticking their noses in this. Your first priority is the stripper. Ms. Drummond, you get on the property records. I expect reports from both of you. All of us will be putting in some overtime. I'm going to find out where Uncle Eddie Payne has been for the past twenty-five years or so and what his possible connection to LaVon was in the old days. Guy disappears from sight for all this time and suddenly turns up dead. So I'm asking myself why this is happening now."

Drummond gathered her gear and started to rise. As Benno got to his feet he said, "You know, if you're wrong, you can get your ass in a crack. You don't need heat from the mayor's office unless it's completely necessary."

"You let me worry about that," Rubin said. "I'm not wrong. I'm sixty-three years old, and alla time I forget shit. My wife is on my ass about forty-something pills a day I'm supposed to take. Next in line for me is the assisted living. I might be a crazy old fart. But in this particular instance, I'm not wrong."

By the time the little girl was six she no longer wanted to be pretty. She wanted to be ugly so badly that sometimes her heart would ache. In first grade she made friends with a grossly obese girl named Teresa and a child named Leslie with a withered arm, in hopes that by associating with the two outcasts she could become as ugly as they were. After two weeks of hanging out with Teresa and Leslie she was still as pretty as ever, so she called them a couple of freaks, reducing them to tears, and said she wouldn't be their friend anymore.

When she wasn't in school her mother left her alone for hours, often all night. During these periods of loneliness she'd practice making hideous faces in the mirror, hoping that her features would freeze into a horrible mask, and she even thought about slashing her cheeks and nose with a knife in order to leave terrible scars. She thought that, if she was ugly, Uncle Eddie might keep away from her.

The first time Uncle Eddie came to her in the night was about two years after she'd seen him set the car on fire. At first she was glad that he was finally paying attention to her. When she was very small, before the incident with the burning auto, it had bothered her that Uncle Eddie ignored her all the time. But back then she'd had her daddy to love her. Now Daddy was gone from her life, and Uncle Eddie was the only man who ever came around. When he did, he would sit with her mother and drink the whiskey that the little girl thought smelled so awful. After a time Uncle Eddie and her mother would lock themselves in her mother's bedroom, leaving the little girl alone with the sounds of sex—the squeaking of the bed, her mother's lustful moans—coming muffled through the door. During those periods the little girl would tightly shut her eyes and pretend that Uncle Eddie had come to play with her. In her dreamworld she'd get out her tiny cups and saucers—the ones that Daddy had given her on the Christmas before he went away—and fix tea just for Uncle Eddie while her mother slept. She imagined that the tea parties would be a secret just between Uncle Eddie and her.

And then one night when she was four, Uncle Eddie came to her for real. It was very late, long after midnight, and at first she thought the opening and closing of the door was an extension of her dream. But there he stood in the moonlight, thick-shouldered and barrel-chested, a heavy, dark-bearded man in boxer shorts, listing some as he grinned at her. She smiled back and immediately thought of her tea set. He sank down on the edge of her bed, his weight making the mattress sag, shifting her in his direction. He called her a pretty little girl. A pretty, pretty little girl. His breath stank of alcohol. When his hand slid between her legs and his fingers probed her most private place, she was so shocked she couldn't breathe.

He stayed for what seemed to her a long, long time, though it was probably not over a half hour, and before he left he told her that she wasn't to say a word about what had happened between them. After he was gone she was sick to her stomach. The following day she bled in the toilet. She never told anyone what had happened, partly from shame and partly because Uncle Eddie had told her not to and she wanted to be good.

Uncle Eddie visited her room fairly regularly after that, late at night when her mother was asleep, and every time he came in her room she was too terrified to move or to resist him. She grew to hate the sight of him, but was sure she could do nothing to stop him. She was only a little girl. He always told her she was pretty, and after a year or two of Uncle Eddie's visits, she didn't want to be pretty any longer. She did want to be obedient, though, so every time he came through the door she stripped off her pajamas and cast her panties aside without being told. She thought if she was obedient he might not stay so long.

She tried every trick her child mind could come up with to stay away from him, even hiding outside her room after Uncle Eddie and her mother had gone to bed, but he always seemed to find her. Always he told her she was pretty before he did the things to her. She wanted to be ugly. She wanted to be the ugliest little girl in the world.

One warm June night shortly before her seventh birthday, after Uncle Eddie and her mother had drunk a lot of whiskey and then locked themselves inside her mother's bedroom, the little girl left the house. She crept out through the front, closing the door softly behind her, and went down the sidewalk wearing her Kermit the Frog pajamas. She lived with her mother in a big Highland Park home with a circular drive and a fountain in front, the same home where they'd lived when her father had died. There was a wooded creek nearby, and the trees and bushes near the water made excellent hiding places. She went down to the creek, snuggled down in high damp grass, and hugged her knees to her chest, hoping to stay there until the sun came up and Uncle Eddie was gone. She rested her head on a big dry rock and dozed.

There was an urgent rustling sound nearby. At first the little girl thought it was the wind in the grass, but the rustling was accompanied by a fluttering noise. The child raised her head from the rock to look. A sparrow hopped around not five feet away, trying to fly, though its right wing hung down at a strange angle, obviously broken. The little girl got up on her haunches and reached for the bird, but it scrambled away from her. She got up and hurried after it as it chirped in terror and scratched the dirt with its claws. She captured the sparrow and lifted it up. The bird's heart beat rapidly against her palm. It lowered its unbroken wing and stayed still, shivering, its injured wing hanging limply down.

There she stood for long moments with the sparrow imprisoned in her hands, and she thought of ways to help the bird. She would have liked to carry the sparrow home and nurse it back to health, but her mother never would have let her do so. Her mother would make her free the injured bird in the woods where she'd found it or, worse, might even kill the sparrow rather than mess with taking care of it. A year or so earlier the little girl's cousin had given her a puppy, and in a week's time she'd trained the puppy to go outside and use the bathroom, but her mother had taken the dog to the shelter to get rid of it. No way would something similar happen to this sparrow that she'd found.

She took the bird's head between a thumb and forefinger and twisted its neck around until the head came off. She held the severed head in her closed fist and felt the beak open and close in reflex until it was still. Then she threw the body and head in the creek and, dry-eyed, sat down on the bank and looked at the drops of blood on her hand and on her pajamas. Then she went back and laid her head on the rock and went to sleep, strangely satisfied.

9

Muscle's, the strip club where Trafficante supposedly worked, was fifteen miles west of Dallas on Highway 157. The stretch of four-lane was nearly deserted, with no other buildings in sight except for a couple of female topless joints down the way. There was a giant billboard outside Muscle's picturing a cartoon guy in his jockstrap, with pumped-up chest and arms. Snow was piled on the roof of the club. Benno parked beneath the sign under an overcast sky.

He hoisted up his briefcase and checked its contents—Morgan Masters' driver's license photo, a couple of the stills from Morgan's BMW featuring her legs wrapped around Trafficante's neck, and a copy of his notes from last night's interview with the man. Benno put the pictures in his inside breast pocket, then started to close the briefcase. He paused, reached inside, and picked up a small square writing pad. On the top page he'd scribbled the number from Morgan Masters' caller ID—Jessica Baldwin's, the woman who'd left Morgan the urgent message. Benno's cell phone was in the glove compartment. He seldom carried the cell, and when he did, he usually kept it turned off. Now he dug out the phone and punched in Jessica Baldwin's number. After three rings he heard a click; then a cultured female voice said, "This is Jessica."

Benno cradled the phone between his jaw and shoulder as he snapped the briefcase closed and shoved it under the seat. "Ms. Baldwin, hi. This is Detective Benno, DPD Metro. I'm calling because we got your number from Morgan Masters' caller ID. Are you acquainted with Miss Masters?"

There was a sharp intake of breath over the line. Jessica Baldwin said, "The police? Is this—"

"Have you read this morning's newspaper?"

"Yes. I've been trying to call Morgan ever since. Where is she?"

"At a hotel, where she'll be until the crime scene unit releases her house. I should also tell you that we listened to your message on her answering machine and found it sort of odd."

Anger flashed in Jessica Baldwin's tone. "Well, I should tell *you* that going around listening to personal messages is bullshit."

"It's procedure, nothing more." He flipped open his .38 and checked the cylinder, found five loaded chambers with an empty under the hammer, then reholstered the gun.

"Still bullshit. How do I know you're the police, anyway?"

"I can give you my badge number and you can call Main Headquarters to check me out. Would you like for me to call back later, after you've had a chance to verify who I am?"

There was a rustling noise over the line. She said, "What do you want with me?"

"To ask a few questions. Can I meet with you in person, ma'am?"

"Ma'am? You sound like a fucking cowboy."

"I don't intend to, ma'am, uh, Ms. Baldwin. When would be a convenient time?"

"I have read the paper. Don't think I'm going to help you screw Morgan. She couldn't have killed anyone."

"That's all I'm trying to determine. How about this afternoon?"

"This afternoon is bad," she said. "I have appointments until six."

"What about later, then? Six thirty, seven? You name the place."

"You're pretty determined, aren't you?"

"I get that way on a case," Benno said. "If you'd feel better about it, maybe you could come to my office."

"I don't think I'd feel that comfortable in a police station. I'll give you a few minutes, but don't expect any revelations. Do you know La Madeleine Restaurant, on Forest Lane at Inwood Road?"

"I can find it," Benno said.

"Six thirty, then. I'll be wearing a gray business suit, and I'll wait for you inside the front entrance. And, uh, Detective . . . Benno, is it?"

"Yes, ma'am," Benno said, then felt like biting his tongue. *Ma'am . . . Jesus . . .*

"Do you know what I do for a living?"

"I don't know anything about you," Benno said, "other than that you called Miss Masters and I got your number off of her caller ID."

"I'm a psychiatrist," Jessica Baldwin said.

"Uh-oh."

"Right. My relationship to Morgan is personal, but I've also given her some counseling. So come on if you want. But I'm good at yelling privilege if you ask a question I don't think I should answer. See you at six thirty, okay?" There was a click on the line as she disconnected.

Benno stared at the phone a moment, then shoved it back in the glove box. He liked her voice, cultured and sexy, combined with a no-bullshit attitude. He opened an appointment book and penciled in Jessica Baldwin for six thirty, picturing what she might look like. She'd be wearing a business dress. Maybe a curve-hugging suit with platform shoes. Sexy . . .

He pushed the door open with his foot and looked around the parking lot. It was only half past eleven, yet there were fifteen or twenty vehicles sitting around—pickups, sports cars, and several SUVs straight from the carpool. Benno pictured mothers dropping off their kids, then heading off to drool over a guy dancing in his underwear.

The building was cinderblock, built low. Benno got out and headed for the entry, flinching some against the chilly north wind. He climbed up on the porch. A sign on the door said that Muscle's was open from eleven a.m. until two in the morning. He pushed his way inside. Loud rock music assaulted his ears. He was immediately hit by the smell of cigarette smoke and beer, dank odors blending in a cauldron of stale air. He was wary and alert, but he felt pretty good, getting back into the swing of being a cop and liking his gradual change in attitude.

He was in a dimly lit entry hall with wooden walls painted black. He walked softly to the end of the corridor to peer inside the club. The bar was on his left, with muscular waiters in tights and vests hustling back and forth, toting drink trays. The club was a whole lot bigger inside than it looked from the parking lot. Tables encircled the room, sitting on five levels leading down, with a sunken stage in the center of the floor. More than half of the tables were occupied, with women screaming their lungs out, swigging mixed drinks or bottles of beer. The room was dimly lit except for a spotlight directed on the stage. A blond hulk wearing a nylon G-string was in the middle of his act, gyrating to "I Shot the Sheriff." As Benno watched, the dancer thrust his pelvis at four ladies seated ringside. They clapped and squealed, and one heavy-thighed woman shoved money into the guy's G-string and then reached for his crotch. He backed away grinning, shook his head and wagged a no-no finger.

A man around thirty years old, walking fast, approached the entry where Benno stood. The greeter was around six feet tall, with thick curly hair hanging below his collar. Too skinny to be one of the dancers, he was dressed in Dockers and a thick fuzzy sweater. He had a small nose, sharp cheekbones, and sparse hair combed over to hide his bald spots. He stopped a few feet away and said, "Ladies only in here."

Benno tried to look friendly but businesslike. "I'm not a customer. I'm a Metro detective. Is the manager here?" Eight years with LAPD, most of them working Homicide, had taught him that he got better results by not throwing his weight around. A lot of cops would have flashed their shield, trying to intimidate the guy. Benno didn't reach for his wallet, but showed a tight firm smile.

The man offered a grin that was more of a smirk. "You got ID?"

Benno maintained his outward calm, but mentally classified the guy as uncooperative. Not that the man's attitude was any big deal; strip club employees often had outstanding warrants downtown and, as a rule, had hard-ons for cops on general principles. Benno handed over his wallet, open with his identification facing out through a plastic window.

The thin man raised a penlight up to ear level,

thumbed the switch, and examined Benno's ID. He shined the flash on Benno's face and compared the cop with the picture. He snapped the wallet closed and handed it back. "Yeah, okay, Detective. Our liquor license is in a frame behind the bar. Don't stay too long, okay? Makes the customers nervous." He turned and started to walk away.

Benno stepped after the guy. "I'm not from Alcoholic Beverage. I told you, I'm Metro."

The man halted and turned. "What's Metro want?"

Benno ducked the question and instead said, "And your name is . . . ?"

"Denzel. I'm the day guy."

"Meaning you're currently in charge. Just the man I'm looking for." Benno was practically yelling so that the guy could hear him over the music.

"Look, Mr. Metro," Denzel said, "I'll give you the quick rundown. We don't allow no drugs, though we don't shake people down for 'em. If we see anybody carrying a weapon we ask 'em to leave. We don't allow none of our customers to grab the dancers' dicks. If anybody's obviously drunk we run 'em off, though with all these women jumping around sometimes it's hard to tell who's drunk and who's just horny. But we try to be legitimate." He put hands on hips. "So what can I do for you?"

Benno was getting just a tad hot under the collar. "Look, Mr. Denzel, I'm not—"

"Denzel's my first name."

"Yeah, sorry," Benno said. "But I'm not here to roust any club. I'm here on a murder investigation."

Some of the wind seemed to go out of Denzel's sails, but not all. "What murder?"

Benno hesitated, then decided not to give a direct answer just yet. "I've got some pictures I'd like to show you. Is there a place we can . . . ?"

Denzel looked dubious, but thumbed over his shoulder. "Office in back." Visible behind him, the dancer finished his performance and ran around gathering up his clothes while women squealed and snatched at his buttocks. "Come with me," Denzel said and marched away down the aisle.

Benno followed between the rows of tables and stayed two paces to the rear as Denzel led him in a circular path around the stage. Cigarette smoke burned Benno's eyes while women interrupted their partying to stare at him. Some looked hostile, others embarrassed. Denzel went through parted curtains into a tiny office with a desk, one visitor's chair, and a file cabinet. He sat in a wooden swivel chair that creaked as he leaned back; then he extended his hand, palm up, toward the visitor's chair. Benno sat down. Denzel said, "This gonna take long?"

Benno reached for the photos from Morgan Masters' BMW. "I don't think so. I'd like you to tell me if you recognize the man in these pictures." He dropped the glossies over in front of the guy.

Denzel blinked rapidly. His eyes were slightly bloodshot, probably because the guy wore contacts. Denzel picked up one of the pictures, looked it over, and then quickly dropped the photo. "This about that shit in the paper?"

Benno stayed deadpan. "What shit is that?"

Denzel blinked. "That killing. You know, involving the rich lady." He blinked again.

Benno's palm itched. He scratched it. "I think you mean the rich lady's daughter. You're pretty sharp, Denzel. I show you a picture, you quickly deduce that the guy is going down on Morgan Masters even though you can't see her face, just her legs. Maybe you've seen the butterfly tattoo before. Maybe I should be running the strip club and you should be the detective, you think?"

Denzel pointed a finger. "We got nothing to do with Morgan Masters other than that she comes here sometimes."

"You're a fountain of information," Benno said. "Now that you've identified the woman after seeing only her legs, could you try to do the same for the man behind the mask?"

"I think you already know who he is. If you didn't, how would you know to come here?"

"You must be bucking for an A in the class," Benno said. "Okay, you asked how long this would take. If you can give me some information about this Zorro and his relationship to Morgan Masters, then I'm out of here."

"These people come and go. Zorro ain't been in lately."

"Oh? Since when?"

Denzel's eyebrows went up. "I gotta tell you exactly?"

Benno paused, then decided to level. "We have information that this Zorro took a trip with Morgan Masters. We know when they got back. When they left is important as hell."

"We don't want publicity on this." Denzel seemed nervous. He fooled with a paperweight, then carefully set it down inside an ashtray from Caesars Palace in Vegas.

"I don't see any newspaper people around here," Benno said, "do you?"

"We got a clientele that doesn't want their names trumpeted around."

"I don't intend to trumpet anything, unless I don't get cooperation. Tell me something. How often does Morgan Masters come in here?"

"Often enough, but I don't keep a sign-in sheet. We got to be discreet in this business."

"Does she come alone, Denzel?"

"Usually."

Benno spread his hands. "You know all your customers by name?"

Denzel shook his head. "Not many. Morgan we know because of a couple of incidents."

"What kind of incidents?"

Denzel squirmed in his chair. "I don't know as I should say. I'd have to talk to the owner."

"Great," Benno said. "Is the owner around?"

"She don't come by much. We have some weekly meetings at her place."

"That's unfortunate, because I don't have a week to wait for an answer. You told me you were the day guy. Does that mean there's also a night guy?"

"Yeah. Vernon."

"So Morgan's both a daytime and a nighttime customer."

"She's liable to walk in here anytime we're open. Listen, I ain't trying to fuck you around. But Morgan Masters is one we got special orders on."

"What orders?"

Denzel's gaze was on the ceiling, the far corner of the room. "I don't think I should say any more."

Benno scooted his chair nearer the desk. "Listen, Denzel, we can do this a couple of different ways. The best way is for you to talk to me, here and now. The other ways you don't really want to discuss."

Denzel's expression hardened. "I'm not a guy that takes to being leaned on."

Benno kept his look bland. "And I'm not a guy that likes to lean. Look, you read this morning's paper and immediately knew there'd be a connection to this club.

Your reaction to the photo tells me you know about Morgan and Zorro. So why not make it easy for both of us? I'm not investigating male prostitution, and I don't really care if you're pimping for a few of the boys out there and getting a piece of the action. Zorro told us a story. All I'm doing is checking it out."

"Hey, Zorro's balling the woman," Denzel said. "I'm surprised he'd say shit to you."

"We're not accomplishing much here," Benno said. "You think if I was to really roust this joint I'd find any dope?"

"Now you're really leaning, ain'tcha?"

"Looks like you're giving me no choice. When did Zorro leave on his trip, Denzel?"

Denzel turned and opened a file drawer. "Jesus Christ, I can get in a world of shit."

"Want to bet I can put you in a bigger world of shit than whoever it is you're so scared of?"

Denzel pulled a piece of paper from the file. "Last Thursday. Five days ago."

Benno wrote the information down. He put his notes away. "That wasn't hard, Denzel. Now I'm leaving. You could have told me that when I first walked in. Christ, fella, why you gotta waste so much time?"

Benno drove out of the parking lot and headed down the highway with semis and bobtails whizzing past in the opposite direction. He dug out his cell. He'd programmed in Tina Drummond's number that morning and now pressed the button to call her. She answered on the first ring. "Trafficante's story checks out," Benno said. "At the time of the murder, he and Morgan were out of town."

"Digging through LaVon Masters' property records bored the shit out of me," Drummond said.

"Find anything interesting?"

"Yeah, pretty much, but I can't talk about it now. Good you called. We have a related homicide."

Benno frowned, and pressed on the gas to pass a slow-moving SUV. He said, "You mean related to the Masters case?"

"Yeah, it's related big-time. Irving PD responded to the call and then contacted us. CSU's already there. Where are you, Benno?"

"I'm just leaving Muscle's, the strip club."

"In Grand Prairie, right?" Drummond said.

"Yeah. I'm on Highway 157."

"Do you have Trafficante's address written down?"

"Zorro? I think so, why?"

"Because Zorro's the related homicide," Drummond said. "Haul ass, Benno. I'll meet you there."

10

Trafficante's place was in the Knollwood section of Irving, on a run-down trashy street lined with fifty- and sixty-year-old apartment buildings. In spite of the cold there were forty or so residents on the sidewalk, men in overalls and mackinacs and women hugging their coats around their shoulders, some of them scratching their heads as if wondering what in hell was going on. Five Irving patrol cars were double parked along with a gray CSU truck, and a fire department ambulance was backed up into the front yard of a two-story orange brick four-unit. The sun was out and the snow was melting, water pouring from the roof gutters and running into the street. Benno recognized Trafficante's dented Ford Escort, squeezed in between a pickup and a sixties-model Volkswagen. He stopped behind one of the squad cars, got out, stuck the magnetic flasher on top of the Merc and then jogged across the lawn. There was a worn-out tire in the yard and the wind plastered a torn piece of newspaper against Benno's coat as he ran. He wadded up the paper and tossed it away. There was an outside staircase leading up, and a uniformed officer in a fur-lined jacket and gloves stood in front of the bottom step with his arms folded. Benno showed his badge.

The cop checked Benno out and then pointed upstairs. "Top on the left. See Patrol Sergeant Stafford."

Benno thanked him and took the stairs two at a time. He entered an overheated apartment with an odor of grease-cooked meat hanging in the air. He looked around as his breathing subsided. There was an old red cloth sofa and a chair with cotton stuffing poking out, along with an ancient Magnavox TV. White-coated techs roamed the room, vacuuming, dusting, and bagging evidence. Over in one corner stood a stocky gray-haired man in an Irving PD uniform with stripes on the sleeve. Benno marched over and said, "Sergeant Stafford?"

The officer had puffy eyes with thick lids under shaggy salt-and-pepper brows. He'd been pointing out something to one of the techs, but now turned his attention to Benno. "Yeah, I'm Stafford. I guess you're Metro, huh?"

"That's me," Benno said.

"Ordinarily I'd rather take it up the ass than call Metro," Stafford said, "but here I had no choice. The vic had your business card. You acquainted with a Gerald Trafficante?"

"He's a potential witness and a possible suspect in a case I'm working. He's also known as Zorro."

Stafford snorted through his nose. "Yeah, there's a mask and cape and shit back there and a couple of publicity photos with the guy posed damned near naked, flexing his muscles. At first we thought maybe he was an actor or something. We're canvassing the neighborhood, but all most of the people around here have to say to law enforcement is fuck you."

"Actually Zorro's a dancer," Benno said. "A male stripper."

"Not anymore he isn't. Can you give us a positive ID on this guy?"

"Yeah, I met him last night. My partner, Detective Drummond, is on her way. By the way, who called this in?"

"Anonymous," Stafford said. "Our switchboard caller ID says it came from the phone in this apartment. Could have been the killer. We're printing the phone."

Benno saw the foot of a bed through an open doorway. "Back there?" he said, nodding toward the bed.

"Yeah. You got gloves?"

Benno nodded, snugging on plastic gloves as he crossed over the threshold into the bedroom. The bathroom was on his left, where blood was spattered on the mirror. There were red smears on the bedroom walls and more stains on the bedsheets. The closet door was open, and Benno could see black capes on hangers and a black hat with a silver-lined brim on a shelf. He supposed the masks were in the closet as well.

A tech was working on a corpse spread-eagled across the bed. The body was that of a muscular male, stripped to the waist, wearing pajama bottoms. The feet were bare and sliced to the bone, from ball to heel. The cuts were a half inch wide and black with clotted blood. There was a large tattoo on the body's upper left arm, a bulldog with USMC underneath, and there was an overnight growth of beard on the face. The upper right side of the man's head was blown completely away, with blood and brain matter smeared across the carpet beside the left ear. In addition to the head and foot wounds there were crisscross cuts on the chest, some a couple of inches deep. The tech had already bagged the corpse's left hand; he now slipped cellophane over the right. The hand was covered in dried blood. Benno looked at the face. Trafficante had died with sort of a grin. Leaving 'em laughing.

Benno said, "Doesn't make sense. Why slash the guy to ribbons if you were going to shoot him?"

The tech's head turned slowly around. She was a pretty Asian woman, thirty-five or so, with short black hair and unblemished skin. Her expression was calm but inquisitive.

Benno said, "I'm Detective Benno, from Metro."

"Yeah, hi, Charlotte Wong. I heard you were on your way." She got up and motioned toward the bathroom. "Best we can determine, the knifing began in there. A razor and a can of Gillette Foamy are sitting on the lavatory, so probably the killer attacked the guy when he was about to shave. And I feel the same way as you. Why not just shoot him from behind and get it over with? Jesus Christ, just looking at his feet sets my teeth on edge."

Benno inched in between the corpse and the bed. "I don't understand the blood on the walls and the mattress."

Wong tossed her head, wiggling her hair. "I don't, either. But he was shot lying facedown and then someone rolled him over, for what reason I won't even speculate. That pool of brains and bone is on the opposite side of his head from the injury."

"I can see that." Benno cupped a hand under his elbow and pinched his chin. "Found any trace?"

Wong finished bagging the corpse's right hand and gently lowered the arm to the mattress. "I'm just getting started here. But there was a long brown hair stuck to his cheek that sure doesn't match this grizzly mug. And unless this guy does a lot of tossing and turning during the night, there were two people sleeping in that bed."

Benno studied the bed. One corner of the formfitting sheet was pulled away from the mattress and all four pillows, two on each side, were rumpled and twisted. The blood smears were all on the side closest to the window. The covers were thrown back on both sides, as if two people had gotten up after sleeping, sex, or both. Benno said, "So he could have been shacked up with the killer all night, and then she did him in in the morning."

"Could have. But this is a big strong guy, so I think it would take a man to handle him. I suppose it could be what some of our less politically correct officers call a *homo*-cide. Personally I lean in that direction, because I don't see anything that would indicate a woman's been in this apartment. No makeup, bras, nothing like that. But there's also nothing to indicate that two guys have been living here. There's only one razor, one bottle of aftershave, you know, stuff like that. Could be a one-night stand, which would mean he could have been getting it on with a woman *or* a man. Won't be able to say for certain if his sleepover buddy was male or female until we analyze whatever body fluids are on those sheets." Wong worked as she spoke, her head down, leaning over for a close look at the carpet. "More brown hairs down here," she said. "And hey, what's this?"

Benno put his hands on his knees and bent over to watch. Wong used a pair of tweezers to lift something from the floor. The object was purple, two different shades. "What is it?" Benno asked.

"A purple flower petal. This guy doesn't look like the gardening type."

"I'd agree," Benno said and started to ask if the

tech was going to bag the flower as evidence. Then he saw that Wong already had a plastic envelope out. He went in the bathroom and looked around.

There was a Bic disposable razor on the counter beside a cylinder of shaving cream with the cap off. The shower curtain was pulled back and the tiles were wet. The nozzle dripped. Benno called out, "Is the dead guy's hair wet?"

"No, and it's tangled and hasn't been washed recently," Wong yelled from the bedroom. "This guy wasn't the one using the shower in there, if that's what you're asking."

Benno wandered back out and looked on the dresser. There were three or four identical photos, all of Zorro wearing his mask and hat, chest bare and flexed, cape over his shoulders and swirling down in back. *Guy thought he was a pretty dashing s.o.b.*, Benno thought. He said, "After you dust these photos for prints, can I have one? Looks like they were taken in a studio."

"Dantley Photography downtown," Wong said. "They do all the strippers. Chicks and guys. They have the lighting setup. Right shadows and whatnot."

"How'd you know that?" Benno cocked his head.

Wong grinned. "Let's say that once I had a dream. Dantley's downtown. Trust me."

Benno went over and looked in the closet. Odd setup. Trafficante's civilian clothes, jeans, sweaters, and T-shirts, were thrown around at random, but all of his costumes and capes were in perfect military order. The masks were folded neatly on a shelf. Some were red, others black. There were three hats on a shelf, side by side, all with silver bands and beaded trim. "Guy could've had his own costume party," Benno said. "Invited half the neighborhood."

"I thought the same thing." Wong snickered. "Jesus

Christ, what's next? The mark of fucking Zorro, huh? Wait'll I tell my boyfriend."

When Benno returned to the living room, Patrol Sergeant Stafford was talking to Tina Drummond. She had on a nice brown leather coat and gloves, which she was pulling off her hands and replacing with latex gloves. She also wore earmuffs with the band over the top of her head. She looked up at Benno and said, "You beat me here."

"I sped. You should call your buddy Randy Dunst."

"Since when did he become my buddy?"

"Since I decided I don't want to talk to the guy. He had a couple of investigators on Morgan Masters at her hotel. We need to find out if she's been there all this time."

Drummond nodded. She pulled out her cell, went to a corner for privacy, and punched in a number, lifting one of the muffs away from her ear in order to use the phone.

Benno turned to Stafford. "The victim's car is the old Ford Escort parked in front of the building. The techs should go over it."

Stafford was looking closely at Benno. The sergeant said, "Wasn't your picture in the paper this morning?"

"I didn't think it was a very good likeness."

"This is connected to that Masters deal, huh?"

Benno moved close in buddy-buddy posture. "I need your help here, Sergeant. That's not for publication."

Stafford pointed to one of the techs, a young guy working with a handheld vacuum. "You should tell those people. That guy recognized you the second you walked in."

Benno chewed his lower lip. Fame was a bitch. "Well, do what you can, okay?"

Stafford shrugged with his hands. "What I can won't be enough. Just remember—if this gets in the paper as being connected to the Masters thing, it's not on me." He stepped toward the exit, then stopped and looked back over his shoulder. "The Escort?"

"The Escort," Benno said, then watched from the doorway as Stafford went down the steps two at a time and started to talk to the uniformed cop on guard. Stafford pointed out Trafficante's car. The uniformed cop yelled out something to a tech standing by the CSU truck. Benno turned from the door. Drummond stood there waiting for him. "What'd you find out?"

Drummond removed her earmuffs, and stuck them in her pocket. "Morgan's at the Doubletree. *Been* at the Doubletree. Those two DA's investigators say they'll stake their lives on it that she's never left. That"—pointing toward the bedroom—"wasn't Morgan's doing."

"That strip club manager was pretty certain," Benno said. "Morgan and Zorro here went partying in Bossier City five days ago. Figuring the time frame, she couldn't have done Uncle Eddie at her place, either."

Drummond rubbed her cheek. She tugged down on a strand of hair. "Morgan's an unlikable bitch. But you know what, partner? Call it intuition or whatever, but I never thought she did it."

Benno felt the adrenaline flow as he followed the techs around, watching them gather evidence, occasionally pointing out something they'd missed, generally supervising a crime scene on his own for the first time in . . . *Jesus*. He was getting really pumped. During the last few years in LA as he'd worked at drugstores, supermarkets, and once even a poker parlor, his self-esteem had sunk lower and lower. But now he was a cop again and this was what his life was all about—that downtrodden shit was history.

He watched a young male tech sift through a trash can; then he had the guy bag a worn-out toothbrush that was rattling around in there. As the tech complied, Benno went out on the porch and breathed in chilly air as he peered down over the rail into the yard. In his mind a crime scene had always included a three-block radius. There was a row of stubby bushes growing near the building foundation, and as Benno's gaze swept the area metal flashed in the corner of his vision. Something was nestled down in the bushes, nearly hidden from sight under the bright green leaves and snowdrifts. He leaned further over the rail and squinted. He couldn't quite make it out, whatever it was.

He yelled at the cop guarding the staircase and motioned for the guy to come over to the bushes. When the cop was directly beneath him, Benno pointed straight down and called out, "There's something hidden in there under the leaves. Careful not to touch it now, Officer."

The uni carefully parted the bushes and crouched for a close-up view. Then, his face turned up toward the landing above, he said, "It's a knife, Detective. A big fuckin' knife."

"Really?"

"I ain't into turkey farming, slaughterhouses and shit, but, yeah, that's what it is."

"Just a minute," Benno said and then stuck his head inside the apartment and yelled for a tech. Charlotte Wong snapped to, shut off a vacuum, and headed for the door. Benno called out to the cop below, "Don't move. We're on our way. And careful. Do not touch a fucking thing."

The thing in the hedge was a thick-bladed butcher's knife with a bloodstained blade and handle. The blade was shiny and new. Charlotte Wong, wearing gloves, held the knife up so that Benno and Drummond could have a look. Drummond inspected the bushes, which were crumpled from a falling weight crashing through. She said, "Looks like someone dropped it from that landing up there. Some of these branches are broken, and the breaks are fresh."

"Or someone threw it there on purpose," Benno said. Then, to Wong he said, "Have it taken straight to the lab. All the tests, okay? We'll want it compared to the cuts on the dismembered corpse from the Beemer's trunk. You know, Morgan Masters' car."

Wong nodded skeptically, then gently carried the knife off in the direction of the CSU van.

Drummond took her earmuffs out of her pocket. "Kind of jumping to conclusions, aren't we?"

Benno shrugged with his hands. "Not that much. We have a dead guy here who's obviously connected to the family."

Drummond fluffed her hair where the earmuff band had covered the top of her head. "Even if it's the weapon used to stab Uncle Eddie, why would someone throw it away right here?"

"Beats me. Could've been hiding it."

"No way, Benno. They would've dumped it in the Trinity River."

"Not hiding it from us. From someone else. Let's say Zorro sneaked out and dropped it so whoever was in his apartment wouldn't find it."

Drummond fitted the band back over her hair. She lifted the muffs away from her ears, then snugged them up. "You're building quite a scenario here. Traficante dumps the knife, goes in, and fucks some woman until she decides to cut him up and shoot him in the head. Why didn't she just hold the gun on him and make him give up the blade, if that's what she was looking for?"

"Maybe he'd already hidden it before she got the drop on him," Benno said. "The tech, Charlotte Wong, found brown hairs on and all around the body."

Drummond seemed thoughtful. "Those hairs couldn't have come from Morgan, could they?"

"Nope. Wrong color. Maybe Morgan's mother's a brunette."

"Jesus Christ, Benno, that woman's nearly sixty years old. You think she'd have the strength to cut up Uncle Eddie, not to mention shoot Trafficante after slashing the shit out of him, and all that after banging him?"

"She might be in pretty good shape," Benno said.

"For what, killing the guy or banging him? At her age, if you ask me, I think she'd need help with either one. I don't know about this. I think maybe your uncle's got you honing in too much on LaVon Masters. Makes you miss certain details you'd otherwise pick up on."

"He's my cousin," Benno said, "not my uncle. Let's see. If LaVon Masters killed Zorro, maybe she had help. LaVon hides the knife in the bushes and then . . ."

"Go on," Drummond said.

Benno looked at the ground in puzzlement.

"Yeah, right," Drummond said. "We're suddenly deciding Trafficante was mixed up in Uncle Eddie's murder, when we already know he was in Bossier City with Morgan Masters at the time. Besides which, we've got no evidence that Trafficante even knew LaVon Masters or that she ever heard of him. That dog won't hunt. Neither will any theory that puts Trafficante in possession of the knife used to cut up Uncle Eddie. If that's the knife we're looking for, someone other than Trafficante brought it here. Just listen to yourself, Benno. What, LaVon Masters goes in and gives Zorro a little nookie, and then takes a shower and offs the guy? What's her motive? I don't think we're fitting our theories to the evidence with a lot of precision here."

Benno shrugged, his gaze drifting in the direction of Trafficante's car. The techs had the right front door open; one squatted on the backseat floorboard while another ran a vacuum over the carpet in front. Benno went toward the Escort to have a look. As Drummond followed he said, "I'm freezing to death. Look, Tina, maybe I haven't got it exactly right. It's a disturbing case. But I'm working on the answers—what can I say?"

She tromped along behind him. "That you don't know your ass from your elbow about what's happened here. That's what I do. Instead of making shit up as you go along, just tell me you don't fucking know."

Trafficante had been a slob where his auto was concerned. There was dirt and trash strewn all over the interior—candy and gum wrappers, Styrofoam cups, a takeout tray from Wendy's Hamburgers, a few Trojan condom wrappers. On the backseat lay a couple fitness magazines. As Benno stood outside the driver's window, the tech who was vacuuming the front floorboard made a sour face. She was a pudgy brunette in her thirties. She gingerly lifted one of the Trojan wrappers and dropped it in an evidence bag.

A flash of color caught Benno's eye. He stood on tiptoes and looked down inside the car. Something was wedged in between the driver's seat and the door, flush against the seat adjustment lever. Benno gently tugged on the handle. The door opened with a click and a protesting squeal of hinges. A flower tumbled out and lay on the pavement at his feet.

A purple flower to match the petal upstairs. The flower was shaped like a rose, only bigger. The petals were pale around the edges and deepened in color nearer the stalk. The flower looked fresh. A blossoming plant in the middle of winter. Benno pictured the inside of Trafficante's apartment. He was pretty sure he hadn't seen any flower vases in there. Nope, he was *damned* sure; Zorro just wasn't a flowery guy. Benno sniffed, then wrinkled his nose in disgust. The flower smelled like some sort of stinkweed. He yelled for Charlotte Wong, who double-timed over from the CSU van. She bagged the flower at his direction, then headed back for the truck shaking her head.

From behind the car, Drummond called out, "Hey, Benno, look at this." Benno went back and stood beside her. She pointed at the bumper and said, "This is the same car he left Morgan's in, isn't it?"

Benno nodded. "Sure. I recognized it the second I got here."

"So it was parked in front of us in the drive when we got to Morgan's last night. Now, think. You pulled up and your headlights shined on the bumper. You remember seeing those?" She indicated two strips of bright chartreuse reflector tape that formed a cross, dead center in the bumper below the trunk lock.

Benno took a thoughtful step back. "No. But I wouldn't have been looking for it."

"I followed Trafficante out to his car to get the videos of him and Morgan in action," Drummond said. "Chartreuse reflector tape I'd remember. I'm pretty observant. I was standing right there when he drove away. All those newspeople with their cameras, the cop car lights . . . nothing was reflecting on that bumper when he left. I'm as sure of that as I'm sure that we're standing here. That tape wasn't on that bumper last night."

"Okay. So what does that tell us?"

"For one thing, it tells us Trafficante made a stop on the way home. Either he stuck the tape on or someone else did. Whichever, the tape would make it easier to follow the guy at night. Zorro had a tail on the way home, Benno. He might or might not have known that he did. But I'm betting he didn't know, if anyone's asking me."

Benno followed Drummond from room to room thinking over what she'd said about his murder theories. He wasn't making anything up as he went along— he was only tossing out ideas. Different possibilities.

What the fuck? Drummond was right. Benno didn't know shit about what was going on in this case. Maybe Drummond had some ideas. He hadn't known her long enough to read her moods.

He cornered Drummond in the bathroom as she looked in at the damp shower walls. "Well, what's *your* take on it?" Benno said.

Drummond leaned inside the shower and sniffed the air. "Body fragrance. Yet there's no container in there. Someone brought their own bath oil, then hauled it away? This is one weird fucking murder, Benno. What's my take on what?"

Benno smelled inside the shower. There was indeed a lingering sweet odor, like lilac or freesia. "This whole scenario so far."

"I think someone's dropping intentional clues and being clumsy as hell about it."

"Like, pointing us in the wrong direction?"

"Sure. Somebody chops up Uncle Eddie in Morgan's bed and then hauls him off in her car, leaving the car abandoned in Oak Cliff where eventually someone's going to find it. Now someone follows Zorro home, kills him, then drops a knife from Morgan Masters' kitchen in Zorro's flower bed. Sounds like they wanted to make sure we made the connection with the other killing, in case we were too dumb to tie the two together on our own. Who'd you talk to at the strip club?"

"The strip club's day manager—guy named Denzel. Why?"

"We'll need to see him again. Trafficante turned a lot of tricks on the side. Maybe not as many as he was bragging about to us, but some at least. We need to know where he stopped after he left Morgan's, where he or someone else stuck that reflector tape on his bumper. Our first guess should be, at that time of night, any stop he made had to do with his whoring. That strip club manager will know who Zorro's been fucking for money, or at least he'll know who does know. If it wasn't for the knife, I'd say this killing could be totally unrelated to the one at Morgan Masters' place. A top priority has to be getting the lab to tell us whether the knife is the one that sliced up Uncle Eddie."

"I told Charlotte Wong to take the knife directly to the lab," Benno said. "I think she's already left. I also think the flowers mean something. But, Jesus, a flower is a flower is a flower."

"By any other name they'd smell as sweet?" Drummond said.

"Not this flower. It's pretty, but Jesus, you should smell the damned thing."

Drummond started to say something more. Before

she could speak, Sergeant Stafford yelled from out in the living room, "You better come, detectives. One of our unis has a witness out here."

In the living room a skinny man was seated in a stuffed armless chair, his forearms resting on his thighs as he kneaded his hands. He had a sallow complexion and a dark, ear-to-ear beard with no mustache. He was dressed in frayed jeans, dirty sneakers, and a pull-over maroon velour shirt that looked twenty years old. The guy was trembling. A pudgy uniformed female cop told Benno and Drummond that the man was Elmer Reed and that Mr. Reed lived next door. Drummond and Benno sat on the sofa facing the man and introduced themselves.

"We understand you might have some information for us," Drummond said.

The man had a high-pitched whiny voice. "I just told the policewoman what I heard." He glanced toward the bedroom. "No shit. Is he really dead?"

"He really is, sir," Drummond said. "Were you and Mr. Trafficante acquainted?"

"Not that good."

"That's understandable. I don't know my neighbors very well, either. Could you possibly just tell us the same thing you told the officer?"

"Just that, well, about six o'clock this morning I heard some noises next door."

Drummond flipped over a page in her steno pad. "You're certain as to the time?"

"I work nights," Reed said. "Get home around five thirty. The reason I noticed I'd fixed myself a nightcap and watched the second half of a *Law & Order* rerun. So it had to be about straight-up six. The guy sleeps all day. Works nights same as I do. He's some kind of entertainer or something."

Benno shifted his weight on the couch, then asked, "What kind of noises did you hear?"

"Music. Some people talking loud. One woman and one man, best I could determine. They sounded pissed off—you know what I mean?"

"Hmm. You see anyone leaving later?"

"Not up until I went to bed. After that, I can't help you."

"What time do you go to bed?"

"Around eight. I gotta be at work at four in the afternoon."

"And you never saw anyone? Anyone at all?"

"Just the meter reader. The electricity guy. He came down the landing, oh, around seven, seven thirty."

Benno made a note to contact the power company, talk to the meter reader. Then he said, "Anything else you recall?"

"No. Just the music and the yelling. At some point somebody turned up the stereo, loud as hell."

"You never heard any gunshots?" Benno asked.

"That music was too loud to hear anything else. So damned loud I wanted to tell them to pipe the fuck down." Reed lowered his head. "Guess it's good I didn't knock on the door, huh?"

Benno and Drummond exchanged a look. Drummond folded up her steno pad and put it away. "Likely fortunate," she said.

Benno gave Elmer Reed one of his business cards, and the skinny guy went back to his own apartment. No sooner had Reed left than Benno's cell phone vibrated in his pocket. He dug out the instrument, pressed the TALK button, and spoke his name into the speaker.

It was Rubin, hacking and clearing his throat before he said, "You at this Trafficante's place?"

"Yeah, Chief. Detective Drummond's here with me," Benno said. Drummond gave him a curious look.

He silently mouthed, "Chief Rubin," at her, then returned his attention to the phone.

"You ID the victim?" Rubin said.

"Sure did. It's our man."

"Ah shit. Keep this under wraps, Detective. No one is to know these homicides are related. I got the skinny on Uncle Eddie Payne. You want to take notes?"

Benno opened his writing pad on his thigh and steadied his pen. "Ready," he said.

"As we talked about earlier," Rubin said, "Uncle Eddie Payne was an old gangster from way back when. A murder-for-hire guy. His last arrest was 1979 with the usual result—charges dropped. After that, he disappears from public records, mainly because shortly after that he did a federal nickel for income tax. I got that from NCIC—the feds have a way of forgetting to update local shit, you know? So I checked Uncle Eddie's family tree. He's got a sister, a Doris Wilmont, who showed up on his visiting list while he was in the federal joint and apparently came to see him once a month while he was in the pen. According to his parole record, when he got released he went to live with this sister. And, *bam,* there's a Doris Wilmont listed in the Greater Dallas phone directory, living in Richardson. I called her up. She's really Uncle Eddie's sister. She even cried when I broke the news to her, so I guess everybody's got somebody who gives a shit, though it's surprising where Uncle Eddie's concerned. I asked Mrs. Wilmont if she knew any connection way back when between Uncle Eddie and LaVon Masters, but drew a blank there. She's gonna claim the body and give it a decent burial. Nice gesture. Better treatment than Uncle Eddie ever gave any of the people he offed, but still a nice gesture.

"Anyhow," Rubin said, "Doris Wilmont says that about five years ago Uncle Eddie began to have these memory lapses and crap. A couple of years ago she moved him into the assisted living—a place called Everlasting Gardens on Walnut Hill Lane across from Presbyterian Hospital."

"Assisted living?" Benno's fingers were beginning to cramp. "People to clean him up after he uses the bathroom . . ."

Rubin coughed, muffled by his palm over the mouthpiece. "Not quite totally assisted. He was seventy-five years old and couldn't remember shit, but he was still self-sufficient. Not wearing diapers or anything, though maybe he'd think he heard a bird tweeting occasionally. He still could drive and had a car at this place. It's one of these arrangements where you retire there on your own, and then when you can't care for yourself any longer they move you to a nursing facility. Kind of ease you out of life in those joints. Myself, I'm not looking forward to it.

"Moving along," Rubin said, "I contacted the retirement center. A week ago yesterday Uncle Eddie stopped his mail and newspaper delivery for thirty days, and nobody at the center's seen him since. His movements between eight days ago and the night Morgan Masters' car turned up are unknown. But the old fart definitely expected to be out of pocket no longer than thirty days. Whether he contacted Morgan, or LaVon, or both, I got no idea."

"Actually, Jeff, uh, Chief," Benno said, "we've got no concrete evidence he even knew either one of them, do we?"

"No. But since Uncle Eddie wound up in the trunk of Morgan Masters' car and got butchered in her bed, I think we're safe to make this wild assumption. You about finished with that crime scene out there?"

Benno looked around the room. The techs were finishing up, closing vacuum and evidence containers.

Two medics were headed into the bedroom, carrying a collapsible gurney and a body bag. "Just about," Benno said. "Listen, we found a knife. I've sent it to the lab. It could be the missing weapon used to slice up Uncle Eddie."

"Great. You are turning up clues out the ass, which restores my faith in putting you on the payroll. As soon as you're through there, you should detour by this Everlasting Gardens joint and interview a guy named Delbert Greene. Nickname is Fishy. Fishy Greene is an old outlaw from Uncle Eddie's era, actually even before that, since Fishy's now up in his eighties. According to Doris Wilmont, Uncle Eddie picked out this particular assisted living because he heard Fishy Greene was there. Assisted living residents are like prison inmates in that they'll pair off. Likely Uncle Eddie told Fishy something that we can use."

Benno said, "I hope he's more talkative than that strip club manager I interviewed earlier."

"He will be, Detective Benno," Rubin said. "I am sixty-three and likely you've noticed I run off at the mouth a lot. Sixty-three rambles a lot, and eighty rambles even more, so you might have trouble keeping your interviewee on the subject. But he will talk to you, count on that. And be prepared. You and Detective Drummond might even have to change a diaper or two."

Drummond snugged her muffs over her ears and led the way down the steps as she and Benno prepared to leave the crime scene. There was a stout woman at the bottom, arguing with the officer on duty about entrance to Zorro's apartment. Drummond paused on the way down and said to the woman, "Is there something I can help you with?"

The woman was in her fifties, with thick calves and swollen ankles. She wore a shapeless wool dress under an equally shapeless cloth overcoat. She had unkempt

gray hair and her nose was red from the cold. "I'm
Mrs. Duncan, the apartment manager here, and I'm
supposed to do a report on any disturbances," she
said.

Drummond hung her head, thinking, and finally
said, "We can't authorize civilian admittance to a
crime scene. But tell you what. If you'd like to return
to your apartment, we'll have the patrol sergeant come
to see you once our techs are finished up there. He
can give you whatever information you need." She
looked a question at the officer on duty. The cop nodded that he'd tell Patrol Sergeant Stafford to give the
manager a thumbnail sketch.

Mrs. Duncan looked skeptically upstairs. "Is it
really a murder?"

" 'Fraid it is," Drummond said. "The sergeant will
be contacting you as soon as they're finished up
there, okay?"

"As if these apartments weren't hard enough to
rent," Mrs. Duncan said. "The owner's gonna shit in
his drawers."

Lovely old thing, Benno thought. His gaze vacantly
roamed the front of the building, resting on locked
apartment doors downstairs, a sign off to one side
reading, LAUNDRY ROOM. Visible through an open
doorway were coin-operated washers and dryers, two
of each. Next to the laundry room were four round
glass meters set in the outside wall.

Drummond handed the manager a business card.
Mrs. Duncan trudged painfully away. Benno stepped
forward and said, "Wait a minute, please."

The older woman turned slowly around, as if movement was an effort. She brushed stiff gray hairs away
from her forehead.

Benno pointed toward the laundry room. "Are
those individual electricity meters?"

Mrs. Duncan followed his gaze. "Yeah. The water's down by the curb. We pay the water; the tenants got their own electricity."

"But you can read all the meters from ground level, right?"

"Sure. Didn't used to be you could, but last year the power company installed those so the meter guy could get all the readings at once. Personally I think the electric company employs a bunch of lazy fucks that won't even climb the stairs to do their jobs."

Benno frowned at Drummond. He said, "The witness, Elmer Reed. Didn't he say he saw a meter reader up there walking around?"

Drummond bit her lower lip. "Yeah, but why would the guy be upstairs when he can read the meters from ground level?" She looked up the steps, did a double take, then turned to Benno and said, "Jesus Christ. The meter guy."

Benno decided that Elmer Reed's tremors were related to alcohol. Reed had poured a stiff one and seemed a lot steadier. He sat on his sofa watching television as Benno and Drummond burst in. A bottle of Jack Daniel's sat on a counter with the top off. Drummond capped the bottle while Benno sat across from the witness and said, "We need something further from you."

Reed gulped and shuddered. He seemed more belligerent. "I told you what I know," he said.

Benno leaned over and retied one of his shoes. "We appreciate that, but something's come up. You said there was a meter reader up here early this morning?"

Reed's pupils looked dilated. "Yeah, sure, a guy in a uniform."

"You sure he was from the power company?"

"Had his name on his pocket," Reed said. "I guess that's who he was."

"Think you could recognize him again?"

"Come to think about it," Reed said, "the uniform was navy blue with a light blue shirt. The name was stitched on the jacket. Could have been a pest control guy. Plumber or something."

"Yeah, but could you recognize him?"

"Maybe. Maybe not."

"I'm hoping you can be more positive," Benno said. "We've ordered a sketch artist to come out here to see you." He took the drink from Reed, walked over a poured it down the sink. "And let's lay off this, Mr. Reed, at least until the artist is through. Once he's finished you can drink to your heart's content. Or go to work. Or whatever. Just get the description right, and then we really don't care what you do."

Reed watched glumly as the booze flowed down the drain. "Coulda been a building inspector," he said. "Maintenance guy, any-fucking-thing. Tell me something—is there a reward?"

Benno handed Drummond the bottle of Jack and motioned for her to take it out of Reed's apartment. She carried it through the door. Benno turned back to Reed. "Not officially," Benno said. "But you help us out, and maybe we'll see what we can do.

11

Drummond had borrowed a motor pool car for the trip out to the crime scene, and now she turned the keys over to one of the CSU people so that she and Benno could ride together to the assisted living center. She sat quietly in the passenger seat as Benno steamed out of Irving on MacArthur Boulevard and took Airport Freeway toward Dallas, with SUVs and tractor trailer rigs parading back and forth on both sides of the median.

Drummond inhaled as if to speak, then lapsed into silence. Finally she said, "I'm about to get nosy." She was studying Benno with a different look, nothing feisty for a change, just a strange hesitation over broaching certain subjects.

Benno eased into the center lane. "Well, I guess since we're partners."

"This is something I probably wouldn't ask any of my old partners. But, hey, it's something that could affect our working together. You know somebody named Bill Nordstrom?"

Benno's chin lifted. "A reporter?"

"Yeah. He's been calling me. The message is, he wants to ask me about you."

"He's poking around," Benno said. "He used to work for the LA paper when I lived out there. I think he's about to print some real shit on me. I told you last night—something could come up."

"What, when you were LAPD you were some kind of big deal?"

Benno thought over his answer. Finally he said, "The West Coast is a different world. Here, a crime's a crime. There it's different, depending on who's involved. I was on some pretty big Hollywood cases that got my name in print. Picture on the TV. Gave me some contacts and made me a helluva lot bigger deal than I should have been."

"Oh? O.J. and things like that?"

"Not that case in particular. But sort of. I caught one guy stalking some actresses and busted a couple of minor stars. In this town it'd be just another case, but when your victim's been in a movie it's different. Any movie. If a guy played a bellhop in some old Frank Sinatra detective picture, then thirty years later he's charged with dope or something, the media will make out like he was a major star."

Drummond adjusted her weapon on her belt. "Is that who you shot?"

"Beg your pardon?"

"The stalker. Last night you said you shot a couple of guys."

"Oh. No, one was early on, about a year after I went on the job, after a supermarket holdup. The other was . . . later. Look, the angle Nordstrom's coming from has to do with another incident. The fact that I'd been in the paper a lot made this other incident a whole lot bigger deal. I wound up getting fired over it, and Nordstrom's about to bring it all up again."

Drummond quietly watched the freeway ahead. She fiddled with her nose. "Is the incident something I should know about? If I'm going to talk to this reporter—and believe me, he'll keep on bugging me until I do—then maybe I should have some ammunition to defend you with."

Benno had a sinking sensation in the pit of his stomach. He wanted to stay on Drummond's good side, but he also didn't want to visit ancient history, the things he'd been trying to live down. "The truth is, you probably should know. But not just now. It's too painful, to tell you the truth," he said.

Drummond's gaze on him was steady. "Up to you," she said. "But I'd rather know in advance instead of reading some asshole's story in the paper. Must have been quite an incident. Hey, Benno, if you need a shoulder . . ."

Benno sighed. "Sure I do. I just don't want to borrow one, okay?"

Drummond suddenly chuckled. "So I guess we're back to *Chinatown*, huh?"

"You could say that." Benno laughed without much humor. "I just don't want to talk about Chinatown yet. I think that might change pretty soon. When it does, you'll be the first to know."

"Seventeen properties," Drummond was saying, "in addition to her Highland Park home. Morgan's house belongs to LaVon, incidentally. But—and this is strange—the older properties are all titled to Harry and LaVon Masters." She was reading from a yellow legal pad, sitting on her ankles with her back against the passenger door. She'd hung her earmuffs over the back of the seat. Her dark facial skin was taut, her eyes narrowing as she squinted at her own writing on the page.

Benno was hunched over the wheel, steering off North Central at the Walnut Hill Lane exit. "Harry Masters has been dead since 'seventy-two. LaVon might be in trouble if she tries selling any of those places. The title companies might not issue a policy." He frowned. "Harry didn't leave a will?"

"The probate records," Drummond said, "are in the same area of the Records Building as property. So I checked over there. Two weeks after Harry Masters' death a case titled 'Estate of Harry Masters' was opened. The docket sheet shows a will admitted to probate, but then there's nothing else in the record. Twenty-seven years later the case is still pending. Procedure is, after two years they're supposed to close the case and make the parties reopen in the event that they want to pursue it, but in the Masters estate this wasn't done."

Benno drove down Walnut Hill Lane past a Centennial Liquor Store and a Dave 'n' Buster's Restaurant, then slowed to read addresses on the fronts of office buildings. "You look up Harry's will?"

Drummond shrugged. "It's apparently misplaced. The docket sheet shows a will admitted to probate, but there's no will in the file jacket. Which is the reason all that property still shows joint ownership. If the estate had been probated, LaVon would be sole owner."

"LaVon, or whoever Harry named as his beneficiary. There would have been a holdup in the proceedings while LaVon answered to murder charges, but after her acquittal she could've gone right ahead and claimed her inheritance, assuming she was sole beneficiary. We need to look at that will. Any idea what lawyer represented the estate?"

"I jotted that down," Drummond said. "Harold Stein."

"Christ." Benno accelerated through a yellow light in front of a Tom Thumb grocery store. Traffic was increasing in volume. He looked at the dashboard clock; it was nearly four and rush hour was underway. "I guess we're gonna have to pay Mr. Stein a visit."

"Bet your ass he'll holler privilege," Drummond said.

"Yeah, well, he might," Benno said. "And we might say he's fulla shit. Privilege only goes so far. By my way of thinking, that's what we got a district attorney for."

Everlasting Gardens was set in behind a grove of trees across the street from Presbyterian Hospital; it was next door to a neat brick four-story with a sign reading, GOODCARE NURSING HOME. The assisted living facility was built in the shape of a horseshoe and had a magnificent entry with round white pillars holding up a peaked-roof overhang. The place looked just like an upscale apartment building, but there were telltale signs that it was really something else: wheelchair ramps, a van parked outside with an invalid lift, an ambulance partway hidden behind a cedar bush. As Benno and Drummond entered the lobby, an old woman with stringy white hair was watering potted plants with a sprinkler can. Her expression was vacant. As the detectives approached the manager's office, Drummond dabbed at her eye.

The rest home manager was named Valerie Clark, a trim woman in her forties with an upbeat attitude. The attitude seemed a bit put on. On Ms. Clark's office wall were photos of Everlasting Gardens' main lobby, dining hall, and rec room. The dining hall photo showed elderly men and women chuckling over dinner. In the rec room picture, people were playing bridge. Benno squinted at the photo. He wasn't sure, but thought one old guy, incredibly skinny with bushy unkempt eyebrows, was holding his cards backward.

Valerie Clark checked Drummond's ID and then handed the card back over her desk. "Someone from the police department called earlier. Has something happened to Mr. Payne?"

"That's what we're trying to determine," Drummond said. "Our information is that he's lived here, what, two years?"

"Roughly. Spring of 'ninety-seven. More like eighteen months."

"Mmm-hmm. What we'd like to do is interview one of the residents who might have been close to him. Mr. Delbert Greene. Did Mr. Payne leave here alone, or was someone possibly with him?"

Ms. Clark reached for a file folder, then opened it up. "Mr. Payne was in what we call our entry level. That means he was free to come and go as he pleased. Residents, uh, graduate up in level depending on the care they require. Some of our wings have full-time nurses on duty. At the upper levels, residents aren't permitted to leave the building unless a guardian or relative signs them out. In Mr. Payne's case that wasn't necessary. He signed himself out. If anyone was waiting for him outside, we wouldn't have a record of that."

"Does a Mr. Delbert Greene live here?" Drummond asked.

Ms. Clark showed a frown of concern. "We have to be careful with that. Above all, we can't be upsetting these people."

"We'll be careful. But in a criminal investigation our priority is getting information. We have to do this, ma'am."

"Oh my. I think Mr. Greene and Mr. Payne were acquainted before they came here." Ms. Clark laughed wittily. "They had nicknames for each other. Mr. Greene called Mr. Payne 'Uncle Eddie,' though it didn't seem that Mr. Payne could have really been— Mr. Greene's almost ten years older. Mr. Payne called Mr. Greene 'Fishy.' They argued all the time, but they were really cute together. It's the kind of camaraderie that Everlasting Gardens likes to see in its residents."

Drummond stayed deadpan. "Maybe it's not exactly the kind of friendship you're used to, Ms. Clark. Where can we see Mr. Greene?"

"He'll be in his room. I'll have one of the staff escort you. Mr. Greene's classification is two care levels up from Mr. Payne. He's hard of hearing. But he's really a love. He's not really fishy at all."

"I'm sure he isn't." Drummond gave Benno an imperceptible nod. Both detectives stood. "Thanks very much for your time, Ms. Clark," Drummond said.

"Don't mention it." Ms. Clark indicated a tray on the front of her desk, holding a stack of business cards. On the card was Everlasting Gardens' logo—a grinning cartoon bear planting a tree—over the words THE JOY OF BEING TOGETHER. Ms. Clark said, "Help yourself to those. Everlasting Gardens is the place to be when it's your time."

Benno gingerly took one of the cards from the tray. He looked at the rec room photo, at the confused old guy holding his cards wrong. "Seems that it might be," Benno said.

Fishy Greene's eyes were puffy and wrinkled. The jowls in his neck hung to his sternum, and he wore the blackest, goofiest-looking hairpiece that Benno had ever seen. The hairpiece was askew so that the part was nearly on top of Fishy's head. Most of Fishy's teeth were missing, and the ones he did have were yellow and crooked. He was hooked up to an oxygen

tank and wore a hearing aid that constantly fell out
of his ear. *Oprah* was on, the volume turned up so
loud that it was difficult to stay in the room. Fishy
yelled in a high cracked voice, "She toldja what?"

"That you might give us some information about
Uncle Eddie Payne," Benno said. He was seated in a
wicker chair while Drummond was perched on the
bed.

"Whadja say?" Fishy sat in a rocker wearing pajamas and a robe. His feet were in slippers. His ankles
were bare, pasty white with a few varicose veins, and
roughly the circumference of a chicken's lower leg.

Benno got up and turned down the volume on the
television. "That you could tell us some things about
Uncle Eddie Payne."

"About who?"

Benno raised his voice so that he was practically
screaming. "Uncle Eddie Payne."

Fishy pulled his robe up so that it covered his knees.
As soon as he let go of the cloth it dropped once
again toward the floor. "Whatcha askin' about that
asshole for? You cops or somethin'?"

"Yes, sir. Metro." Benno didn't reach for his wallet.

Fishy pointed a bony finger at Drummond. "The
nigger gal, too?"

Drummond maintained her calm expression, but did
manage to say, "Yas, suh," with an accent straight
from *Cottonpickers,* an Old South novel Benno'd read
in high school.

Fishy looked even more glum than before. "About
right. Got niggers doin' ever'thing. Used to know their
place, but not no more." The room was about ten-by-
ten, with a single bed, a dresser with a mirror, and a
five-foot-tall armoire with the television set on top.

"Let's talk about your friend Uncle Eddie,"
Benno said.

"Ain't no friend of mine. Ain't no friend to nobody."

"I guess we got the wrong information. The manager told us you and Uncle Eddie spent time together."

Fishy's hearing aid had slipped out yet again. He stuck it back in his ear. "Got the wrong who?"

"Information," Benno said. "We thought you and Uncle Eddie were friends from the street."

Fishy patted the air, palm down. "I knowed the fucker. Back yonder when there was things happenin' in this town. Back then, if I saw Uncle Eddie I might shoot his ass if he didn't shoot mine first. There was some tough assholes in Dallas back then. I mean, really tough. Not like now, with queers and niggers runnin' ever'thing. Back then queers didn' want people knowin' they was queer, and nigger pussy was two bucks a throw. I remember one time me and Scar Hooter, Gandy Wilkes, and a couple of guys went down offa Hall and Thomas Streets where them whores hung out, and we—"

"Look, Fishy," Benno said, "what we're trying to find out is, when Uncle Eddie left here the other day, did he tell you where he was going or who he was going with?"

"Whadja say?"

"Jesus Christ," Benno said.

Fishy grinned at Drummond, showing gaps where his missing teeth should have been. He'd shaved, but he'd missed places, notably on his chin and beneath his nostrils. He said, leering, "How much they gettin' fer nigger pussy these days?"

Benno expected her to come unglued, but she leaned closer to Fishy and tilted her head seductively. "I think it's gone up some since your last time in the saddle, old-timer," Drummond said. "I'm surprised at you, Fishy. Our word from the manager is that you and Uncle Eddie were cute together. We need your help here."

"I wadn' never cute with that asshole. I ain't no queer, if that's what you're askin'."

Drummond teased him with her eyes. "But you knew him back when, right?"

"Shit. Knowed him well enough that he understood Fishy Greene wasn't nobody to fuck with. There was this one time Uncle Eddie was lookin' to waste this kike over in East Dallas, 'cause the guy wouldn't settle up with this bookmaker Ace Darnell. The Jew gimme a hunnerd to stop all that shit. I found Uncle Eddie downtown at the University Lounge, and I says to him—"

"Fishy," Drummond said, "let me ask you something. Did you know a guy named Harry Masters?"

"Know who?" Fishy had once again dropped his hearing aid. Benno found the tiny instrument in the folds of Fishy's robe and replaced it in Fishy's ear. Fishy began to cough and wheeze. Benno turned the knob on the oxygen tank.

Now it was Drummond's turn to yell. "Harry Masters. Did you know him?"

"Shit," Fishy said when his coughing fit subsided. "Know him? Wasn't nobody around didn't know old Harry the movie man. He was a good 'un to know. Wasn't no nigger or Jew like they got doin' ever'thing these days. I remember one time I seen Harry at a standup counter downtown, eatin' a hot dog. I asked him what picture shows was comin' to town that week, and he says to me—"

"How about Harry's wife LaVon?" Benno interrupted.

"Yeah, she was a dish. A looker, that 'un. Liked to spread it around, too—you know what I mean?"

Benno assumed a confidential tone. "Think she might have spread it around to Uncle Eddie Payne?"

Fishy's eyes narrowed. "You look like you might be a Jew."

Drummond snickered. Warmth crept up the sides of Benno's neck. He said, "I don't go to any synagogue, Fishy."

"Good you don't. Maybe you're one of them A-rabs."

"Born and raised in the USA," Benno said. "Uncle Eddie Payne and LaVon Masters—you think they might've been getting next to each other?"

Fishy hacked and spat into a Styrofoam cup. "Uncle Eddie claims he used to fuck her. Mighta been bull-shittin' me. Uncle Eddie claims a lotta stuff. Him and LaVon knowed each other, just like she knowed a lotta people. She used to like to come around them craps and twenty-one games we used to have. Sometimes Harry brung her, but sometimes she come alone. Woman was a gamblin' fool back in them days."

Drummond moved in, watching the old man with a glint in her eye. "Fishy, do you remember when Harry Masters got killed?"

"Who don't? Lotta guys got whacked back then. World'd be better if more of 'em got whacked today. Politicians and shit. Keep their asses in line."

Drummond licked her lips and then said, "We've gotten word that maybe Uncle Eddie Payne might've been in on the Harry Masters job. Do you think he might've?"

Fishy showed an evil grin. "You gonna climb ol' Fishy's pole iffen I tell ya?"

"I don't see how I could resist, with a line like you've got. Come on, Fishy, tell me."

Fishy gulped oxygen. He squinched his eyes tightly shut, then opened them wide. "Don't s'pect it matters

no more, after all them years. Word was out back then
that Uncle Eddie mighta done it. Uncle Eddie's a
prick, but he was a good 'un to get somethin' done if
a body was willin' to pay. Didn't no police ever tie
him to that one, but they never tied him to nothin'
else, neither.'Course, standup people like us, we didn't
go around askin' and guys didn't go around tellin' if
they had any sense. I remember one time after Uncle
Eddie was gonna kill that Jew. The time I put a stop
to it? Right after that me and Uncle Eddie was talkin'
and he said—"

"Harry Masters," Drummond said. "Concentrate,
Fishy. He's the one we're interested in."

"The movie man? Hey, Fishy knows what Fishy
knows. Fishy knows Uncle Eddie claims he was fuckin'
that young wife of Harry's, though I never seen 'em
together. Fishy knows Harry got torched, and that was
the way Uncle Eddie liked to do things back then.
And, hey, Fishy knows that right after that happened,
Uncle Eddie had him plenty of scratch, flyin' off to
Vegas and shit alla time. And later Fishy *heard,* which
is different than Fishy *knowin'*—you know what I
mean? But what Fishy heard was, Uncle Eddie was
callin' on that good-lookin' woman right regular once
Harry was in the ground. So all of it kinda goes together. Tell you one thing, though. Uncle Eddie
mighta been dippin' LaVon, but if he was, she wadn'
the main attraction."

"I hear you," Drummond said. "It was her
money, right?"

Fishy put a finger to his ear. The hearing aid was
still in place. "Hell, no, woman. Whatever money
Uncle Eddie was gonna get, he'd get paid up front
before he done the deed. That was the way things
went back then. But fuckin' a young woman like

LaVon Masters wasn't nothin' to Uncle Eddie, never was. If Uncle Eddie was comin' around after Harry died, Uncle Eddie was interested in that little girl."

Drummond and Benno looked at each other. Benno said, "You talking about LaVon Masters' daughter? She was only a baby."

"Don't matter," Fishy said. "How come you think us standup guys hated Uncle Eddie's guts so much in them days? Eddie was a short-eyes second to none. Ten years old, five years old, didn't matter as long as Uncle Eddie could get his finger in 'em. I remember this one time me and Scar and Ace Darnell was in the University Club, and Uncle Eddie come in and he told us—"

"Fishy," Drummond said, "let's talk about today, more recently. Our word is, you and Uncle Eddie have been pretty close since he's been living in this place."

"Me and that baby-rapin' prick ain't close—never were. He used to come around just bullshittin'. I ain't got no more to do than listen, lessen you and ol' Fishy can get something straight between us, iffen you know what I mean."

"Makes me quiver just thinking about it," Drummond said. "But if we're going to get Uncle Eddie for his sins, we need to know. When he left here last week, did he tell you where he was going or what he was up to?"

"I know what he told me. Told me he was gonna make him a score someplace, but I'll tell you somethin'. Old men like us done made our final score years ago, and we got no more scorin' to do. I think Uncle Eddie was fulla shit. Uncle Eddie was dreamin' like a lotta old farts. Not Fishy. Fishy don't think about that kinda shit no more. I remember one time me and Scar was playin' golf, and Scar says to me—"

"What kind of score was it that Uncle Eddie thought he was going to make?" Benno said.

"Uncle Eddie was talkin' crazy about all this scratch he was fixin' to get offa LaVon Masters. Next thing I know Uncle Eddie's packin' his shit and he's outta here. Serve the stupid prick right if he never makes it back—you know what I'm sayin'?"

"And you got no idea what he was going to do to get this money?"

"Got no idea." Fishy scratched his head. "Things have changed today. Usedta be I'd a thought he was fixin' to waste somebody. But now they got all these niggers runnin' around with bandanas on their heads. Got these—"

"Listen, Fishy," Drummond said, "if anything else comes to mind, will you have the manager downstairs call us?"

Fishy grinned. "You gonna climb the pole iffen I do?"

"I'll be thinking about it a lot," Drummond said. "Be quite a fantasy for me." She looked at Benno. Benno shrugged. Drummond stood. "We'll likely be in touch again, Fishy. We gotta be going now." She stepped toward the door.

Benno got up and extended his hand. "You've been a big help, Fishy."

Fishy clutched at his ear. The hearing aid fell to the floor and the hairpiece tilted dangerously. "Whadja say?" Fishy Greene yelled.

The detectives went back downtown to headquarters. As they entered the ground level, reporters and TV commentators waited in the lobby along with some men in their shirtsleeves who were toting minicams. One of the reporters was Bill Nordstrom, the transplant from LA. Benno looked frantically around for a place to hide.

He ducked into the men's room. Drummond fol-

lowed right on in, brushing past two uniformed male
cops on their way out. She caught up with Benno by
the sinks, and as a guy using the urinal hurriedly
zipped his fly, she said, "No way, José. You're lead.
You gotta give those people something."

"We've got nothing to give them, Tina. Not anything that the chief hasn't cleared."

"So improvise," she said. "Tell them about all these
leads you're working on."

The guy from the urinal splashed water on his
hands, gaped at Drummond as he groped for a paper
towel, then hurried on out. She stood her ground with
hands on hips, looking up at Benno.

Benno paced back and forth. "Don't you understand I'm media shy? I had plenty of that in Los
Angeles. Those people twist your words around." He
checked his watch. Five after six, dark outside. And
there was something he was supposed to do, but he
just couldn't recall.

"So since they're going to twist your words anyway," Drummond said, "it doesn't make any difference what you tell them, does it?"

Benno wasn't really listening. Five after six, five
after six. Somewhere he was supposed to be . . .

Jesus Christ, Jessica Baldwin? The psychiatrist,
Morgan Masters' friend. The sexy telephone voice and
no-bullshit attitude.

Benno bolted for the door. "Gotta go."

Drummond followed fast. "Oh no, you don't."

He pushed out of the restroom and headed for the
building exit, averting his gaze from the media people.
As Drummond came out of the bathroom he called
out to her, "I got an appointment. Very important
meeting. See you in the morning, Tina, okay?"

"Chickenshit," Drummond yelled. She turned on
her heels and stalked toward the reporters. "Hey,

newsies, listen up. You got any idea who just went through that door?"

Benno felt guilty for having left Drummond to face all those reporters, and he didn't blame her for being pissed. Big cases meant big media coverage, and he could expect reporters in his face on a daily basis. They'd gather in the lobby every afternoon and remain there until someone told them something about the progress of the case, and if no one told them anything they'd just make it all up as deadlines approached. He'd dealt with the pressure pretty well for a long time in LA, up until the blowup, and had even had reporters as pals and drinking buddies. Hell, back then he'd looked forward to press conferences. Time after time he'd stood at ease before a bank of microphones answering questions, and had even thrown in some comedy that had made him sort of a local celebrity. The fact that he was well known in the media had made it tougher when the big fall came. No way would he go through that bullshit ever again.

Just the sight of Nordstrom standing there had made his spit dry up. No telling when the big exposé would appear in the *News,* but it was definitely coming. Benno could do nothing about what Nordstrom was going to print about him; he had to put Nordstrom out of his mind and put on the blinders. Easy enough to say, hard as hell to do.

12

La Madeleine occupied one end of a strip center in
an upscale North Dallas neighborhood. It wasn't
Benno's idea of a restaurant for guys. White wrought-
iron tables and chairs lined the sidewalk under an awning, but with the temperature below forty and
patches of not-yet-melted snow clinging to the awning,
no one was eating outside. He peered in through the
window. Service inside the restaurant was cafeteria
style: quiche, gourmet sandwiches, four or five different salads, three kinds of soup. No beef, no gravy, no
boiled potatoes. Over to the right was the pastry bar,
with delicate little cakes, jam-filled croissants, and
chocolate éclairs. Women in fashions from Neiman's
and Barney's sat picking at salads and spooning soup
in careful strokes away from them. And gossiping. Always fucking gossiping. Benno turned off his cell and
left it in the glove compartment. As he went inside he
buttoned his coat to hide his shoulder rig.

And there she stood, no question about it, though
Jessica Baldwin didn't quite fit Benno's impression of
her telephone voice. He had her pictured as fairly tall,

willowy, with a model's shape and exquisite slender neck. The woman who stood just inside the entry was five two or three and looked like an athlete. She had a firm jaw and sturdy shoulders, along with muscular calves bunched tight over tall platform shoes with ankle straps. Light delicate skin, winter pale. Her suit was gray tweed, jacket and skirt, and she wore a white formfitting blouse. She carried a trenchcoat folded over her arm. Her dark hair was layered close to her head, and there were tiny gold studs through her pierced earlobes. Her waist was small, her body well taken care of. She was looking expectantly around the restaurant. He touched her shoulder and she turned to him.

The head-on facial view was pretty stunning. Calm brown eyes, good straight nose—or maybe not completely straight; there was a small hump that didn't detract from the overall picture—all above a mouth that was really the attention-getter. Strange—there was a scar running from just below her nose to just above her chin, bisecting her mouth, so that her smile of greeting was just the slightest bit lopsided. But the smile was the kind you wanted to return. He did so.

"So you've gotta be Detective Benno." Same voice as the one he'd heard over the phone, cultured and smooth, a little hoarse. "You're taller than you looked in your picture in the paper."

"If I'd known this many people were going to recognize me, I'd have struck a more heroic pose. Thanks for coming." He got a whiff of her perfume—not strong, just a hint of scent.

"I got the impression I didn't have a choice," she said, then pointed to the serving line and said, "Trays. Silverware." She strolled ahead of him to take a tray from a stack and slide it along on the rail.

"Nice place," he said, trailing along.

She gave him a sidelong look. "Don't lie to me, Officer. You'd prefer barbecue. Your summons, my choice of food, okay?" She moved on down to the salads, where a girl in a white apron and chef's hat was dishing out the greens.

She had a small Caesar, mixed fresh in the bowl, and a large French onion soup with cheese and croutons sprinkled in. Benno took a long time deciding over the entrées, and finally settled for a ham monsieur—an open-face toasted sandwich, grilled, with thick melted white cheese on top. She took water, Benno iced tea with a lemon wedge. He paid at the end of the line, twenty-one bucks . . . *Christ, that's expensive,* thought Benno. He asked for a receipt and folded it away in his pocket as he followed her over to a small round table with delicate wooden chairs. She set her food out on the table and dispensed with her tray in a rack. Benno, following suit, did the same. He seemed to be the only man in the place. He sat down uncomfortably.

After he'd watched her stir her salad with a fork and take a bite, he asked her, "Do you come here often?"

She chewed and watched him. She had a sip of water. "I come here. I had an appointment nearby."

"A doctor out doing house calls?"

"A psychiatrist. But I don't have what you'd call a normal practice." She sat with her back straight and her legs crossed. She had immaculate table manners.

Benno felt even more out of place. He'd have to be careful to keep his elbows off the table and use the proper forks and whatnot. "What kind of practice do you have?"

"Look, I'd really rather not," she said. "I thought this was about Morgan Masters."

"This is about Morgan. But it's also about you. I got to tell you, we're on a murder scene and there's this odd message on the phone from someone—it makes us wonder."

"So wonder. But unless you're investigating me . . ." She bent her head and got busy with the salad.

The ham monsieur looked pretty good. Benno sawed off a morsel and ate it. The cheese had some spices he'd never tasted before and there was a kind of creamy base mixed in. He swallowed and said, "Investigating a murder—two murders now—isn't exactly like investigating a person. But we do need to know everybody's role."

"I have no role, other than that I'm Morgan's friend."

"You told me on the phone you also had a professional relationship."

She smiled in amusement. A drop-dead look. "It's only going to be professional if you ask something about Morgan I don't want to tell. Which you've already done about me. If your question was about Morgan I'd claim privilege. Since it was about me, I'm saying none of your business."

"I'm a cop. You don't think I can find out about you?"

"Oh Jesus. Look, there's a reason I don't want to go into a lot of detail."

"Anything you say is in confidence, ma'am, unless it somehow connects you."

She rolled her eyes. "Ma'am?"

"Ms. Baldwin, then. But I have to know."

"Try Jessica. I work for the county."

"What, Public Health?"

"The district attorney. I can't have my office know I'm talking to you or that I'm seeing Morgan. So question me all you want, but it's off the record."

"Do you examine criminal defendants for the prosecution? People with insanity defenses?"

She briefly shook her head. "Victims' program. Counseling violent crime survivors. There is a lady who owns a shop down the street whose daughter was murdered last year. They've got the guy and his trial starts next week. She was having problems, so I dropped by. That's what I'm doing in the neighborhood." She looked at her watch. "Not to mention that I've got another appointment when I leave here, and this little conference we're having is going to make me late. So I have to make a call. Excuse me for a moment, will you?" She grabbed her cell, stood, walked to a nearby empty table, and punched in a number.

Benno tried another bite of the ham monsieur while he waited for her to finish. The food was tasting better and better. He couldn't stop watching Jessica Baldwin and wondered what he could say to make her show that smile again. When she'd disconnected and returned to sit across from him, he said, "You met Morgan Masters through a victims' counseling program?"

"No. I met Morgan in a male strip club. Just because I work for the county doesn't mean I don't like seeing a few hard asses once in a while. You got a problem with that, Detective?"

"That's your, uh, prerogative. Muscle's, in Grand Prairie?"

"How did you know?"

"That's apparently Morgan's favorite," Benno said. "Plus, when she got home from this trip she had one of the employees with her." He started to add that this particular employee, Zorro, was now dead, but decided not to. He wanted to hold something back, in case he later found out she already knew the murder in Irving was connected to this case. He felt guilty putting her on, but you never knew. Too many characters involved in this one already.

Jessica Baldwin laid her fork aside. "Oh shit. She had one of those strippers along? I've talked to her and talked to her."

"At the risk of sounding judgmental," Benno said, "I've got to ask. Why is it okay for you to hang out with these male strippers, but it isn't okay for her?"

She tried some of the soup. "I don't hang out with any of those people, and I don't go to those places but once in a blue moon. The night I ran into Morgan I was at a bridesmaids' stag for a friend who was getting married. What's your first name?"

The mention of a wedding made Benno wonder if she was married. She wasn't wearing any rings except for a birthstone on her right hand. He looked at her.

"I don't like calling you 'Detective,'" she said. "Sounds like I'm in a television drama or something. Down at the DA's everybody goes around calling each other Mister or that god-awful Ms. business. Not me. I learn everybody's first name and call them by it."

He bent to cut more of his sandwich. "Ham," he said.

She looked about to laugh. "For real?"

"For real," he said, then went into cop mode, tone flat, as he said, "You were going to tell me about meeting Morgan Masters."

"If your name's really Ham, I think I'll just call you Benno. Is that all right?"

"Sure. My partner does."

"Who'd want to call somebody Ham? Well, Benno, the reason it's okay for me to go to strip clubs and it isn't okay for Morgan . . . do you drink?"

"Not anymore."

"I won't ask why. But you do understand that there are those who can drink and those who can't, don't you?"

"That I definitely do," Benno said.

"Okay. Morgan and strip clubs are sort of the same thing as people who can't drink. We were in this club having a ball, and one of the guys was coming over in hump-you mode, getting money shoved down his crotch and everything. Embarrassed the crap out of most of us, and those of us who did stick a dollar bill in there were looking away, you know, red-faced. Suddenly out of the blue this one chick jumps up from two tables over and lunges at the guy. Jams her hand right on in there and grabs his . . . well, you know. The guy starts screaming bloody murder and the bouncers come to haul her off of him. We all expected her to get thrown out, but all they did was sit her back down. The stripper had to leave the stage, all doubled over and holding himself, yet still she's sitting there. Alone. I thought it was odd that anyone would come to that place alone. It was Morgan. The women I was with were all laughing about it, but then I had a look at her face.

"You'd just have to have seen it," Jessica said. "Shock, but more. Grief. Benno, I've never seen a more pitiful look on a human being. I'd had a few toddies myself and was feeling no pain, but I just had to get up and say something to her. I excused myself from my group and went over and sat with Morgan. I asked her if she was all right, and she just buried her face in her hands and let go of these terrible sobs. It was like she was ashamed and yet she couldn't have helped herself. We call it compulsive behavior. In Morgan's case it's a bit more than a compulsion."

"I've heard of sexual addiction," Benno said. "I think they've even got clinics."

"Close, but not quite accurate. Look, I confess to being a sucker for people with problems. Otherwise why would I be working for the county? I could make three times as much hanging a shingle out and talking to women whose only problem is too much money to spend and a husband that's screwing around. That's not really a problem—clean out the bank accounts and divorce the guy, right? My heart just went out to Morgan. I hugged her and let her cry on my shoulder. Then I told these other women I was leaving and led Morgan out to her car and took her home. We talked on her couch until three in the morning. She scares me, Benno. At the same time she makes my heart ache. What can I say?"

"Hey, I'll level. When I called you this morning we considered Miss Masters our primary suspect. Things have happened to change that. She's not totally in the clear, and she's involved in some way. How long ago was this incident?"

"Three months. Ever since then I've been sort of her confidante. Every time she goes on one of these sexual toots, she calls me later. I'm surprised I haven't heard from her today. I know a lot of think tank panels that would give their eyeteeth to have her as a subject, but I wouldn't make a guinea pig out of Morgan, ever. Some of her behavior is classic. At other times she's totally unexplainable."

Benno thought about the earlier meeting with Fishy Greene at the retirement center. He said, "Any of it have to do with abuse as a child?"

Jessica pushed her salad away, half eaten, and started in earnest on the soup. "Gee, that's where you get into privilege. I swear, Benno, if it comes back to me that you've repeated all this . . ."

"You'd have to define 'repeated.' I won't mouth off to any newspapers, but if I have to use what you say in the investigation, I'll have to. She's not a paying patient of yours, so I don't know that privilege would apply in the first place."

"Maybe not legal privilege. But I look in the mirror

every day. Morgan needs help. If it won't help her, then I won't say anything."

"I don't know anything about helping her mental state. I do know you can help her status in this murder investigation. We got information today that leads us to believe that one of our murder victims might've abused Morgan years ago. That's why I'm asking."

"I suppose I could talk hypothetically."

"Okay. Hypothetically, then."

"Hypothetically . . ." Jessica spooned more soup, uncrossed and recrossed her legs. "There are two kinds of abuse victims. Some remember everything that happened. Their response is frigidity or revulsion to sex. Resigned submissiveness to partners is common—guys, with their usual overall sensitivity, would say it's like screwing a foam rubber mattress. Marriages don't work out. Some of this type of victim get into same-sex relationships even though they're not really gay. Some women respond to counseling, some don't. Many spend their whole lives alone and miserable. The suicide rate in those cases is off the Richter scale.

"Other victims have totally blacked out the abuse," Jessica went on, "and can remember nothing in their lives before a certain age, say six or seven. They become promiscuous early on. Seduce little boys on the playground, that sort of thing. I've seen eight-year-olds pull their dresses up the second a man walks in the room. As adults their behavior is often mistaken for sexual addiction. A lot of the symptoms are the same, but the causes are totally different. These people are responding to things that happened that they can't remember. They perform the kinkiest sexual acts imaginable, and a lasting relationship is impossible. They reject all advances from normal people. After they go on a sexual romp they have deep feelings of guilt, and suicide during those periods isn't out of the question."

Benno had a queasy feeling in his stomach. He pushed his food away. "From what we've learned about her, you're describing Morgan to a T."

"I'm describing a hypothetical patient, Benno. One that is different from other promiscuous cases. This hypothetical patient also hates her mother. That's unusual. Usually they consider their mothers abuse victims as well, but not this patient. I don't consider this patient capable of murder unless it was her mother who was dead. If she were suspected of killing anyone else, I'd say it's impossible." Jessica looked at her watch. "I'm running out of time here." She reached for her coat.

Benno watched the way she moved. "I'll want to see you again."

She'd poked an arm through a sleeve. Her eyebrow arched as she looked at him.

"For more, uh, help on the case," Benno said.

"I've already got cases on the burner. The DA gives me plenty of those." She had both arms in the coat and now adjusted the collar and cinched the belt.

"Well, maybe something more."

"Oh? More than what?" She seemed about to laugh.

He gulped, then spit out, "Hell, I'll go ahead and ask. Are you seeing anyone?"

"I'm seeing lots of people. Every day."

"No, I mean . . . anyone special."

The slightly off-kilter smile again. "Is your name really Ham?" She got up and reached for her purse.

"It's on my birth certificate." He stood away from the table. "Hey, I'll walk you out."

"Okay. Since you're acting interested, let me tell you how it is. I'm leaving here to go see a rape victim whose attacker cut off her thumb. Tomorrow morning at eight I've got a couple coming in whose little boy got kidnapped, sodomized, and thrown into a culvert. After that, it's a lady who's blind because her boyfriend tied her down and poured sulfuric acid in her eyes. I don't make real pleasant dinnertime conversation, Benno. So, no, I'm not seeing anyone, and I suspect my profession has a lot to do with it. Any guy who could battle his way through all that . . ." She started to walk away through the restaurant.

He went after her and caught up halfway to the exit. "I don't exactly deal with the rosy picture in my own job, you know. I might be just the guy."

She stopped, looked up at him with her head canted to one side, and flashed her gorgeous smile. "Might? *Might?* Jeez, I'll be thirty next month, and 'might' is the best I can do?"

Benno watched her walk to a tidy black Nissan in the parking lot, get in, start the engine, and drive away after waving to him through the window. He climbed into his own motor pool–issue Mercury, poked his key in the ignition, and sat there staring at the dashboard.

Jessica Baldwin and her off-kilter, drop-dead smile. A hardworking independent woman, with a contagious, no-nonsense attitude. And sexy . . .

Benno forced himself to think about the case and the two victims thus far: Uncle Eddie Payne and Gerald "Zorro" Trafficante, an old bad guy and a young bad guy, but both definitely bad. And both connected to Morgan Masters. Two more bad guys in Benno's life; they seemed to run in pairs.

Benno'd been chasing two bad guys in California when he'd met Jan—had saved her life, actually, shooting one of the jail escapees as the guy had held a knife to Jan's throat, using her as a shield. It had been in the aftermath of a supermarket holdup; Jan had been unlucky enough to be in the checkout line behind one of the escapees. After he'd cuffed the wounded guy, Jan had clung to him and sobbed onto his shoulder. He'd only known her a couple of weeks before they'd started thinking serious.

Jessica . . . Hell, he'd just met her. He was thinking crazy. Not crazy drunk, the way he used to get, but still crazy. AA had taught him that, years after he stopped drinking, he'd still have periods of off-kilter behavior—dry drunks. Act irrationally.

Benno had known from early childhood that alcoholism was rare among Jews, so when the heavy boozing had started in LA he'd told himself that a nip here and there on the job was only to keep his mind straight. No way did he have a problem with liquor—ol' Ham the Hebrew could take it or leave it. Even the departmental shrink in LA had been stumped, and she'd wound up agreeing that something other than the liquor was causing him to behave the way he did. Later on Benno had decided that the psychiatrist had taken the easy way out in her report to the department, stating that there was nothing really wrong with him other than job stress.

Now, years later, Benno thought he'd hit on the root of his problem through self-analysis—discounting what the shrink had had to say but at the same time relating his behavior to her theories. Benno now believed that his dependence on booze was somehow connected to his religious confusion—being a Jew, but at the same time *not* being a Jew, which meant that he really didn't fit in anywhere.

He wanted to stop blaming his Hassidic father. Maybe someday he could.

When he was in his early twenties he'd developed a few relationships with Jewish women, and each time the woman had sent him packing because he'd refused to attend synagogue or even talk about it. Then there'd been a string of non-Jewish females in his life—one devout Catholic, several Christmas-and-Easter-only Protestants, and two or three women who didn't attend church at all—and those relationships had ended because all those women's families considered him a Jew even though he really wasn't one in the traditional sense.

Jan had been different. Their marriage had been very good for a while, up until shortly after their son was born, but then Benno's drinking had taken its toll. He and Jan had overcome the difference in backgrounds, but by marrying a drunk she'd let herself in for mental abuse—the screaming fights after he'd stopped off for a few. Three different times she'd taken Jacob and gone home to her mother. Finally she'd filed for divorce.

He'd thought back then that Jan was overreacting. Nothing wrong with Japeth's son, Ham, no way. Jan was too emotional—that was all there was to it.

LAPD had swept his behavior under the rug and kept him on the job. In Benno's booze-addled mind, backing from the department had showed he hadn't had a damned drinking problem—and he'd clung to that belief up to the day they'd accused him of being drunk on the job and getting a fellow officer killed.

Now, four years since he'd had a drink, he had a completely different slant on things. A new direction in his life. He could never expect Jan to completely forgive him, but even that relationship was better. She'd agreed to let him have his kid for a while, less than a month from now. He pictured himself showing little Jacob the sights, being a real father for, Christ, the first time ever. Showing the child that his father had changed and that he'd always love his son unconditionally. To Benno's way of thinking, that would be a mammoth step.

He'd even thought lately that he might be ready for a new relationship with a woman. A real, no-bullshit arrangement with both parties giving and receiving in return.

Jessica Baldwin . . .

Jesus, maybe . . .

But probably not. In all likelihood he was only thinking crazy again.

There was a faint ringing noise inside the car, cutting through his trance. The cell phone. He opened the glove compartment and the ringing increased in volume. He grabbed the cell, pressed the button, and said hello.

Drummond was short of breath and out of patience. "Where the hell have you been?"

"I had an appointment. Hey, Tina, I apologize for leaving you with all those reporters. Maybe tomorrow I can—"

"Where are you right now?"

"North Dallas. Inwood area, close to—"

"You know Doubletree Inn, on LBJ Freeway?"

"Where Morgan Masters is—"

"Get there, Benno, in one hell of a hurry. There's been another shooting. Oh Jesus, we've got officers down."

13

Benno stalled behind a mile-long traffic jam on the freeway. The lights at Doubletree Inn were visible two miles in the distance, but the lines of cars and trucks, four abreast, weren't moving. Horns honked and drivers got out to curse and shake their fists. Benno put the flasher on the roof, activated the siren, and bulled his way across two lanes and a strip of grass onto the access road. Then he stepped on it, skirting traffic, running over curbs, whipping through a red light, and very nearly sideswiping a bobtail truck in the process. A hundred yards short of the hotel, traffic stalled again. Now he could see the black-and-whites, a CSU truck, and two ambulances, all crowded together underneath the Doubletree awning. He parked in an office building lot and hoofed the rest of the way.

The media was there, milling around in the driveway, and Nordstrom was right in the middle. The slightly bucktoothed former LA writer was bundled up in a heavy wool coat and a muffler. Benno made brief eye contact with the guy, then skirted the newspeople, head down.

Yellow tape was strung between the awning pillars, and a uniformed cop held the crowd back as medics loaded a shrouded body into one of the ambulances. More white coats labored over a man on a gurney with his coat and shirt cut away. His chest and shoulders were soaked in blood and there was an IV in his arm. Benno badged his way past the officer on guard at the barrier and walked up to a cop with stripes on his jacket sleeve. "I'm with Metro," Benno said. "What the hell's happened here?"

The sergeant was a big broad-shouldered blond with curly hair a bit longer than standard. His nose was red from the cold. "We have two DA's investigators shot down. Wits give conflicting statements, so we're piecing it together. The DA's people were here covering a murder suspect, a woman. Morgan Masters." He looked closely at Benno. "Yeah, you're the guy that's picture was in the paper. Lead on the Masters case, right? Okay, apparently she tried to leave the hotel and the investigators stopped her outside, and that's when hell broke loose. Shots came from a car sitting under the awning. What we're getting is, none of 'em remember the make or license number. Plus, nobody we've talked to got a good look at the shooter because the car had those dark tinted windows. Don't even know if it was a man or a woman. As soon as our guys went down, the shooter hauled ass. Went east on the freeway. Got lost in traffic. *Adios,* motherfucker."

"What about Morgan Masters?"

The cop pointed inside the hotel. "In there. There's a deputy chief from the department."

"Chief Rubin?"

"Yeah, and another Metro. A black chick."

"Where?"

"Manager's office. Go past the check-in desk and turn left. The manager's a fat guy in a suit. He's about to shit his pants. You can't miss him."

Benno jogged toward the hotel entry. He was conscious of a whirring minicam, trained on him from beyond the barrier, and also of Nordstrom watching him. He ducked his head and pushed inside through glass double doors.

The lobby was enormous, with a buffet set up at one end behind a sign reading, POTATO GROWERS. The men lined up for chow looked uncomfortable in coats and ties. There was a four-deep crowd around the front lobby windows, looking out at the cops and ambulances. As Benno went past, one woman said to her companion, "Must have been an accident or something." Benno double-timed around a long check-in counter and went down a corridor on his left. A fat man in a suit paced the hallway, four doors down. Benno made him to be three hundred pounds, minimum. He looked up, terrified, as Benno approached. Benno had his shield raised. The fat man looked as if he might faint.

Benno was concerned for the guy. "Relax. I'm Detective Benno. You okay?"

The man breathed like a cardiac patient. He shoved his hand inside his coat to cover his heart. "Yeah, I'm . . . Ted Haver, the manager. We've never had any . . ."

"You need to sit down and get a glass of water or something. I'm looking for the other law enforcement people."

The man pointed to a closed door. "In there. Man, I need to . . ." He kept his hand over his heart and staggered away down the hall.

Benno went on into the manager's reception area.

Chief Rubin was behind a secretarial desk wearing soft unironed khakis and a pullover sweater. He was shuffling through papers and looked up as Benno came in. "You gotta start keeping your cell phone on," Rubin said. "They had to call you three or four times."

"Yeah, I was in a restaurant," Benno said. "Somebody needs to check that manager out. Looks like he's ready for a heart attack."

"I told the guy to get something from the medics. If he does, he does. The ambulance crew has got its hands full with the wounded guys."

Benno parked his rump on the corner of the desk. "Yeah, I saw. Plus half the reporters in town are out there. If I find out who's leaking shit, I'm having a talk with them."

Rubin looked beat. His eyes were tired. "What about the guys that went down?"

"One of them is dead," Benno said.

"Jesus." Rubin hung his head, then looked slowly up. "I talked to the man with the shoulder wound. The DA's staff has had twenty-four/seven on Morgan Masters ever since she checked in here last night. Their orders were, if she tried to leave the hotel, they were to tell her up front that they'd be following. That way it was her choice to leave the hotel or not to leave, but we wanted her to know we'd be on her until we decided whether or not to take what we had to the Grand Jury. Never mind that we don't have shit. We wanted heat on that young lady. She never came out of her room until about six o'clock this evening. The guys stopped her outside the lobby entrance and just then somebody started shooting."

Benno nodded. "From a car parked under the awning. Wonder how long the shooter'd been sitting there."

"The DA's guys never noticed the car. Hell, there was no reason to. Place like this, there's all kinds of vehicles sitting around at all hours. Best estimate is from the valet parkers. They say the shooter drove up there and stopped, and when they tried to park the car, the driver waved them off. The shooter was there a half hour, max."

"The valets saw the shooter?"

"Not through the tinted windows. All they saw was this hand waving them off. If we ever come up with a witness, I'm finally gonna get a chance to show them one of these." Rubin waved a stack of paper and handed Benno the top sheet.

Benno looked. He was holding a drawing of a young guy with short dark hair, wearing a shirt with a name or logo stitched over the pocket—in the picture it looked like hen scratching. The man wore an earring, left ear. "This from the sketch artist out at the Irving scene?" Benno asked.

Rubin nodded. "The wit next door to Zorro's place. The sketch artist faxed it over with a note saying he's not sure of the wit's accuracy."

"Yeah, the guy was about half drunk when we left him. I told him to lay off the booze, but I'm betting that lasted until about five seconds after we left."

Rubin lifted a copy of the drawing from his lap. "Guy looks Hispanic. Might be we're looking for a Mexican, huh?"

Benno went around and looked over Rubin's shoulder. "Arab, maybe. Sicilian . . ."

"Jew?"

"No way. He doesn't have the soft, understanding eyes."

"You mean like yours?"

"And yours, Chief. The look that's like you're at peace with the world."

"You've got an uncle Ish that looks like he'd whip your ass in a heartbeat," Rubin said.

"I think my grandmother told me Ish had some Greek blood," Benno said. "Where's Morgan Masters now?"

Rubin pointed at a closed door. "In the office with Detective Drummond."

"I'll talk to her," Benno said.

"Don't forget she's a murder suspect. Maybe we should call her lawyer first."

Benno stepped back. He didn't know if this was the time. He decided that it was. "Morgan Masters didn't off Uncle Eddie."

"Now that's just great, since the chief prosecutor of Dallas County has pointed her out to the press. So who?"

"We're working on it. But we've uncovered things that tell us Morgan couldn't have been in on it, at least not directly. When we do find the perp, he or she might tell us Morgan ordered the killing, but I don't think that's the case."

"Yeah, right," Rubin said. "We're beginning to look pretty silly here. I still want you should talk to LaVon Masters. I'm not believing she isn't involved."

"Tomorrow, Chief. We through here?"

"For now," Rubin said. "I'll go take that manager to get checked out before the fat asshole dies on us. You keep your cell phone on." He exited through the door.

Benno went into the inner office. There were pictures of hotels on the wall. Drummond sat beneath a photo of the Doubletree Newport Beach, with the whitecapped Pacific in the background, while Morgan Masters sat in a swivel chair behind the manager's desk, the Doubletree Lake Placid in the background over her head. The chair was double width. Benno pictured the manager's girth and wondered if the guy could fit comfortably in any normal-sized piece of furniture. Morgan appeared tiny in it. She wore jeans and a fuzzy white sweater with a blood smear across the chest, and there were drops of dried blood on her cheek. Her look was vacant, her mouth slack.

Benno said cheerily, "Hi. Mind if I break into this?"

Drummond wore blue sweats with the Nike checkmark on the sides and snow-white sneakers. "Just when we were having fun. Up to you, Morgan. You want to let this lug horn in?" She gave Benno a wink of caution and imperceptibly jerked her head in Morgan's direction.

Morgan studied her palms, then let her hands fall loosely into her lap. She sighed but said nothing.

"Not much dialogue here," Benno said.

Drummond had both feet on the floor. "What perception you have. What can you add to the mix?"

Benno sat down beside Drummond. "Morgan, listen. I'll tell you something you'll like to hear and something you *won't* like to hear. Kind of good news, bad news. Through brilliant detective work, Drummond and I have come to the conclusion that you're no longer a suspect. How does that sound?"

Morgan spoke as if in a trance. "You're the guy from last night."

"Right," Benno said. "And now someone's trying to kill you. That's the part you probably won't like."

"I don't think . . ." Morgan began, then licked her lips and studied the far corner of the room.

Benno said to Drummond, "Has she got any injuries?"

"Negative. She was about two feet away from those DA's investigators when the shooting started."

"Morgan," Benno said, "where were you going when those guys stopped you?"

"Somewhere. Anywhere. I was tired of sitting in

this hotel." Morgan touched her cheek and looked at her finger. "Do you think I could have a wet rag?"

"I'll get her one," Drummond said, getting up. "Your witness, bozo," she said aside to Benno, then went out through the door.

When he and Morgan were alone, Benno said, "What don't you think?"

Her lips parted. She closed her mouth.

"When I first came in here," Benno said, "you said, 'I don't think,' but then you didn't finish."

"I just can't believe anyone is trying to kill me," Morgan said.

"Nobody had any reason to shoot those cops. It had to be you the shooter was after. Care to give me a description of what happened?"

"I came outside," Morgan said. "The two men walked up and said, 'Just a minute. We want to talk to you.' Before they could say anything else one of them goes, 'Gun,' really loud, just like that, and then the other one pushed me down. There were all these explosions then, and I hid my face. When I looked up there was blood on me and the two guys were just laying there. God."

Benno pictured the scene. Okay, the shooter had waited underneath the awning for Morgan to come out. So how had he known where to find her and when she'd be leaving the hotel? Or how had *she* known? Then Benno reconsidered the idea that the shooter might be female; women just didn't kill out in the open with a gun. Maybe poison, a little arsenic sprinkled over the mashed potatoes. So who'd known where Morgan was staying? Dunst, the riding DA. Drummond. Benno himself. And, oh yeah, Harold Stein. Morgan's lawyer. Benno said to Morgan, "You've been through quite a bit. Look, if you'd like to sleep on it, we can ask you questions tomorrow."

Morgan seemed to snap partway out of her trance. "No," she said, "I think I'd rather get it over with."

"And you don't want your lawyer present? I've already told you you're no longer a suspect. I should have added 'at present.' That could change, though I don't see it. But if you want your lawyer . . ."

"No," Morgan said. "I really didn't want that asshole last night, after I learned what was going on."

"Good. You didn't get a look at the shooter?"

Morgan hugged herself and shook her head. "I'm sorry to sound like a dork. No bullshit, I'm pretty scared. Once the gun went off, I kept my head down. When I looked up the car was already gone."

"Anyone would be scared," Benno said. "You said you were going somewhere. What was going to be your mode of transportation?"

"I'd already asked the bellman to call me a cab." Morgan's mouth twisted as realization dawned. "Hey, you can check if you want."

"I believe you, Morgan," Benno said. "See, what we've got could either be a lunatic just wanting to waste somebody, anybody, or a sane person with a specific target in mind. He could have opened fire the moment he drove up, but the valet parkers say the car was there about half an hour. So we've got to figure he was waiting for someone specific to come out. That would have to be you."

Drummond came in with a wet washcloth and handed it to Morgan. Morgan dabbed at her face, wiping off the blood. She hiccupped. Drummond took a seat on the couch and threw one arm over the back.

"So now you should be convinced that this is no game," Benno said, "and that someone really did try to kill you. These aren't random acts. This is someone with a pattern. Everyone who's dead in this case is connected to you. To find out who's responsible, we've

first got to find out why he's choosing the victims."
He studied Morgan. "Am I making sense?"

"None of this makes any sense," Morgan said. "I
went on a trip to Louisiana. That's all I did."

Benno started to say more, but Drummond held up
a hand. Drummond said, "That's all you *knowingly*
did. Come on, Morgan, help us."

Morgan wiped her forehead with the washcloth.
"What is it you want to know?"

"Did you understand it when Detective Benno mentioned killings, plural? You have been holed up in this
hotel for the past day or so, and there has been another murder since you were here."

"All I know is, there was a dead man in my car
and blood in my bedroom. The last I heard, no one
knew who he is."

Drummond looked to Benno. Touchy—they weren't
supposed to put out Uncle Eddie's identity, and
there'd been nothing released to the media that
Zorro's murder was connected to the killing at Mor-
gan's. All the newspapers had was Zorro's real name,
Gerald Trafficante, barely worth a column inch on the
Metro page. "Who had keys to your house, Morgan?"
Benno asked.

"Me. My mother, but believe me, she wouldn't
come over on a bet. I've given keys to a few guys
I've . . . met. Three or four, maybe."

"We're pretty sure the killer came and went
through your back porch entry. Who knew the security code?"

"I have a maid and a general handyman that fixes
appliances, does yard work and shit. Both of them.
But, hey, the code's written down on a piece of paper
tucked over the back door. I forget it myself
sometimes."

Drummond said, "So there were a lot of keys in

circulation and your security code was written down outside, which will make narrowing the field sort of a challenge. If I give you the names of some people, will you tell me what you know about them?"

"If I can." Morgan looked hopeful.

"Have you ever known anyone named Edward Payne? You might've called him Uncle Eddie."

Morgan seemed to think it over, then answered, "I don't think so."

Benno watched her closely; Morgan never batted an eye. Either she was one convincing liar or she was telling the truth. Benno thought about what Jessica Baldwin had said—that some abuse victims blocked out the past. "You would have been a really little girl when you met Uncle Eddie," Benno said. "He could have been a friend of your mother's."

"My mother doesn't have friends. My mother has acquaintances." There was open hatred in Morgan's tone.

"Can you remember when your father died?" Drummond asked.

"No. I know what I've been told. My mother says she had nothing to do with it. She's probably full of shit."

Drummond's tone dripped with sympathy. "You and your mom aren't close?"

"I don't know. Ask her. She sends me a check every month. Other than that, I never hear from the bitch."

"And you're sure you don't know Uncle Eddie Payne?"

"He could have been one of the guys fucking my mother when I was little, I guess. There was a string of those guys. Probably still is."

There was a moment of silence while the detectives thought and while Morgan studied her lap. Benno said, "How long since you've seen your mother?"

"Maybe a year. Since the last time she chewed me out for embarrassing her. I got busted for drunk driving and it got in the paper. Big fucking woo. She's got all those artsy-fartsy people fooled into thinking she's some philanthropist. They sure don't know the old whore very well."

Something nagged at the edges of Benno's consciousness, then went away. "If you are estranged, how come you were using her lawyer?"

"Steinsy's not just LaVon's lawyer. He's mine, too. He handles this trust I've got."

"From your father?"

"I suppose," Morgan said. "Beginning when I was eighteen I've been getting a check every month, coming in an envelope from Stein's office. I asked him about the money once, and he told me he couldn't name the source without LaVon's permission. Since I can't find out the details without talking to my mother, I've decided not to give a shit where the money comes from."

"What kind of account are these checks on?" Drummond's head tilted in curiosity.

"They're Steinsy's checks. Actually they say 'Harold Stein, Trust.' That's why I think I've got a trust fund."

"Just because the lawyer's paying out of a trust account," Benno said, "that doesn't mean you have a fund. It could mean someone gives him money on your behalf, so he sticks it in his account and writes you a check. Let's try something else. After Gerald Trafficante left your house last night, did you hear from him again?"

Morgan looked genuinely stumped. "Gerald who?"

Drummond cut in. "You call him Zorro."

"Oh. *That* disgusting fuck. I hope I never lay eyes on him again."

"That's giving us problems, Morgan," Drummond

said, "that you'd go on a trip with a guy, if you felt that way. Mind if I ask how you got hooked up with him in the first place?"

Morgan had tears in her eyes. "Yeah, I mind. What could my relationship with some guy have to do with anything, anyway?"

Benno answered, "We're only considering different possibilities. I just had a visit with a friend of yours."

"I don't have any . . ." Morgan began, then trailed off before asking, "Who?"

"Jessica Baldwin."

"Jessica?" Morgan was nearly screaming. "*Jessica?* What the fuck were you doing talking to her?"

"We found her name on your caller ID," Benno said. "When we're investigating a murder we talk to anyone who might have information. Look, she's your psychiatrist. She's not going to tell us anything that isn't to your best interest."

"That's not fair! Jessica doesn't know anything about any murder. What in the fuck did you tell her?"

"Nothing she didn't already know," Benno lied. "It was all in the papers this morning."

"I don't give a shit about that. I don't want Jessica knowing I went on a trip with that asshole."

Benno tried skirting the issue. "I'm sure if she's a true friend nothing you do will really bother her."

"She's a lot more than a friend. She helps me." Morgan began to cry. "Oh fuck, how dumb do you think I am? Don't you think I know something's wrong with me? Jessica's working on that. If you fuck that up with all your bullshit—"

"We won't be interfering with what she's doing. We will be protecting you, though."

Morgan had turned off the tears. Her expression of grief turned instantly into a pout. "I'm sick of these questions."

"Just one more thing. This evening, who knew you were leaving the hotel?"

"I don't think . . . oh hell, Steinsy knew. He called up, ordering me to stay put. I told him that I wouldn't, that I was tired of this place, and that he could go fuck himself. I hung up on him."

"Hmm," Drummond said. "What time did your lawyer call?"

"I don't remember. Around five, I guess. Listen, I'm not answering any more questions. I'm going home." Morgan got up and tossed the damp rag on the desk. The blood was wiped from her face, though the red-brown smear was still across her chest like a scar.

"I don't know if you're authorized to enter your house just now," Benno said. "It depends on whether the crime scene people have released the premises."

"They have," Drummond said. "There was a call on my desk when we got back from seeing Fishy. The lab wants us over in the morning to look at what they've come up with."

"It's my house," Morgan snapped. "I guess I can go there whenever the fuck I want to."

Benno studied her. Morgan had changed moods four distinct times in a ten-minute conversation. He wanted to talk to Jessica Baldwin again, get her take from a psychiatrist's standpoint. Come to think about it, he wanted to talk to Jessica regardless. He said, "You can go where you want, Morgan. But you're now an identified target, and we're going to have people watching you."

"What for?"

"Uh, not five minutes ago you said you were scared. Wouldn't you want someone standing by in case—"

"Not so fucking scared that I want someone's nose up my ass. Oh shit, I'll have to call another cab."

"Not necessary," Drummond said firmly. "I'll drive you."

"I don't want to be driven anywhere. I want to be left the fuck alone."

Benno had just about had it. He steadied his gaze. "Let me tell you how it is, Morgan. You are under police protection, beginning now. If that's not satisfactory, we can make it police *custody*. That means you'd have to stay in administrative segregation at the county jail. Now which would you prefer?"

"You can't send me to jail. I haven't done anything."

"Oh yes, we can," Benno said. "Trust me. So your choice. Would you like to have Detective Drummond take you home and post some uniformed policemen outside your house, or would you like for me to call a couple of cops in here to take you downtown?"

Morgan's eyes flashed fire. "You son of a bitch."

Benno spread his hands. "I get that way."

"Nobody's making me stay at that fucking house," Morgan said.

"Yes, they are. And the only way you're going to keep from staying out of jail is to cooperate. The first report we get that you've tried to sneak away without checking with the officers, off you go."

Morgan seemed ready to explode. She expelled a long breath. "We'll see about this." She skirted the desk, stood by the door, and looked at Drummond. "You're the one taking me?"

"That's right," Drummond said. "We'll have so much fun together."

"And fuck you, too." Morgan yanked the door open. "All these fucking questions. Now I wish I hadn't told you a fucking thing." She stalked outside.

Drummond, smirking and shrugging her shoulders, started to follow Morgan out. She paused in the doorway. "The lab at nine in the morning, Benno," she said. "And keep your fucking cell phone on. You can be such an asshole at times."

Benno gave Drummond time to clear the lobby with Morgan in tow. Then he went back down the corridor with his head down, studying the sketch artist's drawing of the suspect in Zorro's killing. The guy in the picture looked like someone who went around blowing up shit, but looks could be deceiving. He might be nothing more than a maintenance man. Plus, the drunk next door to Zorro's could have imagined the guy.

The lobby had cleared out. Cooks and waiters were putting the buffet equipment away. The crowd around the windows had dispersed since there was nothing more to see out under the awning. Chief Rubin stood close to the entrance with two young guys—a square-shouldered black kid with cornrows and a tall thin white kid with an oversized nose—wearing hotel uniforms with VALET stitched across the back. Rubin was holding one of the sketches up while the valet parkers looked over his shoulder. Benno sauntered up.

The black kid was saying, "We told you four times already. The windows were tinted. The driver waved us off."

"Let's try it this way," Rubin said. "Have you *ever* seen anyone that looks like this hanging around here?"

"C'mon, man," the white guy said. "Thousands of people, coming and going . . ."

The black kid pinched his chin. "And this is just a drawing."

"It is an artist's sketch," Rubin said, "made with the help of a witness with perfect eyesight. Look again, will you?"

Benno wondered if Rubin might be just a little bit over the edge on this case. He moved over to the window and looked out. Both ambulances were gone, and only one black-and-white remained underneath the awning. The CSU people were stowing their gear inside the van. A hotel janitor mopped the area where the investigators had gone down. Only a tiny trickle of blood remained. One uniform was taking down the yellow tape. Benno looked beyond the barrier. Nordstrom the reporter was still hanging around, along with a still photographer, camera in hand. The rest of the media had left. Why in hell was Nordstrom still here? Benno went back to Rubin and the valet parkers.

Rubin looked up with a scowl as Benno approached. "I am shooting threes from all over the court," Rubin said. "I'm just not knocking down any." He turned to the valet parkers. "Listen, you think you two could come by downtown tomorrow?"

"Don't want to go identifyin' anybody," the black kid said, "when I didn't see anybody."

"If you look again it might come to you," Rubin said.

"I got class in the morning," the white kid said.

Rubin gave each valet two business cards. "There's my number. Give me yours, there on the back of one of my cards." While the valets wrote down their numbers, flattening the business cards against their thighs, Rubin took Benno off to one side. "I don't know about this," Rubin said. "These two assholes might do better with a lineup, but I wouldn't bet on it."

Benno gazed through the window, where Nordstrom continued to stand. He shoved his hands into his pockets. "What about the hotel manager?" Benno said.

"I think he's okay, but I told emergency medical to take him to Parkland Hospital for a checkup, just in case. I don't think EMU carries enough oxygen for the fat motherfucker."

"Uh, Chief, that reporter Nordstom's still here. I think I'm going to have a talk with him."

Rubin squinted to look outside. "Damned if he isn't. I don't know if you should be approaching the guy. Maybe you should let me talk to his editor."

Benno firmly shook his head. "I want to try this my way first. Going to his boss might make him resentful. I think I'll offer him a deal."

"Suit yourself. Just don't be putting the department in any shit storm, Detective." Rubin headed over to collect the parkers' phone numbers.

Benno pushed his way out under the awning. Cold wind stung his cheeks. The second his foot hit the pavement a flash went off. Benno blinked the glare out of his eyes. The photographer rolled his film and raised his camera once more.

Benno walked over to where Nordstrom stood. "Hi," Benno said. "Talk to you inside a minute?"

He led Nordstrom through the revolving door into the hotel lobby. Halfway between the entry and the check-in desk, Benno faced Nordstrom and said, "You've been calling my partner."

Nordstrom wagged a ballpoint between his first and middle fingers. "Just trying to get a line on you."

"Okay. Why me?"

Nordstrom's chin tilted. "You're news, Detective."

"Old news. How come you're so determined to fuck me?"

"You might be old news out west. You're *new* news here. It's what I do."

"That investigative journalism shit is getting old. So you make this big revelation and then ask how come DPD's employing me. So what? What happened in

California happened, okay? Jesus Christ, forget how
you're going to screw up my life. I don't count. But
you can also screw up a pretty important investigation here."

Nordstrom spread his hands, palms up. "If there's
a story . . . First Amendment, you know?"

Benno jammed his hands into his pockets and
looked toward the buffet. Two waiters rolled the serving table away down a corridor. Benno whirled around
and faced Nordstrom. "Okay, warn me in advance.
When's your smear hitting the paper?"

"Not for a while. Tomorrow I'm talking to Morgan
Masters' lawyer, Harold Stein. He's consented to an
interview."

"During which you'd better roll up your pants,"
Benno said. "Listen, you want a real story?"

Nordstrom's eyes widened in a look of innocence.
"I couldn't compromise my profession."

Benno yanked down on his tie. "You'd compromise
your old lady for a scoop, Nordstrom. Look, right now
you're running around with the rest of the pack. You'll
get what's in the department's daily news conference,
plus some filler bullshit from Stein about how the police have violated Morgan Masters' rights by busting
into her house—the same thing he's going to tell the
other hundred reporters that ask him for an interview.
What if I told you Morgan Masters wasn't even the
primary suspect any longer?"

Nordstrom raised his eyebrows. "Oh yeah? So
who is?"

"I'll level," Benno said. "We don't have a viable
suspect right now. Tomorrow that might change."

Nordstrom studied the floor. "That would be, uh,
interesting. Can I quote you?"

"Not just yet, but maybe. First I want your
agreement not to print anything about what went on

with me in LA." Nordstrom started to shake his head, but Benno pressed on. "Tell you what. I'll bet not a reporter in town even knows the victim's identity. Or that there's been a second murder in addition to this shooting here. Am I right?"

"Well, uh," Nordstrom said, straightening his jacket, "I'd imagine those things will be public shortly."

"Oh no, they won't—not until the department sees that every news organization in the state gets the information at once. Come on, Nordstrom. Main Headquarters, top floor. Deputy Chief Rubin's office. Two o'clock tomorrow afternoon. Whaddya say?"

Two men in Brooks Brothers suits exited the elevators with leather satchels bumping their tailored navy blue pant legs. They passed close to Benno and Nordstrom, then went on outside. Nordstrom kept silent until they were gone, then said, "Are you on the level?"

"I'm as serious as a heart attack. The chief will go along with giving you an exclusive, but only if my past stays out of the paper. We got a deal?"

Nordstrom thoughtfully dragged a finger across his eyebrow. "We might work something out," he said.

" 'Might' doesn't get it." Benno started to walk away, then came back. "And by the way, I'm not telling you your business, but I wouldn't waste any time talking to Harold Stein. Me and Detective Drummond are going to see him, and after that, he might not be so talkative. Also, anything he tells you will be total bullshit. And for a third reason, the information we've got for you just might include some things on Stein that are a helluva lot better than what you can get from him." Benno folded his arms. "So exert the shit out of your First Amendment rights if you want to. Screw me in print and be Harold Stein's stooge-slash-conduit-to-the-public. I can't stop you. But you know what I'd do if I were you? I'd call Stein's office and cancel the appointment. And then at two in the afternoon tomorrow I'd show up at Chief Rubin's office. And in the meantime, I'd go someplace and sit on my hands."

Benno watched through the window as Nordstrom left, motioning to his photographer as he went out onto the driveway. The cameraman folded up his equipment and hustled to keep up with Nordstrom, who was walking fast toward a Nissan parked at the front of the hotel awning. Benno didn't know if he'd done the right thing; if he'd pissed Nordstrom off too much, it could all blow up in his face. He turned back to the lobby, looking for Rubin, wondering what he was going to say to the chief. Rubin hated talking to newspeople. Benno'd made the appointment on the spur of the moment and now his neck was out, yea far.

As Benno walked up, Rubin stuffed the sketch artist's drawings into a satchel as the two valet parkers exited the lobby through the side entrance. Rubin said, "This is not exactly promising." He frowned at Benno. "You call your father yet?"

Benno lifted, then dropped his hands. "Haven't had the time."

"Make time. Japeth's on my ass again. Three calls today. I look like I'm ducking my own first cousin."

"I'll get on it tomorrow," Benno lied.

"See that you do. What'd the reporter say?"

Benno shook his head. "He's tough. Says if we want him to keep the lid on my history, he wants something in return. I don't see how we can give an exclusive to anybody."

Rubin snapped his satchel closed, then lifted it from the floor. "Maybe some exclusive bullshit."

"If we tell him something inaccurate he'll find it out. Then he'll fry me worse when he does go into print."

"We don't lie. We edit. I will give you the benefit of my thirty years of experience fucking with these guys. You tell him real stuff. When he prints it, he doesn't compromise what we've got going. That way he thinks he has an exclusive, but really he's just getting bullshit the same as the rest of the reporters."

Benno did his best to look humble. He slumped his shoulders. "I don't know, Cousin Jeff. I could talk to him. But I might let something out of the bag. I'm a fuck-up when it comes to giving interviews."

"Takes some savvy," Rubin said. "I could step in and have a discourse with the guy."

"That would be imposing on your schedule."

"Not if it's for the good of the department. Tell the reporter to see me."

"Damn, you'll do that? You going to be in tomorrow afternoon?"

Rubin nodded briefly. "I'll make it a point to. Set it up."

"Super idea, Chief," Benno said. "I never would have thought of it myself. Guess it takes experience, huh?"

14

Benno slipped on a patch of ice on his way into his apartment, skinning his knee on the sidewalk. He got up and hopped around, cursing under his breath, and limped on through the gate into the backyard.

Most of the snow had melted during the day, but the thermometer had dipped below freezing after nightfall. There were slick places on the side streets and white outlines on the ground where the houses' shadows had blocked off the sun. The sky was clear and the moon was round and yellow. The widow's home where Benno lived was an old single-story with a high-peaked roof; his private entrance was around in back. She was in her eighties and went to bed with the pigeons. The house was dark, with a single light left on over the stoop so that Benno could find his way in.

Once inside he took off his pants and examined his wound. The skin was ripped away and spots of blood had seeped through. He found some rubbing alcohol and a box of cotton balls, then soaked one of the balls and pressed it against his knee. He threw back his head and bit his lip to keep from screaming out loud. When the pain subsided some, he expelled a long breath and sank back into his chair.

He felt pretty stupid for falling on his ass, but aside from the pain in his leg he was feeling better and better. As far as the job went he was fucking *humming,* getting the hang of it and feeling like a cop once again. The past few years, the various jobs he'd held while kicking alcohol, had been an interruption until he could get on with his life. If Jan could see him now, she might even be proud.

Jesus, my knee. He got another cottonball and soaked it in rubbing alcohol.

As for the case—it was beginning to move, but at the same time there were a lot of unanswered questions. The sketch artist had provided what Benno believed to be a good likeness of the perp, but who the hell was he and what connection could he have to a killing over twenty-five years ago? Morgan Masters claimed to have no memory of a man who'd molested her as a child. Benno couldn't imagine how anyone could forget something like that.

He called Drummond. "How's it going?" he said.

"I'm on the sofa watching a big-screen television. Morgan's upstairs, either going to bed or plotting her escape. She's a lovely person, Benno. She's stopped short of calling me nigger bitch, but I don't think she's missed any other adjective. The dispatcher says he'll have four unis out here within a half hour. Then I'm going home and soak my feet."

"Did you mention Uncle Eddie to Morgan again?"

"Twice. Total blank. I don't think she's bullshitting."

"I can't figure it out, if the guy abused her. I'm going to talk to a shrink."

"I'd be careful you don't wind up paying a big fat

consulting fee out of your pocket. When it comes to approving shit like that, the department's tight as a tick. You gotta send a preapproval form up to accounting and get DiAngelo to sign off on it."

"The shrink I'm talking about already works for the county," Benno said. "I don't think there'll be any charge. Look, you might be there until after midnight waiting on those unis to show up. If you'd like me to fly solo in the morning—"

"No way. I just love seeing the medical examiner, all that blood and shit. You take care, Benno. I'm watching a *Law & Order* here." Drummond disconnected with a click.

Benno held the phone, wondering how many times a day *Law & Order* reruns showed on television. A hundred or so, minimum. He looked at the clock: ten thirty. Jesus, it had been fourteen hours since he'd left his apartment that morning. He wondered how late Jessica Baldwin answered her phone. He used his apartment landline and punched her number in. She answered after the second ring.

"Yeah, hi, this is Detective Benno. I hope I didn't wake you."

"*Detective* Benno? I guess this isn't a social call, then."

"Well, partly. But I have some questions. Is it too late?"

"How can it be too late when I'm still out driving around. I just left the appointment I told you about. The woman with the missing thumb."

"We've had two more murders tonight," Benno said. "DA's investigators at the hotel where Morgan Masters was staying."

"Oh God. Is Morgan . . . ?"

"She's fine. But my questions have to do with her."

Benno held the phone in silence for a beat of four. "I told you earlier that one of our murder victims might've molested Morgan Masters when she was a child. I interviewed Morgan tonight, and the dead molester's name didn't seem to register with her. Any chance that Morgan's lying?"

"I told you, she's blocked out anything that happened to her before she was seven."

Benno carried the cordless phone into the bathroom, opened his medicine cabinet, and found a box of oversized Band-Aids. "I understand she'd block out the abuse. But the guy himself, if he was someone acquainted with Morgan's mother . . . ?"

"Morgan's mother is one of her problems," Jessica said.

Benno was back in his chair, pulling the strips off a Band-Aid, holding the phone between his cheek and shoulder. "I got that impression. But wouldn't she remember the man himself even if she couldn't recall the abuse?"

"Only if he was still in her life after she was seven years old."

Benno smoothed the bandage over his injury, and tossed the strips into a wastebasket. "I'll let you in on something you won't read in the newspapers. We have a description of a suspect that looks pretty good. The suspect's a young guy, but he might be someone connected with Morgan or her mother from twenty-five years ago. That's why it's important to us for Morgan to start remembering. I've heard of abuse victims identifying their abusers years later, after something jogged their memories. Is there any way to help Morgan's recall?"

"These things sometimes happen by accident," Jessica said. "Sometimes they'll have a chance encounter with the abuser, and the sight of this person triggers memory. Hypnosis has worked, but I don't put a lot of faith in it. Where's Morgan now?"

"Under police guard. That shooting tonight? We're pretty sure the perpetrator was aiming at her."

"Oh God. Tomorrow I'll have to run by and see her." Jessica's voice was fainter, and it had taken on a fearful hoarseness. "I've had a lot to swallow in one day."

"Sorry to dump it on you," Benno said. "I should have waited until morning to call. Things are always better after you sleep on them."

"Sleep? I doubt I'll be getting any sleep. Benno?"

He shifted the phone from one ear to the other. "Yes?"

"You told me you don't do booze. Well, I do, and I'm not in the mood to drink alone under the circumstances. Do you drink coffee this late?"

Benno's knee was feeling better. He tugged on the hem of his boxer shorts. "Tell you what," he finally said. "Give me a few minutes so I can brew up some tea."

He took the time to shower and shave and put on cologne, racing through the process in record time. He also put on pressed new jeans and a plaid button-down over a navy turtleneck, and stowed his weapon away. He felt strange without the shoulder rig. It was the first time he'd been without it since he'd come to town.

Jessica Baldwin knocked on the door exactly thirty minutes after Benno'd spoken to her on the phone. Dressed in a white warmup suit and sneakers, she carried a bottle in one hand and a drink in the other. The drink was in a rock glass, ice and amber liquid. She said, "I've started without you," with an off-kilter smile that made him weak in the knees. He stood aside and let her in.

His refrigerator, sink, and stove were in an alcove to one side of his living quarters. He led her to the sink, set her bottle on the counter, opened his freezer compartment, and pointed out the ice trays. He poured hot water from a kettle over tea bags in a cup, added sugar, then led the way to the sofa and set his cup and saucer on the coffee table. She fixed another bourbon over ice, sank down beside him, stretched out her legs, and crossed her ankles beside his cup. His stereo was on with the volume low. Elton John. "Bennie and the Jets."

"You have any trouble with the directions?" he said.

"Not until I got here. I stumbled around in the yard a while before I found the gate. You gotta watch it. There's still some patches of ice." She took a swallow and set her drink down.

He winced as he felt his knee through his pants. "Yeah, I know."

"Just you and the widow living here?"

"Just us."

She winked at him. "I don't suppose you're servicing her, are you?"

"Jesus Christ, Jessica, she's eighty."

She pointed at the stereo. "That music won't keep her awake?"

"She sleeps like a stone," Benno said.

"Good. You've got it pretty warm in here." She stood and, in a series of fluid motions, stripped out of her top and pants. Underneath she wore a green spandex outfit, shorts and halter. Her arms, thighs, and shoulders were ridged with supple muscle. She tossed the warmup suit into a chair and sat back down.

Benno had a sudden tightness in his throat. "You stay in shape," he said.

"Like a fiend. I deal all day with shit. When I finish that, I knock myself out in the gym, then anesthetize with bourbon and stumble into bed. When you called, I was headed to work out."

"That's sure a different outfit than you had on earlier."

"I travel prepared," Jessica said. "I've become an ace at changing at red lights, wiggling around in the driver's seat. Get a few double takes from the other drivers, but hey, I gotta blow off steam."

He bent over and swished the tea bags around inside his cup. "Your appointment after you left the restaurant must have been a downer."

She put one foot flat on the sofa and hugged her knee. "Just a bundle of jollies. This woman's about forty years old. Six years ago this guy started calling her, friendly at first, then more and more menacing the longer he talked to her. He started calling every night, and if she didn't answer he'd leave these really uplifting messages on her answering machine. She spent two solid years terrified. Called the police and got the usual bullshit you heard back then, that he actually hadn't broken any laws. Finally, one night he did break the law. Climbed in through her bedroom window, tied her up at knife point, raped and sodomized her, then whacked off her thumb with a pair of garden loppers. And guess what. The bastard's already up for parole next month. The whole time I visited with her, her hand was in plain sight, the scarry nub where she ought to have a thumb. Just . . . fucking . . . lovely."

"Haven't they changed the law?" Benno asked.

Jessica cut her eyes to look at him.

"Where you can arrest the guy just for calling?" he said.

She laughed, a short, bitter chuckle. "Sure. We now

have the stalker statute. You ever seen anyone try to apply it? It's so damned nebulous that no one really has defined exactly what's stalking and what isn't. When the law first came into being, all it took was a phone call that some guy was harassing a woman, and the police would lock him up. After about sixty trillion lawsuits, that's all changed. It's nearly as bad as before. Jesus, Benno, I don't know how much longer I can do this."

Benno laid the tea bags in the saucer and had a sip. Not quite strong enough for his taste. He dumped the bags back in. "Why *do* you do it?"

She looked about to say something, then turned her head away. "Why are you a cop?" she finally returned.

"That's pretty easy. I've got an older cousin that's one. I always looked up to him. First chance I got, I wanted to follow in his footsteps. He transferred from LA to the Dallas force a few years ago. Here I am, following him again."

She chewed her inner cheek. "Is that the only reason?"

He didn't want to mention his father. "This started out with me asking why you do what you do. Now it's turned around and you're asking me."

"That's my profession, getting other people to talk about themselves. I'm pretty good at not talking about me. Have you been married?"

"Yeah, once. And I have one."

"Child?"

"That was your next question, wasn't it?"

They both stared at the coffee table. Benno had more tea and Jessica downed more bourbon.

She said, "See this?" She put her index finger on the scar bisecting her lips.

"I think it makes your smile attractive as hell," Benno said.

"Some men think it makes me look sort of kinky," she said with a laugh, then turned serious. "That's part of why I do it. I don't care what happened to Morgan Masters as a child—she doesn't have anything on me. I got the lip when I was twelve because I didn't want to drop my panties. And, oh shit, you're the first one I've told that since I was in high school, and even then I didn't want to talk about it. I don't even know why I told you."

Jesus, all this child abuse, first Morgan Masters and now . . . "Sorry. Your father?" Benno said.

"A rootin'-tootin' PhD in literature. I used to sit in the audience at writers' conferences and listen to all these novelists tell how if it hadn't been for kindly old Professor Baldwin they never would have made it. I became a psych major because I was trying to figure that asshole out. Then I went to fucking *medical school* trying to figure that asshole out. I'm *still* trying to figure him out. I can't. Morgan Masters I can figure out. Abuse victims I can figure out. Professor Asshole, I can't figure out." She drained her glass. "I'm going to have another. Sure you don't want one?"

He toasted her with his cup. "I'll stick with this."

She got up and went to the kitchenette and opened the freezer. Ice cracked and then tinkled in a glass. She came back in with a full drink and plopped back onto the sofa. After a good-sized glug of bourbon she set down her glass and said, "Let me give you some of my own self-analysis. I'm a lot more typical of abuse victims than Morgan Masters, who's *a*typical. I told you earlier in the restaurant that my job interferes with any relationships I might be considering, but that isn't quite the whole story. The whole story is that I just don't do relationships well. I've had a few, even with a woman once, because I was afraid that since I couldn't build any emotional attachment to guys, I might be gay. Nothing's ever worked for me, and every time anyone tries to get close I push them away. All it takes is a guy turning sweet and caring, and I feel like the walls are closing in. So you invited me here at the stroke of midnight, which I translate into you're interested. So I'm telling you straight out. You're divorced. You've been off alcohol for a period of time that makes you think about entering into a relationship with a woman. In this corner, you have got the wrong puppy. Do not expect romance with me."

Benno's jaw dropped. "I haven't much thought about it. And since you've now told me off, I don't suppose I'm going to. Take my advice, or don't, but in the future you might wait until a guy makes a move before you—"

"But on the other hand," Jessica said, the dazzling smile popping through, "if it's just casual sex you're interested in . . ." She drank more bourbon, watching him over the rim of her glass.

"—start telling him to hit the road," Benno finished, then folded his arms in a pout.

"Gee, weren't you listening to me?" She looked about to laugh out loud.

Benno straightened on the couch. "Did you say something about sex?"

"*Casual* sex. No heartwarming bullshit, no commitment. No flowers on Valentine's Day or any of that crap. Do you think you can handle casual?" Her firm taut thigh brushed against his leg.

He had a hard time getting his breath. "I could try," he finally said.

She put one arm over the back of the couch, leaned close, and blew in his ear. "Then get a move on, buster," she said. "Jesus Christ, don't make this day any worse than it's already been." She glanced around the room. "And your bed is where?"

Benno jumped to his feet as if his pants were on fire. "You're, uh, sitting on it. You're gonna have to stand for a minute. Won't take but a second, okay?"

It was almost like a battle, a fight, Jessica's teeth bared, wanton, with a look on her face that was almost hatred. She fought him at times, pushing hard on his chest, laying him out, mounting him in a fury, straddling him hard, smiling as if in victory.

For him, it had been so fucking long. It was good. Wonderful.

But Jesus. Exhausting . . .

Later, with the lights off, with Jessica lying naked on her stomach and Benno stretched out beside her on the bed, also bare-assed and with his ankles crossed, she said, "You were raised Orthodox, weren't you?"

He lip-synced Elton John and Kiki Dee as they sang "Don't Go Breakin' My Heart" on the stereo. He turned his head on the pillow to look at her. "Why?"

"I'm going to tell you why you have a problem with booze."

"A departmental shrink in LA already tried. I ended up by telling her she had a problem with psychiatry."

Jessica rose up and leaned on her elbows, her nipples brushing the sheet. "Police departments hire shitty shrinks. I'm a *goddamned good* shrink, with my own neuroses to analyze along with everyone else's. Come on, were you raised an Orthodox Jew?"

"Hassidic. Close, but so far you're oh for one."

She raised her feet up in the air and crossed her ankles, her calf muscles bunching. "Not quite. I knew it was something fundamental and that you weren't Reform. Were you cute in your little black outfit?"

"Just darling," Benno said.

"Okay, here's the thing," Jessica said. "Inner religious conflict as a symptom of alcoholism is pretty common with people raised as Southern Baptists or Campbellites, though with Jews it's really rare. Alcoholics can be chemically and physically dependent, which happens all the time with WASPs whose forebears had drinking problems, but your addiction is purely mental. Growing up you had religion stuffed down your throat. With the Baptists it's praise the Lord and pass the collection plate, and get your ass outta bed for worship Sunday morning or I'm takin' a razor strap after you. I don't know the Jewish worship traditions, but I'll bet you experienced something similar. So I'll guess at some point, probably in your early teenage years, you began to think there might be something in life other than work and walking to the temple—am I right?"

"About the time of my Bar Mitzvah."

"And did you become openly defiant?"

"You'd have to know my father," Benno said. "I wouldn't have dared."

She rolled onto her side, hooked one leg over his, and rested her head on her crooked elbow. "You are not cooperating here, *bubby*. You had to have conflict at home. Later in life, when you started drinking, the conflict accelerated your dependence on booze. That's the way it works. People don't become stumbling drunks because they want to."

"In our house, my father said jump, we all asked how far. I wouldn't have gotten in his face for all the tea in China. There might've been conflict, but it sure didn't involve me rearing up on my hind legs."

"Aha. There *was* conflict of some kind."

"Yeah, but it didn't involve me and my father. It was my mother and my grandmother. She was straight from the old country and spent World War Two in a Nazi concentration camp. Had the numbers tattooed on her arm. She lived with us from the end of the war until she died in 'seventy-five, when I was thirteen."

"Now we're getting somewhere. You had a much revered Holocaust survivor living in your house. And she should have been revered, but I'm betting she made your mom's life miserable by taking over and running things."

"Yeah, my mother's life. Not *my* life, though."

"Not that you realized as a kid," Jessica said. "Did your grandmother kind of take over your upbringing?"

"My religious upbringing, yeah. Read the Torah to me, taught me the three basic principles. The love of learning, the worship, the *tzedakah,* all that, until I could recite them in my sleep."

"And your mother resented that the grandmother took all that over."

Benno chuckled, remembering. "My mother used to make these little sidebar remarks, when neither my father nor my grandmother was listening. When old Ruth—that was my grandmother—passed away, the only dry eye in the family was my mother's."

Jessica shifted onto her back, placed one foot flat on the bed, and rested her other ankle on her knee. "Bingo, buster, that's the conflict. All this time you've thought your problem was someone stuffing religion down your throat, when really it was that you were caught in the middle between your mother and grandmother. You got older, left home, and started to drink. When you'd drink you'd get subconsciously resentful over your situation as a kid, and to feed your resentment you'd drink even more. Something happened to make you hit rock bottom, so you trundled off to Bill W.'s group. Right or wrong?"

"You're condensing a lot of years into a few sentences," Benno said. "But it's close enough."

"What happened to turn you around? Your wife divorce you?"

"She did, but that didn't stop the drinking. It was something that happened a long time after that. Hey, Jessica, you're putting me in a corner here."

She snuggled closer. "That's the idea."

Benno shrugged his shoulders in irritation. "It was something on the job, okay? And, yeah, I'd been drinking. What happened wasn't my fault, but I left myself open by drinking when I shouldn't have been."

"Wasn't your fault?" she asked. "Part of the therapy is that you're not supposed to rationalize."

"And that's the very reason I don't like to talk about it. I'm not rationalizing, but anything I say makes it sound like I am. We had a situation. An officer got killed. I was about half drunk when the situation came down, which made it easier for certain people to point the finger at me. I lost my job and the media blew the whole thing up so that it looked like I was stumbling around drunk and got the guy killed. That's not what happened." He held her chin between his thumb and forefinger and turned her face so that she was looking directly at him. "You got awfully uptight about telling me you worked for the DA's office. I told you that anything we discussed was between us and that your job would never know about you talking to me, counseling Morgan Masters, any of it. Same goes with this deal. I don't want this talked around."

Her tone was firm, but at the same time gentle. "You can give me a dollar's down payment on my fee if you want. Make it all privileged."

The tension left him. He looked at her and grinned. "Isn't there something in the ethics about sex with your patients?"

"I'd leave that part out in any kind of questioning session," she said. "They can grill me all they want to, but I still won't squeal."

Benno stretched out with his head on the pillow and folded his hands over his midsection, thinking. Remembering. He wasn't sure if he should tell her. He didn't like hearing the story himself, even though he'd rehearsed his words in private, over and over, just in case he met someone he thought he could open up to. Benno drew a deep breath and launched into it, fearing that if he hesitated, even for a second, he was sure to lose his nerve.

15

Benno said, "I was lead detective on a West Hollywood murder. This was a plain vanilla drug killing, but the vic was a guy that had played a funny little kid on a sitcom called *Family Tree* twenty years earlier. Hadn't had an acting job since. Was damned near living on the streets and peddling twenty-five-dollar papers of toot to feed his own habit. But when his name hit the paper it suddenly became the case of who offed this great big television star. The newspapers called it the Family Tree murder and tried to make it into another Black Dahlia or something. The LA media's good at that, and the media's a subject you'd best not get me started on. The bottom line was, this dealer fronted the dope to this so-called personality. The so-called personality sold the dope and then stiffed the dealer. So the dealer found the guy, tortured him until he decided he was never going to get his money, and finally shot him in the head. Happens every day. What doesn't happen every day is that the punk used to play a part on a sitcom.

"So the thing comes in the front door as just an-

other dope murder and goes out the back door as a
giant Hollywood mystery. The papers were full of it
every day. Hell, it was no mystery to us. Three hours
after the killing we knew who we were looking for—
this Jamaican dealer named Jared Og—only we
couldn't broadcast this information because if we did,
Jared Og would suddenly be living in parts unknown.
We sat back and waited for Og to turn up, which he
did eventually. When the newspapers called for progress on the case we'd just make up all this crap. As
far as the media knew, we had leads up the ass, but
were keeping them confidential until we were ready
to pounce. Got to be a big joke around the precinct.
The Jared Og case became the J.O. investigation to
us—kind of a takeoff on O.J., you know? The dead
guy's character in the sitcom was Davy Junior, only
this one guy came up with an old publicity photo,
crossed out Junior and wrote Junky in marker, and
then we started calling it the Davy Junky murder. Oh
man, we were hilarious. Only the heavy suits upstairs
weren't laughing. They wanted someone busted, and
damned quick. Held meetings every day and then
rolled the shit downhill on top of our heads.

"So this one afternoon about a week after the murder," Benno said, "I met a guy for lunch at a place
called Beetle's on Sunset. No, that's a lie. I met the
guy for a drink and *called* it lunch. I came in for one
and stayed for a dozen, which I was pretty good at in
those days, and naturally I'd picked a place that was
also a media hangout. By four o'clock in the afternoon
the guy I'd met was long gone, and there I sat knocking them down with this gang of reporters I thought
were buddies of mine." Benno rose up to look at Jessica. "Hey," he said, "I want you to understand
something."

Her chin was propped up on her elbow. "I think

I've got a pretty clear picture. You sneaked away from work one afternoon and got drunk."

"Right," Benno said, stretching back out in the prone position. "But that's all I did. I am not doing a whitewash here. I did wrong. I did not get anyone killed, the way the newspapers made it sound. Granted, if I'd been where I was supposed to be, at my desk waiting for a break in the case, what happened probably wouldn't have. I'm to blame. But I am not *totally* to blame."

Benno paused and listened to her breathe. All these years he'd wanted to tell it his way, yet he never had because he thought no one was going to listen. No departmental bullshit shrink here, no upstairs brass playing to the newspapers. He wanted to get it right, not play down his role in what happened, but at the same time not be giddy with remorse.

"My beeper went off," he said, "right in the middle of some lawyer joke these newspaper guys were telling, and I remember I had to go to this booth in back and yell for quiet so I could call in and the department wouldn't know where I was calling from. Stuff like this was pretty routine for me by now, and the dispatchers all had a pretty good idea where I was and what I was doing, but we played the game.

"Anyway, Jared Og had finally turned up. Some unis had spotted the guy walking around on Eighth Street close to downtown. They'd tried to flag him down and he'd turned tail and hauled it. He was in a third-floor walkup in a pretty shitty neighborhood with these two old women as hostages. I was ready to head out for the scene, but first I had to finish my drink and tell all these reporters what the call was about and where I was going. When I walked out they were in a free-for-all over the pay phone, trying to call their editors. When I got to the hostage location it was like a goddamned movie set with all those cameras and lights set up and television and print reporters hanging around. I was still feeling the booze, but I swear I was functional.

"Naturally with the press out in force," Benno said, "a couple of captains from downtown had gotten in the act, strutting around giving orders. As lead detective I was supposed to call the shots, but in practice, when you're dealing with brass and the television people are around, lead detective don't mean batshit."

"*Doesn't* mean batshit," Jessica said. "I swear, you cops—"

"Yeah, okay. *Doesn't* mean. So anyway, one of these captains orders three SWATs to go charging up the stairs and storm Jared Og, which was dumb to begin with, but which also made for a good scene for all the photographers. I told the captain his idea was bullshit, and if we just sat there and blocked all of the escape routes and called in a negotiator, eventually Jared Og would give it up. I guess all the pops I'd had for lunch made me, uh, what you might call a little belligerent, and I got up in the captain's face pretty good. So now he decides that as lead detective, I'm supposed to go storming upstairs leading the SWATs. Which was an even dumber idea than going in after Og to begin with, but it got me out of the way so the captain could strut his stuff with the media. It's like the captain's promoting himself to leading man and reducing me to the bellhop role, which is the way high-profile cases always play out in LA—who's going to be the grunt and who's going to be the star, and to hell with accomplishing what you're really there to do.

"I did a lot of noisy bitching, but went ahead and stripped off my coat and put on a Kevlar vest. And away we went, me and these three Rambos wearing helmets and carrying assault rifles with ropes coiled over their shoulders, like we were after Fidel Castro in the mountains instead of Jared Og and these two old women holed up in a tenement. I remember those old wooden steps creaked like hell on the way up, and the static on our two-way radio was so loud that if Jared Og couldn't hear us coming he had to be deaf as a stone.

"The kid that died," Benno said, "I never knew his name. He looked maybe twenty-one years old and I remember his hat was too big for him, damned near covering his eyes, and he looked really excited but at the same time really scared. Later I learned he'd just graduated from Special Weapons and this was his first live assignment. He had a cold, phlegm in his throat or something, and I remember his breathing was really ragged. He and I were first up on the third-floor landing. We crouched down and looked out into this really dim corridor with a lot of dust in the air, and three apartments down from the stairwell Jared Og was ready for us. There was a television playing inside the apartment, and for all I knew Jared had seen us enter the building over live action news. He had the door wide-open and this poor skinny old black woman sitting up in a rocking chair with a gun to her head. Us staring in at him and him looking out at us with this little shit-eating grin on his face.

"I kind of knew Jared," Benno said, "because he'd been a street dealer for so long and at one time we'd, you know, run him. As an informant. Had really dark skin, almost coal-black, built like a distance runner, wearing a vest but no shirt and a do-rag over his head. I yelled in at him, 'Give it up, Jared' or 'Lay down your gun,' something like that, but he says in this thick accent, 'Hell no, Beano. Fuck you, mon.' You know how those Jakies talk."

"Sort of a calypso lilt," Jessica said.

"Yeah, right. Just about then the captain comes over the radio, and I had this mental image of him down there in the street with reporters all around, and he says, 'Report, report,' sounding like Patton at the Battle of the Bulge. The kid replies, 'Subject in sight, sir,' loud enough so that Jared Og could hear it the same as I could, which gave old Jared plenty of warning what was about to come down.

"This gave the captain an excuse to say, 'On my signal,' and start counting, 'Ten, nine, eight,' the way he'd seen it in some war movie. Only in the war movies, you've got two groups going in and wanting to move at the same time, but here the countdown was strictly for the media's benefit. And you can't say the reporters didn't get a show—man, did they ever.

"Right there," Benno continued, "I grabbed the two-way and reminded the captain that I was the detective in charge here, but that cut no ice with the guy. I had just enough booze in me to yell out, 'Don't tell us to attack, you dumb cocksucker,' which statement would later get me in trouble, but I was so mad by then I didn't care. I whispered to the kid, 'Do not move, son, not unless I tell you,' but the kid was all caught up in what the captain was saying over the radio and, you know, a SWAT is a guy in uniform, so when a man with bars on his collar talks, the SWATs hop to.

"So the captain counts it all the way down and says, 'Go,' and here the kid hits the corridor running with his assault rifle over his head. He's a wide-open target for about four seconds there, so naturally Jared Og first shoots the old woman in the head and then turns his weapon on the kid. I think the youngster took five slugs, any one of which would have been fatal, and he goes down in a heap with blood spouting from every wound. The last thing he said was, 'Mama.' I swear to Christ, just like a little kid, and the air went out of his lungs and he died right there.

"I've got no clear memory of what happened in the next five seconds," Benno said, "but as much as liquor has hurt my life, I still believe that at that moment it was good that I'd had a few, because if I'd had my head completely on straight I would have turned around, run back downstairs, and throttled that captain in front of God and everybody. But first thing I remember I was across the corridor from the stairwell, flattened against the wall, and I could see these other two SWATs crouched on the top step wondering what to do. I guess we'd all be standing there today looking at each other, but for some reason Jared Og decides to come out shooting. He runs into the hall blazing away at the stairwell entry, and I guess he'd decided to shoot his way through those SWATs and keep on going. He was just about abreast of me before he even saw me. I guess I was supposed to say, 'Halt, you're under arrest,' or something, but I didn't. Hell, I was looking at a dead officer not ten steps away. I put two bullets into the side of Jared Og's head and then he went down, crumpled in the corridor, and I don't think he ever knew what hit him.

"There's nothing like the quiet after gunfire," Benno said. "The other SWATs came in from the stairwell then, and we stood there looking at each other with the odor of burned gunpowder hanging in the air and two dead men for company, plus the dead old lady in the rocking chair inside the apartment. The other hostage, the second old woman, started to scream, and I think that's what snapped me out of my trance. Then there was a crackling sound, the dead

SWAT's radio coming to life, and then the captain's yelling, 'You men up there. What's happened? Report. Report.'

"I never hesitated," Benno said. "I took the dead kid's radio from his belt, thumbed the switch, and said, 'I am reporting, you motherfucker. There are three dead people up here. I am on my way down. You do not move.'

"I went down the steps pretty slowly and knew just what I was going to do all along and came out into sunlight. All of the television crews had cameras aimed at me and there were at least a hundred uniformed cops out there, but I had tunnel vision for that captain like he had a spotlight trained on him. I walked right up, drew back my fist, and was going to cold cock him right then and there, but cops grabbed me, two on either side, and we all went down with me biting and scratching. I could have killed that captain, and I can't swear that if those unis hadn't grabbed me I wouldn't have.

"They dragged me to my feet, and all the time I was yelling motherfucker and cocksucker, real pretty phrases that got bleeped on the evening edition. With the cops to hold me back this captain got really brave. He got up in my face and said, really slowly so the reporters would catch it, 'Is that alcohol on your breath, Detective? This man's been drinking, Officers. Put him in restraints and get him out of here.' Of course, he'd gotten a pretty good whiff of my breath before I'd gone up the stairs, but it had just now gotten convenient for him to point it out that I'd been drinking. The unis cuffed me and loaded me into a squad car—man, was that ever clear on the evening news. They took the cuffs off before we ever reached the precinct, and I was never under arrest, at least not officially, but the captain had gotten what he wanted.

"I can recite the next morning's headlines as if I were sitting around reading them now," Benno said. "In huge type it said, 'Family Tree Killer, Two Others, Die in Shootout,' and right under that headline, in smaller type, it said, 'Officer Arrested at Scene—Police Announce Investigation.' The photo of them loading me into the squad car was damned near all the way across the front page, with this one cop pushing my head down as I went into the back seat. And right there in the paper were quotes from all those reporters I'd been drinking with earlier at lunch. You know, my so-called buddies I'd given all those leads to over the years, clocking my drinks shot for shot. Of course the captain got a lot of ink, telling how an officer drinking on the job was a disgrace, yadda-yadda-yadda. Anyone reading that crap would have gotten the idea that I shot the SWAT kid myself. There wasn't any mention of who actually put Jared Og down, not that it really would have mattered.

"I went on immediate suspension, and the police disciplinary board didn't waste any time in terminating me permanently after a kangaroo hearing. I did get a break in that the brass were so hot to satisfy the public that they made a deal with my police association lawyer to let me keep most of my pension, just so I wouldn't fight them in court, but I was out of a job. My drinking was out of hand long before that, but once unemployed I really turned into a lush. For several months, all I did was drink in front of the television all day until I passed out, which usually happened in the middle of the afternoon.

"I finally woke up four years ago, dead broke and down to my last bottle of whiskey. I hadn't seen my son in months, and the last time I'd talked to my ex-wife she'd threatened a restraining order to keep me away. Plus I'd begun to hallucinate. I'd get up some-

times in the middle of the night, stumbling around
waving my weapon, and it's a miracle I didn't eat the
damned thing. Hey, Jessica, I'm not being really uplifting here."

She sat up in the bed and hugged her knees. "Well,
after the woman with the missing thumb . . ."

"The finish to the story," Benno said, "is that I
finally went to an AA meeting, and then another and
another, and I haven't touched a drink in four years
now. Got a few jobs. Jesus, I've worked in coin-
operated laundries, a miniature golf course . . . I could
make a list. But I got by. Also I missed being a cop
so badly you wouldn't believe. Gets in your blood, I
guess. My cousin transferred from LA to Dallas a few
years back, and he got me on with the Dallas force,
and here I am. Fresh start number one. Hopefully I'll
be here tomorrow as well. For as long as they'll have
me, they've got me. I don't say I'm a bargain, but
I'll do all right as long as I take it a day at a time,
you know?"

Jessica lay beside him in silence.

Benno closed his eyes and exhaled. There was an
empty feeling in the pit of his stomach, a sudden de-
sire for whiskey that he hadn't felt in months and
months. He lay there in the dark and shivered, and it
was several minutes before the urge to drink—to grab
Jessica Baldwin's bottle and let its contents burn their
way down his throat—went completely away.

16

They were silent for a while, Benno listening to Elton John and feeling Jessica Baldwin's upper arm firm against his own. The CD had played all the way through at least twice since she'd arrived, and he thought about getting up and switching to the Bee Gees. But he didn't feel like moving. He wanted to remain there content, with the warmth of a woman beside him. Jesus, how long had it been? Oh sure, he'd slept with a few women in California after his divorce, mostly barroom pickups when both of them had been too drunk to perform in bed, but as far as opening up and having a serious discussion with someone, that hadn't happened since early on in his marriage.

Finally Jessica stirred and said thoughtfully, "The good news is, if you can learn to live with the conflict and accept it for what it is, you might very well be able to drink like a normal person."

"Jesus Christ," Benno said. "Why would I want to do that when I've spent four years kicking the stuff?"

"You might not. But at least there's the possibility.

You don't have any genetic physical dependency on booze. Look at all the fun you're missing."

"You think you're having fun when you drink?" Benno asked.

Jessica was silent for a beat of four. She said, "I don't deny my own hang-ups and I've learned to live with them. I'm functional. I perform in the workplace, and pretty damned well. I'm also an outstanding piece of ass, as long as you don't start sending flowers or come on with any mushy bullshit."

Benno snickered. "I wouldn't say 'outstanding' exactly."

She dug her toes into his calf and stuck out her tongue. "Oh yes, you would. I'm pretty satisfied with myself, actually, and the work I do. I could have turned out like Morgan, but I didn't."

Benno closed his eyes and tried to let the music take over his consciousness. He couldn't. He stared at the ceiling as he said, "Have you had sessions like this one with Morgan?"

"Free analysis?"

"Yeah, something like that. We're working on three murders in the past week, all connected, none making a bit of fucking sense. We're pretty sure our perp is a guy connected to Morgan's past, and her mother's past. If she's done a lot of talking to you . . ."

"Careful, Benno. I wasn't kidding before. I'm not into revealing privileged shit."

"I'm not talking about whether she behaves this way or that way when the moon is in Capricorn."

"I could ask her. If she says talk to you, I can give you anything you want to hear. But she's got to greenlight it. Maybe tomorrow afternoon I can . . . Is she still at the hotel?"

"No."

Jessica rolled over on top of him, her chin pressing

into his chest and her nipples flat against his stomach. "Where can I see her, then?"

Benno thought it over. He'd tell her, but warn her first that there could be trouble. "I got no problem with you seeing Morgan, and I think it might help both her and us. But she's under close guard. Somebody spirited Uncle Eddie Payne out of the assisted living, took him over to Morgan's and cut him up, and until we find out differently we're assuming the killer expected Morgan to be there. There's evidence that someone was there in the house, waiting, and me and my partner showing up might be what scared this person away. If she hadn't been on the trip with the stripper, there probably would have been two dismembered corpses in her car. Tonight at the hotel someone, probably the same guy, tried to shoot her but hit two DA's investigators instead. So if I give you her location you'll be the only one outside the department that knows. It's top secret stuff."

"Oh hell, Benno. I don't know as I've got top secret clearance. But if you want, I could just speak to her over the phone or—"

"No," Benno said. "I'm no psychologist, but I can tell from talking to her that you're big in her life right now. We need information from her, and you might be the only one who can get it. So I'll get you in to see her. I just want you to understand that keeping her location secret is a very big deal."

"So I'm warned," Jessica said.

"Okay. For the moment she's hidden in plain sight, right at her house. Tomorrow or the next day we could move her, depending on whether or not we think she's safe where she is. But we're considering her a primary target for whoever's doing this, so we'll have people on her for the duration. My partner, Detective Drummond, took her home tonight and put two uniformed

cops on her. They'll watch her in shifts, twenty-four/
seven. In the morning I'll get a message to the unis
that you're clear to go in. As soon as I've done that
I'll call you, and you can drop by to see her whenever
you can. Be sure and take ID so the cops'll let you
pass. I'll also give you a list of things we need to know
from her."

"Fine. But I won't tell you anything unless Morgan
okays it. She won't keep any secrets from me. What
she remembers, she'll tell me."

"That's what I'm counting on," Benno said. "Just
like you got me to babble about my mother and
grandmother, and finally to tell you a story I've never
told anyone. Okay, without getting into anything you
think is privilege, can you apply the same methods
with Morgan Masters? We can't complete any list of
suspects without knowing where to start. Family members, friends of her mother . . . you know, anybody
we should know about. I'm accepting the fact that
she's blocked out Uncle Eddie Payne. But how about
somebody who wasn't an abuser? We could be talking
someone who she doesn't consider a threat or have a
bad memory of."

"She's talked about people she knew in school,"
Jessica said, "but school chums don't seem to have
affected her much. She hates her mother—I've already
told you that. There's her lawyer, Harold Stein, who's
been in her life, at least on the fringes, since the day
Morgan was born. Morgan's problems aren't really
rooted in people, per se. Her problems are rooted in
events. As for family members, other than her mother
and her brother, there aren't any. Her mother's folks
all died years and years ago, and Harry Masters' family, what's left of them, all live in California. Morgan's
never even met any of those people."

As Jessica's words seeped through to him, Benno

sat bolt upright in the bed. He looked down at her. "Her *what?*" Benno said.

"Her mother's folks, and her father's. Her mother's are dead, and her father's live in—"

"Did you say *brother?*"

Jessica looked surprised, even amused. "Yeah, sure. She talks to me about him all the time. What, Benno? All this big investigation into her past you're conducting, and you don't even know about him?"

The little girl was almost three. She was still confused over her father's sudden vanishing when her mother brought the baby home.

Ever since the car had gone up in flames in the creekbed nine months ago, the little girl's mother had all but ignored her. The child had been living her life, such as it was, under a nanny's watchful eye. The little girl didn't like the nanny and wanted her daddy to come home.

She'd been told that her father was dead, but the conception of death confused her. She was playing in her room on the day that a policeman came to the house, and she'd overheard the policeman tell her mother that Daddy had been burned. The news had been a relief to the child; she'd burned her finger when she was one, and the finger had subsequently healed. So she assumed that Daddy would come home when his own burn was better.

Two days after the policeman's visit, the nanny had brusquely stuffed her into a starched pleated dress, and she'd ridden in a limousine beside her mother to some-

thing called a funeral. She thought that a funeral was some kind of party because of all the people who came. The service was in a big church with a tall white spire and a bell tower. Inside the church there were a lot of flowers that smelled really nice, and a big shiny box sat at the front of the auditorium. Several people stood up and said nice things about her daddy, and she'd looked around hoping that Daddy himself would appear.

After the funeral she watched from the limo as some men loaded the big shiny box into a strange-looking car with double doors in the rear. Then two policemen on motorcycles led a long line of cars to a big shaded park where a lot of monuments stuck up from the ground. In the park, several hundred people gathered around the big shiny box, and another man said more nice things about her daddy and then everyone prayed. The little girl was bursting to know what was inside the box, but was afraid that if she asked out loud her mother would punish her. When her daddy's burn got well and he finally did come home, the little girl would tell him all about the funeral and the nice things people had had to say about him.

It was several more days before the child got up the nerve to ask her mother, one night at dinner, when Daddy would be better so that he could come home. Her mother's blue eyes turned to flints as she stared at the little girl across the linen tablecloth. Finally her mother laughed a mean laugh and said, "You dumb little bitch, don't you know that he's dead?" The child had seen dead insects before, and once she'd found a dead lizard. She supposed that if Daddy were dead it might be even longer before he came home, and she never asked her mother about Daddy again. As the months went by and Daddy never appeared, his memory became a less frequent comfort to the child.

She created a magic world where bunnies hopped and doggies came out to play, but not even her imaginary haven made life much happier. Her mother grew more and more irritable as time moved along.

Uncle Eddie came by pretty often, but always ignored her, as her mother and Uncle Eddie began to scream at each other all the time. The little girl couldn't understand why Uncle Eddie and her mother were so mad at each other. Uncle Eddie was supposed to be her mother's friend. One day she overheard her mother tell Uncle Eddie that he'd get his fuckin' money, but her mother's words didn't stop Uncle Eddie from being mad. For days thereafter the child hoped that she'd see ponies on the lawn, and in her room she asked her dollies if they'd like for her to pour some fuckin' tea.

The little girl's mother didn't seem to have any friends other than Uncle Eddie, though Steinsy visited often as well. The little girl knew that Steinsy was a lawyer—though she hadn't the slightest idea what lawyers were or what they did—because he'd been Daddy's friend before Daddy went away. The little girl thought that Steinsy was boring. Steinsy never smiled, and when he talked to the girl's mother he used words and phrases that the child didn't understand, such as "codicil," "probate," "evidence," "indictment," and "murder investigation." One day the child heard Steinsy say that Uncle Eddie was a "suspected accomplice." Shortly thereafter Uncle Eddie's visits stopped altogether, while Steinsy continued to come by every single day. It was during one of Steinsy's visits that two men appeared at the door, showing shiny badges and demanding to see the little girl's mother. Steinsy told the men that they couldn't speak to the little girl's mother, only to him, and the men looked very mad as they tromped out to their car.

In the weeks that followed the funeral the little girl's

mother got sick and frightened the child by throwing up in the bathroom every morning. As months went by there were physical changes in her mother as well; her mother's stomach grew and grew until she resembled a toy that the child had in her room—a plastic clown so jolly and round that if you pushed him over he'd pop right back up at you. Her mother's ankles grew big and puffy, her graceful walk turned into a waddle, and she spent a lot of time in the bathroom. Sometimes when Steinsy came over, the child's mother would say that she was too sick to talk to him.

One day about nine months after the fire in the creekbed, the little girl's mother packed a suitcase. As the little girl watched through the front window with the nanny holding her hand, the chauffeur drove her mother out the circular drive and away down the street. For the rest of that day, and through the next day and the next, the little girl's mother didn't come home. The little girl decided that her mother had disappeared from her life just as her daddy had, though in her mother's case the child didn't really care. She spent her time playing with the bunnies and ponies and doggies she'd created in her imaginary world.

On the third morning after he'd driven her away, the chauffeur brought the little girl's mother home. As the child watched her mother come up on the porch with the chauffeur holding her arm, the little girl wondered if something magic had happened. While her mother walked stooped over as if in pain, her stomach wasn't big and round any longer. She carried something in her arms wrapped up in a blanket. As her mother entered the house, the child ran up in excitement to see what was wrapped up in the blanket. She could see a tiny wrinkled face and an arm like a doll's.

When her mother saw the little girl rushing toward her, she turned her back, shielding her prize away from *the child, and snarled at the nanny, "I gotta get some rest. You keep that fuckin' kid quiet and away from me." Then, slowly and painfully, the little girl's mother went upstairs to her room with the chauffeur helping her. The little girl watched from the nanny's side and, for the first time since her daddy had disappeared, started to cry.*

17

The Southwest Institute of Forensic Sciences—an uptown name for the Dallas County crime lab—was nestled in behind Parkland Hospital, the charity facility on Harry Hines Boulevard. Benno got there late, at a quarter past nine, and hustled up the walk picturing Jessica Baldwin in the shower that morning, soaping Benno's back and between his legs. The scratches on his back had stung. As he entered the building, something within him stirred.

Fifteen minutes later he watched through a dirty lab window as a clanging ambulance careened off of Inwood Road and up to Parkland's emergency entrance. Medical techs in overcoats hustled out of the ambulance cab and around to the rear, their breath fogging in the cold.

Benno was concentrating on the outside scenery because he didn't want to look at the table behind him, where moments earlier the lab crew had reassembled Uncle Eddie Payne: legs and arms lined up with bloodless sockets, autopsy stitches forming an upside down Y across the torso, a gaping wound between the shoulders where the head should have been. *What a ghoulish fucking scene,* Benno thought. And the assistant ME wasn't helping, walking around comparing the hatchet with the wounds. The AME was named Joel Schotts, a pudgy bald man in a bloodstained smock with a permanent grin and giant floppy ears. Benno forced himself to turn away from the window just as Schotts slid the ax in between a hip and thighbone and nudged the leg away from the torso, sort of chuckling as he did.

"Well?" Tina Drummond said. Her rump leaned against a wall cabinet and her arms were folded in front of her.

"I'd say it's a hundred percent this is the weapon." Schotts laid the big knife carefully down beside the leg. There was a soft cloth rag wrapped around the handle. "Carved him up like a turkey." He poked at a bloodless thigh. "You want white meat or dark meat?" Schotts said, grinning from ear to ear.

Benno's stomach churned. "What else have you got?"

"Fibers and more fibers," Schotts said. "Fibers from the bedsheets in Morgan Masters' bedroom clinging to the back of one of these legs. Fibers from the trunk of Morgan Masters' BMW stuck to the blade. The wounds in this torso came from the knife you found at the Irving scene. That's not surprising. The knife wounds in the other guy"—here Schotts thumbed toward the autopsy room next door—"also match in size and configuration."

Benno averted his gaze from the autopsy table and concentrated on Schotts' enormous right ear. "You talking about Zorro?"

Schotts had blubbery lips. "The name on the toe tag is Gerald Trafficante."

"Yeah, that's him," Benno said.

Drummond stepped away from the cabinet. "The knife is part of a set from Morgan's kitchen."

"So the killer took an extra weapon along from Morgan's and used it on Zorro. We are looking for the same guy in both homicides."

"Or the same woman," Drummond said. "There was a woman who showered at Zorro's, but I don't think a woman could handle Zorro alone. Maybe with help from the guy pictured in the artist's sketch."

Benno forced himself to look at the body parts. At one time autopsy rooms hadn't bothered him, but it would take time for him to get used to the sight once more. "So other than confirming what we already think, that we're looking for the same killer at Morgan's, Zorro's, and the Doubletree Inn, do we have anything new?"

Schotts went over, opened a drawer, and came up holding two evidence bags. In one was the purple petal found beside Zorro's body, and in the other was the flower that had fallen out of Zorro's car when Benno opened the door. Schotts said, "Believe it or not, these may be the best clues you've come up with."

"They're damned sure distinctive," Benno said. "What the hell are they?"

"My wife would kill for a bulb to grow these babies, and I'd probably have to rob somebody to get the money to pay for 'em." Schotts tossed the evidence bags onto the table along with the body parts. "Hundred bucks for one tuber. You could put in a bed of these for, oh, fifty grand or so. And if I caught anyone planting 'em in my neighborhood, I'd cut the bastards down."

"Purple isn't your favorite color?" Drummond said.

"The flowers are gorgeous," Schotts said. "But they stink like hell."

"Smell like rotten meat," Benno said. "I sniffed one yesterday."

"Just horrible," Schotts said. "Folks, meet the voodoo lily. *Amorphophallus rivieri* if you're into proper names, also known as the devil's tongue or the sacred lily of India. The plants grow about seven feet high. They're as rare as flowers get. And since this one was blooming in the middle of winter, you're looking for someone with a greenhouse."

"If they smell that bad," Drummond said, "then why would anybody want them in their yard?"

"Only someone with more money than sense," Schotts said. "New rich people, old rich people who are just getting into gardening. They want plants to impress their niche of society. Money is the only object with those people—if it costs a lot, it must be something wonderful. I'll take plain old roses any day, thorns and all. You give some hustler a blank check, the first thing he's going to do is load you up with something like voodoo lily tubers. By the time you grow one and get a whiff of the damned thing, the hustler will be out of town or onto some other sucker."

Benno bent over the table and looked through the plastic at the flower. The petals were beginning to wilt. "So how do we find out who around here has got these things growing in their garden?"

"Shouldn't be that hard," Schotts said. "We'll have some of our folks check with rare plant nurseries. They'll definitely have a record of voodoo lily customers."

"That'll take time," Benno said. "We don't have that much."

"Oh hell," Drummond said. "No speculation, Benno, okay? We got three dead guys, plus another DA's investigator in the hospital. Don't be dreaming up any scenarios about voodoo flowers here. I'm as confused as you are. We need to start talking to people. Real live possible suspects and wits. Sitting around wondering who's growing stinky flowers . . . that kind of thinking is counterproductive. We gotta get our heads out of our asses, and start taking positive strides."

Benno started the engine and headed up Harry Hines Boulevard toward downtown with Drummond riding shotgun. He decided that Drummond had been right. Forensics was okay as courtroom evidence, once you had the asshole in custody, but nobody ever caught a perp by talking to the medical examiner. You hit suspects and witnesses hard, to see whose stories didn't match. If you didn't have the perp isolated within forty-eight hours, then there would be a ninety percent chance of the murder case going unsolved. Uncle Eddie had been dead three or four days, Zorro something less than that, not to mention the dead DA's investigator and the other man in intensive care.

As they neared Main Street, with downtown canyon walls on both sides of them, Benno said to Drummond, "I want to clear someone to get in to talk to Morgan." He stopped at a red light behind a county prisoners' van and watched men in jail suits grin through wire mesh and shoot the finger at passersby on the sidewalk.

"Who?" Drummond asked.

"A shrink. Somebody with insight on Morgan's mental state. We gotta notify the unis on watch to let this person through."

Drummond skeptically tilted her head. "This is the same mysterious shrink you told me about on the phone last night? The one who's not going to charge us anything?" She got out her cell, punched a couple of numbers in, then hesitated. "What's this person's name?"

The light turned green and Benno accelerated through the intersection, still behind the county van. "Uh, name?"

Drummond pressed the button to disconnect and dropped the phone into her lap. "Yes, Benno. A name. If I'm going to notify those cops to let someone visit with this woman they're supposed to be guarding, then it would be nice if they knew who they were expecting."

"Dr. Baldwin," Benno said.

"That's a start. This doctor got a first name?"

Benno watched the street ahead. The City Hall tower loomed on his left, a half mile in the distance. He had a sudden cottony taste in his mouth. "Jessica," he said weakly.

Drummond twisted around to face him across the seat. "Jesus Christ, Benno, that's the woman whose number you copied off of Morgan's caller ID. She's a fucking psychiatrist?"

"A crackerjack," Benno said. "A really insightful analyst. Make the call, Tina, will you?"

"Some woman that might be a witness, now you're wanting her analytical opinion. This sounds like a lot of bullshit."

"Has all the credentials," Benno said. "Can get right inside Morgan's mind, pick her brain, tell us what's rattling around in there. An expert."

"Expert what?"

"Psychiatrist. Really, Tina, Jessica Baldwin's credentials are beyond reproach."

Drummond's mouth twisted as she looked at him. "Yeah, I'll just bet." She scooted around to face the front, lifted the cell from her lap, and punched in numbers. As she waited on the line she said, "And you know all about this woman how, Benno?"

Benno cruised in front of Main Headquarters, and eased over to the right in front of the parking garage. He flipped on his turn signal. "We, uh, visited," Benno said.

As they rode up to the top floor on the elevator, Benno hauled out his own cell and punched in Jessica Baldwin's number. He got her voice mail, and when the beep sounded he said, "Jessica, it's me." Then, as Drummond stared daggers in his direction, Benno cleared his throat and said, "Uh, I mean, Dr. Baldwin, this is Detective Benno. I've cleared you to see Morgan Masters. Just present your ID to the officers on guard. Thanks so much for doing this." He disconnected, put the phone away, and faced the front in the position of attention. Warmth crept up the side of his neck.

As the elevator doors rumbled open, Drummond shifted her weight from one foot to the other. She stoically blinked. "Jesus Christ, I'm seeing it all," she said. "Whatever works, Benno. But this investigation's getting too liberal for me."

Drummond's remarks, disparaging as they were, got Benno to thinking. The truth was that he was sticking his neck out pretty far in involving Jessica Baldwin in the case. How did he know she could help? Her counseling Morgan might backfire and send Morgan over the edge. All he really knew about Jessica was what she'd told him, and this from a woman who'd met Morgan in a strip club and who'd also practically dragged Benno into bed on the first day he'd ever met her.

Not that he'd minded, and not that the sex hadn't been good. Terrific . . .

But suppose Jessica was crazy. Suppose she wasn't

even really a psychiatrist, but someone just as off the wall as Morgan Masters and her whole goddamned family.

Benno'd have to figure a way to check Jessica out, make sure she was really someone he ought to be fooling with. Not fooling with in bed, fooling with as far as the case went.

Benno came out of his trance. He was a step behind Tina Drummond, hustling down the top-floor corridor at Main Headquarters. But where the hell were they going?

Ah. Cousin Jeff. Chief Rubin. Headed to report to the chief about progress in the case. Should Benno fill the chief and Drummond in on what he was up to with Jessica Baldwin? He didn't know. Jesus, he'd have to think on it. Whatever he decided would likely be wrong.

Chief Rubin had a corner office at the end of the hall, with a reception room but no receptionist. Drummond waited near the corridor entry while Benno went to Rubin's inner door and softly knocked. Rubin yelled out, "Yeah, come on in." Benno waited for Drummond, then followed her inside.

Rubin had company. His guest was an older man, about seventy, with watery eyes and red marks on either side of his nose. He held a pair of glasses in one liver-spotted hand, and was dressed in a thick plaid shirt, heavy camouflage coat, and lined hunting boots. He sat in a stuffed armless chair across from Rubin, who was reared back behind his desk.

Rubin beckoned for the detectives to come closer. On the wall behind him were pictures of him and the mayor, and a framed certificate from the FBI Law Enforcement Training Center in Quantico. There was also a photo of Rubin accepting a plaque from a gray-haired man wearing a yarmulke, underneath a sign reading, JEWISH COMMUNITY CENTER. Rubin extended a palm-up hand toward the man in the camouflage jacket as he said to Benno and Drummond, "You two drag up a chair. Rusty wants to go back to shooting birds."

The older guy put his glasses on, stood, and extended his hand. "Yeah, hi. Rusty Dobbs. DPD, retired." After the detectives shook his hand and said hello, Dobbs said, "Y'all got it made these days. We used to be in the old place, over on Main. Had all this asbestos in the walls. Too hot in the summer, too cold in the winter." He tugged on his coat. "Dove season. Used to be when I was on the job, huntin' was all I thought about. Now I'm gettin' sick of it." His expression was friendly, but his eyes narrowed as he looked the newcomers over, measuring them up. Old cops and old whores, Benno thought—always on their guard.

Benno dragged two more armless chairs over from by the window. He and Drummond sat down beside Dobbs, and all three faced Rubin.

Rubin rocked forward and leaned on his elbows. "I am assuming you crack investigators are not here to report that you have our killer in custody. So what do you have?"

Benno glanced sideways at the older guy, Dobbs.

Rubin gave a come-on wave. "Speak. Rusty is part of this deal."

Benno nodded. "LaVon Masters had another kid besides Morgan."

Dobbs snickered. "That woman's liable to have kids all over. She ain't what you'd exactly call celibate."

Benno and Drummond looked at the guy.

Rubin said, "Rusty Dobbs was lead investigator on

the Harry Masters murder in 'seventy-two. He got pretty familiar with LaVon back then." He frowned at Benno. "Why is this other kid important?"

"I'm not sure it is important," Benno said. "But it was a boy. Would be middle twenties about now. Since we're looking for a young guy . . ."

"Had her a boy, huh?" Dobbs said. "That's more than we could ever find out."

Drummond scooted her chair closer to Rubin's desk and interjected, "Excuse me. But I've read everything in the newspaper archives about that case, and there's no mention of another Masters child."

Dobbs took his glasses off and massaged his nose. "We never thought it was all that significant. Slowed the hell out of the investigation, though, her bein' pregnant. Me and my partner, Joe DuBose—Joe passed two years ago. Me and Joe used to go by once a week to interview LaVon. Had her lawyer runnin' interference and meetin' us at the door. Since LaVon was in the family way, she got a lot of mileage out of doctor visits, usin' them as an excuse not to talk to anybody. Didn't really matter, tell you the truth. We didn't have a damned thing on her, and for about a year it didn't look like we were about to get anything."

Benno recalled the newspaper wrap-up of the old Masters case. "I thought it was funny that the indictment took a year. So Harry Masters fired a final bullet before he died and knocked up his wife?"

Dobbs vigorously shook his head. "No way it was Harry Masters' child. Old Harry got hisself fixed after the girl was born."

"Whose kid is it, then?"

"All I can swear to is that it's not mine. But my money'd be on Eddie Payne."

Drummond used a hand to brush back her hair. "You were looking at Uncle Eddie all along?"

"From day one," Dobbs said. "We got information that Uncle Eddie and LaVon had been in contact before Harry died. Payne was the number-one button around these parts. Didn't take a genius to add up the numbers."

"His name was never mentioned in the paper," Drummond said.

"Back then we controlled what was in the paper. Not like now, when you turn your case files over to the television news. If we didn't want something out, we sat on it."

Benno had to agree that the old ways were better, at least when it came to talking to the media. "So what happened a year after the murder that allowed the DA to go on with the case?" he asked.

"Easy. Uncle Eddie came on over and decided to talk to us."

"He got immunity from prosecution in a *murder case*? Where he was the button?"

"Sure, yeah," Dobbs said. "You'd just have to have been there to know how that woman thumbin' her nose got the whole county in an uproar. We knew she done it, and she knew we knew. Went around flauntin' all the money she'd come into, like she was laughin' at us. How do you think LaVon Masters got so high society? The murder made her a celebrity. Up until then she was just old Harry's empty-headed young wife, but during the investigation and after the trial she got to be the hottest ticket in town when it come to invites to uppity gatherin's. Crystal Charity Ball, Cattle Barons' Ball, you name it—the party wasn't a success unless LaVon was on the guest list. Back in them days, the district attorney, Henry Wade, he'da done about anything to get LaVon. Plus, we had nothing on Uncle Eddie to begin with. He just walks in one day and says, 'Here I am. You want to visit?' We called the DA over and had us a sit-down."

"Out of the blue?" Benno said.

The older man nodded. "More or less. He didn't have to come in. Was completely in the clear. He got awfully pissed off at LaVon about something. We never knew what. Didn't *care* what. All we cared was that we had us a witness."

"Apparently not much of one," Benno said. "The judge dismissed the case before it went to the jury."

"Hell yes, and the judge did right under the circumstances," Dobbs said. "Uncle Eddie Payne pulled a fast one on the county slicker'n owl shit. He brought a pretty smart lawyer along, Emmitt Colvin, who's dead now along with most of the old gang except maybe me and a few other old farts. Uncle Eddie got immunity in writing at every level, which shows how desperate we were to make a case. We agreed he couldn't be prosecuted for anything he said in private meetings with us. Then when we went to the grand jury, Emmitt Colvin demanded separate immunity in writing on that phase. Not only was Uncle Eddie Payne the star witness, he was the whole case. Without him we had zero. His lawyer knew it and took advantage.

"Up through his grand jury testimony," Dobbs continued, "Uncle Eddie performed like a champ. Laid out more detail than we ever needed. Told how he laid for Harry Masters outside one of his downtown theaters, locked him in the trunk of his car, and drove him way to hell and gone to south Dallas County, beat him to death with a hammer, propped him in the front seat, then set fire to the car. Also told how LaVon Masters gave the servants the night off to eliminate them as witnesses and followed Uncle Eddie out to the boondocks to pick him up after he burned up the car. She even took her daughter along for the ride, because to arrange for any kind of child care would create more witnesses. The little girl wasn't but two, so she didn't understand what was happening out there in the country, and as a two-year-old she wasn't going to have much memory of what went on when she grew up. Uncle Eddie said LaVon paid him fifty thousand dollars. Murder-for-hire carries the death penalty today, though in 'seventy-four, when the case come to trial, the Supreme Court had outlawed executions nationwide. The only question in the DA's mind was how much time LaVon was gonna do, life or twenty-five years or something else. I remember those prosecutors spent all their pretrial time rehearsing their argument for maximum punishment. With Uncle Eddie on the team, conviction was a foregone conclusion."

"You're saying," Drummond cut in, "that Morgan Masters witnessed the murder?"

"As much as a two-year-old could witness anything," Dobbs said. "Hindsight tells you that maybe we shoulda waited until the child was older and used a team of shrinks to jog her memory, but once LaVon got acquitted, nothing mattered. She had double jeopardy going for her. She could stand on the top of City Hall and yell she had done it, and there was nothing anybody could've done about it after the one-eighty Uncle Eddie done at trial.

"I'll give Uncle Eddie credit—he hired one smart lawyer," Dobbs said. "None of the written immunity agreements were tied together. Each phase was a separate deal. The night before he took the stand, we delivered him a third written agreement having to do with his trial testimony. Those agreements were worded so that we couldn't prosecute him even if he changed his story, thanks to our crackerjack DA forgetting to include any escape clause in that regard.

"So when Uncle Eddie took the stand and didn't remember a damned thing, we were left with our pants down and our thumbs up our collective asses. He told the jury he might've met LaVon a time or two, but he wasn't even sure about that, and as far as any questions about the murder and what led up to it, Uncle Eddie said he didn't know what we were talking about. Hell, the judge was right to dismiss the case. If we'd had any idea what Uncle Eddie was gonna say, we never would have been in court to begin with. We were screwed. Thank you very much, ladies and gentlemen. Sorry about all the taxpayers' money we've fucked off here, and on to the next case."

"What do you think happened to make him change his testimony?" Benno asked.

"Got no real clue," Dobbs said. "It's pretty easy to go from A to B to C, though. Eddie got pissed at LaVon about something and came over to see us. Sometime between his grand jury appearance and the trial, LaVon rectified whatever it was that Uncle Eddie was pissed about in return for him having a sudden lapse of memory. End of story. Well, not quite the end, though the rest is anticlimax. We talked the feds into indicting Uncle Eddie for income tax evasion, as kind of a gotcha for what he'd done to us, but the little time he did in some plush federal joint didn't amount to a hill of beans. LaVon could go on her merry way regardless."

Benno said, "And through all of it, you had no reason to wonder about this second child that LaVon delivered?"

"What's to wonder? She got pregnant sometime around the time of the murder. She delivered. We couldn't see what that had to do with the price of eggs."

Benno tugged on his ear. "Did you keep your notes on the case?"

Dobbs waved as if batting mosquitoes. "Sure. Keep all of my notes. Got an archive of them. Maybe I'll sell 'em to the public library for a bundle, like all those presidents do."

"I'm wondering if there might be something in there to steer us to somebody, anybody, who could give us information about this second kid. I doubt LaVon Masters is going to tell us anything. We can check old birth records, but that's assuming she delivered in Dallas County. There are about a hundred places within an hour's drive where she could have gone."

Dobbs scratched his eyebrow. He tugged at his jacket lapel. He bent over and tugged down on his pant leg. "There is this one guy," he finally said.

Benno reached on Rubin's desk for a notepad, tore off a sheet, and brought out his ballpoint.

"A chauffeur," Dobbs said. "This Mexican guy, Oscar Valdez. Drove LaVon everywhere. Brought her to court every day during the trial. Some of our guys tried to get next to him to, you know, maybe flip the guy, but no luck. If she went into labor, bet your last nickel Oscar Valdez drove her to the hospital. Outside of him, I got no idea."

"Got any suggestion as to how we might locate the guy?" Benno asked.

Dobbs shrugged, hands up. "Valdez, that's a pretty common name."

Rubin pointed to the note in Benno's hand. "Give me that," Rubin said. "This is something I can work on. You and Detective Drummond have got plenty on your plates. Incidentally, I faxed a copy of that sketch artist's drawing out to the assisted living center. Fishy Greene says he's never seen the guy before. We're also showing the picture all around Zorro's neighborhood. So we can't even say for certain that this is the guy. Also I can't say he's connected to LaVon Masters giving birth in the distant past. It will be worth it to try and locate this Oscar Valdez."

Benno and Drummond looked at each other. The detectives stood up to leave. Benno said to Dobbs, "Mind if we stay in touch if we need you?"

"Sure," Dobbs said, "if I ain't out shooting birds."

Benno and Drummond went downstairs to the squad room. There was no one in the open bay area, just empty desks and blank computer monitors. Di-Angelo's door was closed with the shades drawn. Inside the lieutenant's office, a light flickered. Benno looked toward his and Drummond's cubicle. A man with greasy black hair and dandruff was standing near Benno's desk, the top of his head visible over the partition. Benno led the way to the cubicle and stuck his head inside. Riding DA Randy Dunst nodded curtly. "Jesus Christ, where have you been? I've been looking all over for you."

Drummond edged past Benno and flounced to her desk. "Gee, Randy, I'm not sure. Just out screwing around."

"I'm checking on your progress. Hoermann wants an update."

"Let's keep him in suspense," Drummond said. "Thanks, Randy, keep in touch." She pressed the button to fire up her computer.

Dunst stood by as if waiting for someone to say something more; then he shrugged and stalked away toward the exit. Benno stepped after him. "Hey, Randy, got a minute?"

Dunst stopped halfway to the railing in front. He leaned on a desk and waited expectantly.

Benno walked up. "I want to ask you something in confidence." He suspected that Dunst resented his treatment at Morgan Masters' place the night before last, with Harold Stein going around like Caesar and Dunst bowing and scraping. Benno wasn't sure how much help the riding DA would be.

"I'll try to show more cooperation than you're giving me. Of course, that won't be hard."

"I mean, *really* in confidence, Randy. It's important."

"Hey, unless you're plotting a crime . . ."

Benno stuck his hands in his pockets. "You do any work with Victims' Services."

"Everybody in the DA's office does work with Victims' Services. Why?"

"Specifically, do you do anything with a shrink named Jessica Baldwin?"

"What, are you kidding? For my money she's the best one over there. Cooperative. Works her ass off, nights, everything."

Benno moved closer. "Between you and me, she's giving us some help on the Morgan Masters thing. I don't want that repeated. It's on her own time. I gotta know how much stock to put in what she says. So you'd vouch for her, right?"

Dunst hooked a thumb under his belt. "I'll tell you something. Most Victims' Services shrinks are lousy psychiatrists, working for the county because they can't make it on their own. Not Jessica Baldwin. The lady's top-drawer. Anything else?"

"No, that's all I . . ." Benno looked toward DiAngelo's office. The door was still closed, the light continued to flicker, and the shades were still drawn. "Say, Randy," Benno said, "when you came in the squad room, was anyone else around?"

Dunst followed Benno's gaze. "They're all in there," Dunst said. "Four or five cops plus DiAngelo. And, hey, they're having a pretty good time. You ought to look in." Dunst stepped toward the exit once more.

Benno said to Dunst's retreating backside, "But Jessica Baldwin. She's okay, huh?"

Dunst never broke stride. He pushed out through the railing gate. "Top-drawer," the riding DA said over his shoulder.

Benno then approached DiAngelo's office, and a male voice said loudly through the door, "Will you look at that ass, man?" Benno had at first intended to knock, but now changed his mind. He pushed open the door and peered inside.

A TV and VCR were set up, the flickering screen illuminating DiAngelo's face as he sat behind his desk, and also casting light on four male detectives' faces as they sprawled around and gaped at the television. Song, the Chinese-American cop who'd shared Benno's cubicle, was in there, along with one black guy and two white guys. All wore shirts and ties but no coats, and all except DiAngelo sported shoulder rigs. DiAngelo had the remote control; as Benno stepped inside, DiAngelo showed a panicked look and put his index finger on the power button. Then his features tightened in recognition. He relaxed and returned his attention to the screen.

The cops were watching the tapes Drummond had taken from Gerald Trafficante. In the current clip, Zorro performed oral sex on Morgan Masters. She lay on top of a bedspread with the Binnion's Horseshoe logo in the center, her head thrown back in rapture, her thighs clamped firmly around Zorro's ears, her fists clenched as she yanked on Zorro's hair.

Benno felt like forty kinds of Peeping Tom. He started to back outside. DiAngelo told him to shut the door. As Benno reached for the knob, Drummond walked in carrying a printout from her computer.

She surveyed the scene, first looking at the television, then at each man in turn, and finally striking a pose with one hip thrust out. "You guys are disgusting," she said.

Song laughed so hard he almost fell off of DiAngelo's desk. "Come on, Tina, you don't like to watch?"

"No, I do not like to watch, especially not with you assholes. If any of you start jerking off I am reporting it upstairs." She turned to Benno. "I have something here on Harry Masters' estate. Would you like to see it, or would you rather wait till the show's over?"

Benno tugged on his collar. "I just came in. I didn't know they were—"

"Hold it," Drummond said. She squinted at the screen and did a double take. "Wait right here," she said, then took off in the direction of her desk.

The cops continued to watch the show. One guy said, "Jesus Christ. Is he hung, or what?"

Drummond returned with a stack of pictures. She flipped the wall switch and the lights came on.

DiAngelo got up angrily. "What the hell you think you're—?"

"Just a second's interruption, Loo," Drummond said, "and then you can go on with your depravity. Benno, look at this." She handed Benno the pictures.

He looked at the top photo. It was one of the pictures from Morgan's BMW, featuring Zorro along with female legs and genitals. Benno handed the pictures back to Drummond and gave her a so-what shrug.

"Come on, are you blind?" Drummond shoved the top photo in Benno's face. She put her finger on the woman's thigh, on the butterfly tattoo. "Butterfly," Drummond said. Then she walked to the television and put her finger on Morgan's creamy upper leg in the videotape, Morgan now rising up to straddle Zorro as he lay on his back. "No butterfly," Drummond said. She pointed to Morgan's face on the television screen. "Morgan Masters," she said, then lifted the photo from the BMW to ear level and said, "Not Morgan Masters. Morgan's got no tattoo. Zilch. Nada. My God, Benno, what I gotta say to get through to you?"

"But if it's not Morgan"—Benno let the picture flutter down from his fingers to rest on top of a stack of paper—"how come Zorro told us it was?"

"He didn't," Drummond said. "I went over my notes. We asked him if he was the guy in the picture, and he said he was. Then we started asking him about the videotapes. We never asked him about the woman in the stills."

Benno and Drummond were back inside their cubicle, facing each other across their butted-together desks. Out in the bullpen, the show now over, DiAngelo's door was open and his light was on. He looked busy as hell, sorting through files. The other cops had returned to their stations, the entire shift now vigilant as watchdogs.

"So we're looking for a female, other than Morgan, with a connection to Zorro," Benno said. "We are also looking for a guy with an earring. Our killer or killers had a stiff one for Uncle Eddie Payne and still have one for Morgan Masters. Our killer or killers might or might not have had a hard-on for Zorro, but I'm thinking Zorro had to go because he knew something having to do with the woman in this picture. The way Harry Masters' estate played out has a bearing, but I doubt if a guy like Zorro would be privy to that information. You found nothing in the newspaper archives about LaVon Masters' second kid?"

Drummond pointed to a stuffed file folder. "Every article mentioning LaVon is in there, through the end of the murder trial. Odd that her pregnancy was such a deep dark secret. You think it's time to see Morgan's lovin' mama in person?"

Benno thought that one over. "Eventually. But we want to be able to hit her with everything at once." He raised one finger. "Let me make a call," he said and punched in Jessica Baldwin's number. He got her voice mail again and told the recorder after the beep, "Jessica, hi, it's Ham Benno again. When and if you get by to see Morgan, we need to know how to find this brother you told me about. Call me as soon as you can." Drummond smirked at him. He disconnected and said, "No cute remarks, okay?"

Drummond rattled a piece of paper from her printer, straightening it out. "I've got something here that's bothering me. One of these properties listed at the county as belonging to Harry and LaVon Masters shows an address at 672 Highway 157, Grand Prairie, Texas. Somehow that rings a bell."

"Give me that address again," Benno said. He was frowning and his fingertips were tingling.

Drummond read off the corporate address a second time.

"Jesus Christ," Benno said. He rummaged through the stack on his desk and came up with a small square of paper. He squinted at the writing. "Did you say 672 Highway 157?"

Drummond read the printout for confirmation. "That's it. Why?"

"That's Muscle's, the strip club." Benno locked gazes with Drummond for an instant, then said, almost under his breath, "Denzel."

18

He was headed toward Muscle's again, only this time he took I-30 instead of the road past Texas Stadium. As he passed the exit that led to Lone Star Park, the racetrack, with semis and bobtails parading past on the other side of the median and Drummond upright beside him in the passenger seat, Benno said, "Something told me not to trust that guy."

"The manager of a male strip joint?" Drummond said. "Probably a pimp, not to mention a drug provider for all the dancers. What clued you in?"

"I should have taken more time in analyzing the guy's statements."

"Maybe you should make adjustments in your future thinking," Drummond said. Then Benno's cell phone buzzed and she said, "I'd answer that, but it might be your girlfriend."

"I'm only dealing with her as a psychiatrist," Benno said.

"Yeah, right." Drummond picked up the cell and grasped the flip-out mouthpiece. "If it's her, I'm going to ask if you two've been fucking."

"Uh, let me take it." Benno snatched the phone, flipped it open, and said, "Benno here."

A female dispatcher told him, "I'm patching someone through, Detective." There were clicks on the line, then a deep male voice with a small-town Texas accent said, "Hello. Hello. Anybody there?"

Benno frowned in puzzlement. "Detective Benno speaking. Were you calling someone from Metro?"

"Benno. Yeah, hi. Sergeant Stafford, Irving PD."

Benno searched his memory bank. Stafford. The Irving uniform in charge of the crime scene at Zorro's place. A stocky guy, with thick puffy eyelids under shaggy salt-and-pepper brows. "How you doing?" Benno said.

"I think we might've caught a break. Elmer Reed called."

Benno closed his eyes. Elmer Reed. The drunk next door, the wit who'd provided details to the sketch artist.

Stafford continued. "Reed said the same guy he saw before was at the complex this morning, nosing around."

"Jesus Christ."

"We sent a squad car out, and we've apprehended the guy."

Benno felt tension grip his chest. "Where is he?"

"Downstairs in interrogation. Looks just like the sketch artist's drawing. Hasn't told us diddly, and we've returned the compliment by not telling him why he's being detained. Thought you might like to talk to the guy before he lawyers up."

"We're on the way," Benno said. He disconnected, slammed on the brakes, and whipped the wheel to the right as they neared the Six Flags/Ballpark-in-Arlington turnoff.

Drummond held the door handle in a death grip.

"Have you lost what's left of your mind? What the hell are you doing?"

"We've gotta take a detour," Benno said.

Police Headquarters in the City of Irving, Texas, is a modest three-story building of sandy brick, across from an idyllic park with picnic tables and a playground.

As Benno and Drummond entered the building's wide, clear glass double doors, they saw a long low counter where uniformed cops worked phones and keyboards. Beyond the counter was a long corridor, where, halfway down, Irving PD Sergeant Stafford held a stiff letter-sized drawing. Benno and Drummond approached Stafford, exchanged greetings, then alternated between glancing at the picture and peering into an interrogation room along the long hallway through a one-way mirror, like people watching a puppet show.

Benno thought that, indeed, the guy in there was a pretty close match with the sketch artist's drawing, all the way down to the earring. The suspect was seated alone at a table, head down, hands folded, and seemed to be shivering. He had an olive complexion and close-cropped, shiny black hair, along with a pencil-thin mustache. He looked to be in his late twenties or early thirties, and his work pants and shirt were matching pale blue. In the artist's sketch the writing over the subject's pocket looked like hen scratching, but the stitched letters on the suspect's shirt read clearly JESÚS.

Benno said to Stafford, "This guy's carrying no ID?"

The Irving sergeant slowly shook his head. "Not a speck. Also the cat's got his tongue. Since our guys collared him he hasn't said a word."

"Where was he, Sergeant?" Drummond asked.

"A block down from the apartment building, walking east. Your wit Elmer Reed rode along in the squad car and pointed out the guy. It's him. At least, the witness is sure that it's him."

Drummond and Benno backed away from the glass for a confab. "I'm smelling bullshit here," Drummond said.

"Doesn't look much like a killer," Benno said. "Not that the guy's got to look dangerous. I guess we hit him with the old one-two."

Drummond led the way to the interrogation room entry and said over her shoulder to Stafford, "We're going in, Sergeant." She pushed on in through the door. Benno followed.

The suspect looked up as the detectives came in. He had deep brown hard-set eyes. As Benno and Drummond sat across from him, he resumed his study of his folded hands.

Drummond crossed her legs and leaned in on her elbows. "I'm Detective Drummond and this is Detective Benno, Metro. Sir, as you probably know, this is a murder investigation. The sergeant outside informed us you've been read your rights, but I'm going to tell you again. You're entitled to have an attorney present. Do you want an attorney?"

The suspect said nothing and continued to watch his knuckles.

Drummond looked at Benno and shrugged.

Benno propped a knee against the edge of the table. "Is your name really Jesús? Hey, pal, look at me."

The suspect glanced up at the sound of his name, but still didn't speak.

"Okay, Jesús, or whatever your name is," Benno said. "Let me spell it out. You can sit there and give everybody the silent treatment, but that won't help you. You were spotted leaving a murder scene yesterday morning. A witness can identify you. Today you returned to the same scene. Not talking will only get you in deeper shit. Detective Drummond just asked you if you wanted a lawyer. That is not a trick or a loaded question. Now. Do you want to speak to an attorney, or don't you?" He favored the suspect with a steely-eyed gaze.

The suspect opened, then closed his mouth. He fiddled with his mustache.

Benno rose partway from his chair and leaned over close. "You are halfway to the joint right now, Jesús. Bullshit like this will only get you the rest of the way there. Now, goddammit, you say something!" He pounded his fist for emphasis.

The pounding of Benno's fist shook the table. The suspect shrank back. Tears welled up in his eyes and rolled down his cheeks to soak his mustache. He held up his hands in a pleading attitude. *"Tengo carda verde,"* he said. *"Pero está a mi casa. Soy legal. Por favor. No English, señor. Por favor."*

Air whooshed out of Benno's lungs. He collapsed back into his chair.

"Jesus Christ," Drummond said. She stalked over to the door, opened it, and stuck her head out in the corridor. "Sergeant, we need an interpreter in here." She shut the door, leaned against the wall, and doubled over in laughter. Her shoulders heaved. She tried to speak, but couldn't. She drew a deep breath. "Guess you meant the old one-two-*three,* didn't you, Benno?" she finally managed to say. "You and me and the interpreter, huh? Jesus Christ, what a waste of fuckin' time."

The interpreter turned out to be a pretty twenty-something named Beverly Cruz, with long hair below her uniformed shoulders. She clearly didn't like the

idea of non-English-speakers being taken advantage
of. As she and Cruz conversed in Spanish, she kept
shooting icy glances across the table at the detectives.
Finally she said, "His name is Jesús Sanchez Maria,
and he's from Santa Re. He's registered and has a
green card, which he's not carrying because he left his
wallet in his other pants. What's he charged with?"

"Nothing, yet," Benno said. "He's a suspect in a
homicide."

She arched an eyebrow, her look meaning clearly,
Why, because he's a Mexican? She said, "He doesn't
understand that. He thinks you're INS and you're
about to put him on a bus headed for the river."

"Tell Mr. Sanchez we're not sending him anywhere.
We want to know why he was at this address, yesterday and today, walking around upstairs." Benno
handed over a card on which he'd written the address
of Zorro's apartment house.

Cruz spoke to Sanchez and showed him the card.
Sanchez' look brightened. He answered her. She
turned back to face Benno and Drummond. "It's his
job. He reads the electricity meters."

Now Drummond spoke up. "He'll have to do better
than that, Miss Cruz. The landlady's already told us
that they have meters installed at ground level in front
of the laundry room. No need for the readers to go
up there."

Cruz held a palm-out hand in Drummond's direction and said something to Sanchez. Sanchez got excited. He answered her with a lot of frantic hand
gestures and probably more words than were necessary. Cruz said sharply, in English, "This landlady. Is
she a portly woman with big doughy ankles?"

"That sounds like her," Drummond said.

"Okay, Detectives," Cruz said. "The power company had those ground-level meters installed at the

landlady's insistence. Two months ago they found out there's a cutoff on the second level to deactivate the meters. She's been charging the tenants full price and paying the company half. The company installed a lockbox on the cutoff, and before Mr. Sanchez reads the meters he's supposed to check the box to make sure no one's tampered with it. I can give you Mr. Sanchez' supervisor's phone number if you want to verify."

Oh, shit, Benno thought. "That, ah, probably won't be necessary. If you would, ask him, yesterday morning early, if he saw anyone up there while he was making his rounds."

"Someone could have asked him that before they put him in custody," Cruz said.

"We thought . . . never mind. Just ask him, please."

She gave Sanchez a conspiratorial wink and talked to him rapidly in Spanish. Sanchez looked very pissed off. He spouted a stream of dialogue, and somewhere in there was the word *"boracho,"* a Spanish term that Benno thought he'd heard before.

Cruz gave the detectives a look that could melt cobalt. She said, "There's a drunk living upstairs."

Now it was Benno's turn to study the table. "We know."

"As Mr. Sanchez was leaving yesterday morning after he'd checked out the meter switch," Cruz said, "this drunk guy came out of his apartment and asked him something he didn't understand. When Mr. Sanchez said he didn't speak any English, the guy went inside and came back out with an empty whiskey bottle and made a bunch of hand signs. Mr. Sanchez got the idea that the drunk was hitting him up for liquor money. When he said no and started downstairs, the drunk yelled that Mr. Sanchez was a fucking asshole."

Cruz flashed a grin. "That much English, Mr. Sanchez understands."

Benno looked at Drummond. Drummond's sides were heaving. Benno lowered his gaze and brushed his hands together. "Guess that clears it up," Benno said.

Benno stood in the corridor and said to Irving PD Sergeant Stafford, "So that's it. Our wit hit the suspect up for whiskey money. When the suspect didn't cooperate, the wit decided to drop a dime on the guy, probably for spite. We called the suspect's supervisor at the electric company. He's one of their more dependable employees. End of story."

"God*damn*." Stafford looked back over his shoulder. Down the corridor, Cruz escorted Jesús Sanchez to the desk to reclaim his valuables. Sanchez was all smiles, head nods, and graciases. "God*damn*," Stafford said again. He waved several copies of the sketch artist's drawing. "What am I going to do with these?"

"Better yet," Drummond said, moving alongside Benno, "what are we going to do with the several thousand we've been circulating? It's a problem, Sergeant. What can I say?"

Stafford thumped the drawings against his thigh. "That witness Elmer Reed? If I ever see the sumbitch again I'm whippin' his ass for him."

The detectives fell in step and headed toward the exit. "Can't say as I'd blame you," Benno said over his shoulder.

They came outside in sixty-degree sunshine, with the remnants of the snow melting fast. Water poured from the rooftops and rushed in the gutters. Benno walked head down, in long determined strides, coattails flying. Drummond had to hustle to keep up.

They'd made it down the steps onto the sidewalk when a male voice on their left yelled out, "Hey."

Benno stopped and turned. Drummond went a couple of paces ahead, then halted as well.

The man approaching them was skinny with a sallow complexion, and had an ear-to-ear beard but no mustache. His hair was wild, and he wore a filthy sweatshirt and jeans. His voice was cracked and hoarse. "Hey, I need to talk to you."

Benno blinked in recognition. It was Elmer Reed, the so-called witness, the drunk who lived next door to Zorro. Benno could smell the whiskey on Reed's breath from five feet away. His hand balled instinctively into a fist. He pictured himself throttling Elmer Reed, banging the guy's head on the pavement over and over.

Benno said, "What the fuck do you—"

Drummond yanked hard on Benno's sleeve. She imperceptibly shook her head, then favored Elmer Reed with her biggest, broadest grin. "Good day, Mr. Reed," she said brightly.

"Yeah, hi." Reed's hands were trembling. "Listen, I, uh, spotted the guy you were looking for. Guess you nabbed him, huh?"

Drummond continued to grin. "We sure did. Man, with citizens like you . . ."

Reed stepped closer and lowered his voice. "Yeah, well, hey, listen. The other day we talked about maybe a reward?"

"Hey, you're sure right," Drummond said. She pointed back toward the building. "Go in there, straight down the hall. Ask for Sergeant Stafford. You know what, Mr. Reed? He told us just a minute ago that he was looking for you."

19

Drummond entered Muscle's at a fast pace, then came to a halt that made her shoe soles squeal like tires. Benno bumped her from behind. A huge black guy, wearing nylon bikini briefs, crouched onstage and gyrated his hips to Michael Jackson's "Billie Jean." Women clapped and squealed. Drummond said over her shoulder, "Is this heaven or what?" Benno took her by the arm and steered her firmly down the aisle. No Denzel in sight.

He herded Drummond past the screaming females at the tables, around the stage, through the curtains in back, and barged into the office without knocking. Denzel was on the phone. His sharp cheekbones cast shadows on his face, and instead of the sparse tendrils covering his bald spots, his head was now shaved. He wore a shirt opened to the third button, showing a sunken chest with very little hair. Benno thought the guy looked better than yesterday. Denzel did a double take as the cops walked in. He said, "Call you back," into the phone, then dropped the receiver into its cradle. "My lawyer says I don't gotta talk to you no more." The music drifted in from the club, the heavy bass muffled and far away.

Drummond and Benno exchanged a look. Drummond said, "Drawers?"

Benno nodded. "Drawers."

The detectives went around the desk, stood on either side of Denzel, and simultaneously yanked the top drawers open and dug inside.

Denzel yelled out, "You got no right! You got no fuckin'—"

Drummond straightened, holding a revolver, and dropped the pistol on the desk with a thud. "Gun," she said.

Benno pulled out a clear plastic Baggie with powder inside. "Dope," he said and tossed the Baggie on the desk beside the pistol.

The detectives went back around and sat across from Denzel, facing him.

Denzel looked ready to explode. "You got no warrant."

Benno shrugged with his hands. "Plain sight. We came in to visit and the stuff was just lying there. You want to take us on, Denzel?"

Denzel looked wildly at the dope and gun. He grabbed the phone. "I'm callin' my lawyer."

"Suit yourself," Benno said. "But first I'll ask you. You got a sheet?"

Denzel had punched in a couple of numbers. He gently put down the phone.

"If you got no sheet," Benno said, "then this is nothing. The coke looks to be gram weight, in the misdemeanor range. If you got a permit for the piece, no big deal. If you don't, weapon possession on a premises serving alcohol is a minor felony, which your lawyer can plead down to nothing. But if you already got a sheet, that's different. Second felony's got some serious minimum time. Third felony is twenty-five years in this state, in case you haven't heard." He took out a pad and ballpoint. "Give me your full name and Social Security number. I can call it in and see if you got a sheet. If you don't, hey, we're outta here. For that minor contraband, we won't waste our time."

Denzel laughed a nervous laugh and said weakly, "The hell is this about?"

"I think you've already got an idea. I'll tell you straight out, if you decide to talk to us instead of some lawyer, you are not going to give us any bullshit. When I was here before, you gave me bullshit. If you've got any more in mind, then you should go ahead and contact your attorney. We'll go from there. Tell the lawyer he should meet you down at the county."

"Come on, Officer. I am a cooperating citizen."

"You'd damned sure better be," Benno said.

Denzel showed a grin that he probably thought was friendly. "No need to go bustin' my balls."

"Good," Benno said. "Detective Drummond, this citizen is showing cooperation. Do you have any questions for him?"

"Several." Drummond pulled out the picture from Morgan's BMW—Zorro and the legs and butterfly tattoo—and also got the printout showing the ownership of the strip club property. "Since I didn't sit in on your previous visit with Detective Benno," Drummond said, "we are starting with a clean slate. My first query has to do with ownership. Who owns this fine establishment, Denzel?"

"I just manage it, lady. Do I look like a guy that'd be buddies with the owner?"

"I'll confess you don't," Drummond said. "But you

do look like a man who might soon be driving a tractor on a prison work farm." She gave Benno a sideways look.

"Dope," Benno said.

"Gun," Drummond said.

"It's, uh, corporately owned. I'm on the board of
directors."

"Great," Drummond said. "Where do you hold
your meetings, in an alley seated on garbage cans?"

"Listen, it's the truth. We got legitimate stockhold-
ers. The corporation leases the club to a holding company. The building belongs to a subsidiary, and we—"

"Denzel." Benno leaned over the table and got up
in the club manager's face. "This is more of the kind
of bullshit I was talking about. We got people getting
dead. We don't care about all these shell games, stock-
holders and subsidiaries. Who is the fucking owner?
Last chance, Denzel. And I'm *not* bullshitting."

"Aw Jesus. I might as well resign."

"That beats the alternative. Detective Drummond,
get the dope and pistol. I'll escort Denzel here out to
the—"

"The rich lady," Denzel choked. "Mrs. LaVon Masters. It's all hers: the building, land, everything. Everything's hers. Hey, I just report."

"You could have saved us a hell of a lot of trouble,"
Benno said, "if you'd just told me that when I was
here the other day. So your current infallible story
begs more questions. Does Morgan Masters know her
mother owns this joint?"

"No way. I told you before, we had special instructions about Morgan as a customer. The instructions
went two ways. We weren't to tell Morgan, or anybody else, the rich lady was involved out here. Been
that way in the five years I been working here."

"I'm having trouble sorting this out, Denzel. Morgan just wandered in here by accident?"

Denzel squinched his eyes closed. He opened them. "That was all Zorro."

"You have these dancers soliciting business?"

"Zorro was a special case. He did a lot of private parties, you know? Even, uh, entertained the owner herself sometimes. I know nothing about how he got together with Morgan. This Morgan Masters has a reputation, you know, for soliciting these guys and then taking pictures while they're fucking her. Zorro ran into her at some outside gig he did. I don't know which one and that's the truth. Then Morgan starts coming here. I don't get let in on all the details. What the rich lady says, I do. And nothing else."

Drummond watched the exchange between Benno and Denzel as if she was mesmerized. She held up the photo from Morgan's BMW, facing Denzel. She said, "I probably already know this. But will you make it official and identify the woman whose legs are featured in this outstanding piece of photography?"

Denzel tugged on his collar. He folded his arms. "Oh Jesus Christ. I got to?"

"Yeah, you got to," Benno said.

"Look, you think I got some control over that old broad? All the time she's asking, don't you think I look a whole lot younger than what I am? Jesus, what can you say? Tell the truth, get your ass fired."

Benno took the picture from Drummond, looked at it, and then faced Denzel. "LaVon Masters? Are you shitting us, Denzel?"

Denzel sagged in defeat. "Two or three years ago she started bugging me about tattoos, like she was some nubile young bunny or something. Bugged me damn near to death. Wanted some artist to come to her house on the q.t. and put a butterfly on her leg. I thought the whole idea was the silliest thing I'd ever heard, but what could I do? Buddy of mine's a tattoo artist. Guy needed the bread, you know?"

On the way back downtown, Drummond said, "So Harry Masters bought the property way back when. I wonder how long the strip joint's been there."

Benno steered one-handed, his free hand resting in his lap. "If we're looking for LaVon's mysterious son, what's his motive? We got a crazy here or what?" Under bright blue skies, the sun on the windshield had a greenhouse effect. Benno cracked the window to let in some air.

"I'd say 'or what,' " Drummond said. "You know Harry Masters didn't make any provision for a kid that hadn't even been born when he died. Especially some other man's kid."

Benno had an uncle who'd left all of his assets to an illegitimate son. The guy's widow had battled the rabbis in court, tooth and nail. Benno'd heard that later she'd joined some Christian Fundamentalist group. "Seems to me that what's important is, who *did* old Harry provide for?"

"The will went in and out of probate," Drummond said. "No copy in the records. After over twenty-five years, maybe there's no copy in existence."

"Yeah, but bet that even if there is no copy, Lawyer Stein can remember the details in the will. A situation like that, where someone likely wanted that will hidden, the guy wouldn't forget that for the rest of his life. Where's Stein's office?"

Drummond dug out one of the business cards that Stein had distributed at Morgan's the other night, in between riding herd on Randy Dunst and standing in between the cops and his client. She held the card in front of her nose. "Thanksgiving Tower," Drummond said. "On Main Street downtown."

They were approaching the Continental Street exit, which led into the business district after dipping beneath an underpass. Benno put his blinker on and moved into the right-hand lane. "Let's go see him," he said.

Drummond slumped lower in the seat. "He'll holler privilege, Benno."

Benno left the freeway and cruised alongside the minimum-security county jail, which at one time was a luxury hotel. "Yeah, maybe," Benno said. "But after I talk to him, he might not say it very loud."

Thanksgiving Tower was a mirror-walled skyscraper connected to an underground tunnel filled with shops and restaurants. Benno used his county sticker to park free in a multiple-story garage on the south side of Main. Then he and Drummond hustled through the tunnel, dodging pedestrians who were ambling along window-shopping. The shops were mostly expensive women's clothing stores, with an occasional high-dollar gift shop thrown in. There was a Don Pablo's Mexican Restaurant, a burger bar, and several standup sandwich places. The walls were alternating panels of chartreuse and bilious yellow. The detectives exited the tunnel, mounted an escalator, and rode up to Thanksgiving Tower's street-level floor.

Stein and Bromberg, LLP, occupied the tower's entire fortieth floor. Benno and Drummond went on a stomach-dropping express elevator ride and stumbled out into a plush-carpeted hallway in front of double glass doors. Visible through the glass was a beige leather wall, supporting the law firm's name in burnished bronze letters. There was an oval receptionist's station, where a chicly dressed woman routed incom-

ing calls. Leather couches and chairs were set up in a
waiting area off to the side. A man sat in one of the
chairs holding a briefcase balanced across his thighs,
and a woman was on one of the couches using her
laptop. The detectives went in and told the receptionist that they wanted to see Harold Stein.

She looked up and said, "Who may I say is calling?"
A tiny mike was suspended in front of her mouth,
supported by a chain around her neck. She was a brunette with layered hair and clear gray eyes.

Drummond reached for her wallet and started to
show her ID, but Benno stopped her with a hand on
her arm. He leaned over the counter and grinned.
"Tell him it's Uncle Eddie Payne." Drummond
backed away a step and gaped at Benno. He kept his
gaze on the receptionist.

The receptionist didn't look like a woman easily surprised, but her eyebrows lifted a fraction. "You're Mr.
Stein's uncle?"

"No, it's, uh, a nickname. We're old friends."

She looked skeptical. She opened her mouth and
started to say more, but then shrugged and got on the
intercom. In a second she said, "A gentleman and a
lady to see Mr. Stein. The man is Uncle Eddie Payne."
She listened and then said, "That's the name I was
given," then listened some more, disconnected, and
pointed to the waiting area. "Have a seat," she said,
then went back to moving her mouse around on her
pad.

Drummond led Benno halfway to the couches and
chairs, then whirled to face him and hissed, "I'm not
going to ask if you've lost your mind. You've already
answered that question."

Benno kept his grin plastered on his face. "Look,
we flash ID, Stein's not going to see us till hell freezes
over. He'll get on the phone to the mayor's office, and

first thing we know we'll get a call telling us to keep away from the guy."

"Maybe, maybe not. But you've just identified yourself as a man that's dead."

"That's the idea. We've kept Uncle Eddie's name under wraps to the media. I want to find out if Stein knows Uncle Eddie isn't among the living. If he doesn't know it, great. But if he does . . . Just trust me on this one, Tina. Okay?"

"No," she said, then stalked over and flopped down in one of the waiting chairs. The woman on the sofa looked up briefly from her laptop, then went back to pounding the keys.

Benno took to the couch alongside the woman with the laptop, rummaged through a stack of magazines. Selecting a *Golf Digest,* he found an article on putting by Dave Pelz, the short-game guru. Benno was nervous as hell, and he halfway expected a couple of IAD cops to come bursting in from the elevators and arrest him on the spot for failure to identify himself as a police officer. He forced himself to concentrate on the article. Dave Pelz recommended that the player position his eyes directly over the target line and swish the putter back and forth a couple of times as a pre-shot routine. Benno wondered when Texas weather would warm enough for him to play. Late February, he'd heard, maybe the first week in March. In about a month he'd haul his clubs out of storage, maybe add a couple of degrees' loft to his driver . . .

A slender redhead in five-inch-high platforms came into the reception area, walking fast. Her hair was done in springy curls. She wore a gray formfitting skirt and white silk blouse and a jacket with padded shoulders. She stopped and said, "Mr. Payne?" She had the same skeptical look as the receptionist. Benno put the magazine aside and stood. Drummond got up as well.

The redhead told them to follow her, then took off for the interior of the offices. Benno let Drummond go ahead of him, then brought up the rear.

The redhead took them through a maze of corridors. They passed small reception areas where admins worked, filing or typing away. Muted sounds drifted throughout the law firm—voices, the whir of a fax machine, the rapid click of computer keys, soft New Age music over the sound system. Benno concentrated on the redhead's walk, her slender hips gently undulating, her pale calves flashing in coordinated rhythm. She reminded him some of Jan, his ex. He remembered that he needed to call her, to confirm Jacob's visit after Christmas.

He thought of Jan in bed with him early in their marriage, their need for each other like ravenous hunger. Jan's long legs in front of his face as she kissed her way down his chest and stomach to take him in her mouth. Jesus, he hadn't been consumed with sex in years. He had to get women off his mind and concentrate on the murders. Focus on the guy who chopped old men into pieces, slaughtered male strippers, lurked outside hotels and shot DA's investigators.

But there was also Jessica Baldwin. *Jesus.*

Her muscled legs squeezing his midsection, her eyes in wanton slits as she matched him thrust for frenzied thrust . . .

First Jan and now Jessica.

Sex. Pressing in on him, taking over his thinking.

They arrived in a corner area where the gold-colored carpet had three-quarter-inch padding. On the wall hung an oil painting featuring a guy who looked a lot like Harold Stein, except that the man in the portrait had a handlebar mustache and wore a monocle. A bronze plaque mounted on the frame read, ISAAC STEIN, 1884–1962. Ceiling-high mahogany bookcases contained a miniature law library—Vernon's *Annotated Texas Statutes, Federal Reporter, 2nd Edition, Shepherd's,* an entire shelf packed with Bar Association periodicals. There was also a big antique desk with a polished top, contrasting sharply with a modern computer workstation. A screen saver on the monitor showed fish swimming past in a never-ending parade.

The redhead never broke stride. She led them to a thick wooden door with an ornate handle. She opened it and stood aside. She asked the detectives if they'd like something to drink. Both said no. The redhead smiled, nodded, and hurried away, and Benno and Drummond went on in.

Harold Stein's office was on two levels, and half again bigger than Benno's apartment. On the level where Benno and Drummond stood was a hand-carved wet bar exhibiting white and red wine along with every brand of liquor known to man, and a seating area consisting of couches and chairs grouped around a glass-topped settee. Straight ahead and two steps down, Harold Stein occupied a desk the size of a handball court. He was short to begin with, but from this distance he seemed about two feet tall. He looked at the two cops. Recognition dawned.

Stein was livid. He stood to one side of his desk and waved a small slip of paper around. "What's the meaning of this?" His iron-gray hair was brushed to perfection, and he wore an Armani suit that was fifteen hundred dollars off the rack, minimum.

"Let me handle him," Benno said softly to Drummond.

"You bet your sweet ass," she said from one side of her mouth.

Then the detectives descended the two steps down
to the lower level. Stein didn't ask them to sit. They
faced him standing, side by side.

"Who's this Payne person?" Stein demanded. His
face grew even redder. "I thought we'd straightened
you two out at my client's home the other night."
Visible behind him through his floor-to-ceiling window, Dallas stretched off into the distance: Reunion
Tower, the Federal Building, the Cadiz Street Viaduct
leading to Oak Cliff and points south.

Benno feigned surprise. "You mean you don't have
an Uncle Eddie?"

Stein picked up his phone. "I'm calling Randy
Dunce," he said and punched a couple of numbers in.
"See what the DA has to say about all this nonsense."

"His name is Dunst." Benno sort of chuckled.
"Hey, didn't mean to upset you, Mr. Stein. Just sort
of joking around about, you know, Uncle Eddie."

"Okay. Ha-ha. I'm busy. Good-bye."

"Hey, I'm sure you are. Got time for a few
questions?"

"Hell no." Stein peered beyond them. "Where's
Diane?" He raised his voice. "Diane, would you show
these people to the—"

"My first question is," Benno cut in, "if you don't
know Uncle Eddie Payne, why did you have your assistant show us in?" He watched the lawyer for a
reaction.

And Benno got more than he'd bargained for. Stein
looked at the call slip as if stupefied. He squinched
his eyes together, then sat down and put his glasses
on. The glasses had stainless steel frames. "I don't
know any . . ." He began, then trailed off. He looked
vacantly out the window.

"See, my thought was," Benno said, "that when I
gave that name at your front desk you'd come back

with something like, Who the hell is Uncle Eddie Payne? But you have us ushered in, no fuss, no bother. And here I was all ready to cross you off our list."

Stein had clipped gray eyebrows and a heavy face with sagging jowls. "What list?" He did his best to sound snappish, but came across as terrified.

"Oh hell, Steinsy, we got all kinds of lists," Benno said. "Suspect lists. Accomplice lists. Lawyer lists. You're on all of 'em." Stein's chin had lifted at the use of his nickname. Benno said, "That's right, we talked to Morgan Masters at the Doubletree, after the guy tried to shoot her. Funny you weren't there, being as how you're representing her. Or maybe you're not. Maybe you're really not her lawyer, but someone else's. Look, you haven't invited us to sit, and Detective Drummond and I are getting tired of standing up." He took a wing chair across from Stein. Drummond sat beside him, looking relieved.

Stein tried to rally. "This isn't the place to be throwing your weight around, Officers."

Benno hesitated. There were times for backing off and times for ratcheting up the pressure. He decided to plunge ahead. "I think you already know that Morgan's not a suspect any longer, which will disappoint your real client, Morgan's mother."

"Are you accusing me of some conflict of interest? Do you know how long I've practiced law in this city?"

"Long enough to know how to fuck people. And no, we're not talking anything as small as conflict of interest. A lot depends on whether you knew Uncle Eddie Payne before LaVon Masters had him kill her husband back in 'seventy-two, or whether you met him later when you pulled whatever legal shenanigans you could in order to get Harry Masters' money into LaVon's bank account. We don't know if you're an accessory to murder or just an accessory to probate fraud.''

Stein sputtered and began to hem and haw. "Anything that remote, the statutes of limitations—"

"Have already run," Benno said. "Or at least you hope like hell they have. But I'm not sure. Conspiracy's different, and if the conspiracy continues to exist today . . . I think even Randy Dunst could research that one. Maybe you should go ahead and call him."

Stein hung up his phone as if the instrument was suddenly red-hot. "Maybe if you'd ask some legitimate questions instead of throwing out all these accusations."

Benno was feeling pretty sure of himself. He winked at Drummond, then pointed a finger at Stein. "Okay. Legitimate question number one: Where have you hidden Harry Masters' will?"

Stein thrust his jaw forward. "How do you know he even had a will?"

"I don't," Benno said. "But you do, since you entered it into probate and then withdrew it."

Stein jabbed at empty air. "Now there's nothing out of line about that. After we admitted the will, we discovered there was a . . ." He trailed off. He looked like a man not used to having his foot in his mouth.

Benno watched Stein. Drummond uncrossed and then recrossed her legs.

"Codicil," Stein finished weakly.

"Now you're over my head," Benno said. "Detective Drummond, what the hell is a codicil?"

Drummond kept on staring at the lawyer. "An amendment," she said. "Something Harry Masters did to change the provisions."

"Ah, this legal crap," Benno said. "If it's an amendment, why don't they just call it that? Okay, Steinsy, your turn. Where's the codicil? Or if you remember what it says, that'll do."

"That," Stein said, more calmly now, "would be privileged."

"Damn." Benno snapped his fingers. "You win, Tina. That's just what Detective Drummond told me you'd do, Steinsy, holler privilege. It's a shame. All these bodies laying around, you obviously right in the middle of whatever's going on, and, *boom,* all you got to do is yell privilege and we're right back where we started. Except for one little thing. What was privileged between you and Harry Masters isn't privileged between you and *LaVon* Masters. Detective Drummond, am I saying it right?"

"You're a little too verbal," Drummond said. "But yeah."

"Aw come on, Steinsy's a lawyer," Benno said. "He's used to verbal. And one more thing. There's damned sure no privilege between you and Uncle Eddie Payne. See, your problem is, you got too many people you're claiming attorney/client relationships with. Somewhere in there you quit being the lawyer and became one of the gang."

"You keep referring to this Uncle Eddie person," Stein said.

"The guy you never heard of, but had ushered into your office? He killed Harry Masters and fucked LaVon silly, at least silly enough so that she agreed to do something pretty drastic to keep him from testifying at her trial. And you know what that something was, Steinsy, don't you?"

Benno didn't like Stein's expression. He'd caught the lawyer off-guard, bulling his way in with the Uncle Eddie alias, but now the shock was wearing off. Stein was now thinking on his feet. Benno could practically see the wheels turning. He had to do something to put the lawyer off his guard once again.

Stein opened his mouth, clearly ready to tell the officers to go fuck themselves.

Benno said quickly, "You know Uncle Eddie's dead, don't you?" On his left, Drummond gasped out loud. Benno wanted to tell her he knew what he was doing, but he wasn't too sure that he did. He was firing blind.

But he had just hit the mark. Air whooshed out of Stein's lungs. The lawyer deflated like a punctured tire. He rocked back in his chair like a fighter on the ropes.

Benno kept on coming. "Sure you know it. I'm not sure if you helped chop his body up and stuff him in Morgan's trunk, but you do know he's dead."

Stein's gaze was vacantly out the window. "I didn't have a damned thing to do with that," he said. "If Uncle Eddie was the body in Morgan's car, this is the first I've heard of it."

Benno wondered if that could be true. He said, "Look at me, Steinsy."

Stein swiveled his head like a man in a trance. His look was now pleading. "I didn't know."

"One jig is already up," Benno said. "That's the one back in the seventies, where you made some kind of under-the-table deal with Uncle Eddie so he wouldn't finger LaVon on the witness stand. Whatever dirty money you got on that transaction is ancient history, but it's connected to what's happening right here, right now. There is a guy running around killing people. For all we know, you're next. Now I'm about to ask and you're about to answer. Or if you don't, Randy Dunst will indeed be out here with a herd of lawyers a whole lot smarter than he is, and the entire county DA's staff is going to go to work on you. If you think you can buck all that, have at it."

Stein licked his lips. He said, "Uncle Eddie Payne had his own lawyer."

"Yeah, we know. A guy named Emmitt Colvin, who's now dead. Please don't tell us we're going to need a séance."

"Let me explain something," Stein said. "I have represented LaVon for decades. I have done things that might've stretched ethics a bit. Those people have so much money . . ."

Benno sat menacingly forward. "Goddammit, Steinsy, no moral soul-searching. We don't care if you were torn between right and wrong, if you went to confession, or any of that shit. We only care what you did, and what you know about what other people did. What did LaVon give Uncle Eddie so he wouldn't testify?"

Stein spread his hands in supplication. "I don't know. That's what I'm trying to tell you. I represented LaVon, both in the probating of Harry's will and the murder charges. As for the will . . . Well, I filed it without the codicil. The codicil was quite a bit more than just an amendment. It completely changed the distribution of the estate. Harry'd decided to leave everything in trust for his daughter. When I discovered the codicil among Harry's personal papers, I withdrew the will from probate. Copies of both the will and the codicil are in my personal safe deposit box. I thought they should be accessible in the event that I might need them sometime in the future. I guess the future is now."

"And in return for you hiding the will and codicil," Benno said, "LaVon jacked hell out of your fee."

Stein looked ready to burst. "I was just getting

started as a lawyer. I'd inherited my grandfather's practice, a drawer full of indigent client files. Grandpa had accounts receivable up to here and zero cash in the bank. So, Christ, yeah, I needed the money back then. You get into these things, you get deeper and deeper."

"You sound just like the assholes in the penitentiary," Benno said. He lowered his chin and deepened his voice. "I'd ah never done it if ah hadn't been in a tight, Judge." He returned to his normal tone. "So Morgan's the one with the money, but she doesn't know it. How the hell did you pull that off and keep LaVon in control of the estate?"

"Through trusteeship," Stein said. "Officially, LaVon is Morgan's trustee, but the trust doesn't exist unless the will goes into probate. If everything goes according to plan, there will never be any need to expose the will. The trust satisfies the terms of the will. Officially the money is Morgan's, and all of it passes to her on her thirtieth birthday. There is an account set up in the name of the trust, and LaVon issues a check every month. I give the funds to Morgan after passing them through my legal trust account. Morgan doesn't know the source of the funds. She asked once, and I told her I'd have to get LaVon's permission to tell her. She's never inquired again."

Benno searched his memory bank. "I think Morgan's twenty-nine, isn't she?"

Stein looked down, then back up. "She'll be thirty in April."

"At which point LaVon goes broke?"

"Not entirely. There are provisions for her lifelong care. But basically she relinquishes control over the assets."

"And if Morgan's not around?"

"I did the planning on Harry's behalf, Detective.

It's all set up with Morgan in mind. There are even provisions for her care if she becomes incompetent. For example, if Morgan were, say, committed to some institution, the trust would shift the assets to that institution's control until Morgan's release. In the event of Morgan's death before the age of thirty, LaVon officially becomes a very rich woman."

"And you and LaVon are aware of all these provisions, but Morgan isn't?"

Stein fiddled nervously with his tie.

"I think you got too many irons in the fire, Steinsy," Benno said. "Let's switch from the dirty little deal to the dirty *big* deal. You claim you don't know what deal LaVon made with Uncle Eddie so he wouldn't testify. How can that be, since you represented her in the murder?"

"That's simple. LaVon didn't tell me, and I don't think Uncle Eddie's own lawyer knew the details. Frankly, after Uncle Eddie appeared before the grand jury, I thought LaVon was toast. I was negotiating with the DA for any kind of plea bargain they'd offer, which at that point was zero. I do know that two days before trial, Uncle Eddie and LaVon talked at length. Then he did a one-eighty on the witness stand. I never asked why. My skirts were clean. I didn't suborn perjury because Uncle Eddie wasn't my witness. He was the prosecution's. Look, I may have gone through life like one of the monkeys with their paws over their eyes, mouths, and ears, but I'm not an idiot. What I don't know, I can't tell."

Benno watched Stein closely. The lawyer's story made sense. "What about LaVon's second kid? What do you know about him?" Benno asked.

"I didn't even know the child was a boy. I thought LaVon's secret delivery was something no one could ever find out. How could you possibly know about it?"

Benno felt Drummond's gaze on him. He only knew about the second child because Jessica Baldwin had told him that Morgan talked about her brother all the time. Simple as that. Benno said, "Morgan knows." He wasn't lying, not exactly; he was only omitting Jessica's role as the messenger.

Stein's surprise looked genuine. He removed his glasses. "How could she? She was only two years old, and LaVon didn't keep that other baby around more than a day or two before she gave it up for adoption."

Benno looked at Drummond for help. Drummond moved up closer to Stein's desk. "We think LaVon's other child may have surfaced, Mr. Stein. He might have killed a guy out in Irving, the same stripper Morgan took to Louisiana. And the same person shot two DA's investigators last night at the Doubletree. We think he was aiming at Morgan, and we also think he murdered Uncle Eddie Payne."

Stein slowly shook his head. "I wish I could help you, but . . . that guy who was with Morgan at her house is dead?"

"Yeah," Benno said. "Poor Zorro. Not that I want you breaking down in grief, Steinsy. You didn't help LaVon with that adoption?"

"I didn't get involved. I didn't want to be involved. And I can't really say anyone adopted the child for certain. All I know is, LaVon was pregnant with Uncle Eddie Payne's child. She had the baby. The baby disappeared. I never asked what happened to it."

"Okay, say we buy that. Who *would* know the details about the birth?"

"LaVon and whoever helped her get rid of it. Possibly Uncle Eddie, since the baby was his. Tie me up and whip me with a cat-o'-nine-tails, Officers. I can't tell you what I don't know."

Benno thought about the chauffeur the old cop had

told them about, the man Rubin was trying to locate. "You ever know anyone named Oscar Valdez?" Benno asked. "Word is, he was LaVon's chauffeur back then."

"I could have known him. Domestics come and go."

"Sounds to me like you've been pretty selective in what you know and don't know," Benno said.

"My profession dictates that I not be aware of certain things. You'd have to ask LaVon if you want to know about that child."

"And she'd refer us to her lawyer," Benno said. "Who is you."

Stein spread his hands.

"Where is LaVon Masters now, Mr. Stein?"

"At this moment? At home, hosting a party for the Dallas Art Society."

"Oh Jesus," Drummond said, "that woman is such a philanthropist."

"She enjoys the role," Stein said.

"Well, she may not enjoy it today. I'm afraid we'll have to crash her party." Drummond stood, then said pointedly, "Unannounced."

"Don't look at me," Stein said. "I'm not about to blow the whistle."

Drummond smiled sweetly. "Oh, I know you're not. If you do, we'll be back for another visit. If you warn her we're coming, that's obstruction. You know it and we know it, and if LaVon even hints that she knew we were coming in advance, your ass is going to jail. And don't worry. We'll just go in disguised as a couple of potential big-time donors referred by you. LaVon will love it. Hell, Steinsy, she might even double your fee."

20

Drummond and Benno hustled back to the lot where they'd stowed the county Mercury sedan. As Benno climbed behind the wheel, Drummond hopped in front and said, "You think that Stein's gonna call her?"

"He might. Depends on whether he's more scared of LaVon or jail. In his case it's probably a toss-up. That's why we have to get there while the party's in progress. Even if she knows we're coming, she won't be able to do anything about it with all those high-toned guests around."

"So let's haul ass," Drummond said.

As Benno followed the exit signs down to the toll-booth, he used his cell to call Jeff Rubin. Rubin clicked on and said, "You haven't called your father. I got another message here."

Benno slowed behind a line of cars waiting to pay, then turned right onto Akard Street. "Well, the day isn't over yet. We may need a search warrant for LaVon Masters' home."

"Now we're getting somewhere. Based on what?"

"Based on . . . Oh hell."

" 'Oh hell' isn't good."

"Well, based on knowledge we have that she's concealed her husband's final will and testament along with a codicil. Her lawyer has a copy in a safe deposit box, but we need the original. But the will and codicil would only be evidence pertaining to Harry Masters' killing in the seventies. It'd be a stretch to make it have anything to do with these current murders."

"She's already been to trial for offing Harry," Rubin said. "Double jeopardy."

"That's why I said, 'Oh hell.' All these people getting dead now are somehow involved in a killing over twenty-five years ago, and whatever's in that codicil has something to do with it. So we gotta see the will and the codicil. We already know that Morgan inherits everything when she turns thirty, which is next year, and which also gives LaVon *beaucoup* motive for what's happening here. I'll lay it out to Randy Dunst. Maybe he can pull off some legal somersaults to make it all fit. We need to go through LaVon's things, Chief."

"Randy Dunst can barely put on his clothes without help. How's he going to make anything fit in a legal brief?"

An SUV finished paying at the booth and moved on into traffic. Benno moved up a notch in line. "Dunst isn't much, but he's all we've got. I don't suppose you've located Valdez, the chauffeur."

"You are not exhibiting sufficient faith in your old cousin. I have indeed located the guy in Waxahachie, thirty miles south of here. He retired to the country five years ago. He wouldn't discuss his employment with LaVon Masters over the phone, but he's agreed to meet. He's on his way in as we speak. Where are you, and where are you headed?"

"We're leaving Harold Stein's office headed for La-

Von's house. That warrant would be nice to take along."

"Impossible, until I talk to the chauffeur. A warrant's not even a cinch after that, unless Valdez gives us something to hang our hats on. Does that car you're driving have a fax machine?"

Benno peered over his shoulder. There was indeed a fax on a backseat floorboard, activated by plugging it into a socket on the dash and then attaching the connector intended for the car phone. "Yeah," Benno said.

"Okay. As soon as I talk to Valdez, I'll call you. If he gives us anything we can take to a judge, I'll rush it through and fax you the warrant. It's the best I can do."

It was Benno's turn to pay at the booth. He pulled up to the window and indicated the free-pass county sticker on the Mercury's windshield, then waited with the motor running while the attendant copied the sticker number down. "If it's the best you can do, Chief, it's the best you can do," Benno said. "But try to do better. We really need the warrant, okay?"

Benno followed the traffic flow north on Akard, and pulled to the curb just short of the exit from Thanksgiving Tower parking to wait for a red light. The Merc was blocking the curbside lane, and a Volkswagen behind him tooted its horn. Benno stuck the flasher on his roof and activated his emergency blinkers. The Volkswagen went around him, nearly sideswiping a Cadillac in the process. The VW's driver, a woman with peroxide-blond hair, stared daggers as she drove past. Benno grinned and waved at the woman.

He drummed his fingers on the steering wheel. The case was a hodgepodge of past and present. Too many characters involved from too many different eras:

Uncle Eddie and LaVon from the seventies, Morgan and Zorro from today. Simple murders were easier: Woman shoots husband, husband shoots lover, passion turns to hatred; domestic cases, easy to figure out and zero in on the perpetrator. There was nothing domestic about this one—everybody involved hated each other. Morgan despised her mother and Stein despised his client. Everybody was capable of killing everyone else. The killer was possibly connected to the Masters clan, possibly not. Possibly Morgan's younger brother, though what could be his motive? Benno had no reason to think the killer was the missing brother, other than that the brother got sent out for adoption a quarter century ago. Judging by what Benno'd learned about LaVon Masters, abandonment might not have been such a bad deal for the kid.

Benno felt like he needed a vacation. That feeling was good and meant that he'd been working hard. Back in LA, he'd always felt like he needed time off, though he'd never taken any as long as the case went unsolved. Being a cop was what he did. Vacations were for guys with office jobs.

His cell phone buzzed. He picked it up, pressed the button, and said his name into the mouthpiece.

Jessica Baldwin said, "How's your back? I scratched you pretty hard."

Benno sat up straighter in the seat. "Sore. Did you get my message?" He glanced nervously at Drummond, who cocked her head and lifted an eyebrow.

"Of course," Jessica said. "Didn't you get mine?"

Benno flipped the phone and looked at his monitor. He activated the scroll-down button. There were three messages. One from Jessica, one from Drummond yesterday, another from ANONYMOUS, probably a telemarketer. He said, "Jesus, I'm sorry. I haven't checked."

"I'm so flattered. When I get you alone, I may whip you silly."

"I'm not into that," Benno said. "Look, are you going to drop in on Morgan?"

"Later. I've already talked to her on the phone and she knows I'm coming. She's also heard from her brother."

Benno had a flash of panic. Uniformed cops all over Morgan's place, yet no one had bothered to put a recorder on her phone. There were lots of directions in which to point the accusing finger, but the phone recorder was ultimately Benno's responsibility since he was lead investigator. He didn't care who received the blame for the foul-up; Benno was a cop who only gave a damn about results. Lack of a recorder on Morgan's line was a fuck-up he never would have committed on the job back in California. "I don't guess we're lucky enough that he told her his whereabouts," he said.

"No, but he did tell her he'd killed some people. She's frightened practically to death, Benno. And I don't feel all that easy about waltzing into her house under the circumstances. Do you think you could meet me there? I'd as soon have a guard while I go in and talk to her."

Benno checked the dashboard clock. "I might could later. Look, you won't be in any danger. There's armed cops all over the place. How soon can you get by to talk to her? It's important."

"In an hour or two." Her voice took on a pleading tone. "I really want people there. Where are you, anyway?"

The light turned green, and Benno rolled forward with his right turn blinker on. "Downtown. Headed for Highland Park. Look, this murder case is popping all over."

"Highland Park?" Jessica said. "You're going to Morgan's mother's house? What for?"

Benno hesitated. He'd gotten her much more mixed up in this case than he'd intended. He considered telling her to forget about seeing Morgan; it would be all he needed to include a civilian casualty to go along with the DA's investigator in the morgue. But Morgan had to start remembering things, and Jessica Baldwin seemed the only answer to help Morgan do so. Benno said, "I'm putting both of us out on a limb. What I'm about to tell you I'm not supposed to tell anyone outside the department. LaVon Masters pulled a lot of shit over twenty-five years ago that's the key to figuring out what's going on today. We have to put heat on her, and right now. I'm asking you to pick Morgan's brain for me. That's just as important as what I'm going to do at LaVon's. But you don't have to. None of this is really your problem, Jessica. If you want to back out, I don't blame you."

"I don't plan to back out of anything. How many cops are at Morgan's again?"

"Four. If they're doing their jobs, one will cover each side of the house. These guys aren't above meeting in the garden for a cup of coffee and a bull session, but normally uniforms are pretty good. Still, this guy's not going to stop at killing cops to get in at Morgan. Do you have a gun?"

"Yes. Carrying one while I'm visiting crime victims is never a bad idea. Occasionally a bad guy might still be after them. I've never had to use it, but—"

"Take it along, and carry it on your person when you go in. I wouldn't let you go to Morgan's if I thought there was really a whole lot to fear, but you gotta be cautious. I think LaVon Masters knows how to contact the killer, if she's not in fact a part of the murder plot herself. Morgan's very likely got infor-

mation stored inside her head that will help us track
the guy down, if you can pry it out of her. I'll come
to Morgan's place the second we're finished with
LaVon."

"How long will you be?" Jessica asked.

"Two or three hours. Four at the outside, considering the drive from Highland Park up to Plano."

"Okay. I'll be there when you come."

"I owe you. No kidding."

Jessica gave a sudden throaty laugh. "And don't
think I won't collect, buster. Maybe we can hash it
out tonight in some way. See you there." She disconnected.

Benno dropped his cell on the seat just as Drummond said, "This is a suspicious circumstance. We're
not supposed to tell God Himself what's going on, but
you're filling this woman in on everything. I'm beginning to think the way to your heart is directly through
your crotch."

"I'm selective in dispensing information."

"Sure. A sixty-year-old fat guy could never pry anything out of you."

Benno'd never been to Highland Park, so he let
Drummond direct him through the city until they entered an area of million-dollar-plus homes. Unlike
new-rich Plano, this neighborhood reeked of old-time
money and reminded Benno of certain sections of
Beverly Hills in LA, where the Gables, Bogarts, and
Garbos had lived in the thirties and forties. Lawns
were gigantic. The houses stood great distances from
the streets, and there were fountains and tall stone
walls in every direction. They passed the kind of manicured country club golf course where everyone fixes
their divots and no one yells, *"Fuck!"* after blowing a
short one. Then they drove over a bridge spanning a

wide deep creek with elms and sycamores growing along its banks in sixty-degree winter sunshine. Drummond directed him down a side street, and they stopped in front of a three-story Colonial with a circular drive and water-spewing cherubs surrounding a fountain. The driveway was full of cars: Mercedes, Porsches, Lincoln and Cadillac SUVs. Expensive autos also lined the street on both sides for half a block in either direction. Benno backed up and parked off the road in front of the creekbank. The detectives got out, crossed over, hurried up the exposed aggregate circular drive, and climbed up on the porch. There was a huge front door with an ornate knocker. Benno found the button and rang the bell.

He needn't have bothered. He'd barely removed his thumb from the button when the door opened and three women came out, lugging coats. Two were overweight, one grossly so, and the other woman was thin as a bulimic. All looked rich, in dresses and heels, and two of the coats bore Neiman's labels. The heaviest of the three wore a glittering diamond necklace. The bulimic was exhibiting a jade bracelet and telling the other two that her husband had brought it from Rome. They nodded, smiled as they passed, and didn't bother to shut the door. Benno and Drummond entered the house and walked in between two pewter urns.

The party was obviously breaking up. Four more women left as the detectives strolled toward the back of the house, stopping to glance at a couple of Egyptian statues and three paintings on the way. One of the oils was a portrait by Dimitri Vail: Steve McQueen in buckskin, fanning his rifle, a scene from the sixties television show *Wanted Dead or Alive,* the series that had transformed McQueen from a nobody into a star. The corridor led to a huge carpeted room set up for a meeting—about fifty padded folding chairs grouped in front of a podium mounted on a removable dais. Richly dressed women made small talk, drinking champagne from dainty stemmed glasses. A couple of jacketed waiters wandered around, collecting the empties. Benno overheard one lady tell a group that she considered her Dali a steal at eighty-four-seven. Drummond looked over her shoulder at Benno and rolled her eyes.

Double French doors opened onto what was obviously a study. Visible through the doorway, LaVon Masters sat in front of a rolltop desk as she entertained four enraptured guests who were sipping champagne. Benno recognized LaVon from her pictures in the newspaper archives and didn't think she looked much older than her photos from decades ago. The resemblance to Morgan was striking; the slightly tilted nose, pointed chin, and smooth round cheeks that, at LaVon's age, had to be pumped with collagen. The blond hair looked as close to natural as possible. She was dressed in a pantsuit whose trousers were snug around tight hips and slim muscular legs. Benno wondered what the woman's bill for cosmetic surgeons and personal trainers might be. Her audience consisted of three ladies in pricey dresses, along with the only man Benno'd seen in the house thus far—other than the waiters. The man wore a snazzy gray suit and looked in his sixties, with perfectly fixed snow-white hair. One of the women handed him a book, which he opened and signed inside the cover. Benno decided that the guy must be the guest of honor, who'd lectured from the now-vacant podium in the larger room. The book had a picture of a flower garden on the cover.

Benno nudged Drummond and nodded his head toward LaVon. "You still think she's too old to bang Zorro?"

Drummond managed to look impressed, unusual for

her. "She could give it a hell of a go," she said. "I do hate to go busting in right now, with all those people around." She snatched a glass of champagne from a tray that one of the waiters carried, sipped, and made a face. She then walked over to one side and did a double take, peering down another hallway. "Jesus, Benno. Come and get a load of what she's got back here."

Benno followed Drummond down a corridor lined with still more paintings, and passed more groups of party guests who were admiring the artists' work. Thirty steps along, the corridor opened up into a greenhouse. Drummond quickened her pace, and the detectives went in among the flowers and greenery.

The foliage was pretty stunning. There were yellow, red, and pink roses, and a bed of caladiums. All along one glass wall, gay impatiens grew. The sun beat down on the glassed-in roof, and a round thermometer showed the temperature to be a steamy eighty degrees. There were four or five women inside the greenhouse, downing champagne as they chatted botany. Benno and Drummond strolled to the back and peered out into the yard.

The grass outside was winter dead, though perfectly clipped and edged, and there were two rose gardens showing bare thorny branches waving in the breeze. The sidewalk led to an eight-foot-high stockade fence in back. Visible over the top of the fence, elms and sycamores showed bare twisted branches like witches' claws. Benno said, "Quite a layout, huh?" Then, receiving no answer, he looked over his shoulder and said, "Quite a—"

Drummond was gone.

Benno backed away and peered up an aisle with greenery and flowers on either side. Drummond was about halfway to the house entry, looking enthralled.

Her champagne glass was at waist level and her lips were parted. Benno went up and asked her what was going on.

"Ever see anything like those before?" Drummond said.

Benno followed his partner's gaze. She was looking at a six-foot-high plant with purple flowers sprouting from the branches. The flowers were shaped like oversized roses. The petals were pale around the edges, and deepened in color nearer the stalk. Benno scratched his head. "Jesus, they're—"

"Voodoo lilies," Drummond said. "That forensics guy gave a good description of the main bush, huh?" She offered her glass, and when Benno took it she leaned over and sniffed. "Motherfuckers stink like hell," she said. "And look, a couple of those branches are clipped. I wonder . . ."

As Benno stood holding the champagne glass, Drummond peered surreptitiously up and down the aisle. There were two women talking near the exit leading to the house, but otherwise the detectives were alone. Drummond grasped a stem near the base of one of the flowers, broke it off, and jammed the lily into her pocket. She snatched her glass from Benno's hand, drained it, and wrinkled her nose at him. "If those stinkers are as rare as the lab guy said they were," Drummond said, "and if old LaVon refuses to cooperate, we've got the same rare plant here that was in Zorro's car. Quite a coincidence, huh? I'm thinking grounds for a search warrant, babe. How 'bout you?"

When the detectives returned to the main house, the party had broken up for real. In the meeting room, three waiters hustled around folding up chairs and stacking them in the corner, while two men in coveralls worked with wrenches tearing the dais down. The double French doors were still open but the study was empty, save for a Hispanic maid using a feather duster. Benno and Drummond went down the corridor past the portrait of Steve McQueen and into the entry hall. LaVon Masters stood by the door in between the pewter urns, pressing flesh with stragglers who were slow to leave.

LaVon was saying, "So glad y'all could make it. So glad, really. You come back to see me, now." She shook hands with a heavyset woman wearing a fox stole and turned to do the same with a tall lady with blue-white hair.

The detectives exchanged a look. Drummond nodded, then went up and touched LaVon Masters on the arm. LaVon turned and showed a quizzical smile. Drummond said softly, "We're Metro detectives, Mrs. Masters, that gentleman and I. Can we have a word?"

The smile froze on the older woman's face, and in a fraction of a second she seemed to age a dozen years. Then her features softened and the gentle look returned. She looked back to her departing guests. "Can y'all excuse me for a minute?" She stepped over in between Benno and Drummond, frowned, and hissed, "You got a lotta fuckin' nerve comin' in here uninvited. What the hell do you want?"

Drummond kept her cool and looked LaVon in the eye. "We won't take much of your time."

LaVon eyed Drummond, head to toe. "You won't take *any* of my time, honeybun. Can't you see that I'm entertainin' here?"

Drummond's spine straightened, almost imperceptibly. She glanced at the women waiting at the door for their hostess, then stepped up close to LaVon. "I can see that, lady," Drummond snapped. "What you can't see is, we're *investigatin'* here. Investigating you. You can talk to us about Uncle Eddie Payne, along with some other stuff, right now, or you can wait and tell it to a judge. Your choice, Madame Masters. What's it going to be?"

LaVon staggered in place. She drew a deep breath and let it out. She turned halfway back toward the departing guests, then faced Drummond once more. LaVon's face was suddenly ashen. "In my study," she finally said. "Wait back yonder in my study. Do I need my lawyer?"

Drummond smiled sweetly. "You mean old Steinsy? Oh, we've already spoken with him. And if you're asking me, Harold Stein would be in the way. We'll wait for you in your study, Mrs. Masters, until you finish bidding those people goodbye. You don't take too long now, *honeybun*."

Benno cooled his heels in an overstuffed chair while Drummond stalked around LaVon Masters' study, steamed to the gills. She paced this way and that, picking up shelf items, putting them down, worrying with her skirt and then her hair. "Honeybun's ass," she muttered. "I'll honeybun her, the damned ol'—"

"You're blowing your cool, Tina," Benno said.

"Fuckin' A," Drummond said. "Wait'll I get the bitch alone."

The words were barely out of Drummond's mouth when LaVon came in, walking fast. Benno studied the woman, the set to her mouth, the firmness of her stride, the total lack of fear in her look. She looked like one tough old bitch, Benno thought. Drummond whirled from a bookcase where she'd just picked up a glass goblet. Benno decided he'd better get it in gear before Drummond smashed the goblet over LaVon's head. He got up quickly and said, "Have a seat, Mrs. Masters." He kept his tone friendly but firm.

She went to her rolltop desk and flowed into a chair. Drummond set the goblet down and stood menacingly near LaVon. Benno shook his head and pointed to a sofa. Drummond sat down, looking pissed. Benno watched his partner in puzzlement; in other situations—the interview with Makepiece at the county jail, the time they'd grilled Zorro at Morgan Masters' place—she'd been cool under pressure, and Benno had yet to see a chink in Drummond's armor. He thought he had the answer to Drummond's current behavior. When Drummond's antagonist was a woman, her demeanor changed. Benno mentally filed the information away for future reference, then concentrated on LaVon.

Benno leaned forward and rested his forearms on his thighs. "I'm Detective Benno, and this is my partner, Detective Drummond. We are on an intensive murder investigation here, and I'll tell you we're bypassing a lot of the usual protocol because we think more lives may be in danger. As far as we know, one of the lives could be yours. I'll also advise you that you are on our list of suspects and that you may want to terminate this meeting until your lawyer can be present. If you choose to do so, you will need an attorney other than Harold Stein. As Detective Drummond told you in the entry hall, we've already interviewed Mr. Stein and consider him a suspect as well. We won't recognize him as a go-between."

Benno was pleased with his opening remarks, most of which were lies. The detectives had no legal basis for being here, something a lawyer would tell LaVon in a heartbeat. And suspect or not, if Harold Stein were to show up, the cops would have to respect his presence. Working with little or no ammunition, Benno'd let the bullshit roll trippingly off his tongue.

LaVon picked up a pen from her desk, set it back down. Her fingers were trembling slightly. She said, "Cops have talked to me before, hon."

"I know that, Mrs. Masters. I will tell you what else we know, and our reason for being here. Your dead husband left a will with a codicil. We want to see it. We believe there is something in its contents that might help us find the person or persons responsible for three murders in the past week and who may very well be responsible for more murders in the future. I'm sure you know that whatever happened more than twenty-five years ago is a dead issue and that you're not in any danger of repercussion in that regard. In the current circumstance, though, I can't promise you any safety net. If you give us the documents, you will have to sign a statement that you understand all of what I'm telling you."

LaVon chuckled nervously and fiddled with the pen once more. "If you're sayin' this will exists, and I'm not agreein' with you that it does, but if you're sayin' it exists and can cause me problems, why would I want to give it to you?"

Benno kept his gaze steady. "Your daughter may be on the killer's list, for one thing."

LaVon seemed a little confused. She said, "You mean Morgan?"

"Yes."

LaVon's eyes were like bright blue flints. "That little bitch doesn't act like any daughter to me. Why would I care about that?"

Benno coughed to hide his surprise. A daughter despising her mother was one thing. It was rare, but it happened. A mother hating her own offspring, and openly admitting the animosity, was something he'd never seen before. Whatever secret flowed between these two women must be something else. Benno said,

"Well, you might want to protect yourself, Mrs. Masters."

The surprise factor was wearing off. LaVon's chin was set in a regal tilt. "I'm sure as hell not in any danger from anybody. You're bluffin' to beat hell, sugar. I'm not showin' you a damned thing."

Benno studied her. The ploy hadn't worked. He didn't know why he'd ever thought it might. This woman had spat in the system's face over a quarter century ago and gotten away with it. Success brewed confidence. He and Drummond were wasting their time. Even if Dunst could figure out a loophole to get a warrant, Benno doubted if the papers would be anywhere on LaVon's premises. If she hadn't destroyed them years ago, she'd certainly do so now. Benno opened his mouth, ready to end the interview.

From her seat on the couch, Drummond said, "What about your other kid, *sugar*?"

Benno's head jerked in surprise. At the same time, LaVon's features rearranged themselves like Play-Doh. Her mouth twisted. Her head went down, then came back up. She swiveled her chair toward Drummond. LaVon's features relaxed, and she looked self-assured once again.

"What kid is that?" LaVon said.

Drummond stood up. "The one you got rid of. Uncle Eddie Payne's kid. If you think Morgan hates your guts, what about your abandoned child?"

Benno's first reaction was to cut Drummond off and get her out of here. But why? His own attempt had failed, so why not let his partner have a go? He sat unmoving and watched the two women.

LaVon looked at the wall. She blew air from between her lips. She said, almost to herself, "Boy, Steinsy really did spill his insides." She glared at Drummond. "That's none of your damned business."

Drummond walked closer to the older woman. "Let's be clear, LaVon. Everything about you is our business. We have dead people, one of whom we've got you fucking in a photo. The same guy who, less than twenty-four hours earlier, was over in Bossier City fucking your daughter and who also worked in a strip joint that you coincidentally own. We have evidence that between leaving Morgan's house and getting killed, this guy paid you a visit. Excuse me for being curious. Us cops like to know about things like that."

LaVon showed a twitch at the corner of her eye but otherwise remained stoic. She gave a dry laugh. "Why, I don't know what you're talkin' about. If you've got evidence that some man's been callin' on me, let me see it. Don't try to bullshit me, honeybun."

Benno's gaze automatically shifted to the pocket where Drummond had stuffed the voodoo lily.

Drummond said, "We have the evidence, LaVon. Trust me. Talk to us and show us what we want to see."

LaVon pushed away from her desk. She rested an elbow on an armrest and propped her chin on her lightly clenched fist. Now she looked amused. "You two are borin' me," she said. "Show yourselves out, will ya? For a pair like you, I wouldn't even send the fuckin' maid to the door."

Drummond sighed loudly in frustration and looked to her partner. Benno met Drummond's gaze and shrugged. Drummond nodded and jerked her head toward the exit.

As they walked down the drive toward their car, Drummond cut her eyes toward Benno and said, "Dunst?"

Benno had his hands jammed into his pockets. He grimly nodded. "It's our only chance," he said.

Drummond paused to look both ways before crossing the street, the Merc now visible across the way, parked alongside the creekbed. She stepped down from the curb. "Not much of one," she said.

21

Jessica Baldwin had never been so terrified. The blindfold blotted out all light, and the tape plastered over
her mouth forced her to breathe through her nose. To
make things worse her nasal passages were congested;
mucus dripped on her upper lip, ran down her face,
and wet her chin. There was a rough burlap bag over
her head, secured by a rope around her neck. The
cord wrapped around her wrists and ankles bit into
her flesh, and the pain made her whimper against her
gag. The bottoms of her feet felt as if they were on
fire. Every time the car turned a corner, centrifugal
force flung her against the spare tire. There were small
lacerations on her scalp where she'd banged her head
against the jack.

The driver jammed on the brakes and the car halted
with a squeal of rubber. Jessica rolled onto her back,
pinning her hands beneath her. Muffled inside the
trunk, she could hear the sound of the car door opening and then slamming shut. Jessica moaned through
her gag. A key scraped in the lock, and then the trunk
lid opened. Sunlight brightened the darkness inside

her blindfold. Hands like vises gripped both of her upper arms and pulled her toward the opening. She tried to scream, but all that came out was a muffled choking sound, thanks to the rags stuffed in her mouth.

Something hard jammed against her skull. She tightly shut her eyes, terrified. Panic welled in her throat as she heard the *click-click* of the gun's hammer going back. Then an explosion rocked the car and she smelled the faint odor of gunpowder. She lost consciousness as blood ran down the side of her head to soak her blouse. Then, for Jessica Baldwin, there was nothing but blackness and total silence. Mercifully, she felt no further pain.

LaVon Masters watched through the window drapes as the detectives hustled toward their car parked on Lakeside Drive, the tall athletic male cop walking alongside the small, lithe African-American woman. As the man climbed behind the wheel and the woman went around to the passenger side, LaVon let the curtain fall back into place. She thought that the tall cop was a sexy hunk and wondered what might get him off in bed. She'd wondered the same thing about nearly every man she'd met since she was twelve years old. Pleasing men in the sack was the best way to get them to do anything she wanted, so LaVon had become an expert at a very early age.

She thought the black woman had been a little bit on the uppity side, but she accepted the fact that modern coloreds were different from the Arkansas niggers she'd known in her youth and now considered themselves on equal footing with white people. And never mind which detective was a sexy man and which was an uppity nigger. Fuck 'em both. LaVon Masters had grown up in poverty, in the toughest part of Little Rock, and what she had she'd earned the hard way.

Police hadn't scared her before, and they didn't scare her now.

She went back down her corridor lined with paintings, and through the room where she'd hosted the Art Society group—a bunch of high-toned bitches so caught up in the idiot who'd written the gardening book that LaVon had expected them all to start in finger-fucking themselves while the old fart held the podium. She didn't know shit about art and even less about gardening; she only feigned interest in both because she had enough green to cover up her hard-scrabble background. She'd become a philanthropist on Harold Stein's advice, shortly after putting Harry in the ground. And she had hated every minute of it. Her donations to charity were all a front; the truth was that LaVon hadn't a charitable bone in her body. She liked the attention her donations brought her and got a charge out of seeing her name in the society pages, but if it wasn't for the publicity she never would have given a dime. She passed a photograph of herself and Harry, taken thirty years ago, dining along with a couple of movie stars. She remembered the evening well. After dinner, while Harry did business downtown, she'd taken one of the stars to bed and fucked him silly. She smiled at the memory.

The black detective had been right about one thing. The thought of LaVon's second kid being on the loose made her nervous. She wondered how much the police knew about her second pregnancy. If Harold Stein was their only source of information, then that was well and good, because Harold didn't really know shit about the kid. But if the truth ever got out, LaVon could be definitely screwed.

She interrupted the workmen and waiters in the middle of cleaning up after the party and told them all to leave and return tomorrow. They didn't argue, hurrying to put brooms and tools away. LaVon then dismissed the maid for the rest of the afternoon. She wanted the house to herself.

She climbed the stairs to her bedroom, pausing before the mirrors on the way up to pat her hair and adjust her clothing. Last night she'd stood naked in her bedroom and pinched an inch's thickness of skin around her waist. Her weight was up four and a half pounds. She had to get the trainer over and get her ass in gear. At fifty-eight, LaVon Masters could run four miles at a steady pace and do a thousand sit-ups. The older she got, the harder the workouts became, but she was determined to stay in shape until the day she fucking died.

Once inside her room she went to the walk-in closet and pulled a padlocked box from the very back of the shelf. The box was heavy, made of thick polished oak and inlaid with brass fittings, and LaVon grunted from exertion as she lugged it over to her bed. She dug through her bottom dresser drawer and located a key, unlocked the strongbox, and then carried some papers from within over to her vanity. She hadn't read over the documents in twenty years, but knew their contents as well as she knew her name. Just thinking about Harry and his will made her seethe. She'd never seen the papers until four days after Harry died, and if he hadn't placed copies with his banker—a man with old Republic National before it went broke and became part of the NationsBank chain—as well as with Harold Stein, she'd have burned the fucking things. The banker was now retired in California and Harold had used the leverage contained in the will to remain her attorney over the years, and both had kept their copies in safe and secret places. LaVon couldn't fault the bastards for keeping the copies. If they hadn't, they'd both be fucking dead.

Fuck Harry, the banker, and the lawyer, and above everyone else, fuck that goddamn Eddie Payne. Of all the events that had happened over the past few weeks, the thing that pleased LaVon the most was that Uncle Eddie was finally gone. But in the bastard's place, LaVon's secret kid had now returned to haunt her. If her luck hadn't been so rotten lately, she'd have no luck at all.

LaVon carefully read the will and codicil, searching for a loophole even though she knew she wouldn't find one. Goddamn Harry Masters all to hell. LaVon got up and paced her bedroom, so tense with worry that she failed to hear the doorbell ring downstairs. The visitor had to press the button several times before LaVon finally stalked down the steps to see who in hell was bothering her. Fuck the new visitor as well. Whoever stood on the porch pressing the button over and over, they were about to get a piece of LaVon's fucking mind.

The longer Morgan Masters stayed home under police guard, the antsier she became. Her skin was crawling. She'd even thought of suicide. She stalked from one end of her bedroom to the other. She smashed a glass against the wall. She pulled her own hair. It was difficult to breathe.

She looked down out of her window, watching the uniformed cop out back patrol the fence and pool area. As the sun had continued to shine and the air warmed during the day, the cop had stripped off his lined uniform jacket and hung the garment on the end of the diving board. Now he walked to and fro in front of the fence, one hand resting on the butt of his pistol in an old-time Western gunslinger's pose. His billed cap was tilted back on his head. The guy was obviously trying to look alert, but Morgan suspected that the cop was bored. Maybe all of them were bored to death—the guy in back, the two at either side of the house, and the man covering the front. If their attention wavered enough, maybe Morgan could get away. Go somewhere and party.

Stoney, her chocolate Lab, lay on the pool deck and watched the cop with interest. The cop had been back there all day, walking around, waiting for something to happen that, Morgan was sure, never would come to pass. Likely the officer needed something to spice up his day. Morgan thought about stripping down to her panties, standing at the window and flashing the guy. Anything to break the monotony.

Last night, after Detective Drummond had brought her home and then surrounded her with what seemed like half the fucking police force, Morgan had slept on the daybed shoved against the wall in the guest room. No way would she get a wink of sleep in her own bed, because that was where they'd found all the blood. Being upstairs in the house where someone had butchered a corpse into pieces was creepy as hell. Creepy, but somehow exciting. Morgan had stretched out on the daybed and imagined the killer in the bedroom, chopping away with an ax. At times she even envisioned herself as the killer. Once when she did that, she screamed out loud.

She wondered who the dead guy might be. She hadn't a clue. Her memory of the past week was so foggy she wasn't even sure at times where she'd gone or what she'd done. She vaguely remembered the trip to Bossier City with the nasty guy. She recalled patches of sex with the man, the video camera running, but her memory of the events was as if she'd only been an observer. A hidden watcher inside the room, staring in excitement while two strangers got it on.

She'd spent a lot of her time on the daybed trying

to sort her behavior out, just as Jessica Baldwin had suggested, but Morgan's mindset hadn't reached the point where she could deal with the facts. She understood that she had mental problems, and wanted desperately for the problems to go away. "Mental problems," she knew, was a fucking PC expression meaning that someone was crazy as hell.

Morgan was sick and tired of wondering whether she was insane. She'd never felt normal in her life. Ever since she could remember, she'd thought of herself as weird.

She'd tossed and turned on the daybed for more than half of the night and had watched the clock's digital numbers flash at three a.m. She must have fallen asleep shortly after that, because her next recollection came when she'd snapped awake at eight in the morning. She'd seen the clock at three and again at eight. So in between, she reasoned, she must have been asleep.

Somewhere in there she'd dreamed. The dreams were horrible. Morgan pressed her nails into the fleshy parts of her hands.

She'd been dreaming often lately. It scared her that the dreams might be subconscious recall of things that had really happened in her life. Jessica Baldwin spoke often of the relationship between dreams and reality. The thought that the things Morgan saw while asleep might actually have occurred made her insides quiver.

Her dreams involved being a little girl and sleeping alone in a gigantic room. The dream had sporadically repeated itself throughout her life—two or three times, in fact, within the past month or so—and sometimes when she was awake she could recall the details. Last week she'd told Jessica about the dreams. Jessica believed it would help for Morgan to remember everything she'd seen while asleep. Morgan had tried, but total recall was just too damned frightening.

In the dreams, a man would come to her. He was a thick-chested hairy man with liquor on his breath. As he slid into bed with her, he grunted and groaned. Sometimes in the dreams, Morgan believed the man was her father. At other times she thought he was her uncle. But she'd never had an uncle, and her father had died when she was too young to retain any memory of him.

Hadn't he?

Sometimes, Morgan wasn't sure. She needed for Jessica Baldwin to explain these things. She needed to recall her early childhood. But there was a barrier of some kind in her brain, blocking out the past. Jessica said that before she could be completely normal, she had to tear that barrier down.

But doing so was just too scary. That's why, when she was alone and would have snatches of memory, Morgan would do the unexplainable things she did to drive the demons away. Such as take off for Bossier City with the scuzzy guy. Such as bring a series of strangers home, tape them while they . . .

Morgan hugged her midsection. She had to do something to make herself happy. Maybe go downstairs and visit with the cops on the lawn. Maybe fix herself a drink. Maybe call the officers in and ask them to party. Maybe even fuck them all.

But sex never made her happy. In the aftermath of sex, she was always miserable. Often after one of her toots she cried for days.

She was certain of one thing. Normalcy was her goal, the ultimate pot at the end of the rainbow.

She went into the guest room and flopped down on the daybed. Earlier, on the phone, Jessica had told her she was coming by today. Until Jessica arrived and the two could talk things over, Morgan was afraid to move. Seeing Jessica would help, just as it always did.

Morgan Masters stretched out on the daybed and began to sob. She was so fucking tired of being insane.

22

Randy Dunst watched the voodoo lily as if he expected the flower to slither out of the Ziploc bag and piss in his eye. Finally he said, "Come again?"

Drummond left Dunst's desk, stalked halfway to the door, then came back waving her hands. "Sorry, Randy. I just don't see what's so fucking difficult. This is a rare-as-hens'-teeth flower, found growing in LaVon Masters' greenhouse. It is identical to the flower left on the floorboard of a murder victim's car. We would like a search warrant, sometime before this flower shrivels up and dies. We're talking apples and apples here."

Dunst pyramided his fingers under his chin. "Not quite the identical flower. The same *species* of flower. Try it this way. You bring me half of a Louisville Slugger found at one location, then bring me the other half of the same Louisville Slugger found someplace else, and the broken ends match, then we've got something to talk about. But you find one Louisville Slugger at one place and another Louisville Slugger at another place, so what? You're talking more like, oh, golden delicious apples and winesap apples. Am I being clear?"

Drummond sat on the corner of the riding DA's desk. "This evidence is a little more definitive than a fucking baseball bat. Do you know how many people in this city of one-million-something grow voodoo lilies?"

"I didn't know anyone did," Dunst said.

"Not two in half a million. Maybe not *one* in half a million. The flowers reek. No real gardener wants them anyplace on their property. This establishes that Zorro made a stop at LaVon Masters' place on his way home. That gives us probable cause in a murder investigation to search the premises."

"What did the guy want with a flower?" Dunst said.

"Fuck if I know," Drummond said. "The point is, he had one."

Benno was seated off to one side, letting Drummond carry the ball while he tried to call Jessica Baldwin. It was the third time he'd punched her number in since leaving LaVon's, and the third consecutive occasion on which he'd gotten her voice mail. He frowned in puzzlement as he flipped the mouthpiece closed.

Benno rested his ankle on his knee, his other knee pointing off to one side. "We both know the lily at Zorro's came from LaVon's. It's too much of a coincidence. LaVon Masters isn't going to kick you in the nuts, Randy. Get us the fucking warrant. We expect bullshit from suspects, but you're supposed to be a teammate."

Dunst opened a legal pad and took out a pen. His nails were spotless, freshly manicured. "Well, here's something else to occupy your mind. Before I take this to a judge, particularly regarding the premises of a woman as powerful as LaVon Masters, I want my ducks in a row."

"Oh Jesus Christ," Drummond said. "Here we go again with the social register. We don't have time to fuck around, Randy. People are dying here."

"I agree there's little time, so let's not waste what we have." Dunst drew a numeral one on the page and circled it. "The flower in the Ziploc. You came in possession of it how?"

Benno and Drummond exchanged a look. Drummond said, "We were invited guests at an Art Society meeting. It was an open house."

"Nobody's going to swallow that you were invited guests," Dunst said. "Not even some judge."

"How about, we displayed a keen interest in the finer things?" Benno said.

"Even less believable," Dunst said. "I mean, look at yourselves. You are not art aficionados, nor are you gardening experts. A judge is going to interpret that you were nosing around uninvited, looking for clues. Which you were. We need some basic premises here. What prompted you to go to Mrs. Masters' in the first place?"

"Her lawyer told us all about Harry Masters' will. We went there looking for the original."

"That won't fly," Dunst said. "You just described a specific purpose for being on the premises. Stealing a flower from her greenhouse establishes a completely *different* purpose. Unless you can establish a connection between the two . . ." Dunst gave a hands-up shrug.

"A canvass of the flower suppliers nationwide showed us that LaVon ordered voodoo lilies," Drummond said. "How about that for a connection?" Benno frowned at her. She guardedly winked at him.

Dunst picked up his pen and made another note. "Closer. But still a tough one."

Drummond got up, put both hands on Dunst's desk, and bent over close to the lawyer. "Read my lips, Randy. They are all tough. And if you don't start preparing the warrant documents, and right now, we are going out to LaVon's and break a window. Then we're going to climb in through the broken window and toss the joint. And when the shit comes down we're going to swear that we did all this on the advice of Randy Dunst, honcho legal expert. How's that sound?"

Dunst swallowed hard. "You'd do that?"

"In a heartbeat," Drummond said.

Dunst read over his notes. His mouth twitched. "Let me think on this."

"No," Drummond said. "I will let you get on that computer and start typing the papers. That is all I will allow."

Benno's cell phone buzzed in his pocket. *Ah. Jessica.* He pulled out the instrument and checked his caller ID. His features sagged in disappointment. Rubin calling. Benno answered.

Chief Rubin said, "What am I supposed to do with this reporter waiting to see me?"

Benno checked his watch. Two o'clock on the nose. He tightly shut his eyes. Christ, Nordstrom. He'd forgotten about the guy. "Be there in a minute, Chief," Benno said. He closed up his phone. "I gotta go upstairs."

Drummond and Dunst were watching him. Drummond said, "For how long?"

"Just a few minutes," Benno said. "Chief Rubin's got a problem with the media. While I'm gone, Randy can get us the warrant."

Dunst looked uncertain. "I haven't agreed to that. Not without consideration."

Drummond walked around and switched on the riding DA's computer. "You bet your ass he's going to," Drummond said. She clicked on an icon. A legal form with some blanks to fill in appeared. "Come on, Randy," she said. "You gonna type in this shit or am I?"

On the way down the corridor to the elevator, Benno tried Jessica again and once more got her voice mail. This time he left a message. He wondered if she were already inside Morgan's and had possibly left her phone in her car. He checked a note in his pocket and called the landline at Morgan's house. After two rings a cop answered, Officer Thomas Binell.

Benno said, "Yeah, Detective Benno. Metro. You have the woman's name you're supposed to let in to see Morgan?"

"Miss"—there was a rustling noise over the line—"Jessica Baldwin, right?"

"Right. You seen her yet?"

"No one's been here. Is there a problem with letting her through?"

"No, no," Benno said. "Look, when she gets there, tell her to call my cell. She has the number. No big deal, okay? Just tell her I want to check on her."

As Benno walked through Rubin's deserted reception area, he could see Nordstrom inside the office sitting across from the chief. As Benno approached, Rubin offered the reporter a mint from a bowl. Nordstrom declined the offer. Benno came in and said, "You two making connections?"

Rubin waved a hand for Benno to sit. "I was just telling him LaVon Masters was the major suspect in her husband's murder up until the state's prime witness did a turnaround."

"No fooling," Benno said, sitting down.

"And this is supposed to be a scoop?" Nordstrom rocked his foot up and down. "Sounds more like a stall."

"I'm, uh, just getting to the major revelations," Rubin said. He threw Benno a help-me glance.

"Has Valdez the chauffeur gotten here yet?" Benno asked Rubin.

"No sign of the guy," Rubin said.

"He should be here, if he's just coming from Waxahachie," Benno said.

Rubin brushed his hair back. "I was thinking the same thing."

Nordstrom got on the alert. "What chauffeur?"

"A witness who can blow the lid off the case," Benno said. "Maybe you should hang around a while, interview the—"

"You told me to be here at two," Nordstrom said. "It is after two. I have deadlines to meet."

"Meaning," Benno said, "that if you don't get something pretty quick, you're going to fuck me in print, right?"

Nordstrom spread his hands. "You called this meeting. I'm just going along."

Rubin asked, "Have you considered what you might do to our investigation here by dragging up this old Los Angeles crap?"

"I have considered a lot of things," Nordstrom said. "I am considering that I know things pertaining to Detective Benno here that nobody else has got. If I'm going to agree not to print them, I got to have something for a substitute. At this point I haven't received anything from you but the runaround." He flipped his notebook closed.

Benno scratched his chin. He looked thoughtfully at Rubin. He said to the reporter, "How about this—LaVon Masters is likely guilty of probate fraud?"

Rubin sat forward, frowning.

Nordstrom found a blank page in his notebook. "I don't think that's an equal offense to murder."

"How about," Benno said, "that for over twenty-five years she's been hiding the fact that the money she's got isn't really hers. That actually it belongs to her daughter."

Nordstrom brushed his pant leg. "That would be interesting as a side item, possibly. It would not be as interesting as, say, a story that the lead detective on the case got fired once, from a major department, for being drunk on the job. Or as interesting as knowing who's a suspect in this current mess. Detective Benno, you told me at the Doubletree that Morgan Masters is no longer the prime target. Okay, who is?"

"We are not ready to name that individual," Rubin said.

"Then I don't see we've got that much to talk about," Nordstrom said.

Benno felt anger building inside him. He tried to control it, which was tough to accomplish. The AA people talked all the time about dry drunks, times when anger boiled even after the drunk had stopped drinking. Benno pictured himself grabbing Nordstrom by the throat and throttling the guy.

Rubin pinched the bridge of his nose. "Detective Benno, this reporter knows what he wants. I guess I have to give it to him."

Benno frowned. Give Nordstrom what? What was Rubin talking about?

Rubin dug in his drawer and slid one of the sketch artist's drawings across to the reporter. "This guy."

Mentally, Benno looked at the ceiling and pounded

his own forehead. Physically, he did nothing. He just sat there, speechless.

Nordstrom picked the drawing up and looked at it. "Who is it?"

"The killer," Rubin said mysteriously. "Nobody in the media's got that but you. We'd planned to distribute it, but if you'd like, I can wait a couple of days."

Benno said, "Uh, Chief."

Rubin held up a hand in Benno's direction. "I know," Rubin said. "It's tough to do this. But Mr. Nordstrom here has got us by the short hairs. We have to cooperate, Detective."

Benno said, "But that's not—"

"And this is no bullshit?" Nordstrom cut in.

"This is no bullshit," Rubin said. "That is the guy, and this is currently exclusive to you."

Nordstrom put the drawing away and stood. "This is the way I like to do business, Chief. I gotta try for tomorrow's edition. So if you'll excuse me." He went out, walking fast.

Benno said, "Uh, Chief."

Rubin expansively spread his hands. "You see what I was talking about? First you give them reluctance. Then you give up the goods. This is the way you handle the media."

"There's a problem, Chief."

"What problem could there be? It's information we were going to disseminate anyhow. So we've given Nordstrom a little jump, though not much of one, and at the same time we've gotten your chestnuts out of the fire. We have performed a double dip here."

Benno inhaled. He swallowed hard. "That's not the guy, Chief."

Rubin's expression didn't change. "What?"

"The guy in the drawing. It's not the killer. We got back from Irving earlier, where they'd apprehended that particular suspect, and we got a look at him. That individual is guilty of reading electricity meters."

"You're saying we've given Nordstrom bullshit."

"Pure and unadulterated," Benno said.

"Which he will print immediately."

"And get our asses in a crack. Lawsuits . . ."

"Ah," Rubin said. "This is even better."

Benno shifted around in his chair. "How can that be?"

"Hear me out. Nordstrom prints this bullshit. Tomorrow his editor learns it's bullshit, and now the paper's calling its defense attorneys, shoring up the walls and shit. So what's the paper going to say then, when Nordstrom tries to give them a story which smears the lead detective on the Masters case? They're not going to touch the story with a fifty-foot pole." Rubin leaned closer and jabbed the air with his finger. "And you are absolutely certain that the guy in the drawing is not the killer and that we have just given Nordstrom total bullshit?"

"I'm not sure what the results are going to be," Benno said. "But, yeah, the guy in the drawing is not the killer."

Rubin expansively spread his hands. He grinned from ear to ear. "Oops," Rubin said.

Benno stood in Rubin's doorway while he called Drummond. Drummond picked up and said, "We're in Randy Dunst's car, headed for the Crowley Courts Building."

"Has he got a judge picked out?" Benno said.

There was a click and then static sounded over the line. Drummond came back on and said, "He says he's got an in at District Court Number 373. Judge Gaines. Says it'll take only a couple of minutes."

"Okay," Benno said. "I'll wait for you in the lot to

the side of the building. I suppose we'd better take Dunst along to serve the warrant." Benno disconnected and looked at Rubin. Rubin showed a glum expression. Benno said, "You'll call me as soon as you talk to the chauffeur, won't you, Chief?"

"I will if you'll keep your goddamned phone turned on," Rubin said. "You been neglectful in that regard, Detective Benno."

Benno pulled out his cell and waved it around. "I gotcha. Actually I'm expecting a call from you and one other person. Until I hear from the both of you, this line will never be unavailable, okay?"

Benno steered out of the parking garage, turned north until he reached Elm Street, and then headed west toward the criminal courts. Traffic was light downtown, since most of Dallas business had moved out beyond the Loop years ago. The center of the city mostly housed lawyers and cops, along with county and federal employees. Benno was feeling pretty low after kowtowing to Nordstrom. Once he put this case to bed he might quit and not give a damn what the reporter put in his column, but he owed it to his cousin to keep embarrassing crap out of the newspapers until these current murders were history. It was his and Drummond's case. He'd make certain they shared equal credit. Drummond was turning out to be one hell of a partner. As he went down the incline alongside the Texas Schoolbook Depository, nearing the underpass beneath Stemmons Freeway, he tried Jessica again on the cell.

Fucking voice mail again. Benno waited for the beep, then said, "Are you dodging me or something? Listen, I've hit a few snags, and it's going to be a while before I can get to Morgan's. Call me, huh?" He flipped the mouthpiece and dropped the phone on the seat beside him. A nagging worry crept into the back of his mind and then went away as he pulled into the Crowley Building lot and saw Drummond coming fast, waving the warrant, with Randy Dunst tight on her heels.

23

Benno knew that there were people who turned it on when the cameras pointed in their direction. Tiger Woods, of course—Palmer and Nicklaus back in the old days. Some actors, a few politicians. Maybe a cop or two, even Benno himself when he'd worked in LA, before the blowup that had gotten him fired. Thirty seconds after he pulled the Merc into LaVon Masters' circular driveway, Benno added Randy Dunst to the list.

On the drive out from downtown, Benno watched the riding DA in the rearview mirror. Dunst sat in the backseat, breathing though his nose as if he was terrified. The warrant lay faceup in Dunst's lap, and occasionally he'd snatch up the paper and hold the judge's signature an inch from the end of his nose, as if he was afraid the jurist had used disappearing ink. When he wasn't verifying that the warrant was actually signed, Dunst's lips would move as if he was silently rehearsing a speech. Which Benno thought Dunst probably was. *Two* speeches, in fact: one of gushing apology that he'd use when serving the warrant on

LaVon Masters; another to recite in telling his superiors, if this whole thing blew up in their faces, how these two incompetent detectives had pressured Dunst into going for the warrant to begin with.

As Benno braked to a halt in front of LaVon Masters' pillared porch, two on-the-spot television reporters skirted the fountain with cameramen in tow, coming fast. The reporters were both good-looking women with perfectly coiffed hairdos. They'd jumped out of the driver's seat of a van parked in front as the cops had arrived, and the cameramen had burst from the rear double doors. One picture taker was a thin man in sweater and jeans; the other was a guy wearing a bush jacket.

As the entourage approached, Benno sat bolt upright. "Who the fuck is that?" he said.

Dunst shifted around in back. "I think they're with the television station."

"I can see that, Randy. Who called them?"

Dunst had the backseat door shouldered partway open. "I think, possibly, John Hoermann. Come on, Detectives, let's get it in gear." The sudden change in his demeanor was remarkable. He straightened his tie. He leaned sideways, looked in the rearview, and bared his teeth for inspection. He rolled the warrant into a cylinder. Dunst shoved the door open and marched onto the porch. Benno and Drummond threw glances back and forth as if to say, *Jesus Christ, what's with this guy?*

The cameramen shouldered their minicams and aimed at Dunst. Dunst gave Benno and Drummond a wave. "Follow me, Detectives," he practically yelled. One of the on-the-spot reporters steadied a steno pad on her thigh, and wrote something down.

For a couple of seconds, neither detective moved a muscle. They peered through the windows as Dunst marched up to the heavy oak door and pounded with the knocker. Dunst's shoulders were squared, his stride was long and forceful, and his butt twitched like a peacock's. He looked over his shoulder toward the Merc. "Come on, Officers," he said, even louder than before. The minicams continued to whir.

Drummond emptied her lungs. "You think he even needs us?" She pushed her door all the way open. "What a fuckin' ham," she said.

Benno snickered, got out, and followed Drummond up on the porch. As the detectives approached, Dunst banged the knocker three more times. The women stood by taking notes. Dunst was spelling for them, "D . . . U . . . N . . . S . . . T." Both women nodded. One underlined Dunst's name on her pad.

Drummond stepped around the DA and the reporters. "Gee, Randy, you tried the bell?" She depressed the button. Chimes inside the house played the opening bars to "New York, New York." Drummond stood back and folded her arms.

Benno stuck his hands in his pockets and stood off to one side. As he watched the street, a second motor pool car—a Ford—came around the corner and parked behind the Mercury. Four men in suits piled out. One was Song, the Chinese-American cop in the unit, and another was Lieutenant DiAngelo. Benno didn't recognize the other two. On the way out he'd called the dispatcher and asked for backup to aid in the search, but he hadn't expected her to send the shift lieutenant. DiAngelo looked pissed. Benno nodded and smiled at the guy.

One on-the-spot reporter said to Dunst, "And you're what, assisting with the warrant?"

"I'm the prosecutor in charge of the investigation," Dunst said.

"Hmm. I got the impression the other night at Mor-

gan Masters' house that John Hoermann was personally handling it."

"John?" Dunst coughed and cleared his throat.
"John and I are coordinating."

Drummond said irritably, "What's wrong with this
woman? Why the hell doesn't she answer her door?"
She rang the bell again.

The on-the-spot reporter wrote something down,
then scratched her nose. "So you and Hoermann—
you're *jointly* in charge?"

"John and I work together a lot," Dunst said.

DiAngelo came up close to Benno and hissed, "So
now you've got the dispatcher telling me to come out
here and report to you. What's next, you taking over
my job?"

"Just plodding along, Loo," Benno said peacefully.
He looked around for Drummond.

She'd left the front door and moved to the side to
stand on tiptoes and peer in through the window. "Oh
Jesus." She drew her weapon and smashed the glass,
then reached in to unlock the door from inside. "Get
all these media people out of the way," she called out.
"Jesus Christ, Benno, there's blood all over in there."

One of the pewter urns had overturned and rolled
heavily away as the detectives pushed in through the
door. There were smears of blood on the walls, across
the tiles, and even some spattered on the ceiling. They
followed the trail toward the back of the house.

LaVon Masters lay dead beneath the portrait of
Steve McQueen. Benno and Drummond stood side by
side as they looked down at her. Behind them, Randy
Dunst said, "Christ, I'm going to be . . ." Then he
held both hands over his mouth as he bolted back
toward the entryway.

LaVon had absorbed the worst beating that Benno
had ever seen. The right side of her face was caved

in and her eye hung out of its socket. Her left upper
arm was bent at a ninety-degree angle, as if she had
two elbows, and grayish bone poked out from the torn
sleeve of her pantsuit. The weapon, a tire iron, lay
beside her in a lake of blood. There were marks on
her legs where the killer had battered her over and
over, probably after she was dead. Bloody sneaker
footprints led away from the body toward the back of
the house. The shoes' treads were diamond-shaped.
Weapons held ready, Drummond and Benno prepared
to follow the trail.

DiAngelo came into the corridor and stared down
at the body, "My sweet fucking God."

Drummond snapped, over her shoulder, "Don't just
stand there, Loo. Call the fucker in."

The trail led past the study, through the corridor
lined with paintings, and on into the greenhouse. The
greenhouse door stood open, rocking in the wind. The
detectives passed the voodoo lily plant on their right,
then warily moved outside. The footprints faded step
by step as they continued down the sidewalk to the
open back gate. Near the top of the gate was a single
handprint, clearly outlined in blood, and a faint diamond outline, where the killer had braced a shoe
against the gate to push it open. Drummond gave a
follow-me gesture and went out behind the garage,
with Benno following close behind.

The melting snow had left a thin residue of mud in
the drive, a perfect cast for the fresh tire tracks leading
in, then back out, through the alley. The detectives
holstered their weapons.

And there was more to see. Benno pointed down, at
a spot behind the place where the killer had obviously
parked. "Look at this, Tina." She came over and stood
beside him, shoulder to shoulder.

There was a path through the mud leading back

toward the house, as if someone had dragged something heavy in through the gate. Also there were dark spots in the dirt that could have been drops of blood. Benno and Drummond followed the path back into the yard, heads down. Halfway up the walk, the drag marks faded, and then completely disappeared. Drummond found a piece of chalk in her bag and marked the sidewalk on both sides of the drag impressions.

As they reentered the greenhouse, they encountered DiAngelo. The lieutenant was looking at the voodoo lily plant. He put hands on hips as the detectives walked up. "Nasty-smelling bastard, huh?" DiAngelo said.

"Yeah, it's rare," Benno said. "We searching the house?"

DiAngelo raised a hand in a sarcastic salute. "I've dispatched the troops, General."

"This is no time for wiseass," Benno said. "You're my superior. Nobody's trying to steal any of your thunder, Loo."

"You couldn't prove it by me. Jesus, did you look at that dead woman?"

"LaVon Masters. Somebody hated her guts, didn't they?"

"Mashed her face like a fuckin' bug," DiAngelo said. "Last time I saw—"

"Hey," Drummond said loudly, from twenty paces away.

Benno looked. Drummond had moved up an aisle perpendicular to the main greenhouse walkthrough and now stood peering down at something hidden behind a thick bush with waxy leaves. Benno raised his eyebrows in a question.

"Better get over here," Drummond said. "We got another dead woman."

The body was sprawled facedown across three

planting boxes of Asian jasmine, smashing the plants down to the potting soil. It was a woman wearing an expensive-looking business suit, but no shoes or panty hose, her feet protruding out into the aisle. There was a burlap bag over her head, tied loosely around her neck. One side of the bag was dark with blood. Several deep cuts crisscrossed the bottoms of her feet. As Benno stood with Drummond on his right and DiAngelo on his left, all three cops looking down at the body like people watching a flea circus, Benno said, "Wonder what happened to her feet. I never saw anything like that before."

DiAngelo lifted his coat and packed in his shirttail in back. "I saw stuff like that in combat training. Pictures of some Nam camp survivors. The gooks would cut their feet like that, and while they were questioning the prisoners, they'd stick needles down in the cuts. Guy told me, it's more painful than gettin' a tooth pulled without Novocain."

"Jesus Christ," Benno said. He stepped up beside the body and shoved a planter aside with his foot. "Let's roll her over and have a look at her face." He grasped the corpse's shoulder.

"Hold it," DiAngelo said. "I think we should wait for the crime scene unit. We might fuck up some evidence or something."

"We got no time for that, Lieutenant," Benno said.

"Well, we're makin' time, *Detective*. That's the rules. We don't touch shit until the lab crew's been over everything. I'm not gettin' my ass in a crack listenin' to you two."

"CSU's a half hour away, minimum."

"We wait for half an hour, then." DiAngelo stoically folded his arms.

Benno stood away from the body. "We've got a lawyer here. Let's ask him."

DiAngelo frowned. "You mean Dunst?"

"Yeah, Dunst. John Hoermann's special representative."

"Who went outside to lose his cookies," DiAngelo said.

Now Drummond cut in. "Well maybe he's recovered enough to give us a legal opinion. Come on, Loo. Go get Randy and let's ask him. Maybe we've got imminent danger or something."

DiAngelo took two steps in the direction of the house, then stopped and turned. "Oh no. I'm not leavin' you two alone with this body. For all I know, by the time I get back you'll have the evidence fucked up to hell and gone."

Benno had already tensed in preparation for rolling the body over as soon as DiAngelo went away. He relaxed and stepped back.

"Oh Jesus Christ," Drummond said, "*I'll* go get Randy." She stalked away toward the house. "Keep the lieutenant company, Benno. Maybe you two can share a dirty joke. Prisoner torture stories. Anything to keep you entertained."

While DiAngelo hovered over the body like Rumpelstiltskin guarding the gold, Benno strolled halfway up the aisle and tried to call Jessica. The voice mail again. Benno said after the tone, "I don't know where you are, but listen up. If you haven't gone to Morgan's yet, don't. This situation's turned dangerous as hell. Don't make a move until you talk to me." He disconnected just as Drummond hustled into the greenhouse with Randy Dunst in tow.

The riding DA's face was the color of chalk. He was wiping his mouth with a handkerchief. He followed Drummond to where the body lay; he had to peer around DiAngelo to have a look. Dunce made a choking noise, said, "Oh Christ," and then stepped away as if he might throw up again. Benno looked quickly around for an empty flowerpot or bucket.

Dunst turned his back so he wouldn't have to look at the corpse. "Who is it?"

Drummond got in between Dunst and DiAngelo and gestured with her hands. "That's what we're trying to find out, Randy. We sure as hell can't see her face with that bag over her head. The loo's telling us not to disturb the body until CSU gets here. We say we got to disturb it. This could be one of LaVon Masters' party guests, but we don't think so. We saw drag marks out back that look like the killer may have hauled the body in here from outside. We can't know until we have a look. Give us some legal guidance here."

Dunst chanced a look over his shoulder at the corpse. He coughed into his cupped hand. "I don't know if I've got . . ." Dunst trailed off.

"Sure you have the authority, Randy," Drummond said. "You are John Hoermann's personal representative on the scene. You have the media in the palm of your hand. I could suggest possibility of imminent danger, but you're the lawyer."

Now Dunst looked interested. "Imminent danger of what?"

"We have a lunatic killer running around. Viewing this dead woman, determining her identity if we can— that might prevent more people dying. And in that regard, I am not bullshitting one iota."

Dunst looked to DiAngelo. "Lieutenant?"

DiAngelo stepped back from the corpse and raised both hands. "Do not be putting it off on me. If you people fuck up trace evidence moving that corpse around, it's you doing it."

Dunst said, "Christ."

"And if we don't roll her over," Drummond said,

"and more people get killed while we're fucking around waiting for CSU, that's going to be on your head. So which do you want: heat from some CSU honcho or a report in the newspaper that you allowed more people to die?"

"Christ," Dunst said. He managed to look at the body from the corner of his eye. "Just . . . do it," he croaked, then stepped away and retched.

As Dunst threw up all over a bed of gardenias, Benno's cell phone buzzed in his pocket. He snatched up the instrument and checked the caller ID. Chief Rubin. Benno answered.

"I got the chauffeur here," Rubin said.

"That's good news, Chief. Hold on, will ya?" Benno depressed the HOLD button, shoved the phone into his pocket, and nodded to Drummond.

With DiAngelo glaring nearby and Dunst wiping vomit from his mouth, the two detectives grabbed the corpse and rolled it over. One of the planters overturned, spilling Asian jasmine plants and potting soil all over the floor. Benno used both hands to undo the rope around the woman's neck, then tugged the bag from over her head. He straightened up and blinked.

The dead woman had a soft round face and tiny nose. There were fat wrinkles under her throat. In spite of the bullet wound in the side of her head, she had a sort of peaceful look. Benno looked to Drummond and shrugged.

"Me, neither," Drummond said. "I never laid eyes on her before."

From behind the detectives, Randy Dunst said, "Jesus Christ. Oh Jesus fucking Christ." He was putting his soggy handkerchief away.

"I don't know how in hell we're going to ID this victim," Benno said. "You ever seen her, Randy?"

Now Dunst managed to appear angry, a pretty good

trick for a man who'd just thrown up all over the place. "What are you talking about, Detective? It's Jessica Baldwin, from Victims' Services. You told me earlier you'd been working with her. Christ, another law enforcement person down." He breathed like a cardiac patient.

Benno frowned in irritation. "You're full of it, Randy. Jessica Baldwin's a fitness freak. Doesn't even resemble this person." He mentally snapped his fingers. Jesus, the chief. He yanked out his cell and pressed the TALK button. "Sorry, Chief, we got all kinds of shit going on. Listen, we'll be heading out to Morgan Masters' house in Plano. I think we'd better get some firepower out there, pronto. LaVon Masters is dead and so's an unidentified female over here. This killer's likely to have Morgan next in his sights."

"I'll get on the horn and send some people," Rubin said. "Listen, I have got Mr. Oscar Valdez seated across from me as we speak. He was LaVon Masters' chauffeur for fifteen years."

"He have anything spectacular to add?" Benno asked.

Dunst was staring at him. The riding DA pointed at the corpse. "This is definitely Jessica Baldwin, Detective."

Benno shook his head and held up a just-a-minute finger.

Rubin said, "A lot was just what we thought. Mr. Valdez did take LaVon Masters up to Denton County, where she delivered a child in a private hospital. Checked in under an assumed name. Brought the baby home two days later."

"That could help," Benno said. "Maybe Denton County has birth records where we could pick up on the assumed name she used. Might help us in locating the kid. Listen, Chief, we'd better talk about this later. Anything else?"

"Yeah," Rubin said. "There is this one more thing. You can quit looking for a guy. According to Mr. Valdez here, LaVon Masters' second baby was a girl."

The little girl was in third grade and almost nine. Her IQ was a hundred forty-seven. She was also emotionally disturbed, dangerously so.

On one occasion the assistant principal, a man named Jackson Barr, found the girl naked under the gymnasium bleachers, singing songs and staring into space while a gang of boys fondled her privates. Barr threw his coat over her and whisked her into his office, and there she asked him if he'd like to touch her just as the boys had done.

Not only was the child obsessively promiscuous, she was physically violent as well. Once in the lunchroom, after an argument over a place in line, she pulled out clumps of another child's hair. In a playground altercation over a volleyball, she threw another little girl to the ground, straddled her, and pounded the child's head hard enough to give her a concussion. The school counselor thereafter noted that she'd never seen such an angry child in her twenty-seven years with the district.

Mr. Barr recommended to the principal that the little girl be barred from attending public school. The princi-

pal responded that the little girl's mother was a wealthy and powerful woman and that to take such action would cause problems with the school board. However, as the child's behavior continued to deteriorate, the principal finally agreed to look into the matter. He talked to the board, who conversed with their lawyers. In short order, a motion was filed in County Family Court.

Two days after the school board filed its motion, as the chauffeur brought the little girl home from school, a strange vehicle was parked beside her mother's Porsche. The vehicle was a rusty old Ford with a broken tailpipe. Though she'd never seen the car before, its presence somehow frightened her. Her mother being home was unsettling as well; normally her mother wasn't there when she got home from school; she almost never arrived before the nanny had put the little girl to bed. The little girl shivered from the top of her pigtailed head to the bottom of her Mary Jane patent leather shoes.

The nanny met the little girl at the front door, grabbed her by the hand, and hustled her off past mirrors, Egyptian statues, and paintings by Dali and Vail. "Your mama's got company, child," the nanny said. "You play in your room and stay out of the way." The little girl cried and held back, but the nanny tugged her along.

As they passed the study, the child could see her mother through the open doorway. Her mother was seated at her rolltop desk, and there was a man in there with her. The man was dark-complected and hairy, with thick shoulders, neck, and arms. The little girl had seen him before, though she couldn't recall where or when. The sight of the man brought fears to the surface that the child couldn't have explained, and as the nanny tugged her past the library, the little girl whimpered out loud. Her mother glared daggers at her. The nanny put the child inside her room, went out, and closed the door.

As soon as the nanny was gone, the little girl crept out of her room and down to the study. She hid behind one of the French doors and listened.

Her mother was saying, "They already served the fuckin' papers, Eddie. Hearin's next Tuesday. They're fixin' to commit the little bitch. I can't have that. You know what happens then."

The man's deep voice was familiar to the child, though she still couldn't quite place him. "They'll come out to get her if she don't show up at the hearing, Vonnie," he said.

"I got that covered," the mother said. "Harold Stein's preparin' voluntary commitment papers to a private sanitorium. All we gotta do is provide a copy to the county and the school district, and then as far as they're concerned, we've handled the problem without any interference. What we really do with her don't matter to them, as long as they got that paper to stick in the file. Fuck 'em. Buncha bureaucrats."

The little girl had no idea what her mother and the fearsome man were talking about, but she did know that she had to sneeze. She put both hands over her mouth and nose. "Ahh-choo!"

From inside the study, her mother said, "What the fuck was that?"

The child left her hiding place and ran as fast as she could toward her room. She heard heavy footsteps behind her and looked fearfully over her shoulder. The heavyset man was coming after her. The little girl lowered her head, tightly shut her eyes, and tried to run faster.

The man caught up with her just outside her room. He snatched her up from the floor. She struggled and kicked and cried for help, though she knew there was no one in the house who might assist her. The man clamped his hand over her mouth. She bit him as hard as she could. He slapped her one, two, three times. The little girl fell silent and hung limp in his arms as blood ran from her nose. She thought she might wet her pants, but held back in fear that the man might hit her again.

He carried her as if she were weightless, past the study and toward the front of the house. Her mother came out of the study and followed along.

The man said, breathing hard, "Wonder how much she heard."

"Don't matter," the little girl's mother said. "Where she's goin' she can't do shit about it. Just get her the fuck on outta here."

He carried her out of the house and into the drive, threw her into the backseat of the rusty old Ford, and slammed the door. The little girl tried to get out of the car, but the rear inside handle was broken off. She sniffled in fear as she looked around.

In the front passenger seat was a second child, also a girl. The other little girl was younger than she and seemed in a trance. The two children looked at each other over the top of the seat.

The front passenger door opened and the man hauled the second little girl outside. Then he climbed behind the wheel, threw the car in gear, and burned rubber as he pulled away down the drive. The car bumped and rattled, jostling the little girl from side to side. She cried out in fear and pain, looking fearfully out the back window as her mother took the second child by the hand, hauled her past the fountain and on toward the house. As the Ford rounded the corner and her home disappeared from view behind a neighboring house, the little girl screamed at the top of her lungs.

24

Oscar Valdez didn't know the exact date of LaVon Masters' secret delivery. The retired chauffeur was sure, however, that it that was early April when he'd driven his employer to the private hospital in Denton County. Chief Rubin got on the horn to the neighboring county's records division, threw his weight around until he got the head honcho on the phone, and demanded that he receive, via E-mail, a record of all Denton County births during the first two weeks of April in '72, pronto, cut the crap, do not screw around.

In short order he had computer photos of sixty-two birth certificates, including the infants' weight and length along with images of tiny footprints. Forty-six of those records described male babies. Of the remaining sixteen, the birth certificates named both parents on all but four. One of the single mothers was Hispanic, and another was black. The Caucasian births were Avery Louise Holbert, mother's name Yvonne, and Sandra Denise Hershey, whose mother was Sue. Both certificates listed the father as unknown.

Rubin printed out the two likely certificates, hustled

downstairs to the warrants section, and bullied one of the clerks into casting her work aside to put both infants' names into the National Crime Information Center data bank. Rubin wanted the Holbert child checked out first because her mother's name, Yvonne, seemed to him like a pseudonym LaVon Masters might choose. But no one named Avery Louise Holbert was wanted in any jurisdiction, so the clerk typed Sandra Denise Hershey's name into the data bank. The NCIC computer burped and beeped, then lit up like neon.

Morgan Masters couldn't sit still. She prowled back and forth between her bedroom and guest room, scratching the back of her neck and both upper arms until welts appeared. She flopped down on the daybed. Ten seconds later she abandoned the bed and straddled a chair. She stalked in, sat at her vanity, and looked in the mirror. Her eyes were puffy and she wore no makeup. She uncapped a lipstick and smeared some on her mouth. She grabbed a Kleenex, dipped it in cold cream, and wiped the lipstick away.

She knew the term for her own behavior—obsessive-compulsive—and had its symptoms memorized, but knowing what was wrong with her and doing something about it were two different things. She itched as if stricken with hives. She had to get out of this fucking house. She went to her closet, got her video camera, and tossed it on the bed, then lay on her back and wriggled into tight jeans. It wasn't so much that she *wanted* to go out—she simply *had* to.

She snatched up her phone and punched in the number for Jessica Baldwin's cell. After three rings she got the voice mail and waited for the beep. She then screamed into the phone, "Fuck you, Jessica. You told me you were coming here. You don't really give a shit about me, do you?" She slammed the receiver down and put on a sweater that fit snug over her boobs.

At times like this, Morgan could be very cunning. She had a fertile mind and could dream up the most logical excuses for going out. After she'd finished high school her mother had sprung for a strict girls' college off in Virginia, and Morgan had dreamed up countless excuses—family deaths, do-or-die emergencies—so that school officials would let her leave the campus. Once she'd driven into DC, gone home with three guys she'd met in a bar, and stayed with them in their apartment for fourteen days. On that occasion, when she'd finally returned to the campus, she had been dropped from all her classes and was sent packing for home. She hadn't given a shit at the time, and for that matter, neither had LaVon. LaVon had only sent her away to get rid of her, and once Morgan returned to town, her mother sprang for rent on an apartment as far across the city from her Highland Park home as possible. Ever since then, Morgan had lived alone.

But those cops downstairs weren't going to listen to any dying grandmother stories. If she were going to get away, Morgan would somehow have to sneak past them. Her Mercedes was parked in the front driveway, and she'd have to get past the uniformed officer on the porch in order to get behind the wheel. Or she might slip past the guy patrolling the back of the house, run around to the side, vault over the fence beside the electricity meter, and . . .

She had to get away. Only when she was out and about would her skin stop crawling. She clawed impulsively at her upper arms.

Morgan went over to the window and looked down at the pool. Stoney the Lab was out there, sniffing around for a likely spot to pee, but the cop on guard was nowhere in sight. A portion of roof overhang was directly beneath her window. Maybe she could run across the roof to the corner of the house and shinny down a drainpipe. She put on a light cotton jacket, got her video camera, and hung the strap over her shoulder. Then she raised the window. Cool wind billowed the drapes. As she lifted one foot onto the sill, there was a slight creaking noise behind her. Morgan backed away from the window and turned around.

A woman stood in her bedroom, just inside the door. Morgan gasped in shock.

The woman was short and very pretty, with muscled arms and legs. She wore a spandex workout suit with short pants and a sleeveless top, along with jogging shoes. She had delicate, winter-pale skin and her dark hair was layered close to her head. Morgan thought the woman was beautiful. Diamond studs glinted on her earlobes. A scar bisected her lips so that one side of her mouth was higher than the other. Her eyes glowed like vicious bright coals. She pointed a pistol at Morgan's midsection. On her arms and sleeveless top were stains that looked like blood.

Morgan's throat tightened in fear. "Who are you? What do you want?"

The woman's upper lip curled into a sneer. "Who am I? Who are *you*, bitch?"

Morgan placed a hand on her own breastbone. "I'm Morgan Masters, and you are in my—"

"That is not your fucking name. That is my fucking name. And this isn't your house. It's rightfully mine." The woman raised the pistol, and at the same time pointed toward the king-sized bed. "Lay down over there. And don't call yourself by my fucking name, not ever again."

Morgan moved over to the bed and stretched out, her thoughts a jumble, the fear in her gullet like bile.

The woman came over, grabbed Morgan's wrist in a painful grip, and produced a pair of handcuffs. Morgan looked wildly toward the doorway. A long-handled ax was propped against the jamb. The woman snapped a cuff around Morgan's wrist and yanked her hand toward the bedpost. As she did, a siren wailed in the distance.

The woman's chin lifted at the sound. Her mouth twisted in hatred. She bent close and placed her lips an inch from Morgan's ear. "The police won't save you, bitch," she fiercely whispered. "No one else will, either, so don't start hoping. There's nothing in the world that'll save your ass from me."

Chief Rubin patched Benno through to a drawling Tennessee Bureau of Investigations officer named Dennis Oglethorpe. Benno activated the speakerphone in the Merc so that both he and Drummond could hear. Using the speaker freed up both of Benno's hands so that he wouldn't wreck the fucking car as he went north on Highway 75 headed for Plano. The magnetic roof flasher was on, the siren blaring full volume, and the speedometer needle hovered near ninety. Seen up ahead, pickups, bobtails, and tractor/trailer rigs scrambled to get out of the way of the speeding cop vehicle. "I've got my partner Detective Tina Drummond on here with us," Benno said.

"I'm pleasured, ma'am," Oglethorpe said in a baritone, and Benno pictured the guy tipping the brim of his trooper's hat. Jesus, the way Oglethorpe sounded over the phone he *had* to be wearing a trooper's hat, along with some gigantic hogleg revolver, the holster strapped to his leg, quick-draw fashion, as he gazed out his window at hazy Blue Ridge peaks in the distance.

Drummond showed a mischievous grin. "I'm pleasured, too, Sheriff."

"Oh no, ma'am, I'm not the sheriff. I'm just—"

"Our Deputy Chief Rubin tells me," Benno cut in, "that you're the expert on Sandra Denise Hershey—am I right?"

"Can't say as I'm an expert, exactly. But I've handled her more'n once over the years. That's one little gal a man could feel plumb sorry for."

"Afraid we don't share that feeling," Benno said.

"Sandra's origins are down in Texas—did you know that?"

"We're just finding it out," Benno said.

"First time we handled her she was twelve. The time she killed her foster parents? That was some people deservin' to die, not that I'm saying that officially, you understand. Kept her tied up in a trailer house, and I suspect that son of a bitch—excuse my language, ma'am, but I suspect her foster father done some sexual things to that child. Hell, I know he did. Our people found Sandra wanderin' down the highway a mile from the trailer house, and she led 'em back to where her foster parents were shot through the head. The girl had some physical injuries, in particular on her mouth. If you're interested in physical ID characteristics—"

"She has a scar bisecting her lips," Benno said, feeling his stomach churn.

"Right, you got that already. The child didn't give our patrolmen no trouble at all. Her foster father was named Jerome Payne, and he had outstanding warrants down your way."

"Several," Benno said. "His brother was a guy named Edward Payne aka Uncle Eddie. I've just gotten a thumbnail on this, but apparently Uncle Eddie was funneling money to keep the girl hidden and on the road."

"Somebody was," the Tennessee lawman said. "For three years Jerome Payne and his woman traveled from state to state with that little girl, and with no visible means of support that we ever found. Maybe some rich oilman down there had an illegitimate daughter he wanted kept out of sight, you figure?"

"Actually it was a rich woman, the girl's real mother," Benno said.

"Had to be something like that. Our folks identified the child through a birth certificate found inside the trailer. Funny thing was, Sandra kept sayin' her name was something different than was on the certificate."

"Morgan," Drummond said, bending closer to the dashboard speaker.

"That's sure right, ma'am. Our folks never knew if it was supposed to be her first name or her last name, and the child had been chained up so long and had so many mental problems they didn't pay her much mind. We thought it was probably a name that Jerome Payne and his woman dreamed up for the girl, to hide her real identity. Our people booked her into state juvenile custody as Sandra Denise Hershey, the name on the birth certificate. I personally did an extensive search trying to locate her real family. I tried both last names, Hershey and Morgan, but never came up with anything solid. This Edward Payne you were talking about?"

"Uncle Eddie," Benno said. "Currently deceased."

"Do tell. My memory on the case might not be the best. It's been seventeen years. But I did talk to Edward Payne, because he was Jerome Payne's brother and the only relative we could locate. He said he didn't know anything about any child, and truth is, I had no reason not to believe him. My recollection is, he was in federal custody at the time."

"Doing a nickel on income tax," Benno said. "To speed up some of this, most of it we can piece together. The girl was mentally screwed up to the point where she was dangerous, and the school she was attending in Dallas was threatening to commit her involuntarily to a public asylum. Her mother couldn't afford to have her committed, because it would mean loss of control over a pretty sizable fortune. The mother and Uncle Eddie made a deal with the fugitive brother to hide the girl, and in the meantime substituted another child and passed her off as Morgan. She's *still* passing as Morgan and doesn't know who she really is."

"Do tell. What kind of a mother would do something like that?"

"A real degenerate bitch," Drummond said.

Traffic slowed to a standstill, blocking the freeway up ahead. Benno took to the shoulder and stepped on it, the siren continuing to wail as the Merc whipped underneath 635. "The child they substituted was one the mother'd had with Uncle Eddie. She'd been living with Uncle Eddie since she was born. After she made the switch, the mother enrolled her in private school to keep her away from anyone that knew her before, and the substitute child *became* Morgan Masters. Apparently, pedophilia runs in families, or at least it did with Uncle Eddie and his brother. Both of those girls were abused to beat hell. Unfortunately, we don't have time to feel sorry for them. We've got to put on blinders and deal with the current situation. I'm assuming that when you talked to Uncle Eddie in prison, up to then he didn't know the girl's whereabouts?"

"Said he didn't. Said he didn't even know his brother was keeping any kid. I told you, Detective, I had no reason to suspect that he did."

"But that's the way Uncle Eddie knew how to keep up with her from then on," Benno said. "He just would have had to contact the Tennessee justice system periodically."

"Roger that," Oglethorpe said. "Sandra Denise stayed in state custody till she was eighteen, and according to the juvenile custodians she was one handful. Got in all kinds of difficulty, attacking other juvenile inmates. Tougher than most of the boys they ran across, and that's saying something when you consider some of these street kids in the program. Sandra Denise had a real volatile streak. The truth is, our folks screwed up by releasing her when she reached eighteen. She wasn't on the street on her own a year before we handled her again. Over the past ten years she's been in and out of our women's facility in Nashville. The last time she did four years and just got out this fall."

"Violent crimes?" Benno asked.

"Sure as hell were. Picked up men in bars and then mugged them. More than mugged them: beat some of those old boys practically to death. Tortured the bejesus out of 'em till they gave up the gold. The more she got away with it, the worse she treated her victims. Our head doctors tell us, if she hadn't got caught when she did, we would've had a string of dead bodies on our hands."

"Did she slice up the bottoms of their feet?" Benno asked.

"Yeah, and stuck needles down in the cuts. It's an old North Vietnamese prison camp technique. And Sandra was a whole lot more violent than what was necessary just to get their pocketbooks. This one old boy told me that even after he gave up his money she kept on jabbing those needles in."

"All that, and your prosecutors let her off with a four-year sentence?"

There was a pause. Oglethorpe finally said, "Tell me something, Detective Benno, have you ever met her personally?"

Benno glanced to his right. Drummond was watching him. His ears warmed. "A couple of times," Benno said.

"Then you know she's a pretty young woman, built up like that gal who used to be on television, was associated with the rasslin'."

"Chyna," Drummond said. "Really knows how to handle old boys." She looked pointedly across the seat at Benno.

"That's the one. Smart, too. Sandra Denise has done a lot of reading while she was locked up and has no trouble at all passing herself off as a woman of some sophistication. Some of those old boys she laid the hammer to? Doctors and lawyers, all of 'em married. A couple of them told me personally, they thought she was a medical student when they ran across her. She always had a past invented for herself."

"She told me her father was a literature professor," Benno said.

"She's used that cover more than once. Told some of 'em her daddy was a doctor or lawyer, but always it was that her father was a professional man. Our shrinks say that's significant, that she's covering up the truth about her family background, even to herself. The diagnosis is that someday she might run across her real family, and when she does, she's likely to slaughter those folks."

"That's what's happening here," Benno said. "Uncle

Eddie Payne looked her up when she got out of jail and brought her down to Texas to use as a hammer to get money out of her mother. The mother pays, Uncle Eddie doesn't blow the whistle on the identity switch. She pretended to go along with the scam until she got him alone in her half sister's house, then killed him and chopped his body to pieces. Then she laid in wait for her sister inside the house. Strictly by chance us cops happened by, checking out a stolen vehicle report, and scared her off before the sister got home. So far she's killed Uncle Eddie and her mother, along with a couple of other people. Right now she's holed up in a house with the sister as hostage. Unless she's already killed the sister."

"I don't want to be in your shoes," Oglethorpe said, "if this little gal's on a rampage. Those prison shrinks? They predicted that someday it might come down to this. These weren't any low-class bars where Sandra Denise met those fellas she mutilated up here in Tennessee. Thing was, none of 'em wanted to testify and hang their dirty underwear out in public. And not only that, our crime scene people botched some evidence pretty bad. I get pissed off about prosecutors lettin' people off light, same as you, but in this instance the DA's hands were tied. Making the deal beat the alternative, which likely was letting Sandra walk altogether."

"Do you think she could impersonate a psychiatrist?" Drummond said.

"In a New York minute," Oglethorpe said. "Sandra Denise knows as much about psychiatry as most professionals. The times I've interviewed her? She could tell me everything there is to know about her own condition, how being abused caused her to act the way she does. Unbalanced she definitely is. Dumb she definitely ain't. Tell you something in confidence. One time, when my wife and I were on the outs? Sandra Denise gave me some pointers on how to smooth out those difficulties. And you know what? Our own psychiatrists told me later, what Sandra Denise said to me was right in line with what their own analysis would be. You have to watch yourself with her. She's able to charm the pants off an old boy."

"I think I may know an old boy that's happened to," Drummond said, batting her lashes.

"Is she currently wanted in Tennessee?" Benno asked.

"Just a parole warrant. She hasn't reported to her officer since she got released. Apparently she's been down there creating some difficulty for you folks in the meantime. Still and all, I can't help feeling sorry for that little gal."

"We can't do that," Benno said. "We're too worried that she'll kill some more people." The Plano exit loomed ahead. Benno slowed and moved into the off-ramp lane.

"Oh, she'd murder folks in a heartbeat, right enough. But she's darned sure a charmer—you know what I mean?"

"Indeed I do," Drummond said.

"Look," Benno said. "We'll have to be back in touch. We're on our way to arrest her if we can."

"Well you look out she don't charm your pants off," Oglethorpe said. "She's done that to more than one of our folks."

"Some of our folks, too," Drummond said, grinning at Benno. " 'Preciate your help, Sheriff."

"Pleasured, ma'am," Oglethorpe said.

25

The scene in front of Morgan Masters' house gave
Benno a flashback to LA, the time he'd crept upstairs
along with the SWATs and Jared Og had killed one
of the guys. Uniformed cops had Morgan's street
blocked at both ends with traffic barriers, and two
mobile news units sat behind the barriers with cameras
and on-the-spot reporters standing around, ready for
action. Jesus Christ, the press was having a field day:
first LaVon Masters' home and now this. Benno
counted four Plano black-and-whites, and there were
a couple of cruisers from the far North Dallas precinct
as well. He caught a flash of captain's bars on a uniform collar and recognized the same Plano captain
who'd been on the scene the other night and also had
attended the conference room meeting the morning
after. An ambulance with its rear doors open sat behind one of the squad cars. Cops were crouched down
behind the cars with their weapons trained on the second story of the house. There was a van full of
SWATs as well, muscular, in-shape-looking guys wearing blocked-off hats, toting AK-47s and coiled ropes

around their upper arms. Benno recognized John
Hoermann from a block away, the tall chief ADA
standing behind the captain, both men stooped over,
using the ambulance as cover from the house. Benno
parked at the curb short of the barriers, and he and
Drummond jogged toward the scene. When they were
twenty steps short of the ambulance, something
flashed in an upstairs window. A millisecond later
there was a sound like a firecracker, and something
dug up turf a foot from Drummond's shoe. The detectives dived for cover behind the ambulance.

The first time Benno had seen John Hoermann, he'd
thought the ADA carried himself like a man thirty
years younger than he was, but now Hoermann
seemed bent and old. His pointed nose was down and
there was a glint of fear in his eyes. He grabbed
Benno's elbow, pulled him up close, and indicated the
cell phone in his hand. "Chief Rubin called. He tells
me LaVon Masters is dead."

"Right," Benno said softly. "Along with several
other people. What's happened here?" He thought he
saw movement in the upstairs window where the shot
was fired. Drummond crouched nearby, her breathing
slow and even. Benno looked her a question. She
shook her head—she was okay. Benno expelled a relieved sigh.

Hoermann squatted down. "The unis guarding Morgan Masters allowed a visitor in. They tell me you'd
okayed that, Detective."

Benno didn't want to get in a finger-pointing con-
test. "That's on me. I thought it was someone other
than who it was. I got fooled, okay? How many people
are inside the house?"

Hoermann's eyebrows moved closer together. "Do
you know the shooter's identity? These unis say it's
a woman."

"Yeah, it is. LaVon Masters' daughter."

"Hell no, detective. That's who the shooter's got hostage up there."

"No, it's . . . I got no time for a drawn-out explanation, Mr. Hoermann. That's who it is. And the hostage isn't really Morgan, but that's what we'll keep calling her for now. Who's in there besides the perp and Morgan?"

The Plano captain, who was on his knees on Hoermann's left, now butted in. "One of the officers on guard went in with the visitor and hasn't come out. Shortly after that, the cops outside heard a gunshot. The officer in there might be dead, might also be a hostage. He had a rifle with him. I think that's what the shooter's using up in that window."

"So it's three people in there, maximum, and one is a cop?"

"That's my understanding," the captain said. "We're going to deploy half of our tactical squad to one side of the house and half to the other."

Benno looked down at the pavement, considering. "I don't think that's a good idea, Captain."

"We have to move. I don't think she's killed anyone in there yet. People in the shooter's situation need warm bodies as hostages."

"*Most* people in the shooter's situation," Benno said. "I'm not sure this particular individual gives a damn. She wants Morgan Masters dead, and I don't think she cares what happens to her own ass, one way or the other. What effort's been made to contact the shooter?"

"I called the main line inside the house. No one answers. The phone is hooked up to an answering machine. I left the message that there's no way out of there, but I have no idea if the shooter was listening."

"I don't think it would matter if she was," Benno

said. "I think the odds are fifty-fifty that she's already killed Morgan, along with the cop that went inside with her. If the hostages aren't already dead, sending in SWATs will be sure to get them killed."

The captain looked resentful. "You've got all kinds of ideas about what *not* to do, Detective, but you're not suggesting any alternative."

"First, I'll have to talk to the shooter," Benno said. He pulled out his own cell and, as Hoermann and the captain gaped at him, punched in Jessica Baldwin's cell phone number.

The real Morgan Masters, the woman he'd known as Jessica, answered after the second ring. "Did you come for me, lover."

Benno kept his voice calm. "Your sister's not to blame for anything that happened. She was a victim, the same as you."

"*Half* sister, Benno. And don't try mind-fucking me. Do you think I'm supposed to love that little bitch?"

"You ought to feel sorry for her."

"No one's ever felt sorry for me," she said. "Have you got any idea what it feels like to be ten years old and have a drunken old man's cock shoved inside you while his hag of a wife pins down your arms? Do you?"

"I've got a pretty good idea what you went through. Don't kill anyone else—it isn't worth it."

"Was that your partner I nearly shot a minute ago? The black girl."

"Yeah."

"She's kind of cute. Are you fucking her?"

"No."

"I won't be jealous if you are. I told you sex was casual with me."

Benno massaged his forehead. "Listen, is Morgan still alive?"

"Morgan? *Morgan?* I'm Morgan, you asshole. I don't like you any more than the rest of those cops out there."

"Okay, *Morgan,* sorry. Is your *half sister* still alive? If she is, we can always negotiate."

"Negotiate? Is that the part where you send in a pizza for me to eat and pretend you're trying to arrange a getaway helicopter, and then we spend the next couple of days bullshitting each other while you send cops sneaking in through the windows? You are such a fucking bore, Benno. Uncle Eddie was a mean old fart, but at least he was interesting. Had all kinds of arguments about why I shouldn't chop his arms off. But you? You're even more boring than those Tennessee doctors and lawyers. Pompous assholes. I suppose you know about them."

Benno closed his eyes. "I just talked to an old friend of yours. A guy named Oglethorpe."

"He's a nice enough cop, but an ignorant shit," she said. "I've got no plans to leave here alive, lover, and never have had any. When my job is finished, so am I."

"Goddammit! Is your sister alive?"

"Why would she be?"

"Are you saying she's dead?"

There was a pause. Then she said, "Hold on." There was a rustling noise. Then, as if from far away, there was an earsplitting scream followed by loud sobs of pain. The killer came back on the line. "Does that answer your question, Benno? I can hurt her some more, if you're not convinced."

"You can get out of there alive if you cooperate."

"I don't want out of here alive. There's only one reason this little bitch isn't dead. Don't you know what that is?"

Benno held the phone. He looked at Drummond,

then at Hoermann. Finally he said into the mouth-piece, "No, I don't. Why don't you tell me?"

"I can see all four sides of this house from here, Benno. If one cop tries coming in here from any direction, the bitch is history. But you're the exception, lover. You can come right in."

"How about if we exchange your sister for me?"

"Fuck no. You come in, everybody else stays outside. I endured your cock, lover. Fucking you made me sick to my stomach, but I had to do it to get information from you. I hate your guts, and I want you up here now. You can try to kill me. Or I might kill you. Either way, it's over. You want it all over with, don't you?"

"Not that way. Listen, you don't have to—"

"You've got five minutes, lover. If you're not moving toward the house by then, alone, this bitch is positively dead."

The Kevlar vest was too tight, so Benno adjusted the Velcro strap. Drummond paced back and forth in front of him. "This is insane. She'll blow your brains out and then kill Morgan to boot."

"The hostage is named Sandra Denise Hershey. Hey, I know it's confusing. And if I don't go in, she's history anyway." Benno checked his watch. Three minutes gone. He checked the clip on his Glock. Hoermann and the Plano captain stood behind Drummond, both men watching the house. The cops still crouched behind squad cars with weapons aimed. Another front was blowing in. The wind was strong and growing colder by the minute. Benno reached for his coat, then changed his mind.

"She may cut you down before you're halfway across the yard," Drummond said.

"She won't do that," Benno said. He holstered the

Glock at the small of his back and winked at Drummond. "Guess I'm ready," he said.

"At least let me cover you." Drummond had a pleading look.

"Cover me from what? She won't shoot till I'm inside. Trust me."

She faced him with hands on hips. "You're a real putz, Benno—you know that?" Her expression showed concern.

"I can't argue with that." He left the cover of the van and jogged toward the house. "Happy Hanukkah, Tina," he said over his shoulder. "From a putz to a shiksa, okay?"

He went around to the side of the house, the same direction he'd gone on the day he was checking out the stolen vehicle report, and stepped up on the bricked-in electric meter to boost himself over the fence. He landed with a thud on winter-dead Tiff and righted himself. He spotted the Lab huddled against the house, its tail between its legs. It whimpered in fear. Benno patted the dog and trotted on to the back. He skirted the pool and went up on the porch. The sliding kitchen door was open, the light on the security panel flashing green. He pulled his weapon, held it ready, ducked inside, and crouched behind the kitchen counter. Pots, pans, and butcher knives still hung suspended from a rack. The light on the answering machine blinked. A faucet dripped nearby.

He'd been in plain sight from the upstairs window as he'd trotted across the front lawn and around to the side of the house. So he had to assume that she knew where he was. Holding his breath, his heart threatening to pound its way through his breastbone, he flattened against the kitchen doorframe, rolled into the den, and came up in a crouch, Glock held ready.

There was no one in sight. Bubbles rose in the saltwater aquarium, and the sixty-inch television screen stared at him like a giant unseeing eye. A faint sheen reflected from the leather sofa and chairs, and his features reflected from the concert grand piano's polished wood. A sliver of daylight slanted in from the entry hall, dust motes swirling in the beam like confetti. Moving cautiously, his weapon held out in both hands in firing position, he crept through the den into the entry hall and took cover beneath the staircase banister, his feet sinking into the softness of the Oriental rug. The pendulum in the six-foot-tall grandfather clock rocked back and forth, ticking and tocking, shattering the silence. A pane was missing from the floor-to-roof leaded-glass window, the pane that Drummond had broken out when they'd first entered the house. Jesus, it seemed like years ago. Visible through the window, cops crouched behind squad cars with rifles trained on the second floor.

The dead uniformed cop lay faceup with his head in the entry hall and his feet inside the dining room. He was partially bald, with a thick muscular neck. There was a bullet wound in his forehead, directly between the eyes.

Benno whirled out of his hiding place and mounted the bottom step, weapon slanted upward. "I'm here. Come on, give it up and save us both a lot of shit." His voice cracked at the end.

Stony silence was the only thing that met him. The grandfather clock continued to tick. Slowly, carefully, lifting first one foot and then the other, he took off his shoes.

He mounted the stairs two at a time until he reached the landing. He pointed his weapon this way and that. The upstairs corridor stood silent and empty. He searched his memory bank: guest bedrooms on his left and directly ahead; the master bedroom and bath

at the end of the hall, three doors down. The door to
the master bedroom stood open. Benno crept down
that way, flattened against the wall, and leaned forward to peer inside.

The girl he'd known as Morgan was spread-eagled
faceup on the bed, her wrists and ankles cuffed to the
head and footboards. The bottoms of her bare feet
were sliced from ball to heel. Blood seeped from the
wounds and dripped on the bedspread. Her eyes were
open, the lids fluttering in pain. A bloody kitchen
knife lay next to her on the pillows. Visible beyond
the bed, a rifle was propped against the windowsill.

Benno looked left and right, seeing no one except
the helpless girl. He crossed the room and knelt beside
the bed. The girl whimpered through her gag. Benno
placed a reassuring hand on her arm and, for an instant, lost focus as he gazed in pity at the fear in her
eyes. He wanted to reach out and help her.

With a shriek like a braking train, the woman he'd
known as Jessica Baldwin came at him from the master bath. Her lips peeled back, the cords in her neck
taut with exertion; she hefted an ax over her head.
Benno crouched there frozen as the blade came whis-
tling down.

He moved just in time to save his hand from being
severed, but not quickly enough to keep the wooden
handle from smashing into his wrist. His arm went
instantly numb. The Glock flew from his fingers, skit-
tered across the bed, and clattered to the floor on the
other side.

Benno and the woman faced each other, both
breathing hard. Benno's arm hung limp at his side.
Her biceps tightened as she raised the ax to strike
again.

Benno blocked the ax's descent with his good hand,
gripping the handle hard. The blade bounced off of

his thigh, opening a gash through his pants. Now both his arm and upper leg were numb. He tried to twist the weapon away from her. She shook him off, aimed a kick as hard as a horse's at his knee, backed away a step, and regrouped. She raised the ax again, this time aiming for his head.

Helpless, he weakly raised his arm for protection, the blade descending as if in slow motion, the sharpened edge swishing directly toward his skull.

A gunshot rent the stillness. A hole appeared in the woman's face, just in front of her ear. The bullet exited from the back of her head, spraying red mist and bone matter. She went instantly limp and crumpled to the floor, the ax blade bouncing harmlessly from Benno's shoulder, the weapon thudding to the carpet. The woman tried to lift her arm, then let it fall limply back. She tried to speak and died that way, her lips parted in an unspoken question, her eyes staring vacantly at nothing.

Benno stood numbly over her, holding his wounded leg as the pungent odor of gunpowder filled the room.

Tina Drummond walked in from out in the corridor, her service weapon pointed ahead of her. She came over and stood beside Benno, both detectives now looking down at the dead woman.

Drummond holstered her weapon, stepped over to the girl on the bed, and reached out to strip the tape away from her mouth. She turned her face to Benno as she pulled the tape away. "I told you I'd cover your ass," Drummond said. "How come you never listen to me?"

26

They learned a lot from items turned up at the real Jessica Baldwin's place, a two-story modern town house in the Valley Ranch section of Irving, just down the road from the Dallas Cowboys' practice facility. Randy Dunst secured a warrant and, using a key found in Jessica's pocket as she lay dead in LaVon Masters' greenhouse, Benno and Drummond drove out to Valley Ranch and let themselves in a good half hour before the county evidence gatherers arrived. Drummond entered first and Benno followed, limping. EMU techs had bandaged the thigh laceration he'd received when the ax had barely missed killing him; they told Benno that the blade had only nicked the muscle and had missed an artery by a hair. The wound was superficial. Nonetheless, it hurt like hell.

Jessica Baldwin's town house had shag carpet, dainty French provincial furniture, and shiny black-surfaced Maytag appliances in the kitchen. The killer had made more of a mess than Benno would have imagined—he still thought of her as a professional woman, a psychiatrist, and it would be a while before

he had her true image rooted in his mind: a psycho-
path, smarter than most but stone-cold crazy nonetheless. The trash compactor and pantry wastebasket
overflowed with crumpled frozen dinner cartons, takeout pizza boxes, and bottles of Heineken beer. The
counters were littered with plates, some containing
chicken bones, some with half-eaten turkey and
mashed potatoes, and others with dried lasagna clinging to their surfaces. A small TV in the breakfast room
was on, showing CNN with the volume muted. The
detectives went upstairs to the bedroom, where the
killer'd held Jessica prisoner.

Jessica Baldwin—the real Jessica Baldwin, the
woman who'd cared more about helping victims of
violent crime than making a financial killing in her
own practice—had spent the final two days of her life
in a cramped twin bed with her wrists and ankles
cuffed to the posts. There were marks on the wood
where the metal had scarred, likely as Jessica had
writhed in pain while the killer jabbed needles into
the cuts in the soles of her feet. The bottom portion
of the bedsheet was stained with blood. There was a
thick writing pad near the headboard, where the killer
had made notes while Jessica told her things—likely
begging for her life as she did. Benno snugged on
rubber gloves, then picked up the pad and thumbed
through the pages while Drummond checked the
closets.

The notes were neatly written and easy to deci-
pher—names of patients, appointment times, brief de-
scriptions of the crimes that had turned normal people
into victims. The story that the phony Jessica Baldwin
had told Benno in the restaurant was real—there was
really a woman whose attacker had cut off her thumb.
On the fifth page down was a description of Morgan
Masters' mental condition, which the killer had then

recited to Benno, practically word for word, the night they'd made love on Benno's sleeper sofa. Morgan's name on the pad was scratched through with violent strokes of the pen, and in its place the killer had written SANDRA. Benno shook his head. Jesus, it was hard to keep Morgan's, Jessica's, and Sandra Hershey's identities straight in his own mind; he wondered if the killer had possibly gotten up every morning not sure who she was. He pictured her sitting there with Jessica Baldwin gagged on the bed, using Jessica's cell phone to learn all about Morgan's whereabouts from Benno. With Benno on her side and under her spell, the killer could have tracked Morgan anywhere. But Morgan was really Sandra, wasn't she? This case report would be a bitch to write.

There was a folded slip of paper shoved in between the written pages. Benno smoothed it out and read it. This was a ruled spiral notebook page, containing Jessica's address and phone number along with directions to Valley Ranch from Trafficante's dilapidated apartment building in Irving. Benno would have to check his own notes from the interview with Zorro on the night the man had returned from the casino trip, but was pretty sure Trafficante had known who the real Jessica Baldwin was. He had told Drummond and Benno that all during the trip Morgan had kept calling the woman for advice.

The killer's steps from there were fairly easy to put together. She'd killed Uncle Eddie, driven his body to Oak Cliff, then returned to the Plano house to wait for Zorro to bring her half sister home. If Benno and Drummond hadn't stumbled into the house, the killer would have done away with the stripper and her own half sister, then and there. As it was, she'd waited somewhere near the Plano house, followed Trafficante to LaVon Masters' place, and then to his apartment, where she'd captured, tortured, and then killed him. She'd gotten Jessica Baldwin's name from him, then driven to Valley Ranch and taken Jessica prisoner. Benno wondered briefly why Zorro had taken the voodoo lily from LaVon's. Likely to sell the fucking stinky flower. Somehow, Benno couldn't feel sorry for the guy.

The first time that Benno had spoken to the phony Jessica Baldwin over his cell, he'd told her that her half sister was holed up at the Doubletree. It all fit. Benno had met the woman he thought was Jessica at the restaurant at six thirty in the evening. The two DA's investigators had gone down around six. From the Doubletree to La Madeleine was a fifteen-minute drive.

Jesus, she'd played him like a harmonica.

He wondered about her analysis of his own problem with alcohol, the advice that she'd given him on his sofa sleeper. He'd talk to a departmental shrink about it. He suspected that what the killer'd told him would be right on target. The Tennessee cop had told him and Drummond that Sandra Denise Hershey had read a lot. Benno suspected that she had, and then some.

Drummond came out of the closet carrying a pair of jeans and a sweater. Both garments were spattered in dried blood. "Bet me the blood types don't match Uncle Eddie and Zorro," she said.

"They will," Benno said. "Does it look like any of the real Jessica's clothes are missing?"

Drummond nodded. "There are empty hangers twisted around on the racks. Also looks like a couple of pairs of shoes may be missing. Some shoes jumbled around on the shelves, drawers open, panty hose pulled out and dropped on the floor."

"Instant psychiatrist's wardrobe," Benno said. "Jesus, Tina, I feel so fucking dumb."

"Maybe that's because you've been *acting* dumb," Drummond said. She dropped the clothes on the bed. "Ah hell, Benno, don't feel bad. You were acting like a man. The way to a guy's heart is through his zipper, my mama used to tell me. Also unlocks the door to whatever's on his mind. Some things don't ever change—what can I say?"

It took a couple of weeks to sort out the probate mess, and by that time, Benno and Drummond were working on a Dart Rail Transit shooting, but they kept abreast of the Harry Masters estate by clipping out the daily newspaper stories and reading them to each other over lunch. It irritated Benno that Harold Stein hadn't gotten totally screwed, but Drummond opined, what the hell, the guy was a lawyer. He would always win out in the end. And besides, Harold Stein was the only person familiar enough with the details to keep all the various names and pseudonyms straight, so that the judge could eventually understand what the fuck was going on.

The fact that LaVon Masters and Morgan Masters—who'd lived most of her life in the Tennessee justice system as Sandra Denise Hershey—were both dead negated the trust Harry'd set up for his daughter. Furthermore, since Harry's will contained no provision in the event that both his wife and daughter were deceased at the time of probate, the will was likewise negated and the assets turned over to the court registry for distribution. Here things became complicated because Harry's only still-living relative was a brother in California, a non compos mentis who resided in a nursing home. Since the real Sandra Denise Greene—who likely continued to think of herself as Morgan Masters—wasn't related to Harry by blood, she was originally to receive nothing. Zilch. Nada. Her only

legacy was whatever Uncle Eddie Payne, her real father, had owned, which turned out to be a saggy bed
and some clothes at Everlasting Gardens and against
which the assisted living facility had a claim for one
month's rent that was in arrears. Benno thought it
was unjust that Sandra Denise/Morgan wasn't getting
anything out of the estate. Drummond thought, what
the hell, the bitch should try living on a cop's salary
for a while.

Just as the court was ready to ship the bulk of Harry's estate off to the brother in California, Harold
Stein entered the fray with both fists flying and his
Superman's cape whipping in the breeze. He filed a
motion on Sandra Denise/Morgan's behalf that, despite its obvious legal deficiency, had the potential to
grind the case to a standstill for a year or more. Stein's
position: As Harry Masters' surviving spouse, LaVon
would have been entitled to half of the estate had she
been alive; therefore her only living survivor, Sandra
Denise/Morgan, now became heir to whatever her
mother would have gotten. Stein's reasoning in his
brief was in direct contrast to Texas law; however, as
Stein pointed out, probate statutes in California were
different, and since the brother was to inherit under
California law, that state's practices should prevail in
a Texas court as well.

Stein's position was, as a matter of law, total bullshit. His motion prevailed. Or at least it was scheduled
for a hearing, which was enough to make the brother's
California attorneys throw in the towel. The brother—
or at least the guardian representing the brother—was
in financial straits and couldn't wait another day for
his money, so the West Coast faction settled. Sandra/
Morgan walked off with half of Harry Masters' assets.
Harold Stein's fee wasn't stated in the newspaper, but
as was mentioned in a small item in the financial

pages, he tendered an offer for a small shopping center on the same day as the settlement.

At lunch, Benno tossed the article aside. "What a guy, huh?"

Drummond sprinkled hot sauce on her scrambled eggs. "Good news for the strip joints," she said, "if Morgan's gonna stay in the chips. Come on, Benno, eat up. If we're gonna earn our twenty bucks an hour, we gotta get our asses in gear."

That afternoon, Benno was in the squad room cubicle going over ballistics reports when Randy Dunst dropped by. Drummond had gone to the can, so the riding DA sank down in her empty chair. He tossed a stapled sheath of papers into Benno's in-basket. "Thought you'd want to see this," Dunst said.

Benno put the reports aside while he read what Dunst had brought. It was a copy of a petition for a restraining order. The district attorney was asking the court to freeze Harold Stein's fee from the Masters estate, pending a criminal investigation into the lawyer's activities in regards to the Morgan Masters trust fund. If tried and convicted, the petition argued, Stein could face a heavy fine, and seizure of the fee would protect the county's interest should conviction become a reality. Benno tossed the papers aside. "Aw shit, Randy," he said.

"We're gonna fry his ass," Dunst said.

"No, you're going to hope he doesn't fry *your* ass. Next is going to come a lawsuit where Stein alleges police negligence in protecting his client, by letting that woman into her house when they were supposed to be guarding her. Bet me. The DA's just trying to get the jump on the guy. If Stein agrees not to sue, all this other shit will disappear."

"Are you into practicing law now? The DA is dead

serious. I'm to stay on top of this matter with diligence."

Benno wanted to tell Dunst that, if the district attorney were really intent on going after Stein, then someone else would end up prosecuting, other than Randy Dunst. But Benno didn't have the heart to say what was on his mind. Instead, he just looked at the guy.

"I'll whip Harold Stein's ass in the courtroom," Dunst said.

Benno picked up the sheath of paper and thumbed through it. He tossed the whole mess back into his in-basket. "Tell you what, Randy," Benno finally said. "If you're a betting man, I'll lay you eight to five."

When Dunst had left, Benno leaned back and rubbed his eyes. He massaged his cheeks with the palms of his hands. He looked up at the ceiling, toward the building's upper floors, and thought of his cousin, Chief Rubin. Jesus, Benno had promised the chief. Today, without fail.

He stared at the phone as if afraid the receiver would jump out of its cradle and smack him in the nose.

He pushed his chair back from his desk and stared some more. The phone continued to sit there.

Benno picked up the receiver and punched in a number in the 580 area code. He hunched over his desk as the line began to ring. Benno had a nearly uncontrollable urge to slam the phone down, but he held his breath and kept on waiting.

There was a click on the line. An elderly male voice from fifteen hundred miles away said, "Allo?"

Benno's throat constricted. He sucked in air.

The elderly voice said, "Allo?" a second time.

Benno expelled a long regretful sigh. "Hi, Pop," he finally said.

ONYX

A KISS GONE BAD

Jeff Abbott

"A BREAKTHROUGH NOVEL."
—*New York Times* bestselling author Sharyn McCrumb

"Rocks big time...pure, white-knuckle suspense. I read it in one sitting."
—*New York Times* bestselling author Harlan Coben

A death rocks the Gulf Coast town of Port Leo, Texas. Was it suicide, fueled by a family tragedy? Or did an obsessed killer use the dead man as a pawn in a twisted game? Beach-bum-turned judge Whit Mosley must risk everything to find out.

"Exciting, shrewd and beautifully crafted...A book worth including on any year's best list."
—*Chicago Tribune*

0-451-41010-6

To order call: 1-800-788-6262

S425/Abbott